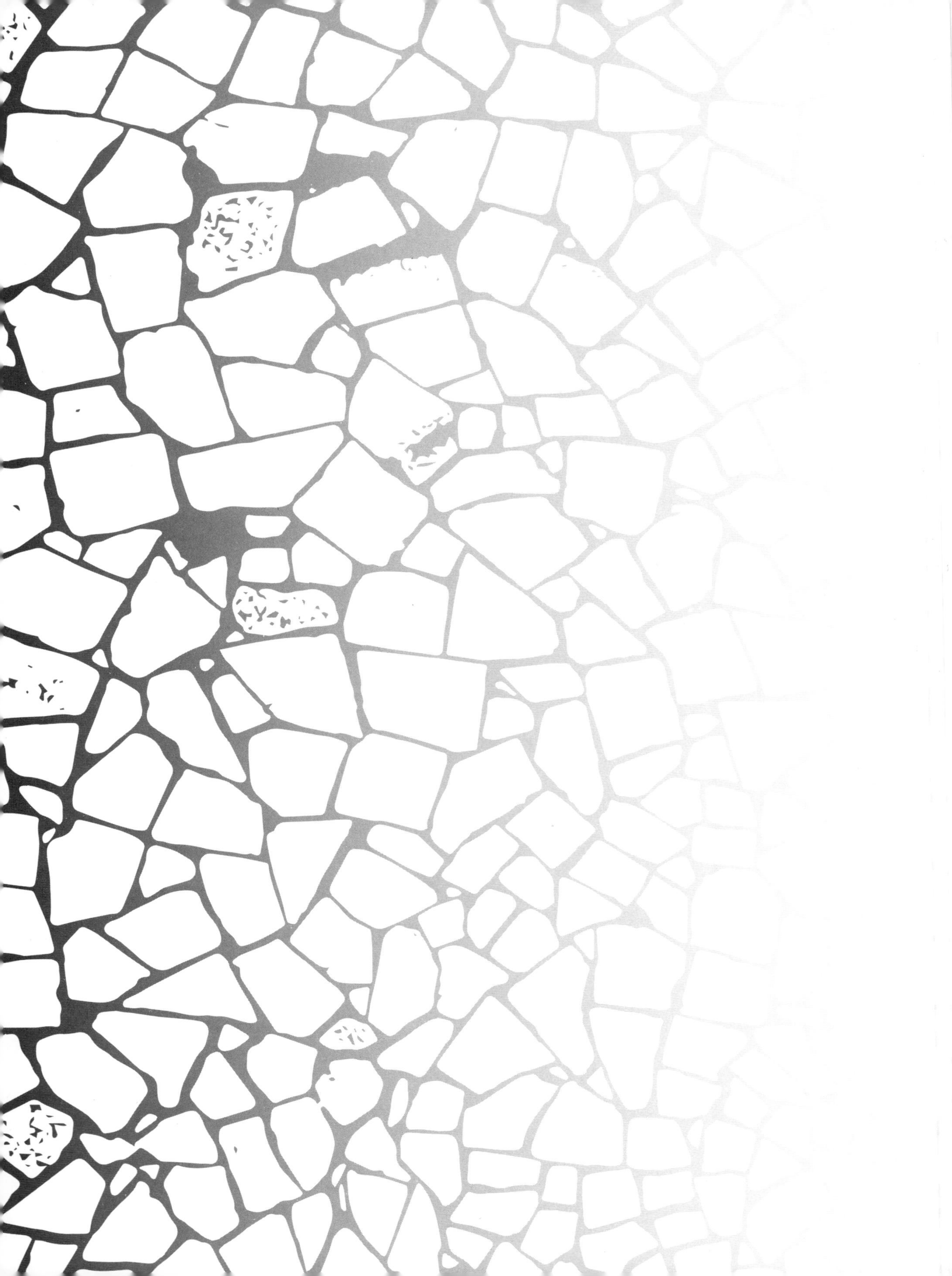

El Torres ↓ Jesús Alonso Iglesias

THE GHOST of GAUDÍ

THE MAGNETIC COLLECTION

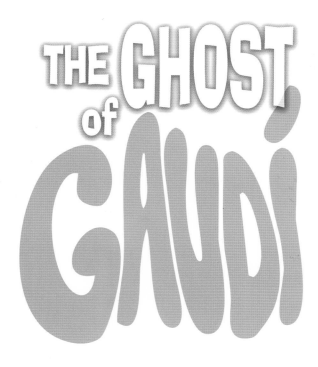

THE GHOST of GAUDÍ

Written by El Torres
Illustrated by Jesús Alonso Iglesias

Translation by Esther Villardón Grande
Localization and editing by Mike Kennedy

A comic inspired by Ricardo Esteban

THE GHOST OF GAUDÍ Original Graphic Novel Hardcover
September 2017. FIRST PRINTING

ISBN: 978-1-942367-16-1

Published as part of The Magnetic Collection by The Lion Forge, LLC.
Originally published in Spain as EL FANTASMA DE GAUDÍ.

www.LIONFORGE.com

Names: Torres, El, 1972- | Alonso Iglesias, Jesús, 1952- illustrator. | Villardón Grande, Esther, translator. | Kennedy, Mike (Graphic novelist), editor.
Title: The ghost of Gaudí / written by El Torres ; illustrated by Jesús Alonso Iglesias ; translation by Esther Villardón Grande ; localization and editing by Mike Kennedy.
Other Titles: Fantasma de Gaudí. English
Description: [St. Louis, Missouri] : The Lion Forge, LLC, 2017. | Translation of: El fantasma de Gaudí. Madrid : Dibbuks, 2015. | "A comic inspired by Ricardo Esteban." | "Published as part of the Magnetic Collection ..."--Title page verso.
Identifiers: ISBN 978-1-942367-16-1 (hardcover)
Subjects: LCSH: Gaudí, Antoni, 1852-1926--Comic books, strips, etc. | Ghosts--Comic books, strips, etc. | Murder--Comic books, strips, etc. | Precognition--Comic books, strips, etc. | LCGFT: Graphic novels.
Classification: LCC PN6777.T67 F3613 2017 | DDC 741.5946--dc23

As above, so below

A few years ago, I found myself trapped by a strange obsession. I had gained access to several twelfth- and thirteenth-century Arabic texts in which was explained how certain ancient architects had endeavoured to reproduce, on the face of the Earth, the heaven's most recognizable constellations.

Apparently, their purpose was to draw energy from the stars toward mankind. And so I, of course, decided to find these reproductions. By following this thread, I discovered that even the Christians of the Middle Ages were familiar with such vision. I soon learned that the masters who erected the first Gothic cathedrals in the French Champagne region did so by mimicking the Virgo constellation, no doubt in an effort to link their temples to the "Virgin stars."

What surprised me the most, however, was to read that this idea was rooted before the first millennium. This "cosmic architecture" was in practice even in Ancient Egypt, with the sole purpose of enacting an age-old axiom first attributed to the god Thoth, and then to the Greek Hermes Trismegistus: that the order of the universe required all that is in the heavens above to also exist below, here on Earth.

This obsession of mine ended up materializing in a novel titled *The Templar Doors*. It was published in the year 2000, and seven years later it prompted one of the strangest conversations that I can remember. It took place in Tortosa, when a bookseller named Esteban Martín approached me with that glint in his eye that almost invariably foreshadows something important…

"I've read your novel about the cathedrals," he said, "and I think you should know something. The architects of Chartres did not disappear in the twelfth century!"

Martín explained that he had discovered the same technique of reproducing in stone what lies in the skies… in the works of Antoni Gaudí! Over lunch he explained in detail that Don Antoni's main modernist buildings in Barcelona traced, on a city plan level, the geometric pattern of Ursa Major; and that his findings were so surprising that he intended on using them as the central argument of a novel. His work, as he announced to me, saw the light in 2007 under the title *La Clave Gaudí* and was published in seventeen countries.

But his idea, as was to be expected, soon spread beyond the literary sphere. Proof of this is in this very work you hold in your hands. A story that should not be read as mere criminal intrigue but as a reflection on how our remote ancestors' magically-inclined mentality is as alive as ever in this era of science and technology. Gaudí was enraptured, at the beginning of the twentieth century, by a vision of the world far beyond conventionalism, and it is precisely this spirit that has been understood and revived by the authors of this comic. But it is in the hands of you, the reader, of course, whether or not to participate in this vision that transcends the apparent. The same vision that, incidentally, captures the soul of Toni, the heroine of what you are about to read. But, if I were you, I would not pass up this chance to truly SEE…

Javier Sierra
Summer 2015

Javier Sierra is a journalist and writer, best known for his works La Cena Secreta (Plaza & Janes, 2014), El Maestro del Prado (Planeta, 2013), and La Pirámide Inmortal (Planeta, 2014). All his novels have the common purpose of solving historical mysteries, based on documentation and field research, focusing on the mysteries of history that, according to him, "have waited for centuries to be revealed."

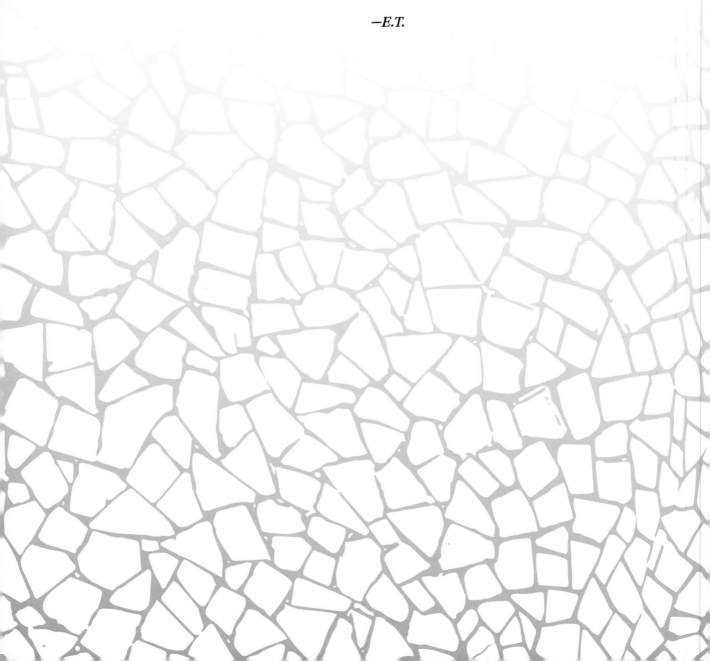

To all of those who believed I could do it and almost convinced me of it.

To my family and those two little things that make me sleep little and get up very early.

And to Paloma, "cause you're like my mirror."

       —Jesús

To Paqui.
Each and every one of them have always been for you.

       —E.T.

Chapter 1
Casa Vicens ⋄ Güell Pavilions

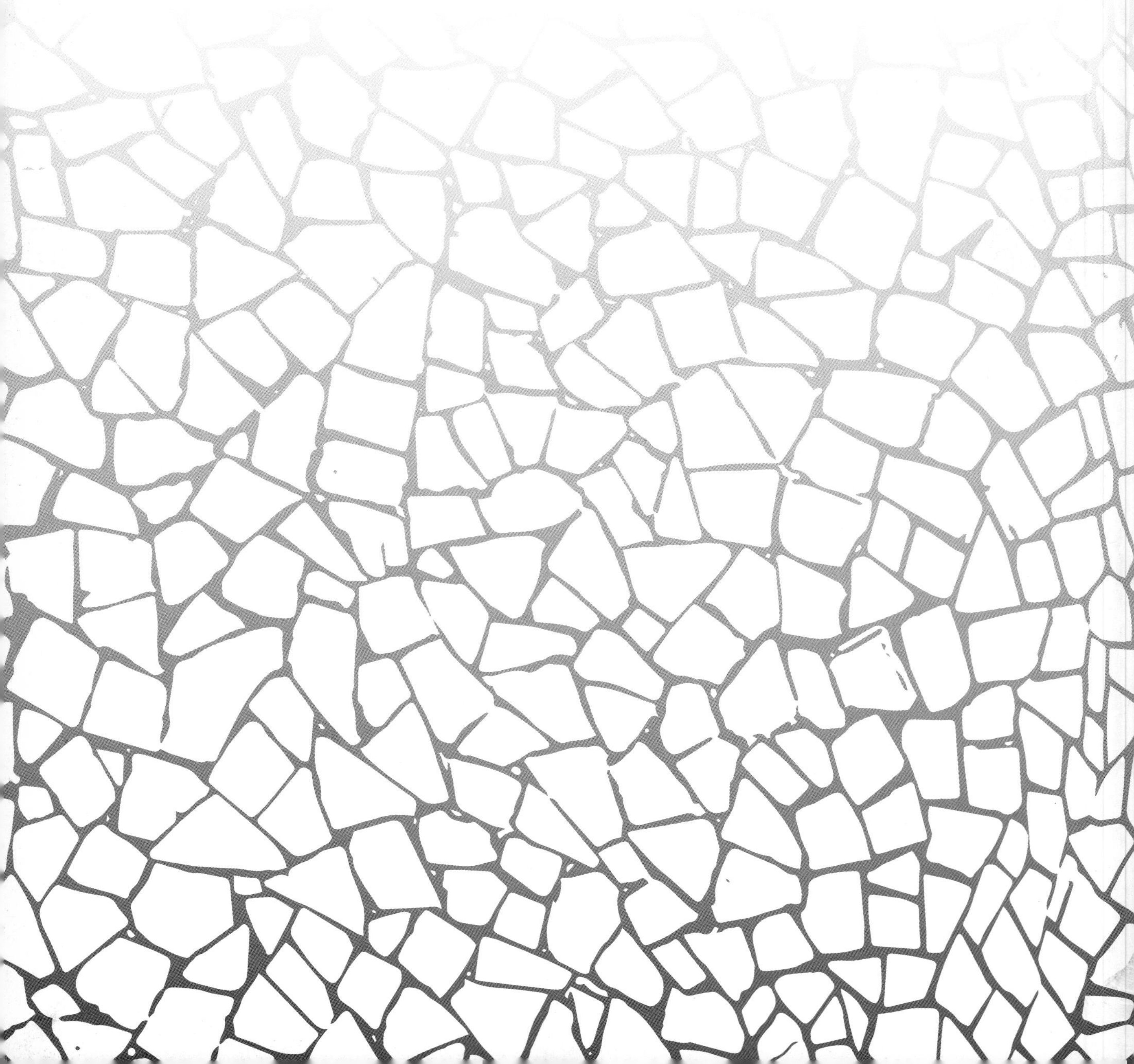

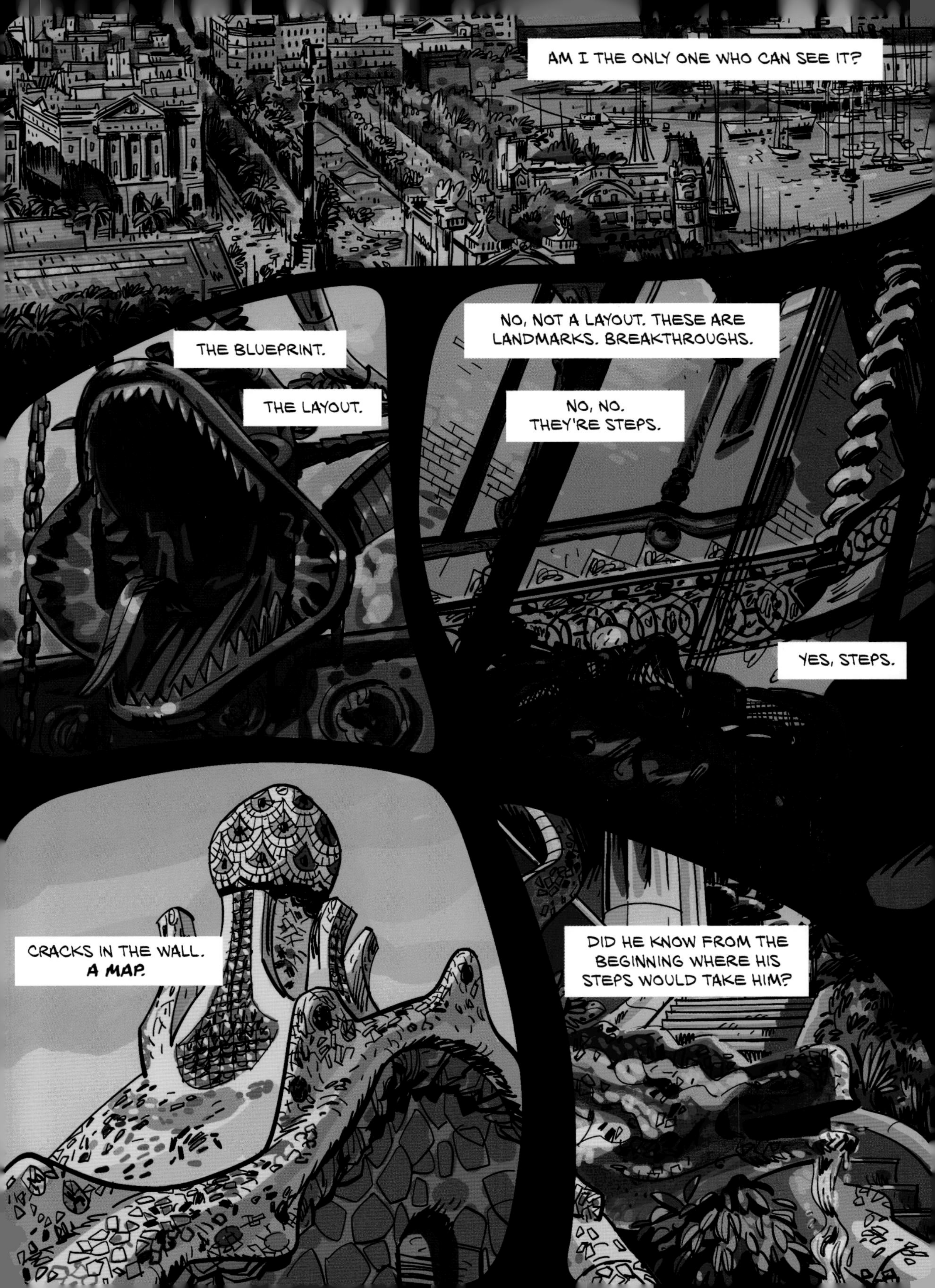
AM I THE ONLY ONE WHO CAN SEE IT?
THE BLUEPRINT.
THE LAYOUT.
NO, NOT A LAYOUT. THESE ARE LANDMARKS. BREAKTHROUGHS.
NO, NO. THEY'RE STEPS.
YES, STEPS.
CRACKS IN THE WALL. **A MAP.**
DID HE KNOW FROM THE BEGINNING WHERE HIS STEPS WOULD TAKE HIM?

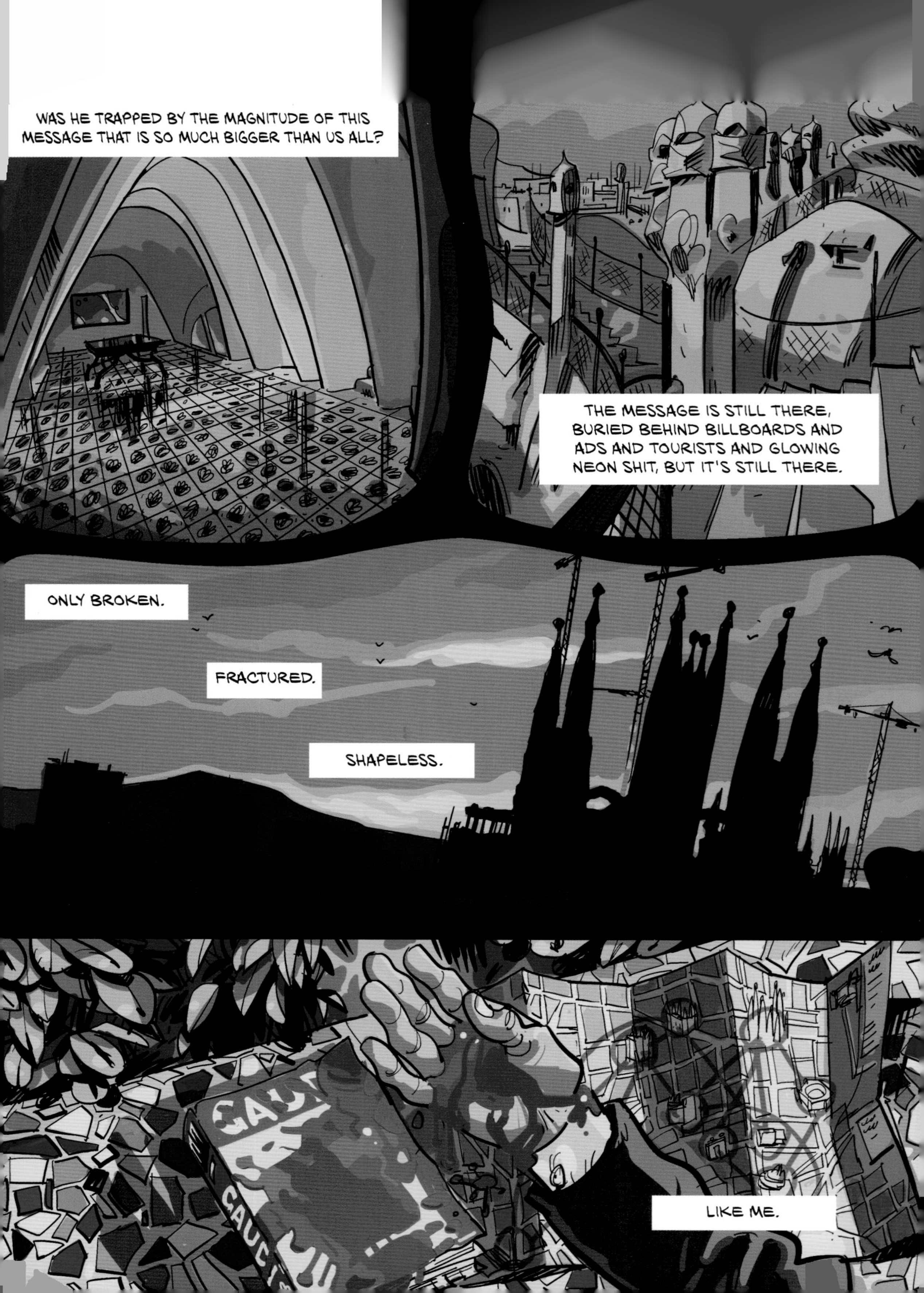
WAS HE TRAPPED BY THE MAGNITUDE OF THIS MESSAGE THAT IS SO MUCH BIGGER THAN US ALL?
THE MESSAGE IS STILL THERE, BURIED BEHIND BILLBOARDS AND ADS AND TOURISTS AND GLOWING NEON SHIT, BUT IT'S STILL THERE.
ONLY BROKEN.
FRACTURED.
SHAPELESS.
LIKE ME.

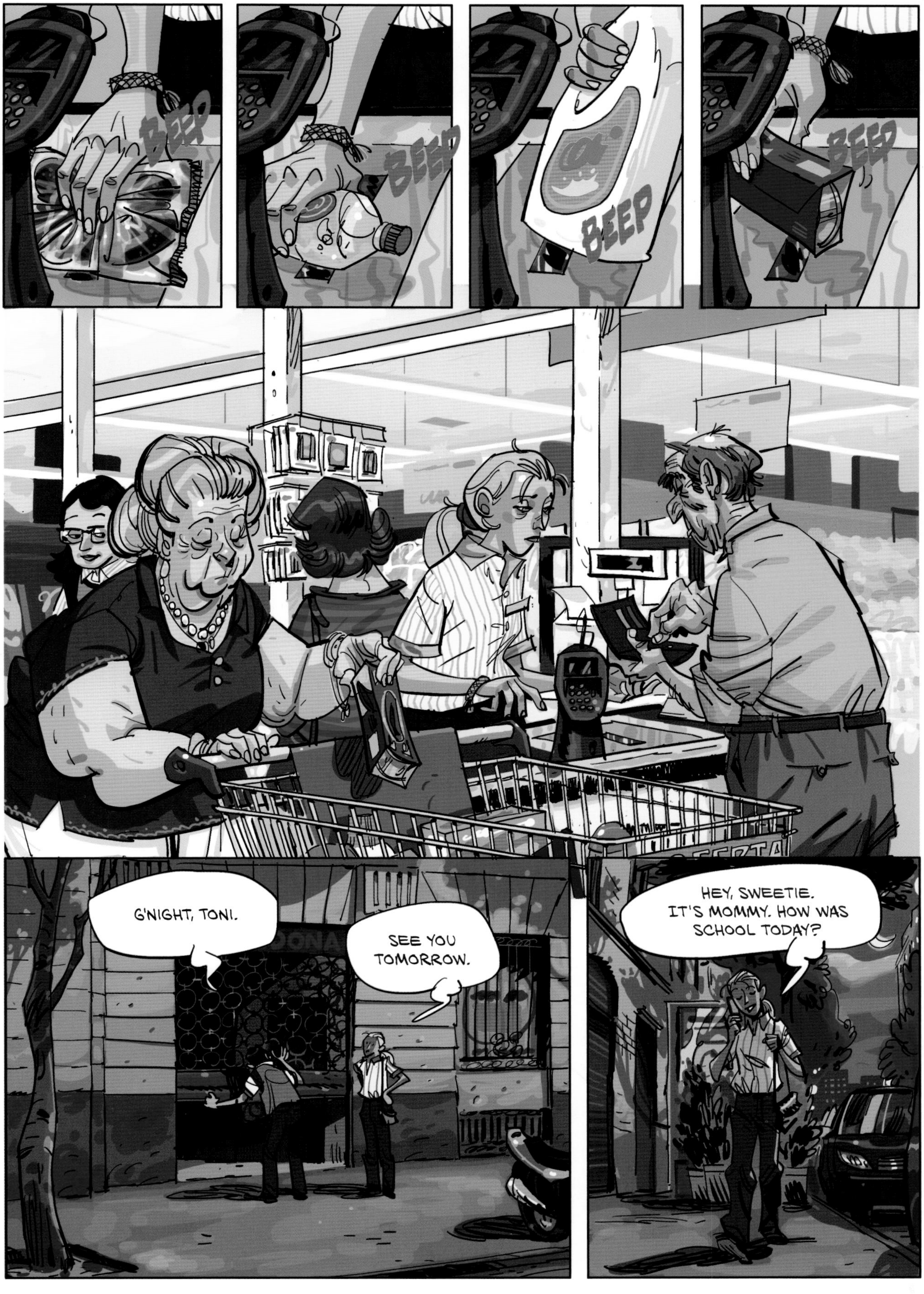
BEEP
BEEP
BEEP
BEEP
G'NIGHT, TONI.
SEE YOU TOMORROW.
HEY, SWEETIE. IT'S MOMMY. HOW WAS SCHOOL TODAY?

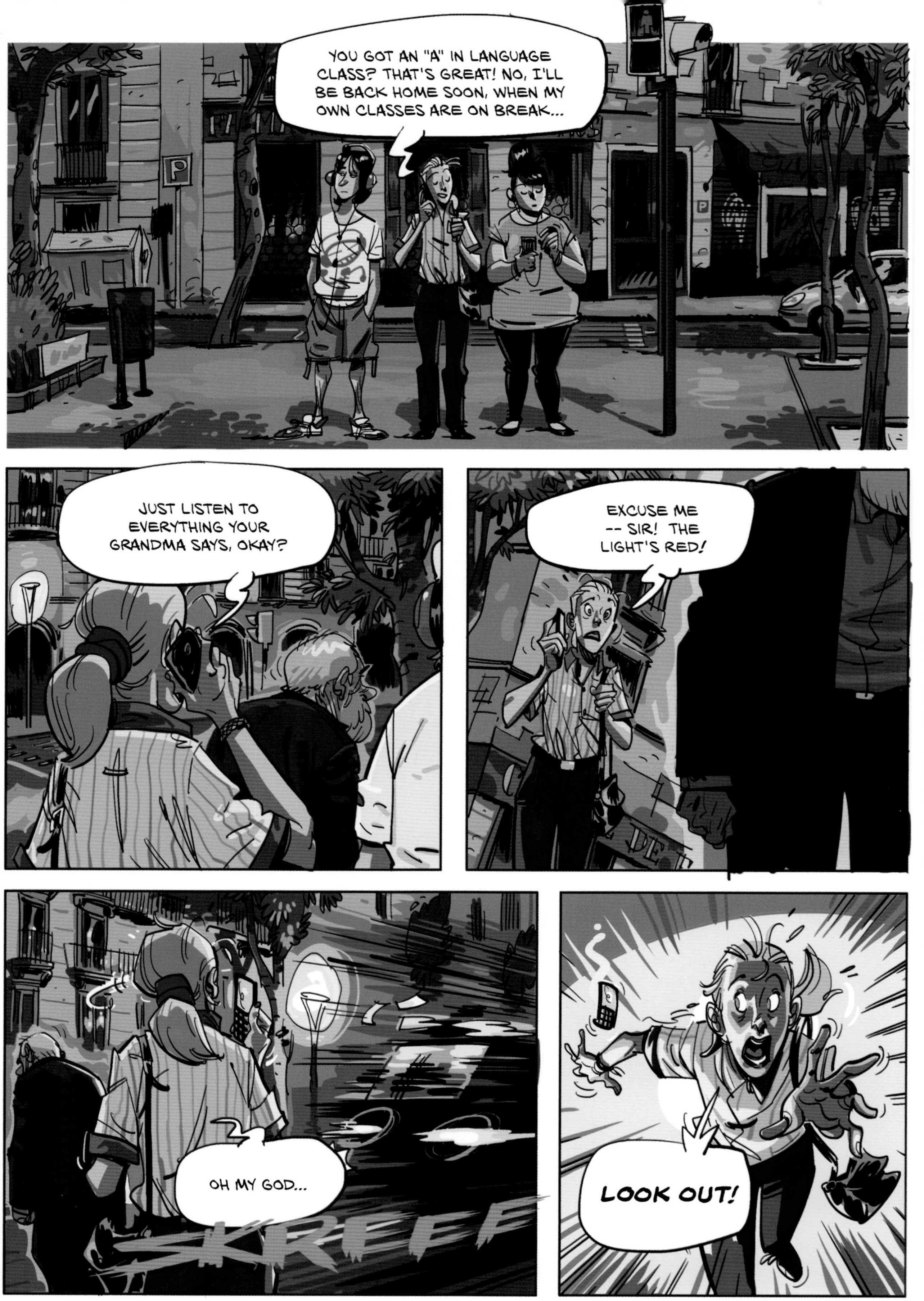
YOU GOT AN "A" IN LANGUAGE CLASS? THAT'S GREAT! NO, I'LL BE BACK HOME SOON, WHEN MY OWN CLASSES ARE ON BREAK...
JUST LISTEN TO EVERYTHING YOUR GRANDMA SAYS, OKAY?
EXCUSE ME -- SIR! THE LIGHT'S RED!
OH MY GOD...
SKREEE
LOOK OUT!

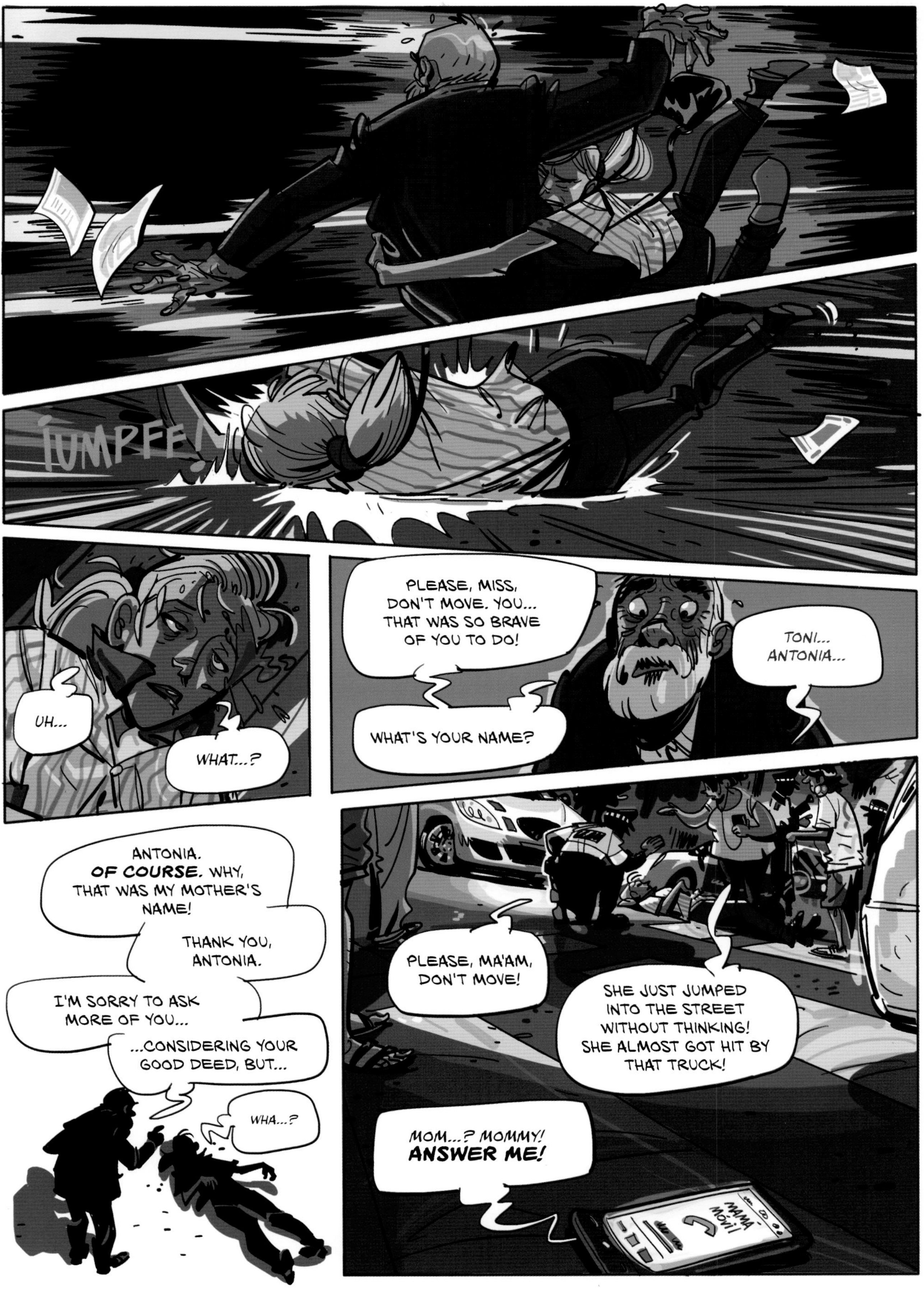
ÍUMPFF!
UH...
WHAT...?
PLEASE, MISS, DON'T MOVE. YOU... THAT WAS SO BRAVE OF YOU TO DO!
WHAT'S YOUR NAME?
TONI... ANTONIA...
ANTONIA. **OF COURSE.** WHY, THAT WAS MY MOTHER'S NAME!
THANK YOU, ANTONIA.
I'M SORRY TO ASK MORE OF YOU...
...CONSIDERING YOUR GOOD DEED, BUT...
WHA...?
PLEASE, MA'AM, DON'T MOVE!
SHE JUST JUMPED INTO THE STREET WITHOUT THINKING! SHE ALMOST GOT HIT BY THAT TRUCK!
MOM...? MOMMY! **ANSWER ME!**
MAMÁ MÓVIL

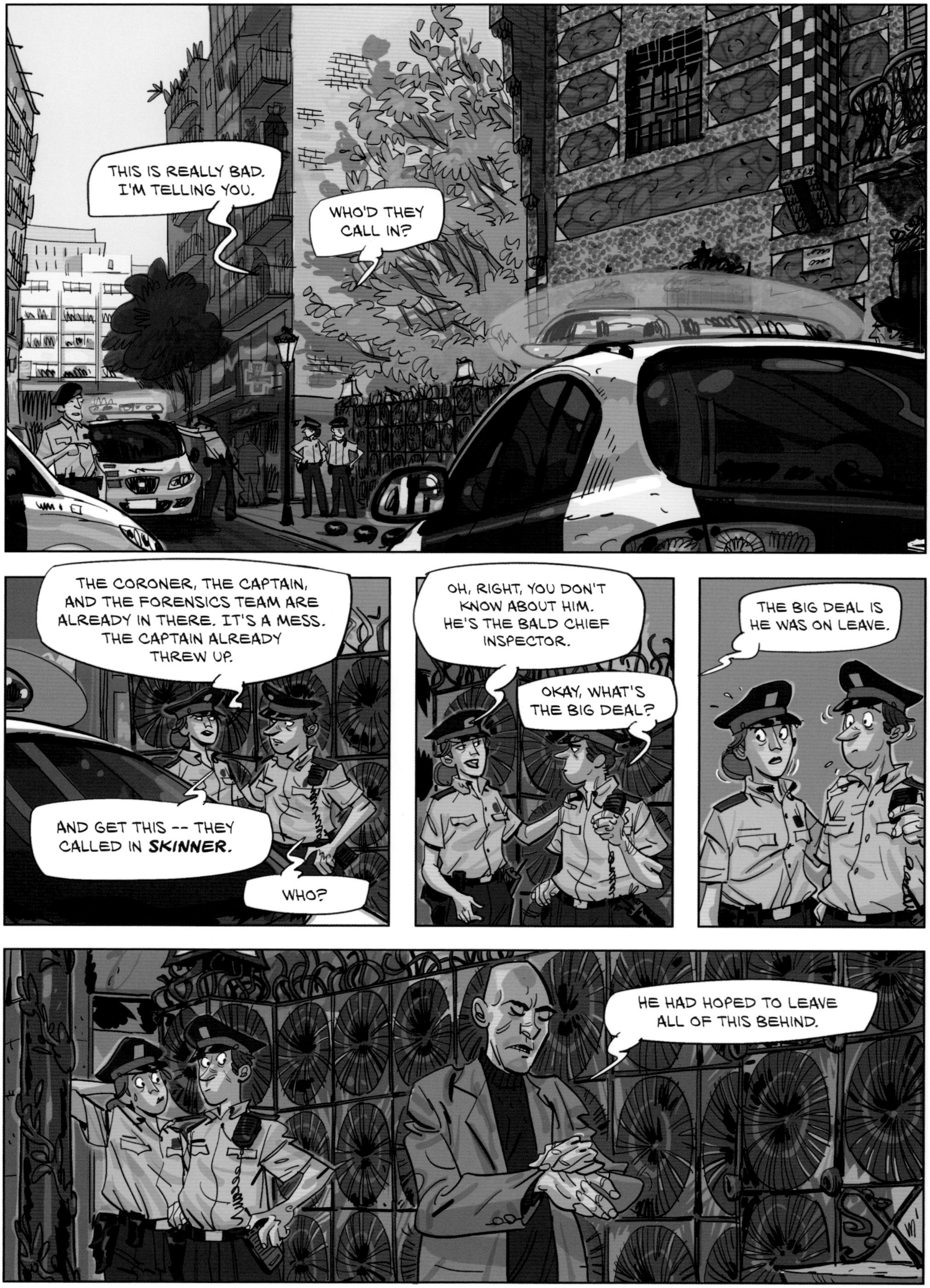
THIS IS REALLY BAD. I'M TELLING YOU.
WHO'D THEY CALL IN?
THE CORONER, THE CAPTAIN, AND THE FORENSICS TEAM ARE ALREADY IN THERE. IT'S A MESS. THE CAPTAIN ALREADY THREW UP.
AND GET THIS -- THEY CALLED IN **SKINNER.**
WHO?
OH, RIGHT, YOU DON'T KNOW ABOUT HIM. HE'S THE BALD CHIEF INSPECTOR.
OKAY, WHAT'S THE BIG DEAL?
THE BIG DEAL IS HE WAS ON LEAVE.
HE HAD HOPED TO LEAVE ALL OF THIS BEHIND.

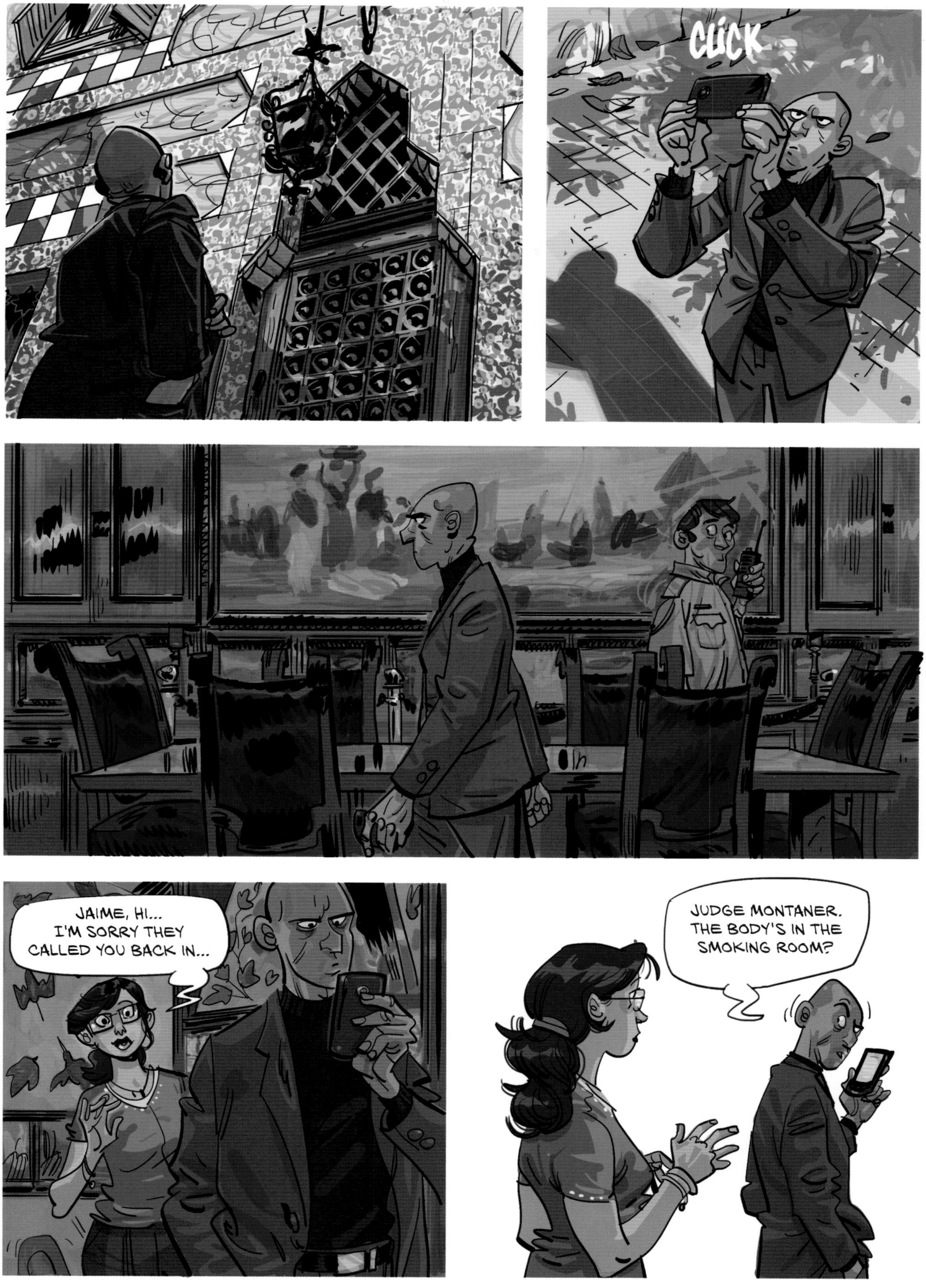

CLICK
JAIME, HI... I'M SORRY THEY CALLED YOU BACK IN...
JUDGE MONTANER. THE BODY'S IN THE SMOKING ROOM?

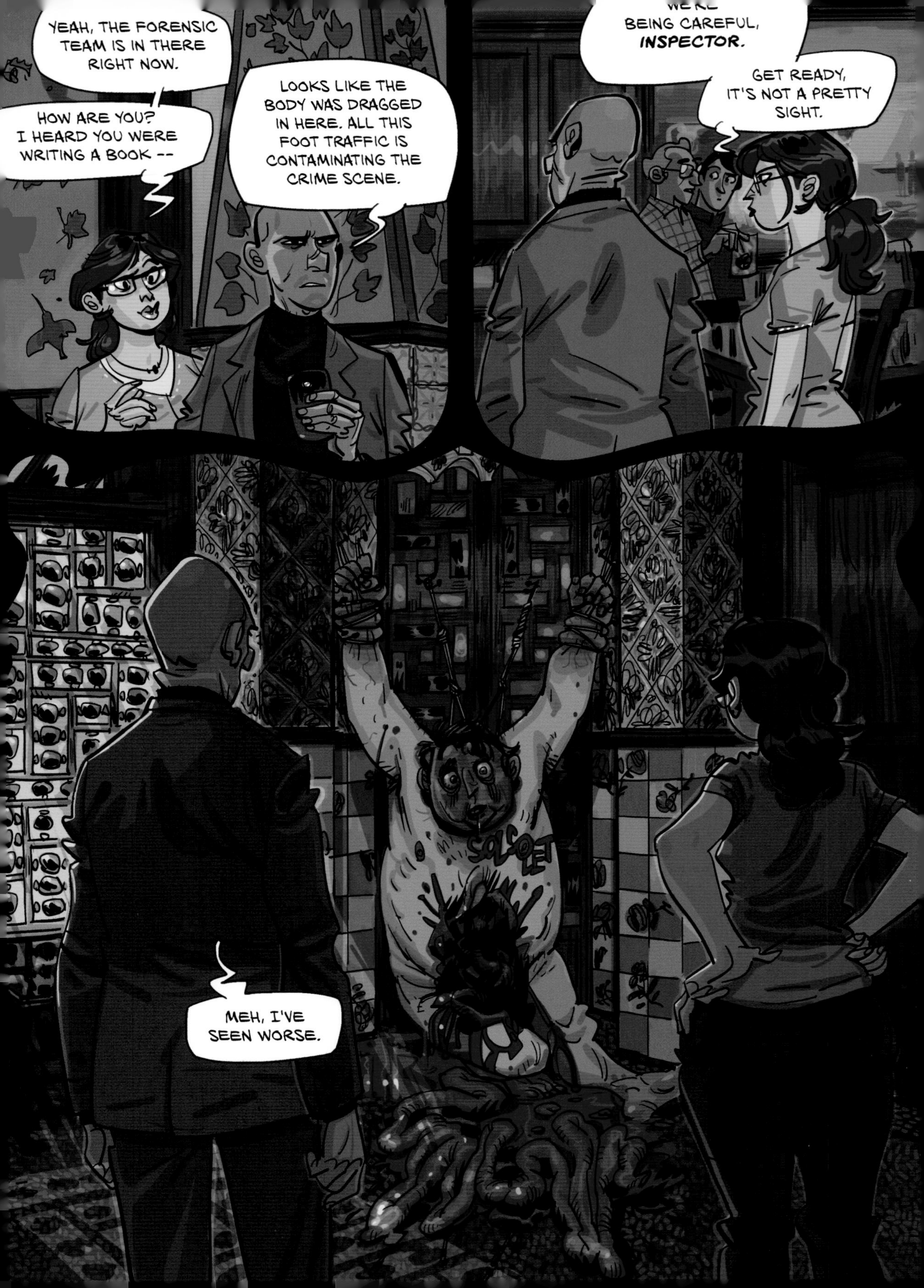
YEAH, THE FORENSIC TEAM IS IN THERE RIGHT NOW.
HOW ARE YOU? I HEARD YOU WERE WRITING A BOOK --
LOOKS LIKE THE BODY WAS DRAGGED IN HERE. ALL THIS FOOT TRAFFIC IS CONTAMINATING THE CRIME SCENE.
BEING CAREFUL, INSPECTOR.
GET READY, IT'S NOT A PRETTY SIGHT.
MEH, I'VE SEEN WORSE.

AH!

RELAX, ANTONIA. YOU'RE IN THE HOSPITAL. THERE WAS AN ACCIDENT AND YOU SUFFERED A MILD CONCUSSION, BUT YOU'RE FINE NOW. YOU CAN RELAX.

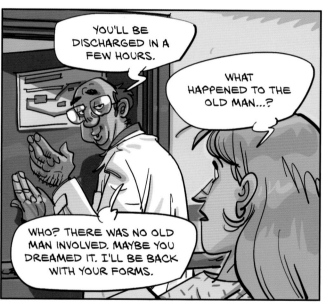

YOU'LL BE DISCHARGED IN A FEW HOURS.

WHAT HAPPENED TO THE OLD MAN...?

WHO? THERE WAS NO OLD MAN INVOLVED. MAYBE YOU DREAMED IT. I'LL BE BACK WITH YOUR FORMS.

A DREAM...? HUH. WHERE'S MY PHONE --

WHAT HAPPENED TO YOU, BLONDIE? HIT BY A CAR?

ALMOST. AN OLD MAN WAS CROSSING GRAN VIA WITHOUT LOOKING, AND WE WERE BOTH NEARLY HIT.

HA -- JUST LIKE GAUDÍ.

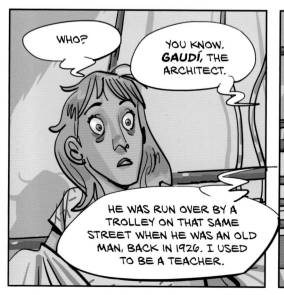

WHO?

YOU KNOW. GAUDÍ, THE ARCHITECT.

HE WAS RUN OVER BY A TROLLEY ON THAT SAME STREET WHEN HE WAS AN OLD MAN, BACK IN 1926. I USED TO BE A TEACHER.

THERE MUST BE A CURSE ON THAT SPOT.

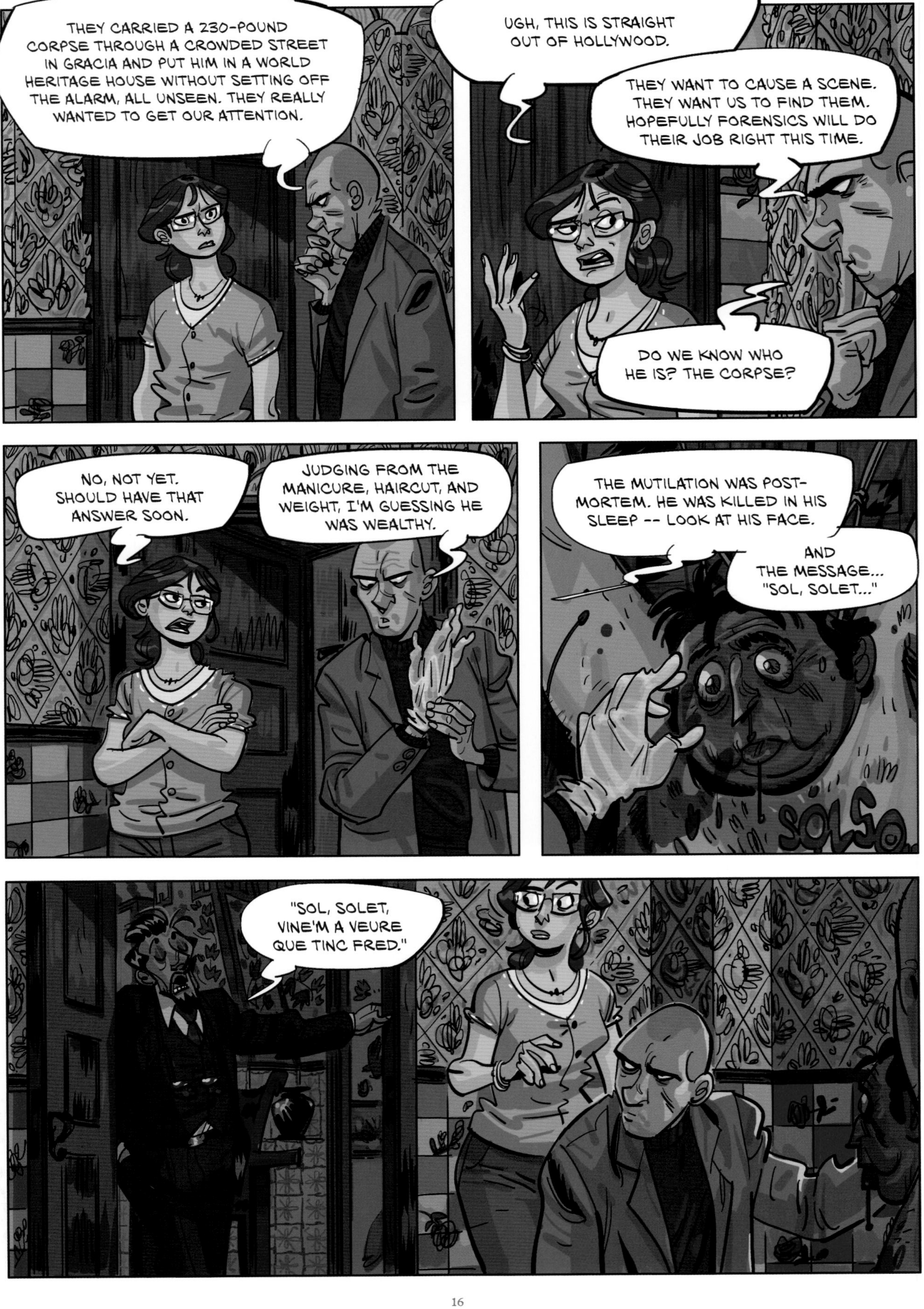

THEY CARRIED A 230-POUND CORPSE THROUGH A CROWDED STREET IN GRACIA AND PUT HIM IN A WORLD HERITAGE HOUSE WITHOUT SETTING OFF THE ALARM, ALL UNSEEN. THEY REALLY WANTED TO GET OUR ATTENTION.
UGH, THIS IS STRAIGHT OUT OF HOLLYWOOD.
THEY WANT TO CAUSE A SCENE. THEY WANT US TO FIND THEM. HOPEFULLY FORENSICS WILL DO THEIR JOB RIGHT THIS TIME.
DO WE KNOW WHO HE IS? THE CORPSE?
NO, NOT YET. SHOULD HAVE THAT ANSWER SOON.
JUDGING FROM THE MANICURE, HAIRCUT, AND WEIGHT, I'M GUESSING HE WAS WEALTHY.
THE MUTILATION WAS POST-MORTEM. HE WAS KILLED IN HIS SLEEP -- LOOK AT HIS FACE.
AND THE MESSAGE... "SOL, SOLET..."
SOLSO
"SOL, SOLET, VINE'M A VEURE QUE TINC FRED."

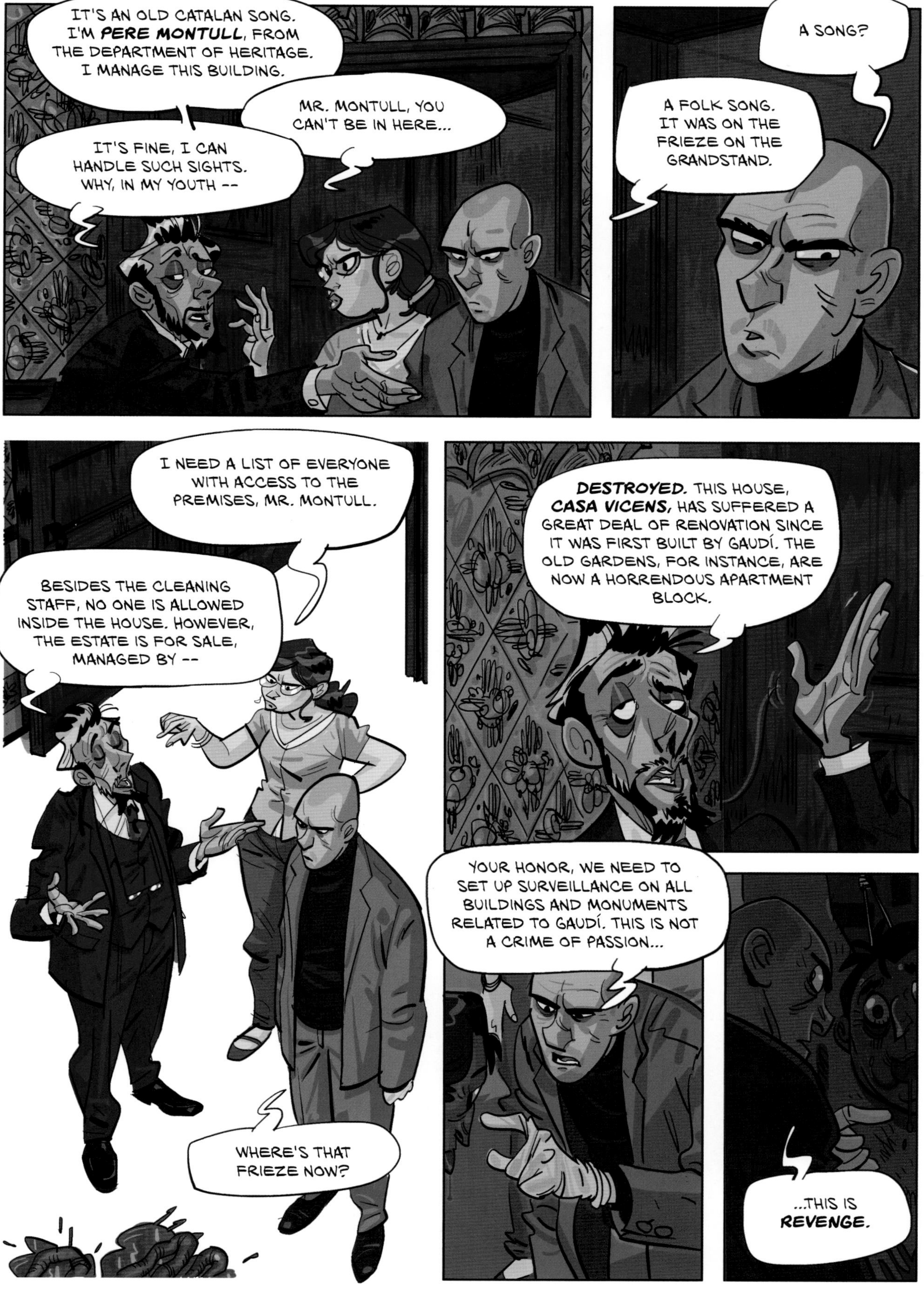

IT'S AN OLD CATALAN SONG. I'M PERE MONTULL, FROM THE DEPARTMENT OF HERITAGE. I MANAGE THIS BUILDING.
MR. MONTULL, YOU CAN'T BE IN HERE...
IT'S FINE, I CAN HANDLE SUCH SIGHTS. WHY, IN MY YOUTH --
A SONG?
A FOLK SONG. IT WAS ON THE FRIEZE ON THE GRANDSTAND.
I NEED A LIST OF EVERYONE WITH ACCESS TO THE PREMISES, MR. MONTULL.
BESIDES THE CLEANING STAFF, NO ONE IS ALLOWED INSIDE THE HOUSE. HOWEVER, THE ESTATE IS FOR SALE, MANAGED BY --
WHERE'S THAT FRIEZE NOW?
DESTROYED. THIS HOUSE, CASA VICENS, HAS SUFFERED A GREAT DEAL OF RENOVATION SINCE IT WAS FIRST BUILT BY GAUDÍ. THE OLD GARDENS, FOR INSTANCE, ARE NOW A HORRENDOUS APARTMENT BLOCK.
YOUR HONOR, WE NEED TO SET UP SURVEILLANCE ON ALL BUILDINGS AND MONUMENTS RELATED TO GAUDÍ. THIS IS NOT A CRIME OF PASSION...
...THIS IS REVENGE.

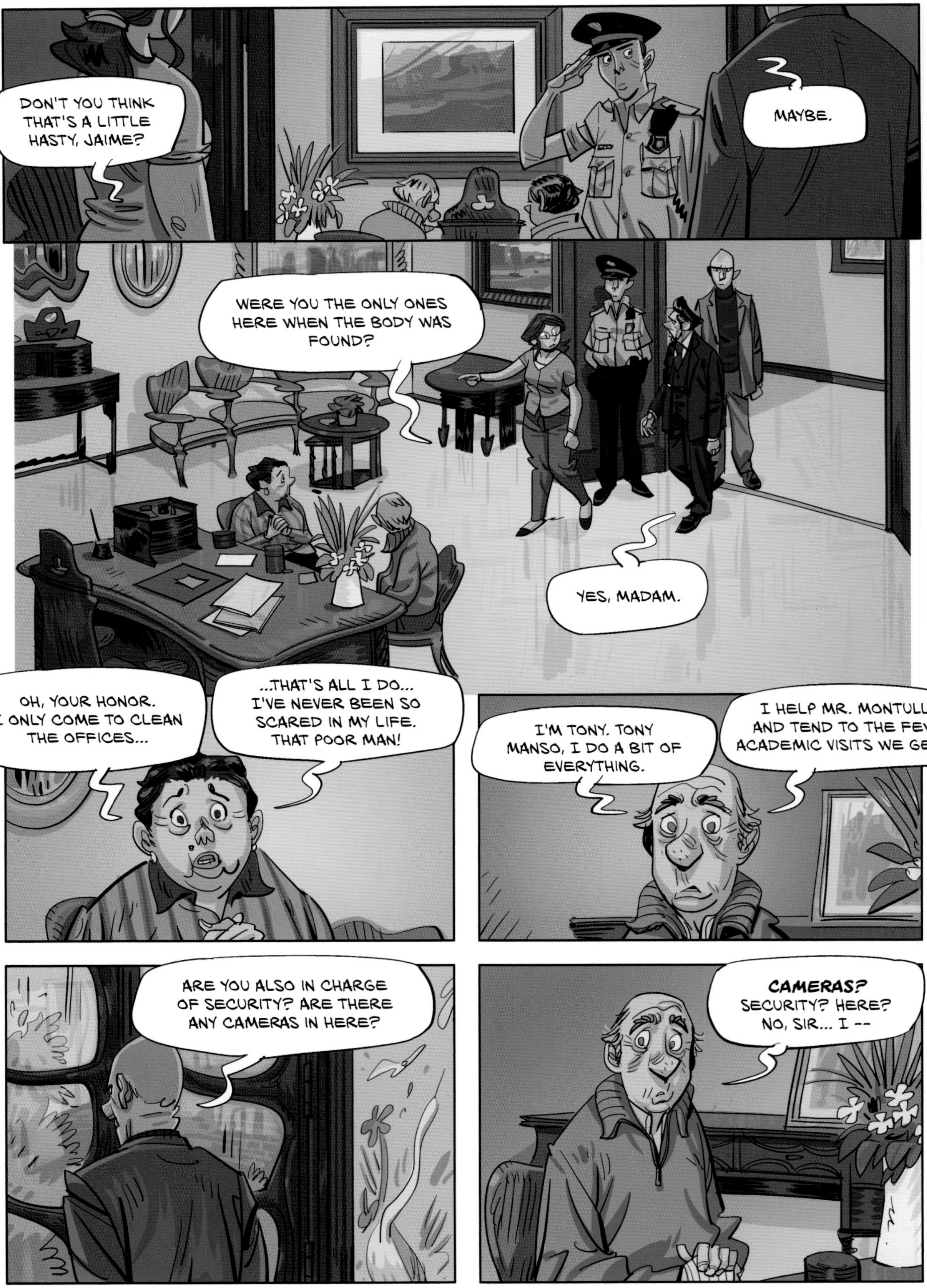
DON'T YOU THINK THAT'S A LITTLE HASTY, JAIME?
MAYBE.
WERE YOU THE ONLY ONES HERE WHEN THE BODY WAS FOUND?
YES, MADAM.
OH, YOUR HONOR. I ONLY COME TO CLEAN THE OFFICES...
...THAT'S ALL I DO... I'VE NEVER BEEN SO SCARED IN MY LIFE. THAT POOR MAN!
I'M TONY. TONY MANSO, I DO A BIT OF EVERYTHING.
I HELP MR. MONTULL AND TEND TO THE FEW ACADEMIC VISITS WE GET...
ARE YOU ALSO IN CHARGE OF SECURITY? ARE THERE ANY CAMERAS IN HERE?
CAMERAS? SECURITY? HERE? NO, SIR... I --

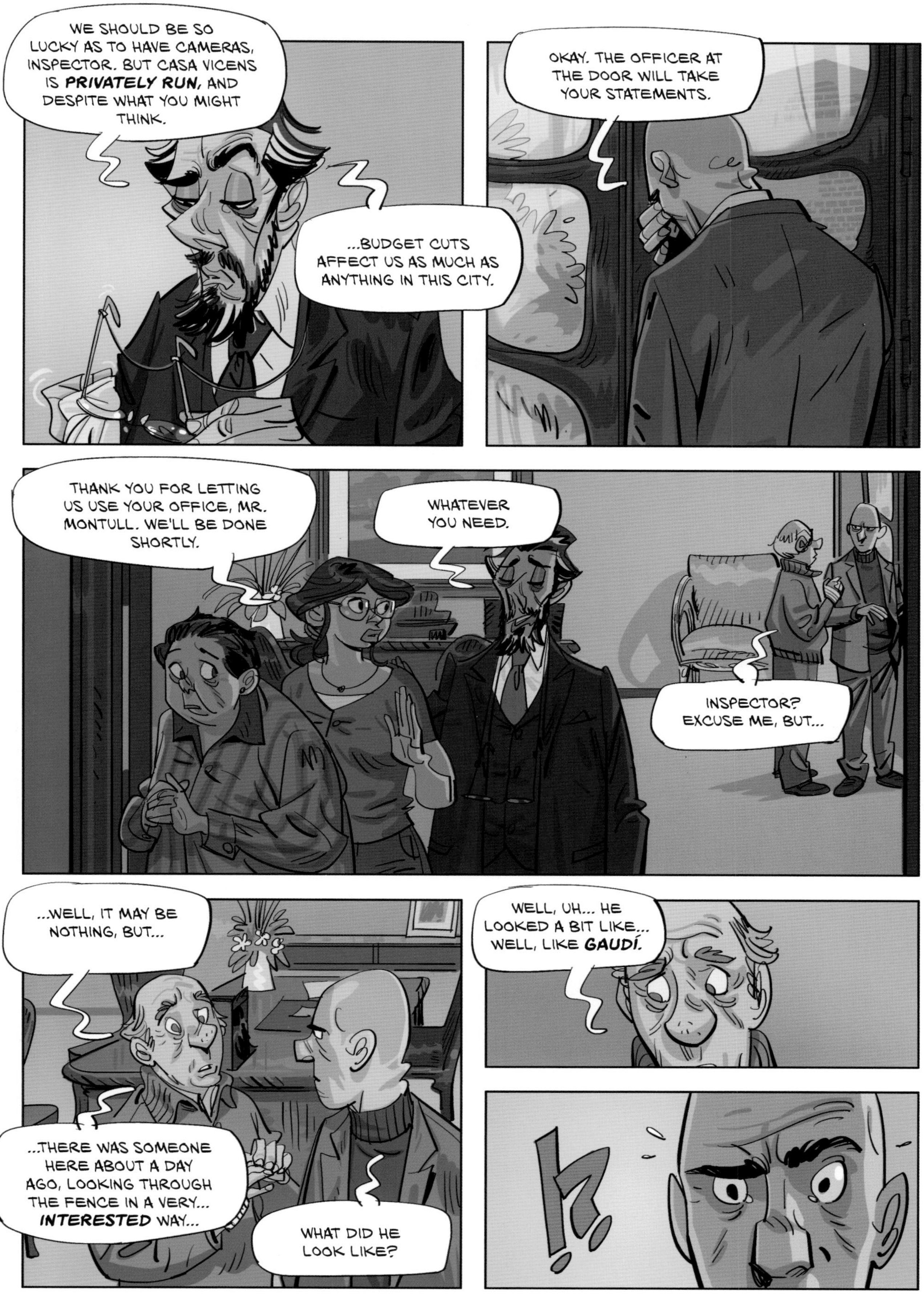
WE SHOULD BE SO LUCKY AS TO HAVE CAMERAS, INSPECTOR. BUT CASA VICENS IS **PRIVATELY RUN,** AND DESPITE WHAT YOU MIGHT THINK.
...BUDGET CUTS AFFECT US AS MUCH AS ANYTHING IN THIS CITY.
OKAY. THE OFFICER AT THE DOOR WILL TAKE YOUR STATEMENTS.
THANK YOU FOR LETTING US USE YOUR OFFICE, MR. MONTULL. WE'LL BE DONE SHORTLY.
WHATEVER YOU NEED.
INSPECTOR? EXCUSE ME, BUT...
...WELL, IT MAY BE NOTHING, BUT...
...THERE WAS SOMEONE HERE ABOUT A DAY AGO, LOOKING THROUGH THE FENCE IN A VERY... ***INTERESTED*** WAY...
WHAT DID HE LOOK LIKE?
WELL, UH... HE LOOKED A BIT LIKE... WELL, LIKE **GAUDÍ.**
!?

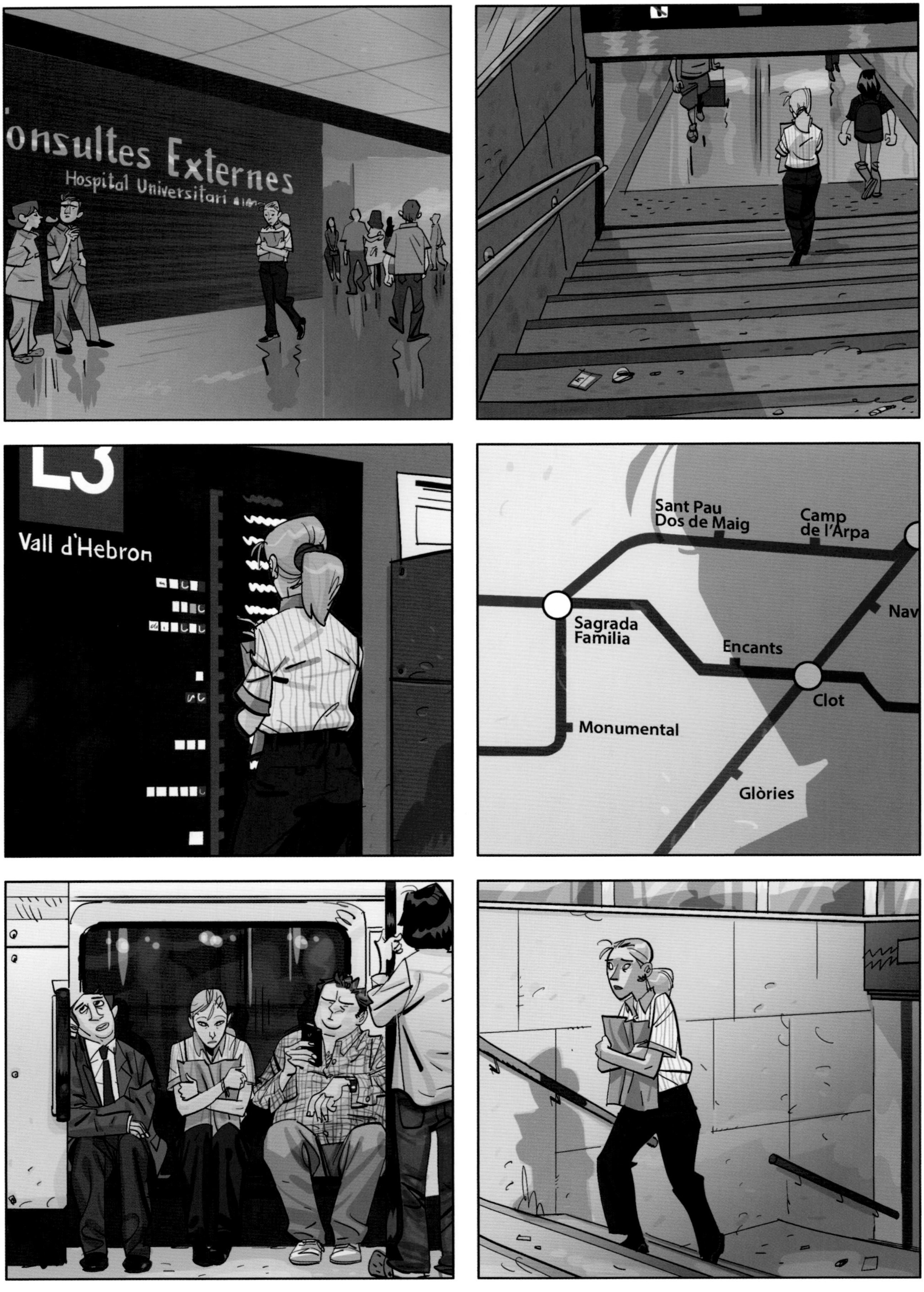
onsultes Externes
Hospital Universitari
Vall d'Hebron
Sant Pau
Dos de Maig
Camp
de l'Arpa
Sagrada
Familia
Encants
Clot
Monumental
Glòries

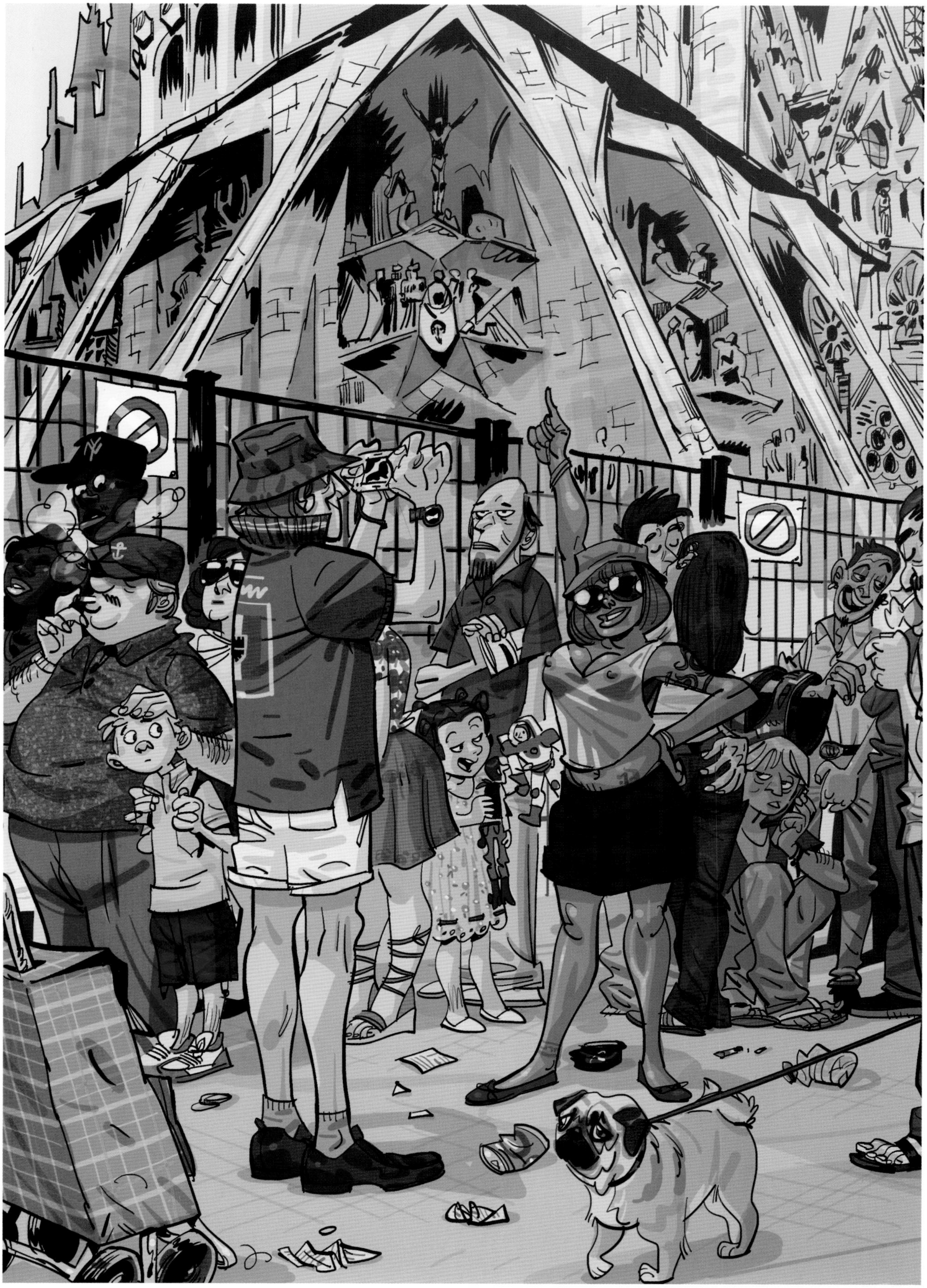

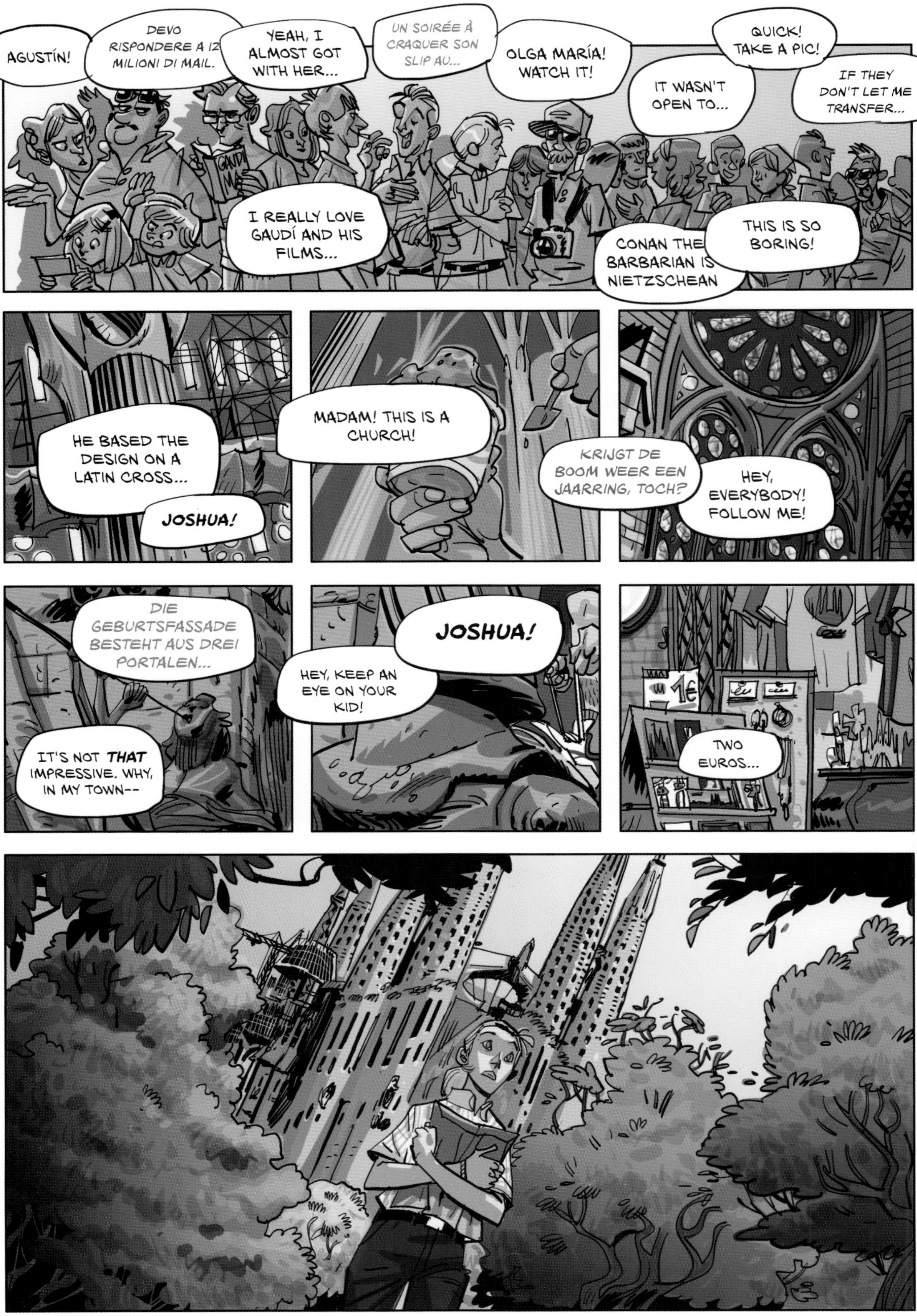
AGUSTÍN!
DEVO RISPONDERE A 12 MILIONI DI MAIL.
YEAH, I ALMOST GOT WITH HER...
UN SOIRÉE À CRAQUER SON SLIP AU...
OLGA MARÍA! WATCH IT!
QUICK! TAKE A PIC!
IT WASN'T OPEN TO...
IF THEY DON'T LET ME TRANSFER...
I REALLY LOVE GAUDÍ AND HIS FILMS...
CONAN THE BARBARIAN IS NIETZSCHEAN
THIS IS SO BORING!
HE BASED THE DESIGN ON A LATIN CROSS...
JOSHUA!
MADAM! THIS IS A CHURCH!
KRIJGT DE BOOM WEER EEN JAARRING, TOCH?
HEY, EVERYBODY! FOLLOW ME!
DIE GEBURTSFASSADE BESTEHT AUS DREI PORTALEN...
IT'S NOT THAT IMPRESSIVE. WHY, IN MY TOWN--
JOSHUA!
HEY, KEEP AN EYE ON YOUR KID!
1€
TWO EUROS...

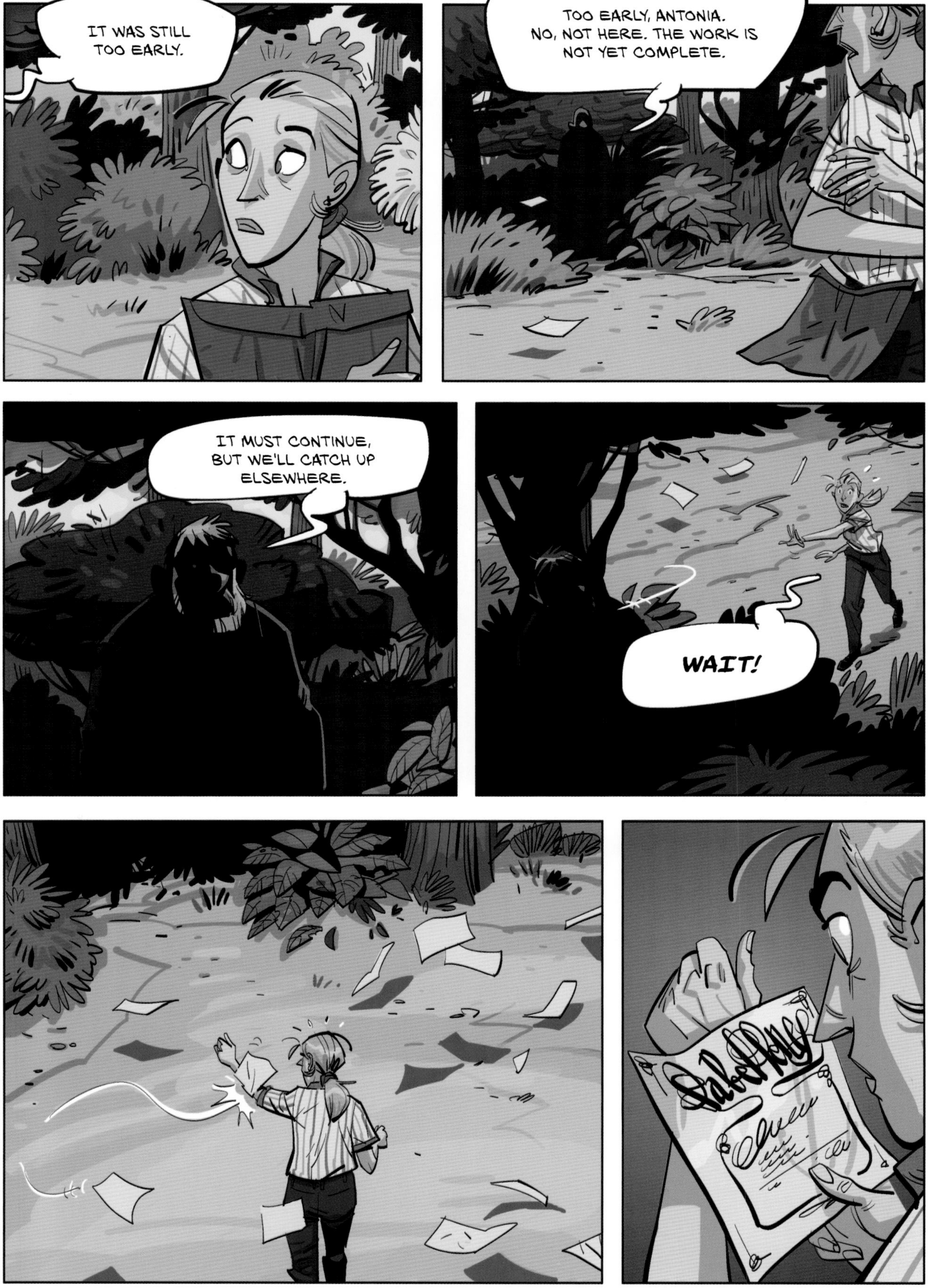
IT WAS STILL TOO EARLY.
TOO EARLY, ANTONIA. NO, NOT HERE. THE WORK IS NOT YET COMPLETE.
IT MUST CONTINUE, BUT WE'LL CATCH UP ELSEWHERE.
WAIT!

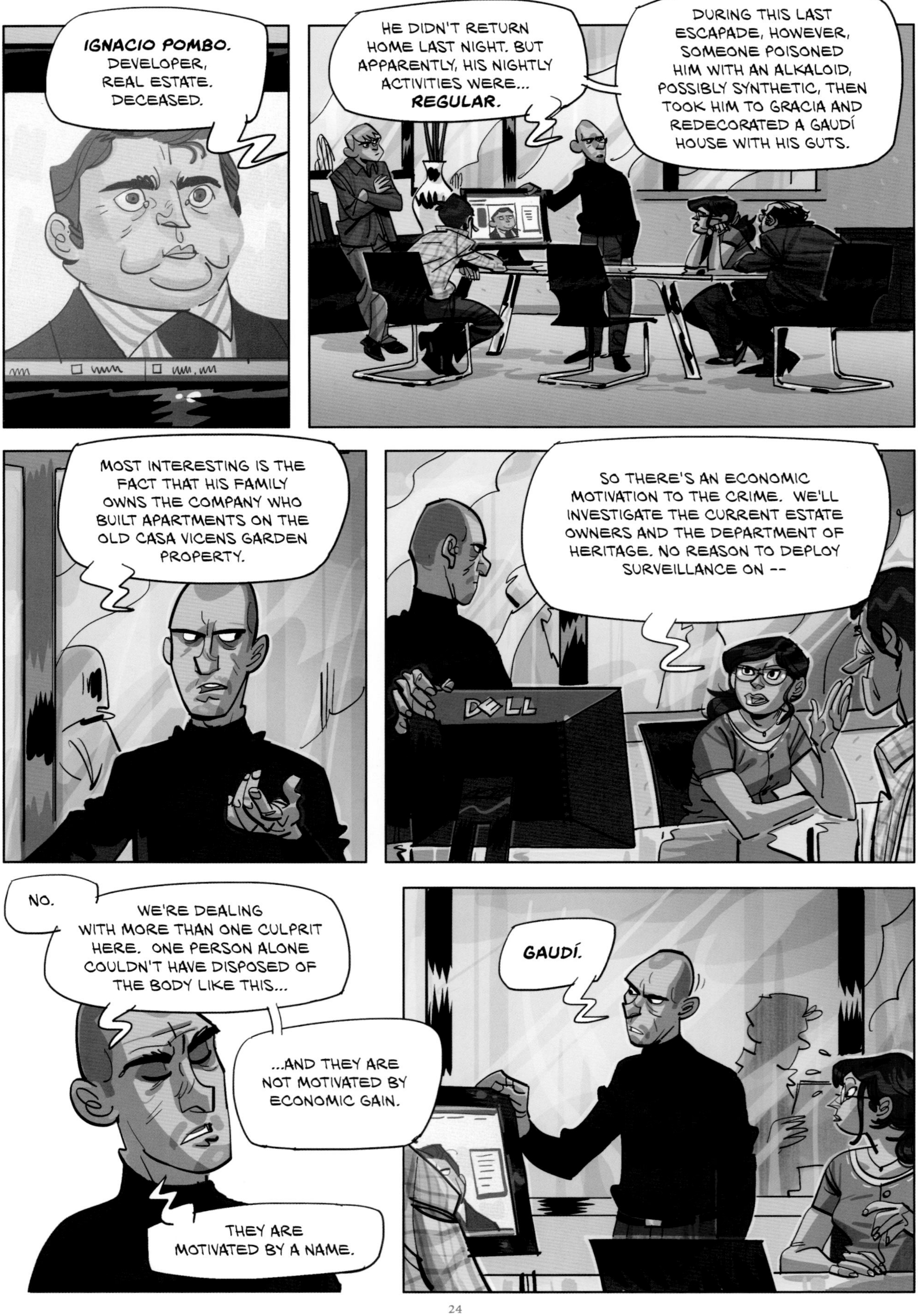
IGNACIO POMBO. DEVELOPER, REAL ESTATE. DECEASED.
HE DIDN'T RETURN HOME LAST NIGHT. BUT APPARENTLY, HIS NIGHTLY ACTIVITIES WERE... REGULAR.
DURING THIS LAST ESCAPADE, HOWEVER, SOMEONE POISONED HIM WITH AN ALKALOID, POSSIBLY SYNTHETIC, THEN TOOK HIM TO GRACIA AND REDECORATED A GAUDÍ HOUSE WITH HIS GUTS.
MOST INTERESTING IS THE FACT THAT HIS FAMILY OWNS THE COMPANY WHO BUILT APARTMENTS ON THE OLD CASA VICENS GARDEN PROPERTY.
SO THERE'S AN ECONOMIC MOTIVATION TO THE CRIME. WE'LL INVESTIGATE THE CURRENT ESTATE OWNERS AND THE DEPARTMENT OF HERITAGE. NO REASON TO DEPLOY SURVEILLANCE ON --
DELL
NO.
WE'RE DEALING WITH MORE THAN ONE CULPRIT HERE. ONE PERSON ALONE COULDN'T HAVE DISPOSED OF THE BODY LIKE THIS...
...AND THEY ARE NOT MOTIVATED BY ECONOMIC GAIN.
THEY ARE MOTIVATED BY A NAME.
GAUDÍ.

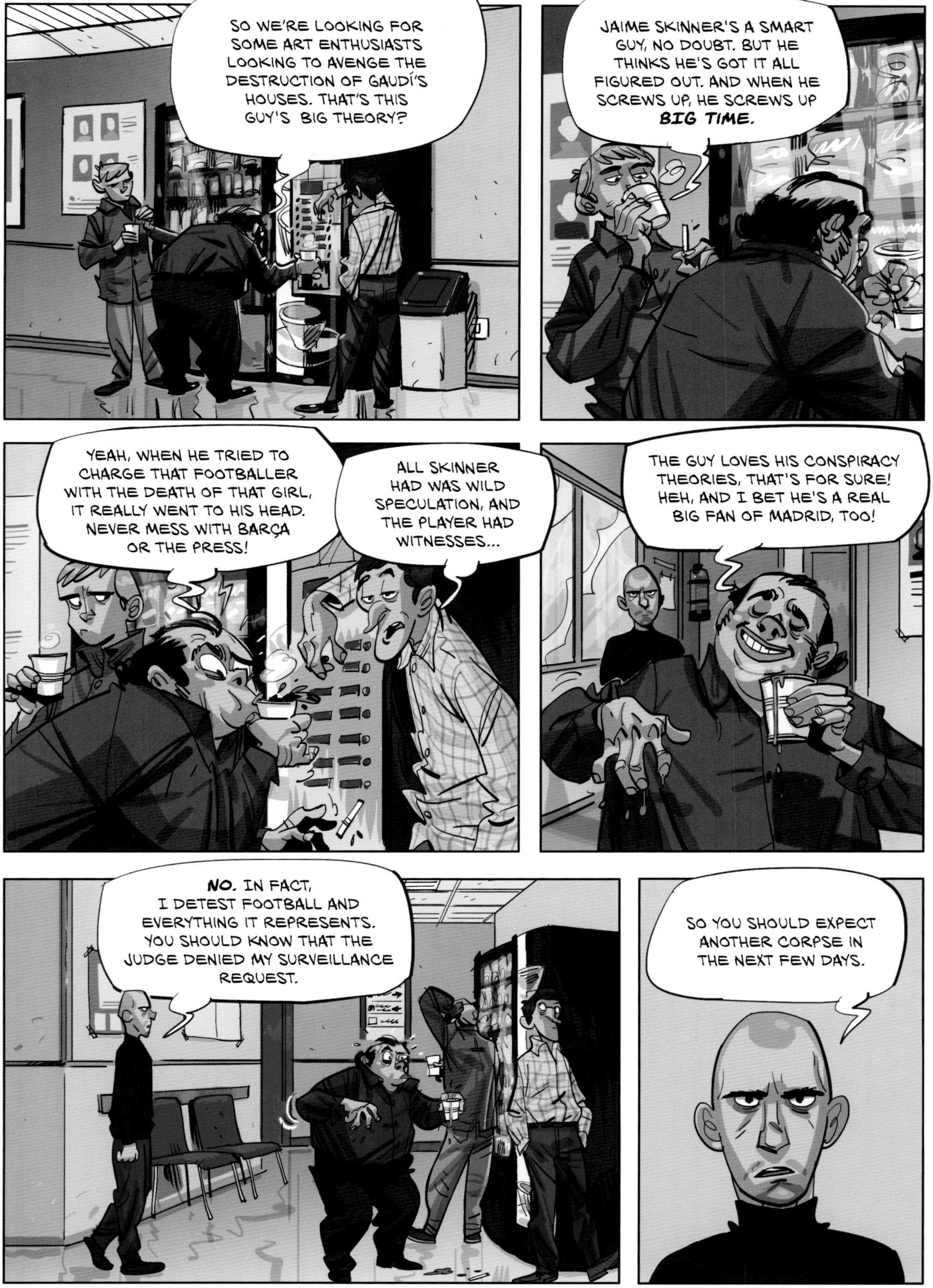
SO WE'RE LOOKING FOR SOME ART ENTHUSIASTS LOOKING TO AVENGE THE DESTRUCTION OF GAUDÍ'S HOUSES. THAT'S THIS GUY'S BIG THEORY?
JAIME SKINNER'S A SMART GUY, NO DOUBT. BUT HE THINKS HE'S GOT IT ALL FIGURED OUT. AND WHEN HE SCREWS UP, HE SCREWS UP BIG TIME.
YEAH, WHEN HE TRIED TO CHARGE THAT FOOTBALLER WITH THE DEATH OF THAT GIRL, IT REALLY WENT TO HIS HEAD. NEVER MESS WITH BARÇA OR THE PRESS!
ALL SKINNER HAD WAS WILD SPECULATION, AND THE PLAYER HAD WITNESSES...
THE GUY LOVES HIS CONSPIRACY THEORIES, THAT'S FOR SURE! HEH, AND I BET HE'S A REAL BIG FAN OF MADRID, TOO!
NO. IN FACT, I DETEST FOOTBALL AND EVERYTHING IT REPRESENTS. YOU SHOULD KNOW THAT THE JUDGE DENIED MY SURVEILLANCE REQUEST.
SO YOU SHOULD EXPECT ANOTHER CORPSE IN THE NEXT FEW DAYS.

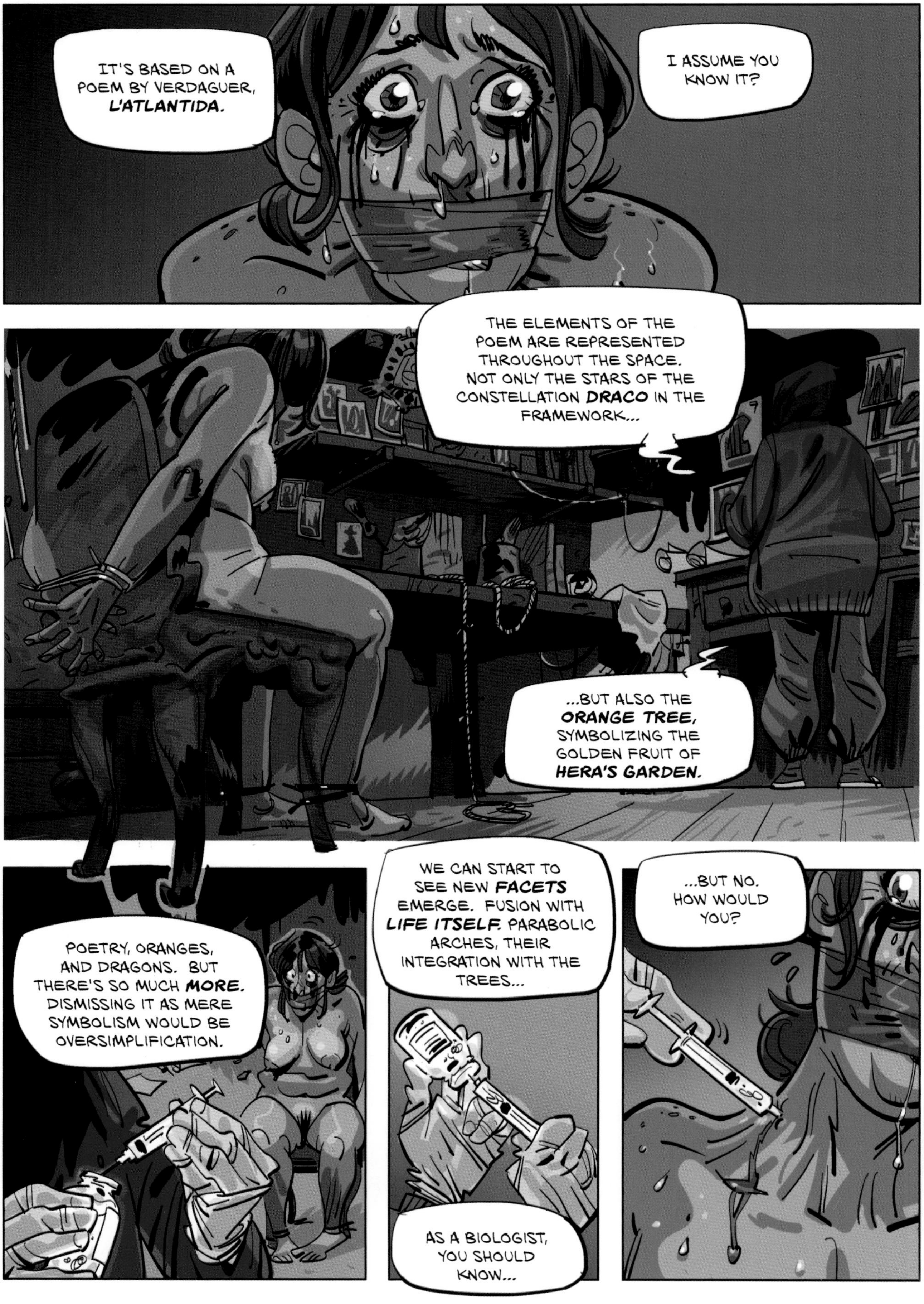
IT'S BASED ON A POEM BY VERDAGUER, **L'ATLANTIDA.**
I ASSUME YOU KNOW IT?
THE ELEMENTS OF THE POEM ARE REPRESENTED THROUGHOUT THE SPACE. NOT ONLY THE STARS OF THE CONSTELLATION **DRACO** IN THE FRAMEWORK...
...BUT ALSO THE **ORANGE TREE,** SYMBOLIZING THE GOLDEN FRUIT OF **HERA'S GARDEN.**
POETRY, ORANGES, AND DRAGONS. BUT THERE'S SO MUCH **MORE.** DISMISSING IT AS MERE SYMBOLISM WOULD BE OVERSIMPLIFICATION.
WE CAN START TO SEE NEW **FACETS** EMERGE. FUSION WITH **LIFE ITSELF.** PARABOLIC ARCHES, THEIR INTEGRATION WITH THE TREES...
AS A BIOLOGIST, YOU SHOULD KNOW...
...BUT NO. HOW WOULD YOU?

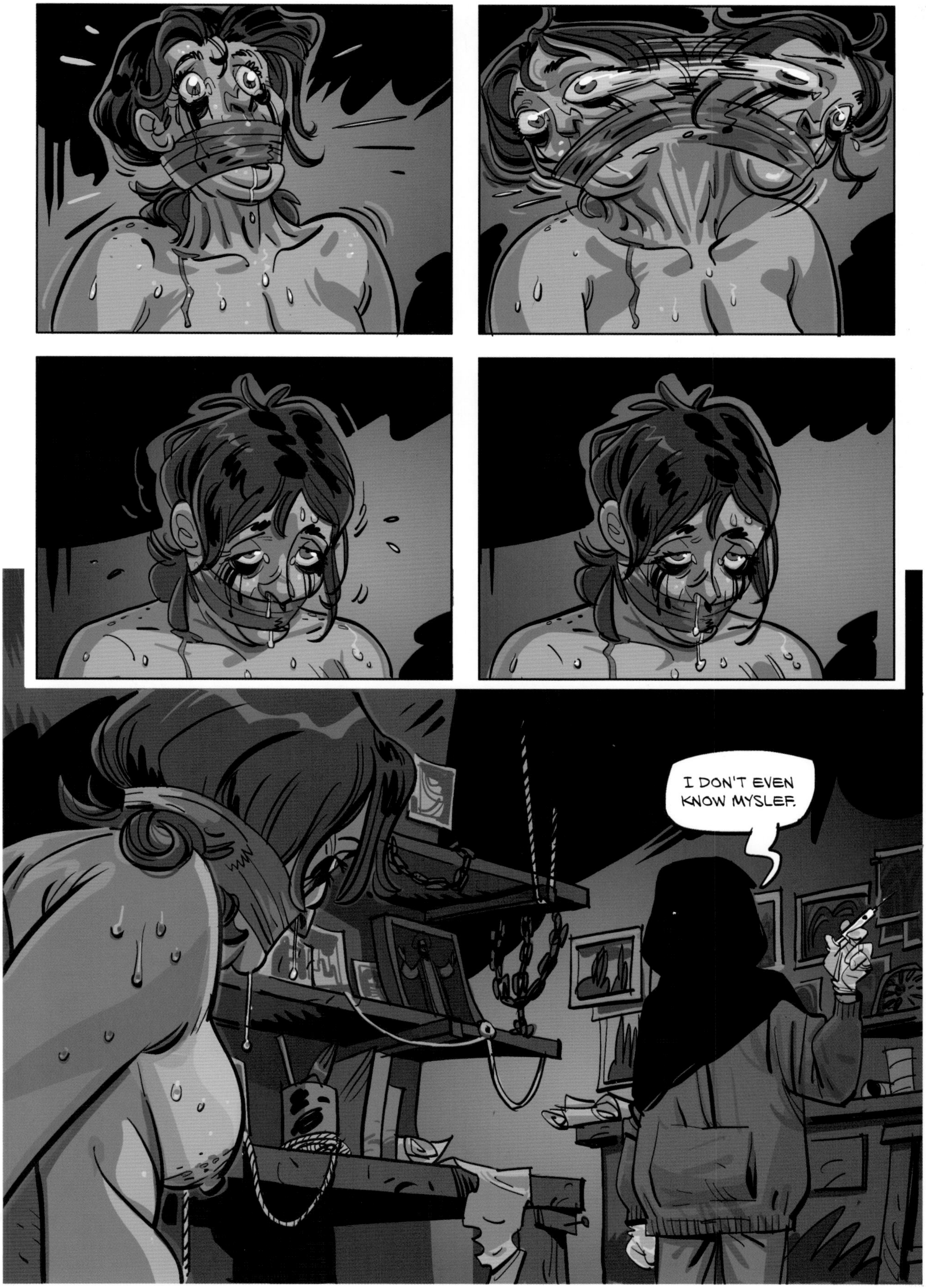
I DON'T EVEN KNOW MYSLEF.

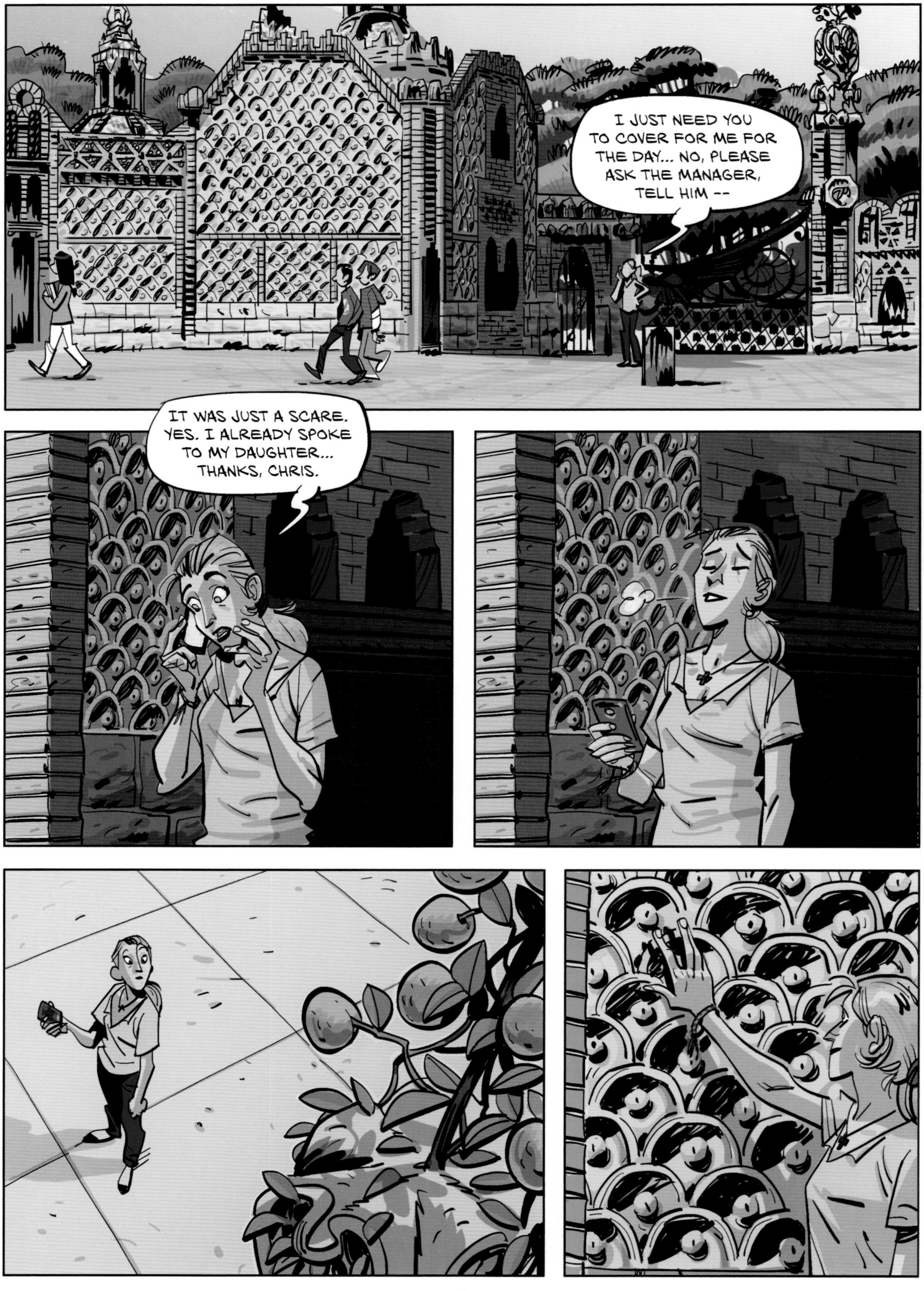
I JUST NEED YOU TO COVER FOR ME FOR THE DAY... NO, PLEASE ASK THE MANAGER, TELL HIM --
IT WAS JUST A SCARE. YES. I ALREADY SPOKE TO MY DAUGHTER... THANKS, CHRIS.

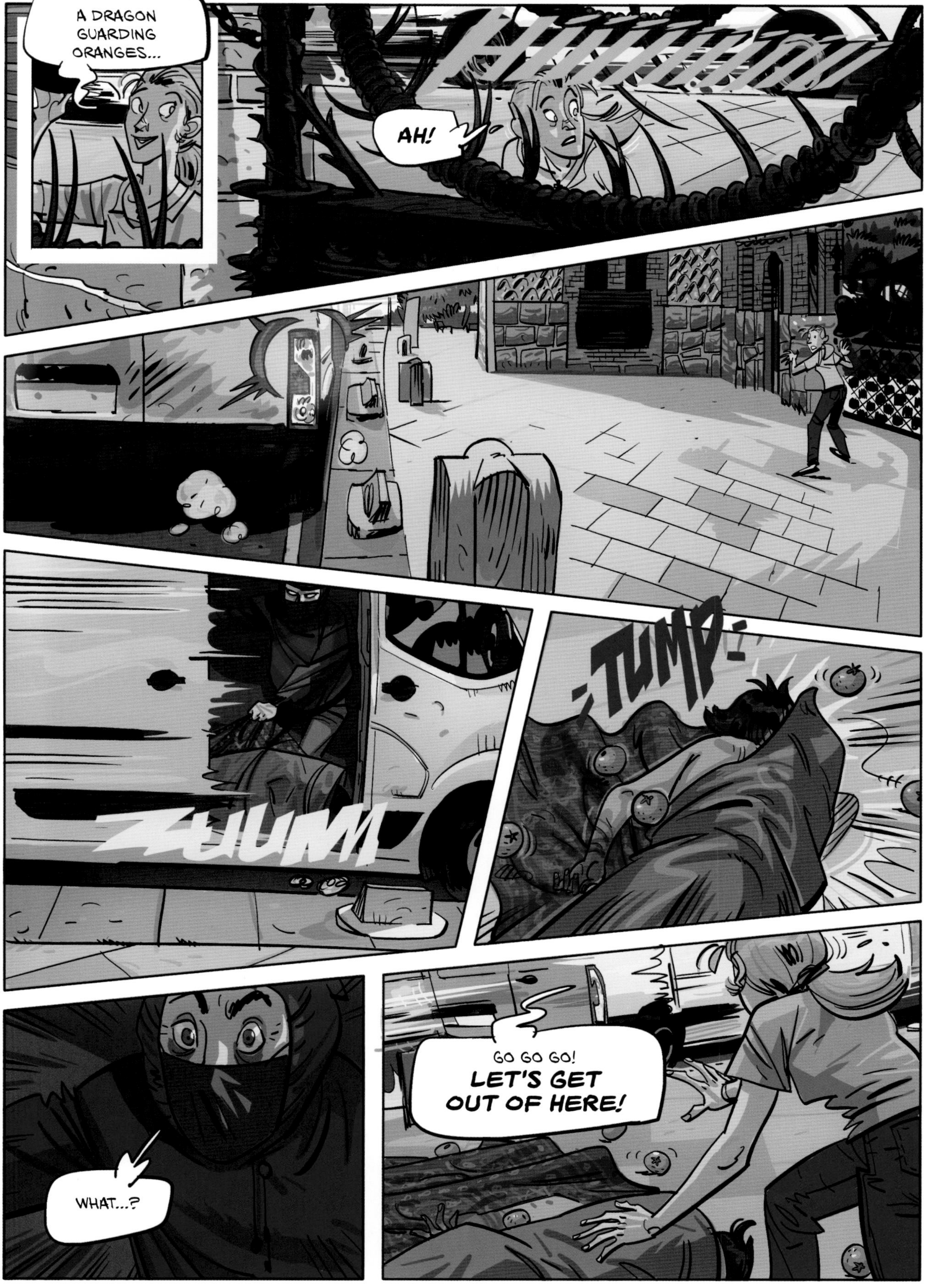
A DRAGON GUARDING ORANGES...
AH!
TUMP
ZUUMM
WHAT...?
GO GO GO!
LET'S GET OUT OF HERE!

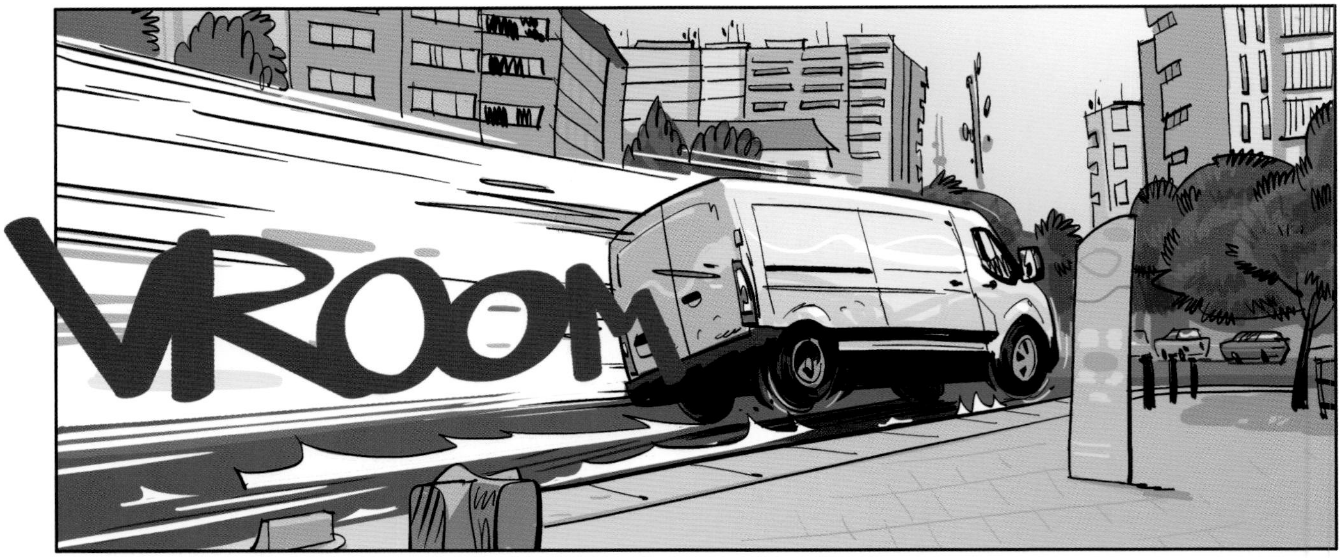
VROOM

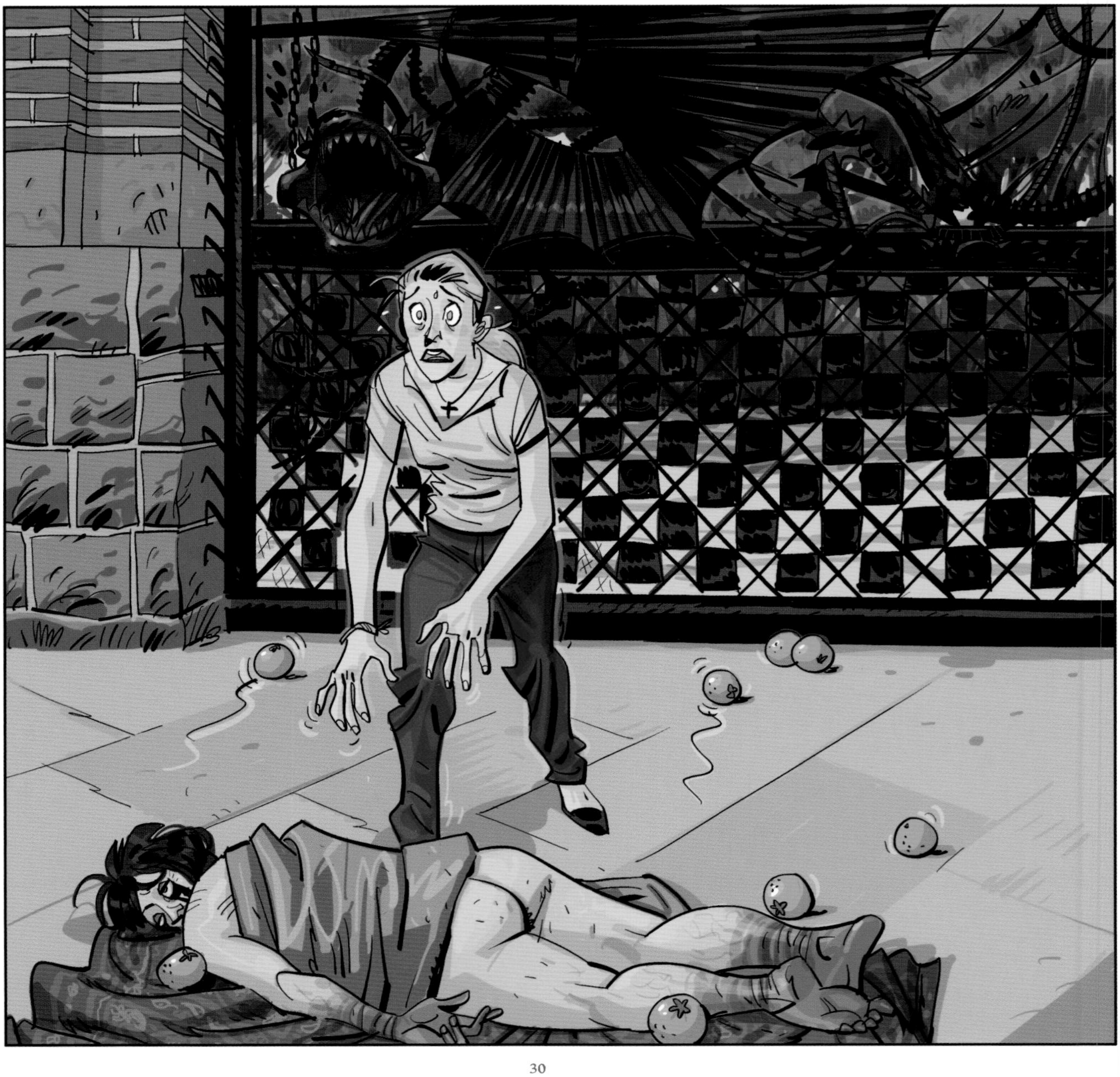

Chapter 2

Güell Palace ⋄ Casa Calvet
Park Güell

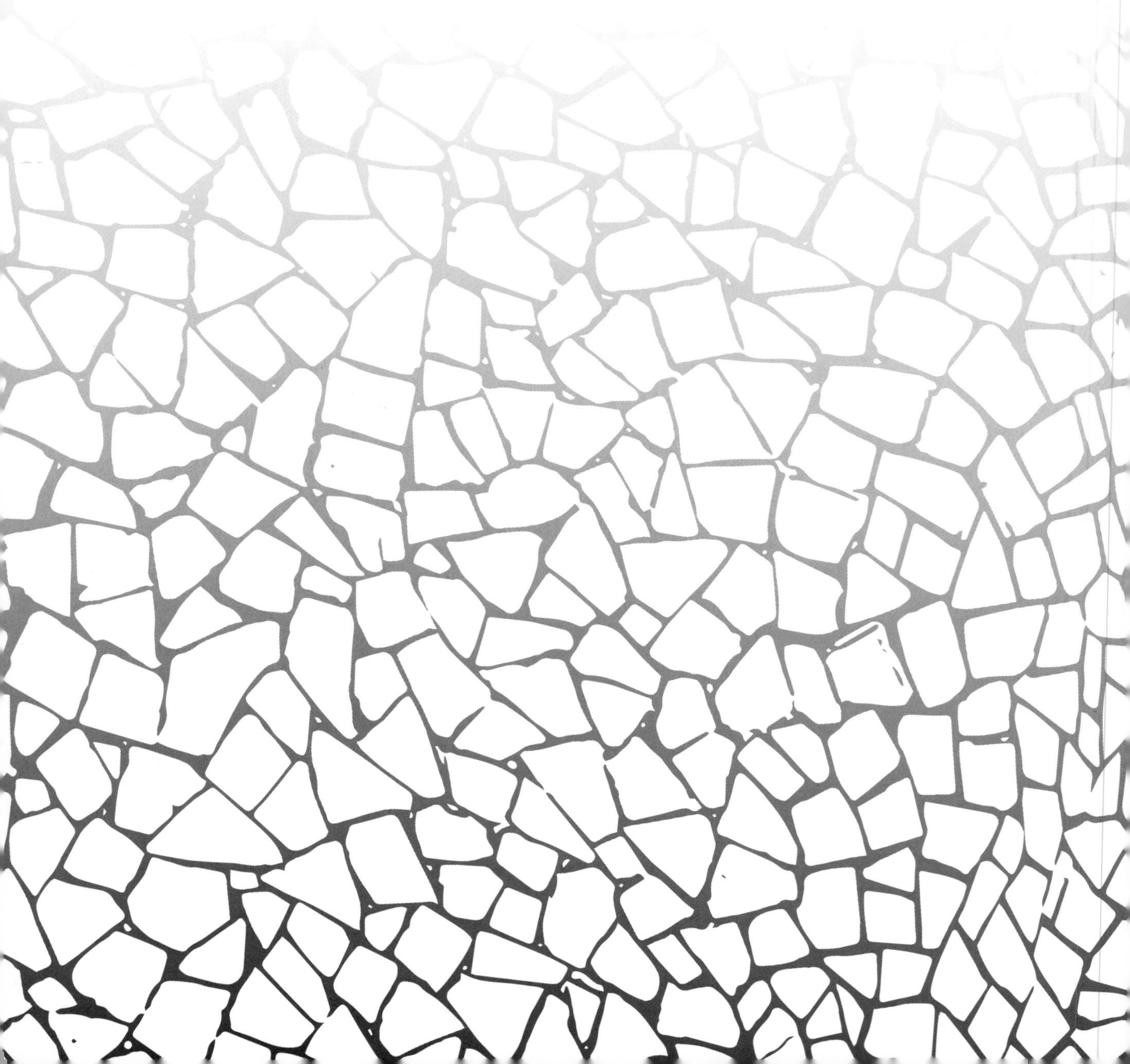

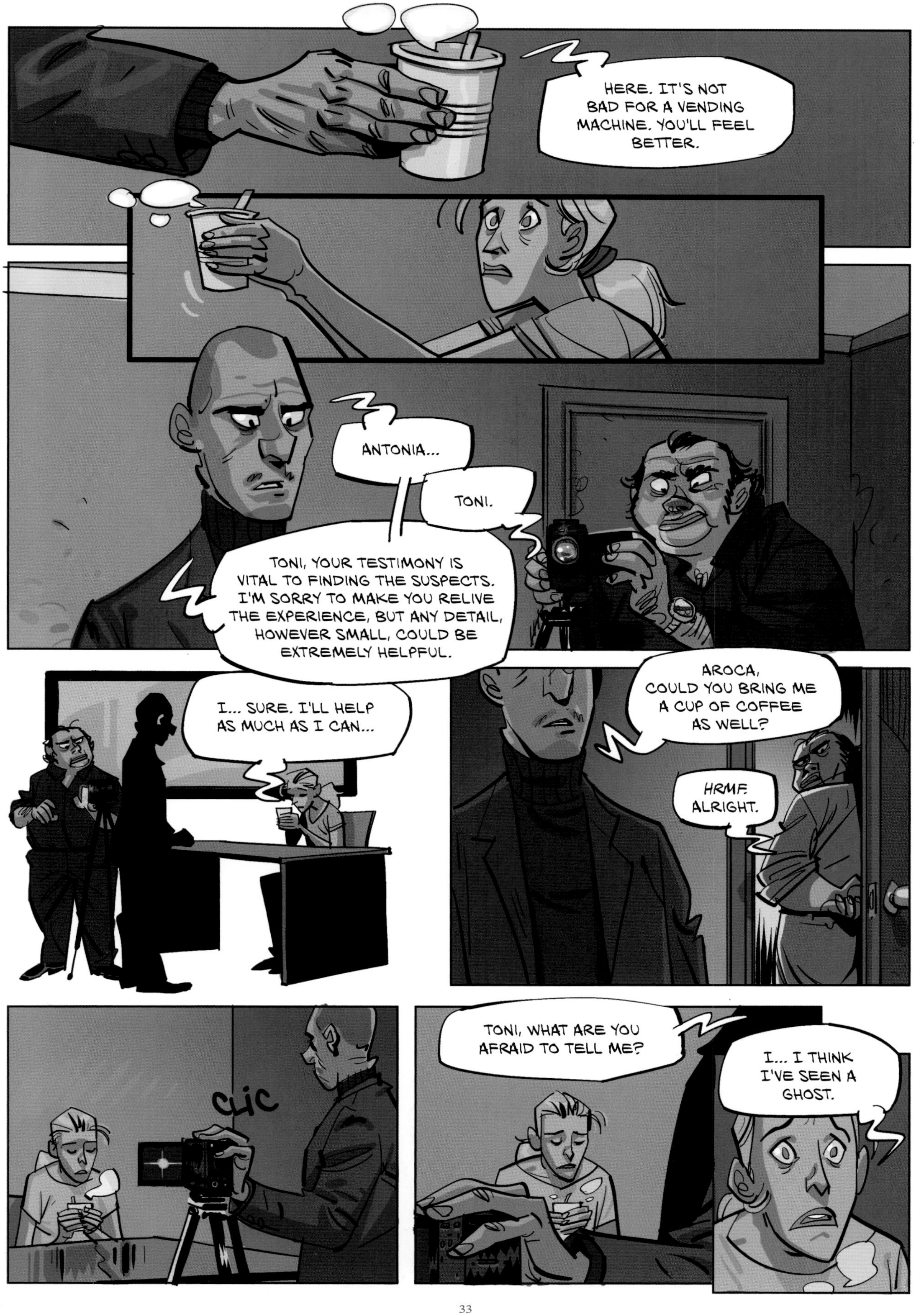
HERE. IT'S NOT BAD FOR A VENDING MACHINE. YOU'LL FEEL BETTER.
ANTONIA...
TONI.
TONI, YOUR TESTIMONY IS VITAL TO FINDING THE SUSPECTS. I'M SORRY TO MAKE YOU RELIVE THE EXPERIENCE, BUT ANY DETAIL, HOWEVER SMALL, COULD BE EXTREMELY HELPFUL.
I... SURE. I'LL HELP AS MUCH AS I CAN...
AROCA, COULD YOU BRING ME A CUP OF COFFEE AS WELL?
HRMF. ALRIGHT.
CLIC
TONI, WHAT ARE YOU AFRAID TO TELL ME?
I... I THINK I'VE SEEN A GHOST.

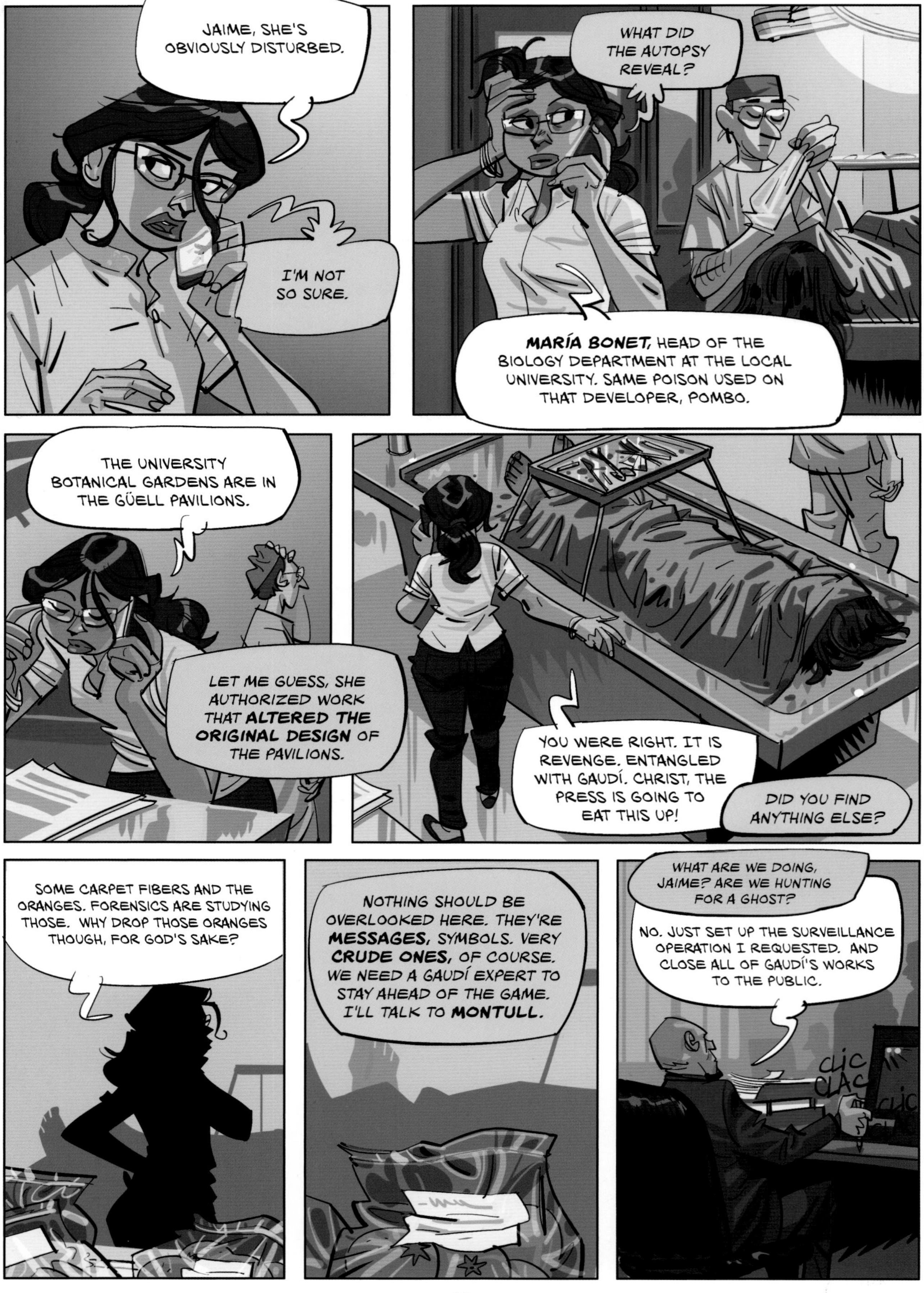
JAIME, SHE'S OBVIOUSLY DISTURBED.
I'M NOT SO SURE.
WHAT DID THE AUTOPSY REVEAL?
MARÍA BONET, HEAD OF THE BIOLOGY DEPARTMENT AT THE LOCAL UNIVERSITY. SAME POISON USED ON THAT DEVELOPER, POMBO.
THE UNIVERSITY BOTANICAL GARDENS ARE IN THE GÜELL PAVILIONS.
LET ME GUESS, SHE AUTHORIZED WORK THAT ALTERED THE ORIGINAL DESIGN OF THE PAVILIONS.
YOU WERE RIGHT. IT IS REVENGE. ENTANGLED WITH GAUDÍ. CHRIST, THE PRESS IS GOING TO EAT THIS UP!
DID YOU FIND ANYTHING ELSE?
SOME CARPET FIBERS AND THE ORANGES. FORENSICS ARE STUDYING THOSE. WHY DROP THOSE ORANGES THOUGH, FOR GOD'S SAKE?
NOTHING SHOULD BE OVERLOOKED HERE. THEY'RE MESSAGES, SYMBOLS. VERY CRUDE ONES, OF COURSE. WE NEED A GAUDÍ EXPERT TO STAY AHEAD OF THE GAME. I'LL TALK TO MONTULL.
WHAT ARE WE DOING, JAIME? ARE WE HUNTING FOR A GHOST?
NO. JUST SET UP THE SURVEILLANCE OPERATION I REQUESTED. AND CLOSE ALL OF GAUDÍ'S WORKS TO THE PUBLIC.
CLIC
CLAC

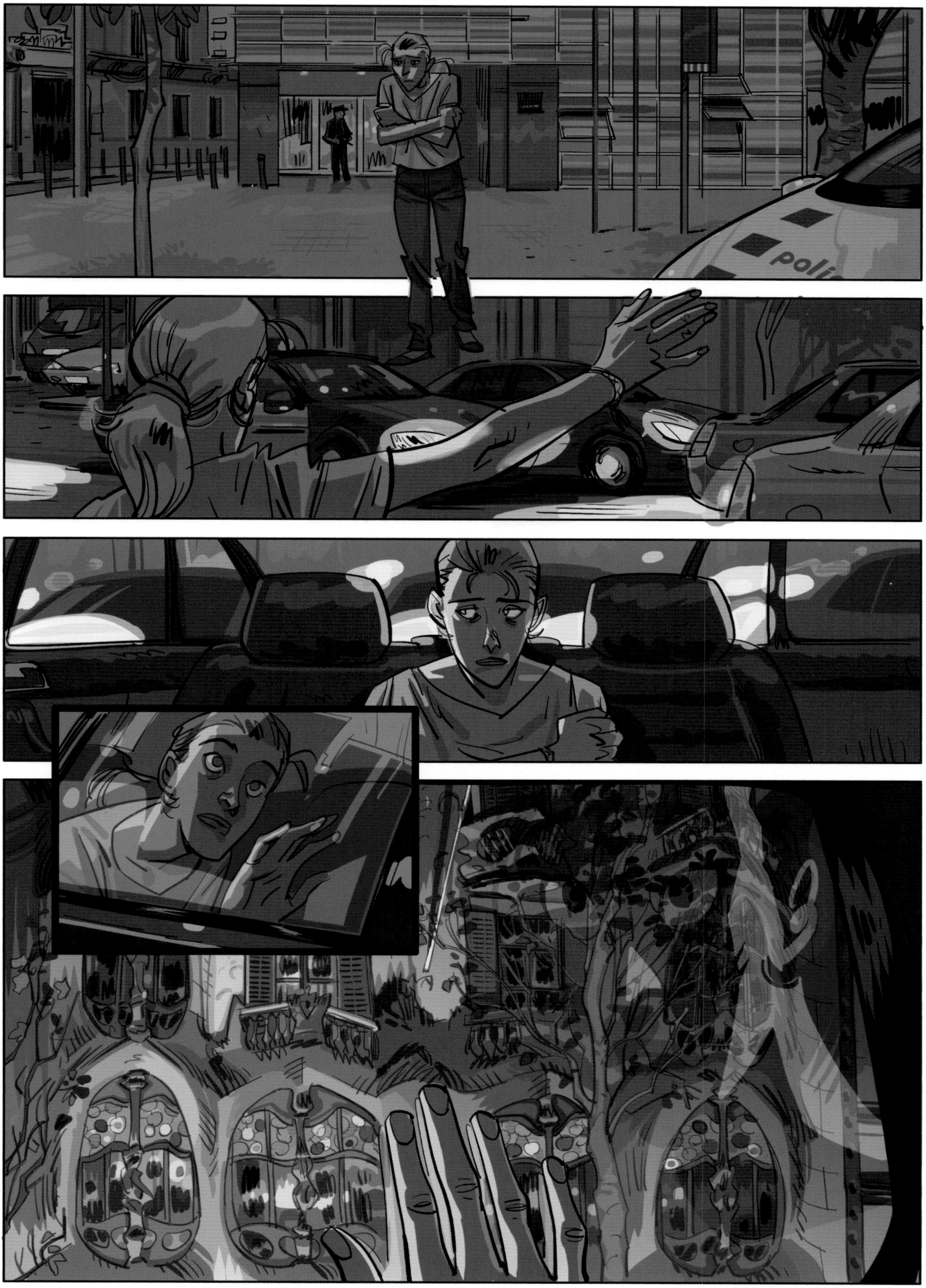
polic

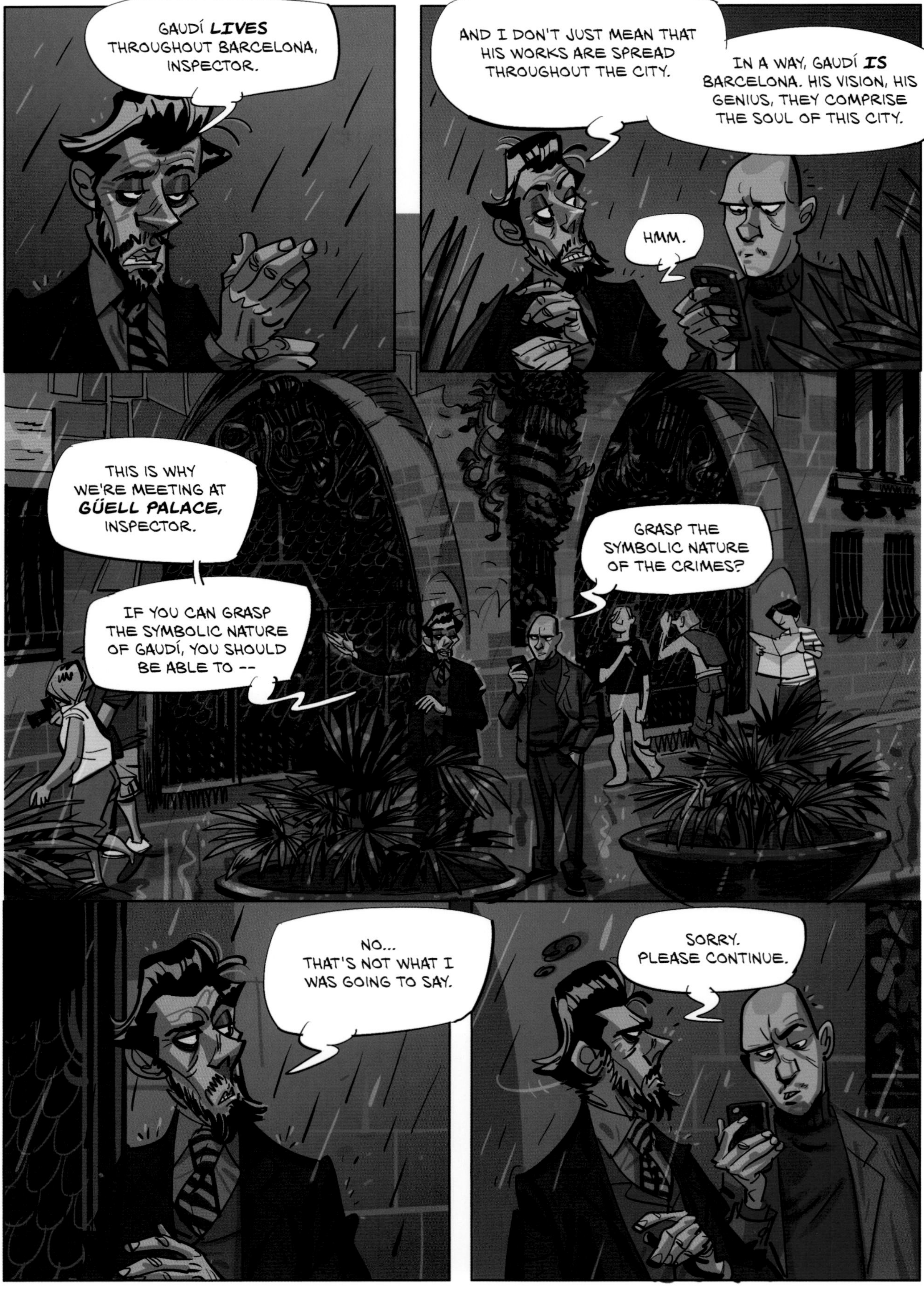
GAUDÍ LIVES THROUGHOUT BARCELONA, INSPECTOR.
AND I DON'T JUST MEAN THAT HIS WORKS ARE SPREAD THROUGHOUT THE CITY.
IN A WAY, GAUDÍ IS BARCELONA. HIS VISION, HIS GENIUS, THEY COMPRISE THE SOUL OF THIS CITY.
HMM.
THIS IS WHY WE'RE MEETING AT GÜELL PALACE, INSPECTOR.
IF YOU CAN GRASP THE SYMBOLIC NATURE OF GAUDÍ, YOU SHOULD BE ABLE TO --
GRASP THE SYMBOLIC NATURE OF THE CRIMES?
NO... THAT'S NOT WHAT I WAS GOING TO SAY.
SORRY. PLEASE CONTINUE.

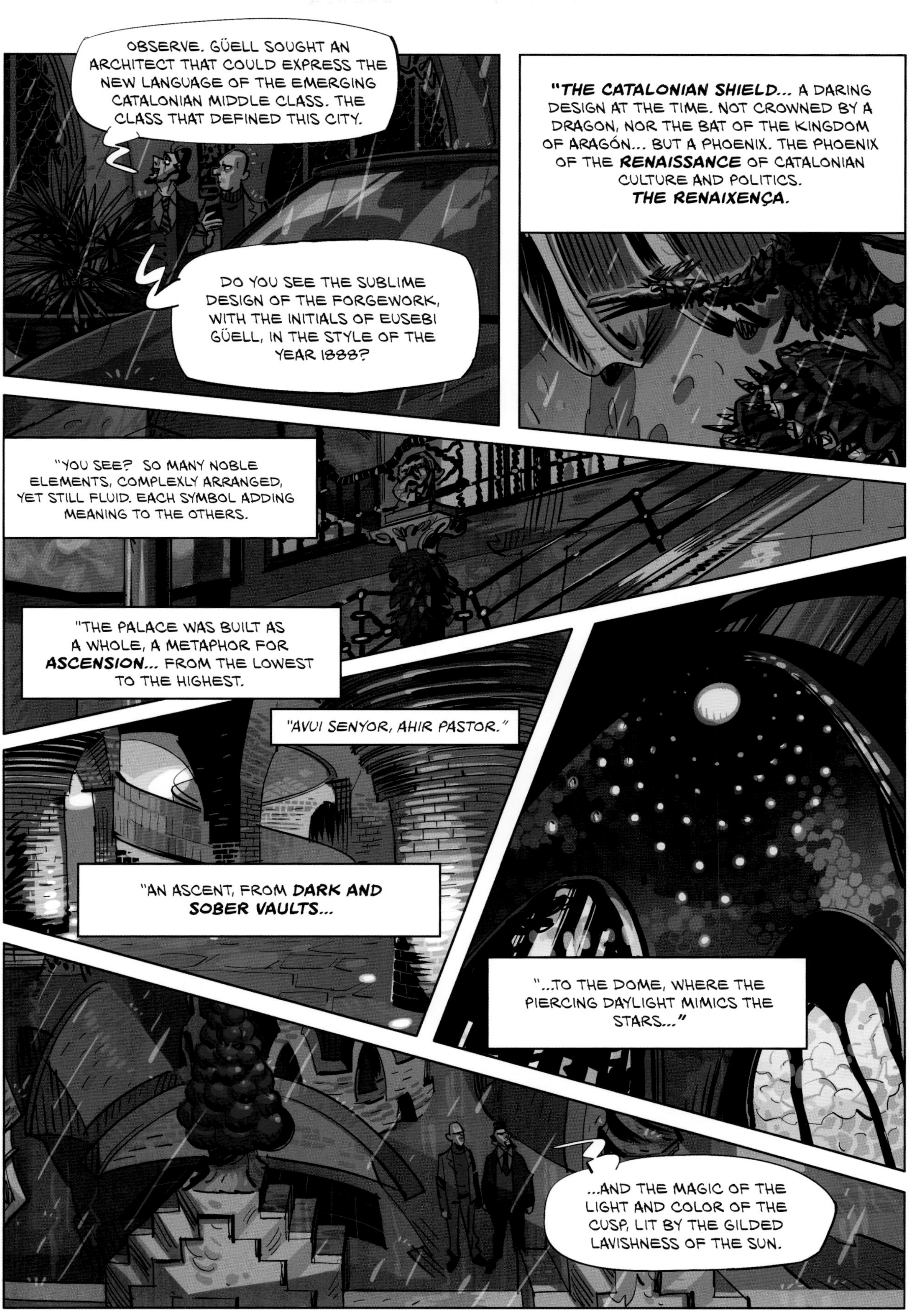
OBSERVE. GÜELL SOUGHT AN ARCHITECT THAT COULD EXPRESS THE NEW LANGUAGE OF THE EMERGING CATALONIAN MIDDLE CLASS. THE CLASS THAT DEFINED THIS CITY.
DO YOU SEE THE SUBLIME DESIGN OF THE FORGEWORK, WITH THE INITIALS OF EUSEBI GÜELL, IN THE STYLE OF THE YEAR 1888?
"THE CATALONIAN SHIELD... A DARING DESIGN AT THE TIME. NOT CROWNED BY A DRAGON, NOR THE BAT OF THE KINGDOM OF ARAGÓN... BUT A PHOENIX. THE PHOENIX OF THE RENAISSANCE OF CATALONIAN CULTURE AND POLITICS. THE RENAIXENÇA.
"YOU SEE? SO MANY NOBLE ELEMENTS, COMPLEXLY ARRANGED, YET STILL FLUID. EACH SYMBOL ADDING MEANING TO THE OTHERS.
"THE PALACE WAS BUILT AS A WHOLE, A METAPHOR FOR ASCENSION... FROM THE LOWEST TO THE HIGHEST.
"AVUI SENYOR, AHIR PASTOR."
"AN ASCENT, FROM DARK AND SOBER VAULTS...
"...TO THE DOME, WHERE THE PIERCING DAYLIGHT MIMICS THE STARS..."
...AND THE MAGIC OF THE LIGHT AND COLOR OF THE CUSP, LIT BY THE GILDED LAVISHNESS OF THE SUN.

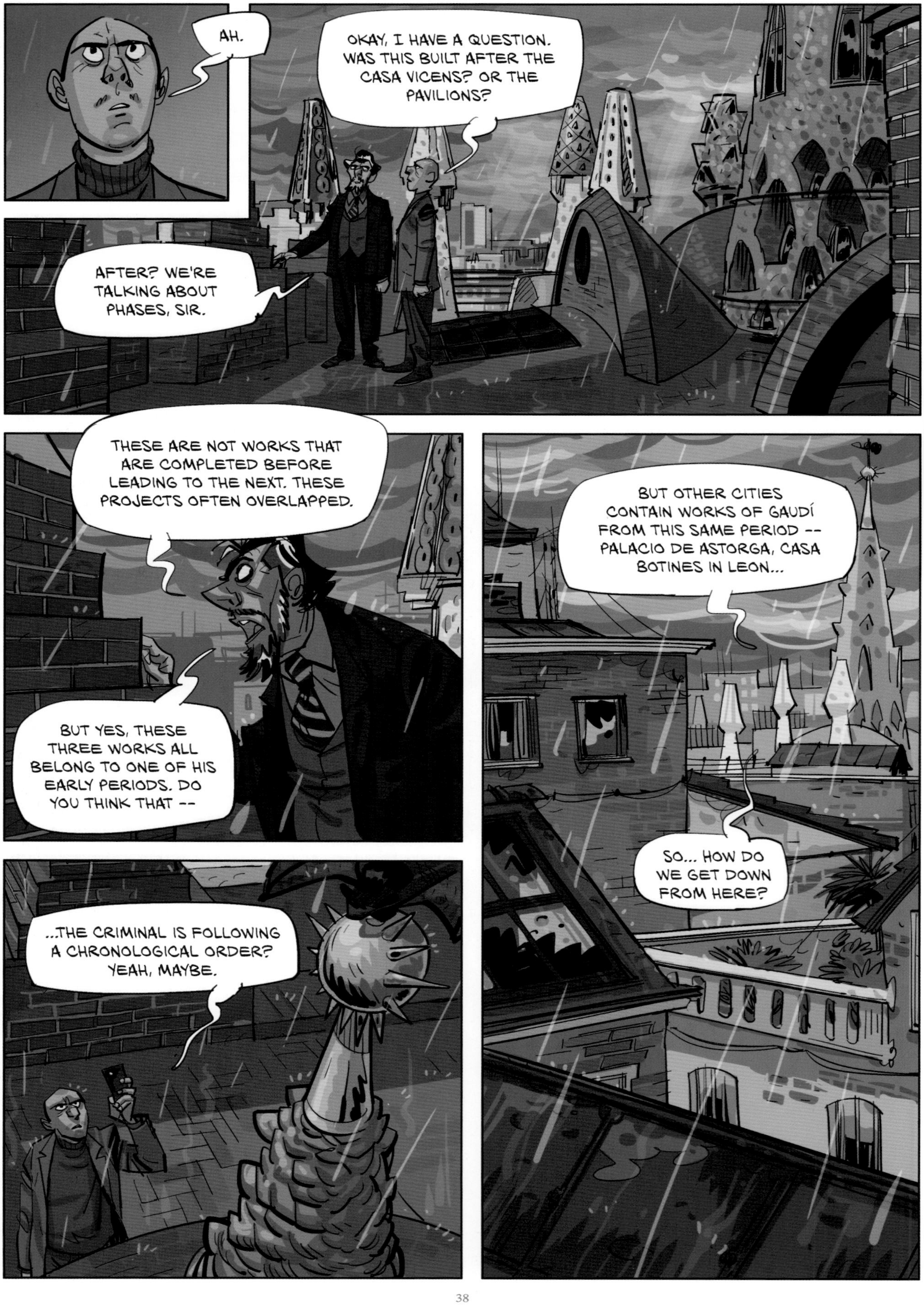
AH.
OKAY, I HAVE A QUESTION. WAS THIS BUILT AFTER THE CASA VICENS? OR THE PAVILIONS?
AFTER? WE'RE TALKING ABOUT PHASES, SIR.
THESE ARE NOT WORKS THAT ARE COMPLETED BEFORE LEADING TO THE NEXT. THESE PROJECTS OFTEN OVERLAPPED.
BUT YES, THESE THREE WORKS ALL BELONG TO ONE OF HIS EARLY PERIODS. DO YOU THINK THAT --
...THE CRIMINAL IS FOLLOWING A CHRONOLOGICAL ORDER? YEAH, MAYBE.
BUT OTHER CITIES CONTAIN WORKS OF GAUDÍ FROM THIS SAME PERIOD -- PALACIO DE ASTORGA, CASA BOTINES IN LEON...
SO... HOW DO WE GET DOWN FROM HERE?

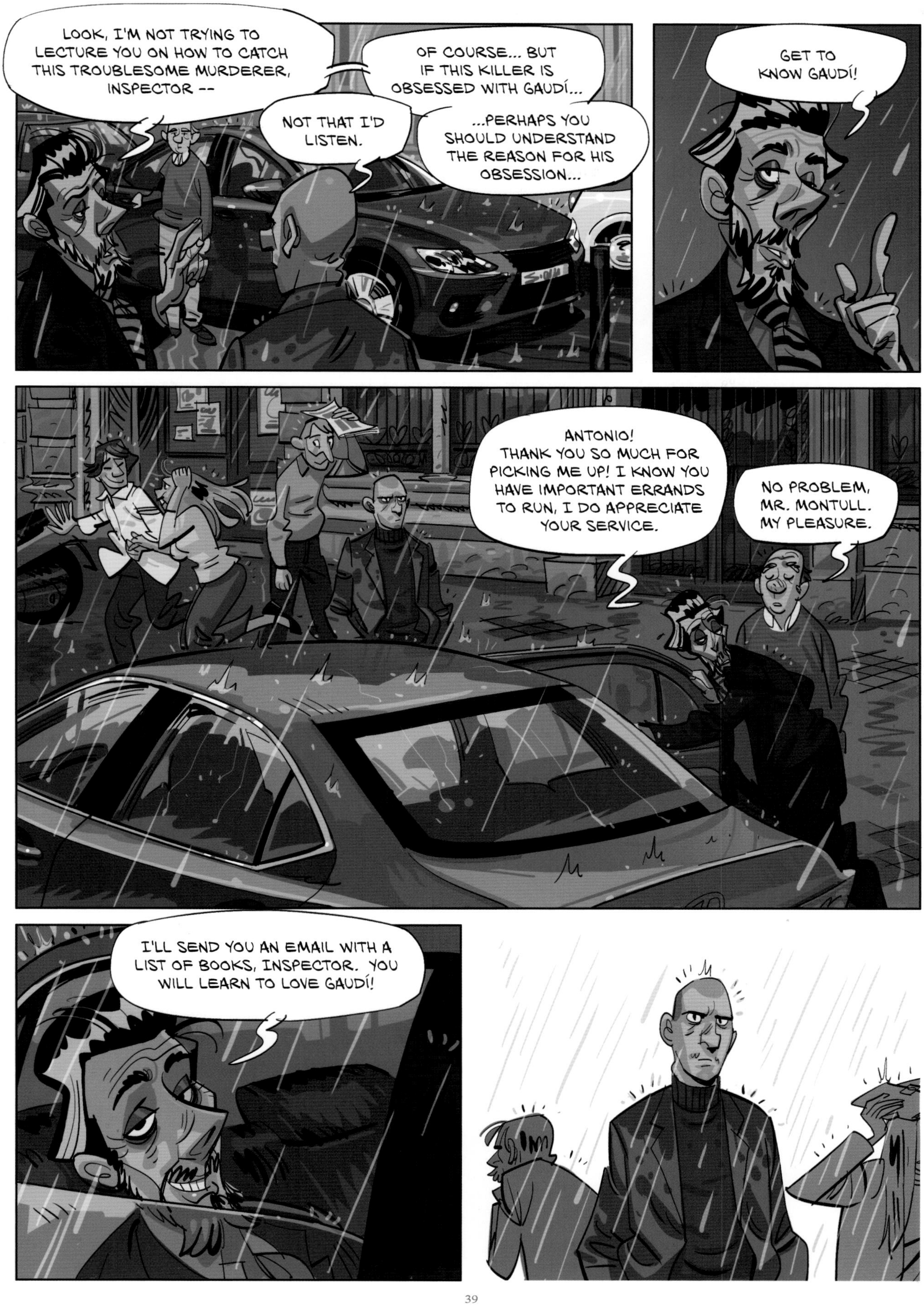
LOOK, I'M NOT TRYING TO LECTURE YOU ON HOW TO CATCH THIS TROUBLESOME MURDERER, INSPECTOR --
NOT THAT I'D LISTEN.
OF COURSE... BUT IF THIS KILLER IS OBSESSED WITH GAUDÍ...
...PERHAPS YOU SHOULD UNDERSTAND THE REASON FOR HIS OBSESSION...
GET TO KNOW GAUDÍ!
ANTONIO! THANK YOU SO MUCH FOR PICKING ME UP! I KNOW YOU HAVE IMPORTANT ERRANDS TO RUN, I DO APPRECIATE YOUR SERVICE.
NO PROBLEM, MR. MONTULL. MY PLEASURE.
I'LL SEND YOU AN EMAIL WITH A LIST OF BOOKS, INSPECTOR. YOU WILL LEARN TO LOVE GAUDÍ!

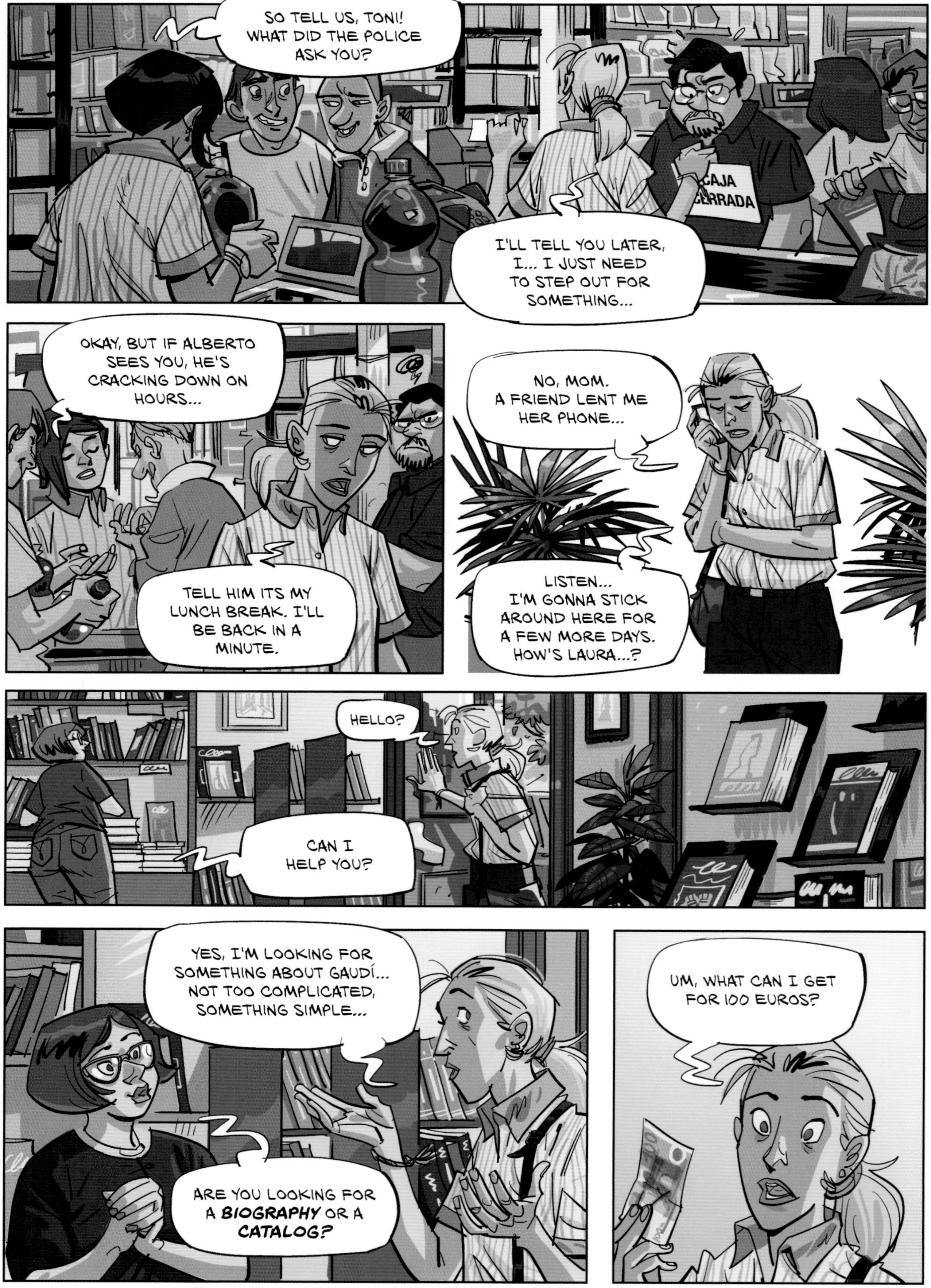
SO TELL US, TONI! WHAT DID THE POLICE ASK YOU?
CAJA CERRADA
I'LL TELL YOU LATER, I... I JUST NEED TO STEP OUT FOR SOMETHING...
OKAY, BUT IF ALBERTO SEES YOU, HE'S CRACKING DOWN ON HOURS...
TELL HIM ITS MY LUNCH BREAK. I'LL BE BACK IN A MINUTE.
NO, MOM. A FRIEND LENT ME HER PHONE...
LISTEN... I'M GONNA STICK AROUND HERE FOR A FEW MORE DAYS. HOW'S LAURA...?
HELLO?
CAN I HELP YOU?
YES, I'M LOOKING FOR SOMETHING ABOUT GAUDÍ... NOT TOO COMPLICATED, SOMETHING SIMPLE...
ARE YOU LOOKING FOR A **BIOGRAPHY** OR A **CATALOG?**
UM, WHAT CAN I GET FOR 100 EUROS?

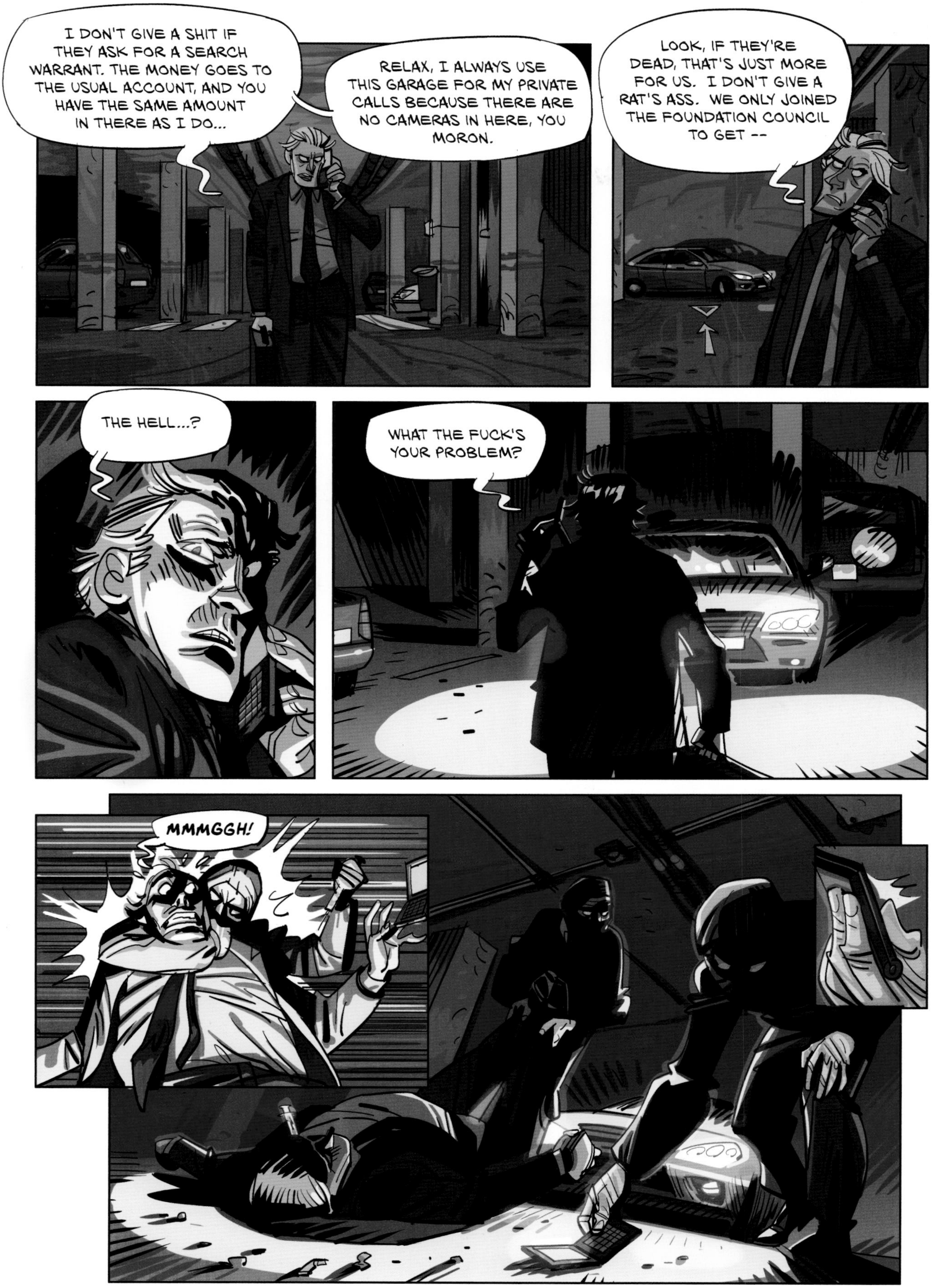
I DON'T GIVE A SHIT IF THEY ASK FOR A SEARCH WARRANT. THE MONEY GOES TO THE USUAL ACCOUNT, AND YOU HAVE THE SAME AMOUNT IN THERE AS I DO...
RELAX, I ALWAYS USE THIS GARAGE FOR MY PRIVATE CALLS BECAUSE THERE ARE NO CAMERAS IN HERE, YOU MORON.
LOOK, IF THEY'RE DEAD, THAT'S JUST MORE FOR US. I DON'T GIVE A RAT'S ASS. WE ONLY JOINED THE FOUNDATION COUNCIL TO GET --
THE HELL...?
WHAT THE FUCK'S YOUR PROBLEM?
MMMGGH!

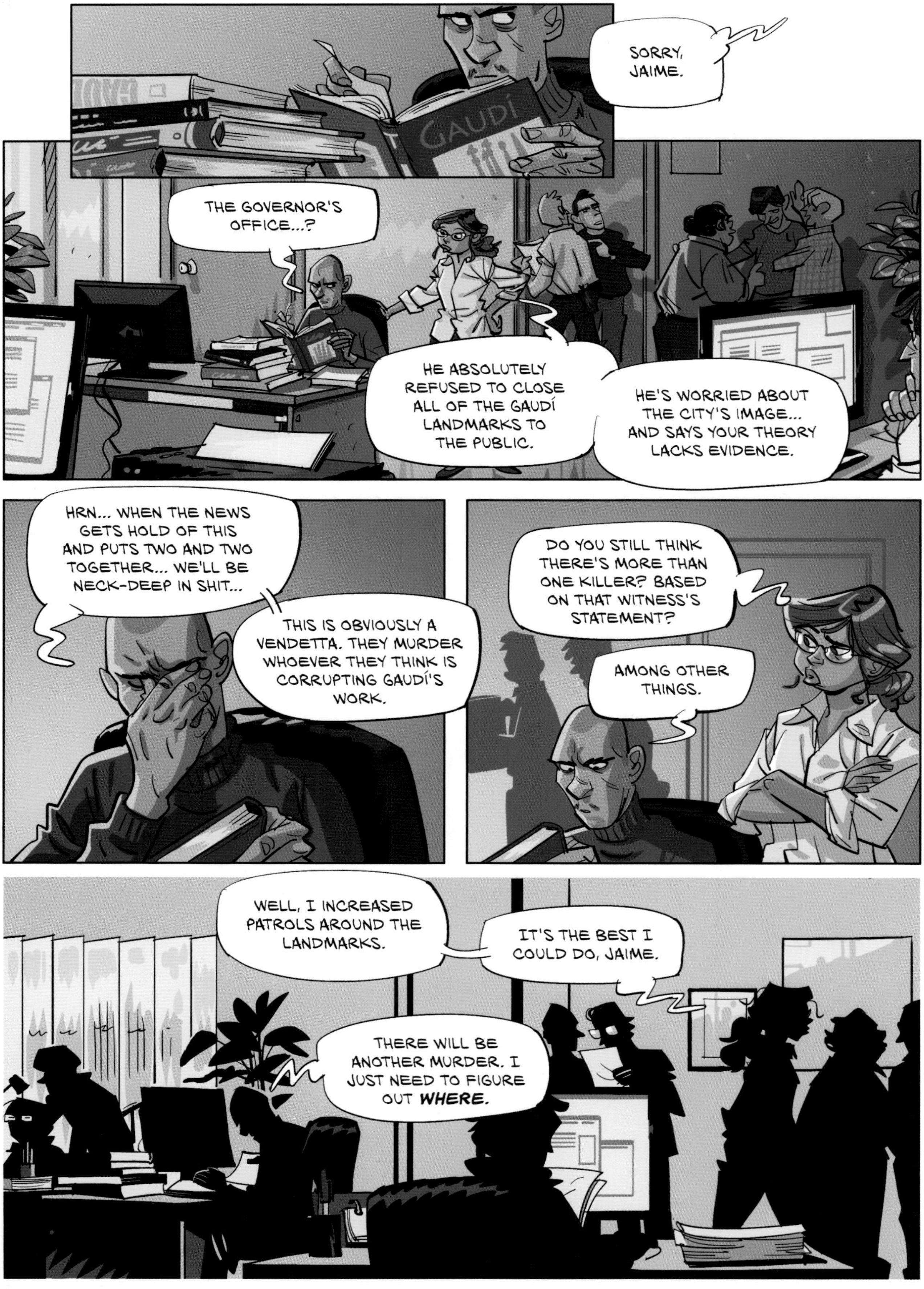
SORRY, JAIME.
THE GOVERNOR'S OFFICE...?
HE ABSOLUTELY REFUSED TO CLOSE ALL OF THE GAUDÍ LANDMARKS TO THE PUBLIC.
HE'S WORRIED ABOUT THE CITY'S IMAGE... AND SAYS YOUR THEORY LACKS EVIDENCE.
HRN... WHEN THE NEWS GETS HOLD OF THIS AND PUTS TWO AND TWO TOGETHER... WE'LL BE NECK-DEEP IN SHIT...
THIS IS OBVIOUSLY A VENDETTA. THEY MURDER WHOEVER THEY THINK IS CORRUPTING GAUDÍ'S WORK.
DO YOU STILL THINK THERE'S MORE THAN ONE KILLER? BASED ON THAT WITNESS'S STATEMENT?
AMONG OTHER THINGS.
WELL, I INCREASED PATROLS AROUND THE LANDMARKS.
IT'S THE BEST I COULD DO, JAIME.
THERE WILL BE ANOTHER MURDER. I JUST NEED TO FIGURE OUT **WHERE.**

WELCOME TO **CASA CALVET**. DO YOU HAVE A RESERVATION?

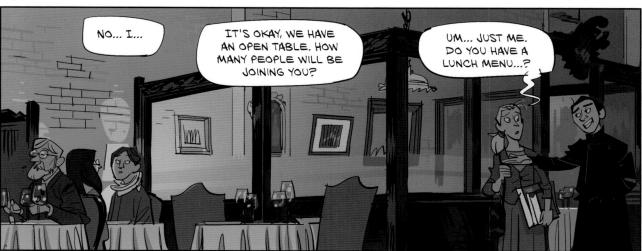

NO... I....

IT'S OKAY, WE HAVE AN OPEN TABLE. HOW MANY PEOPLE WILL BE JOINING YOU?

UM... JUST ME. DO YOU HAVE A LUNCH MENU...?

I SEE YOU LIKE GAUDÍ. PLEASE, FOLLOW ME.

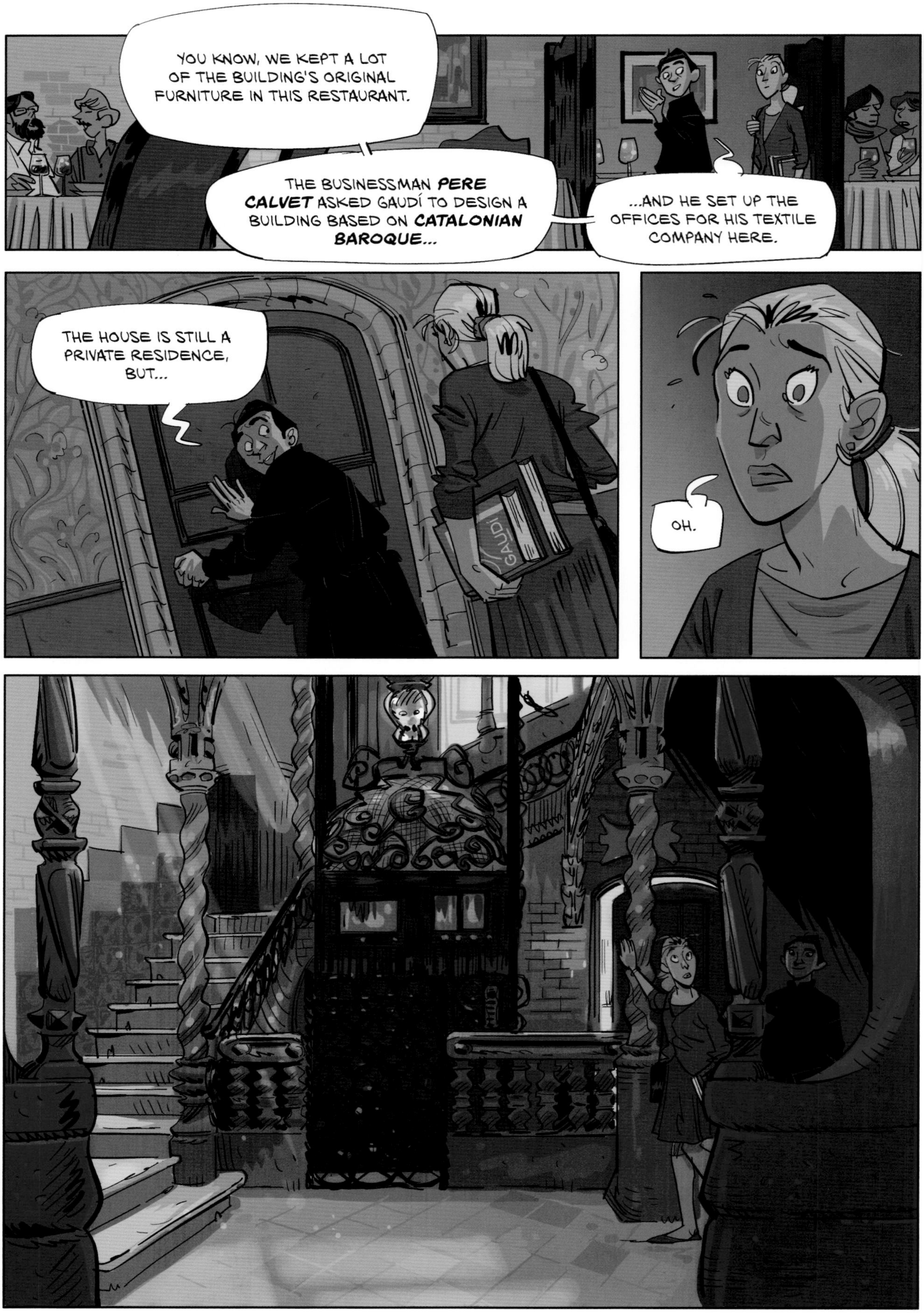

YOU KNOW, WE KEPT A LOT OF THE BUILDING'S ORIGINAL FURNITURE IN THIS RESTAURANT.
THE BUSINESSMAN PERE CALVET ASKED GAUDÍ TO DESIGN A BUILDING BASED ON CATALONIAN BAROQUE...
...AND HE SET UP THE OFFICES FOR HIS TEXTILE COMPANY HERE.
THE HOUSE IS STILL A PRIVATE RESIDENCE, BUT...
GAUDÍ
OH.

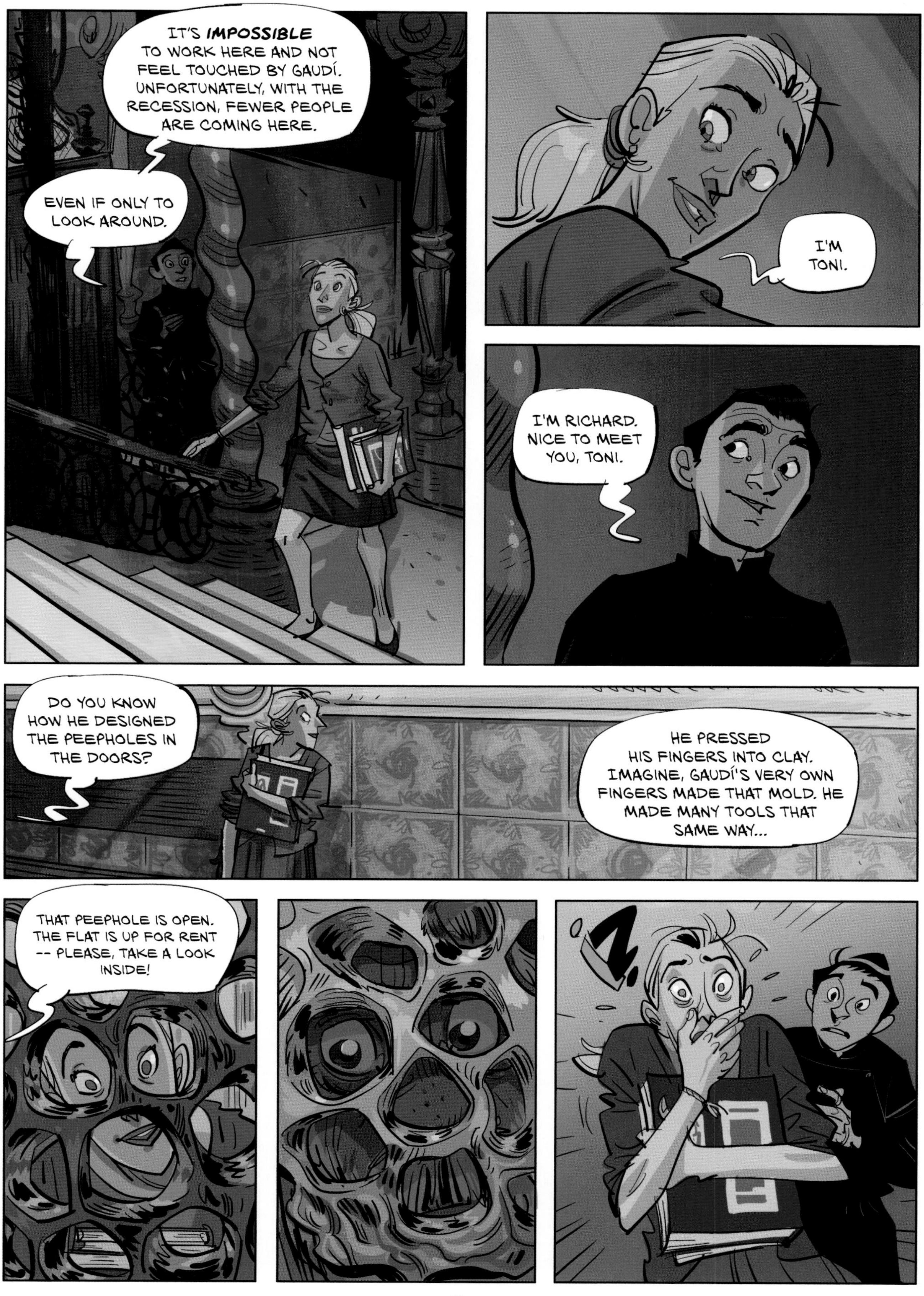
IT'S IMPOSSIBLE TO WORK HERE AND NOT FEEL TOUCHED BY GAUDÍ. UNFORTUNATELY, WITH THE RECESSION, FEWER PEOPLE ARE COMING HERE.
EVEN IF ONLY TO LOOK AROUND.
I'M TONI.
I'M RICHARD. NICE TO MEET YOU, TONI.
DO YOU KNOW HOW HE DESIGNED THE PEEPHOLES IN THE DOORS?
HE PRESSED HIS FINGERS INTO CLAY. IMAGINE, GAUDÍ'S VERY OWN FINGERS MADE THAT MOLD. HE MADE MANY TOOLS THAT SAME WAY...
THAT PEEPHOLE IS OPEN. THE FLAT IS UP FOR RENT -- PLEASE, TAKE A LOOK INSIDE!

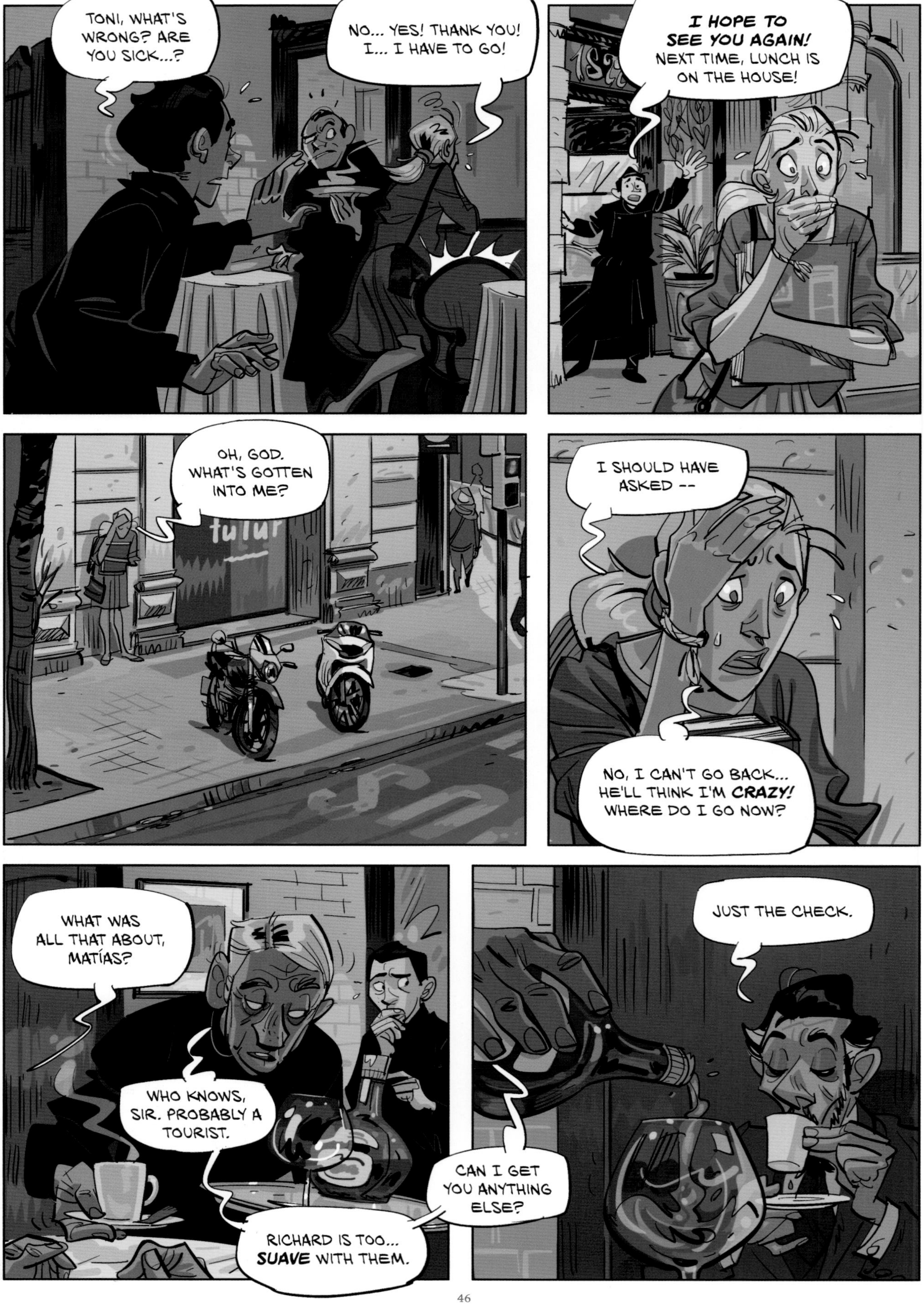
TONI, WHAT'S WRONG? ARE YOU SICK...?
NO... YES! THANK YOU! I... I HAVE TO GO!
I HOPE TO SEE YOU AGAIN! NEXT TIME, LUNCH IS ON THE HOUSE!
OH, GOD. WHAT'S GOTTEN INTO ME?
I SHOULD HAVE ASKED --
NO, I CAN'T GO BACK... HE'LL THINK I'M CRAZY! WHERE DO I GO NOW?
WHAT WAS ALL THAT ABOUT, MATÍAS?
WHO KNOWS, SIR. PROBABLY A TOURIST.
RICHARD IS TOO... SUAVE WITH THEM.
CAN I GET YOU ANYTHING ELSE?
JUST THE CHECK.

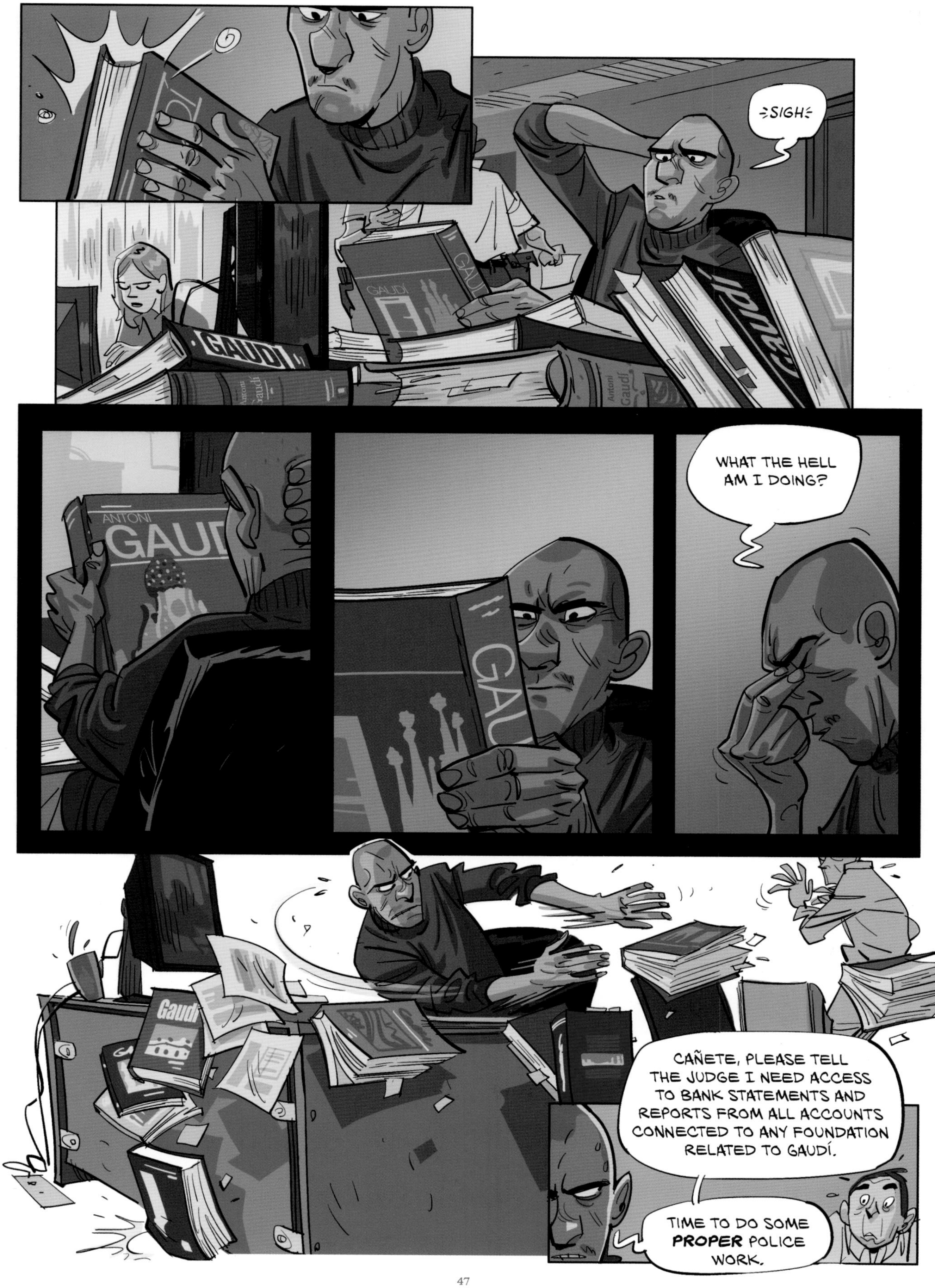

SIGH
WHAT THE HELL AM I DOING?
CAÑETE, PLEASE TELL THE JUDGE I NEED ACCESS TO BANK STATEMENTS AND REPORTS FROM ALL ACCOUNTS CONNECTED TO ANY FOUNDATION RELATED TO GAUDÍ.
TIME TO DO SOME **PROPER** POLICE WORK.

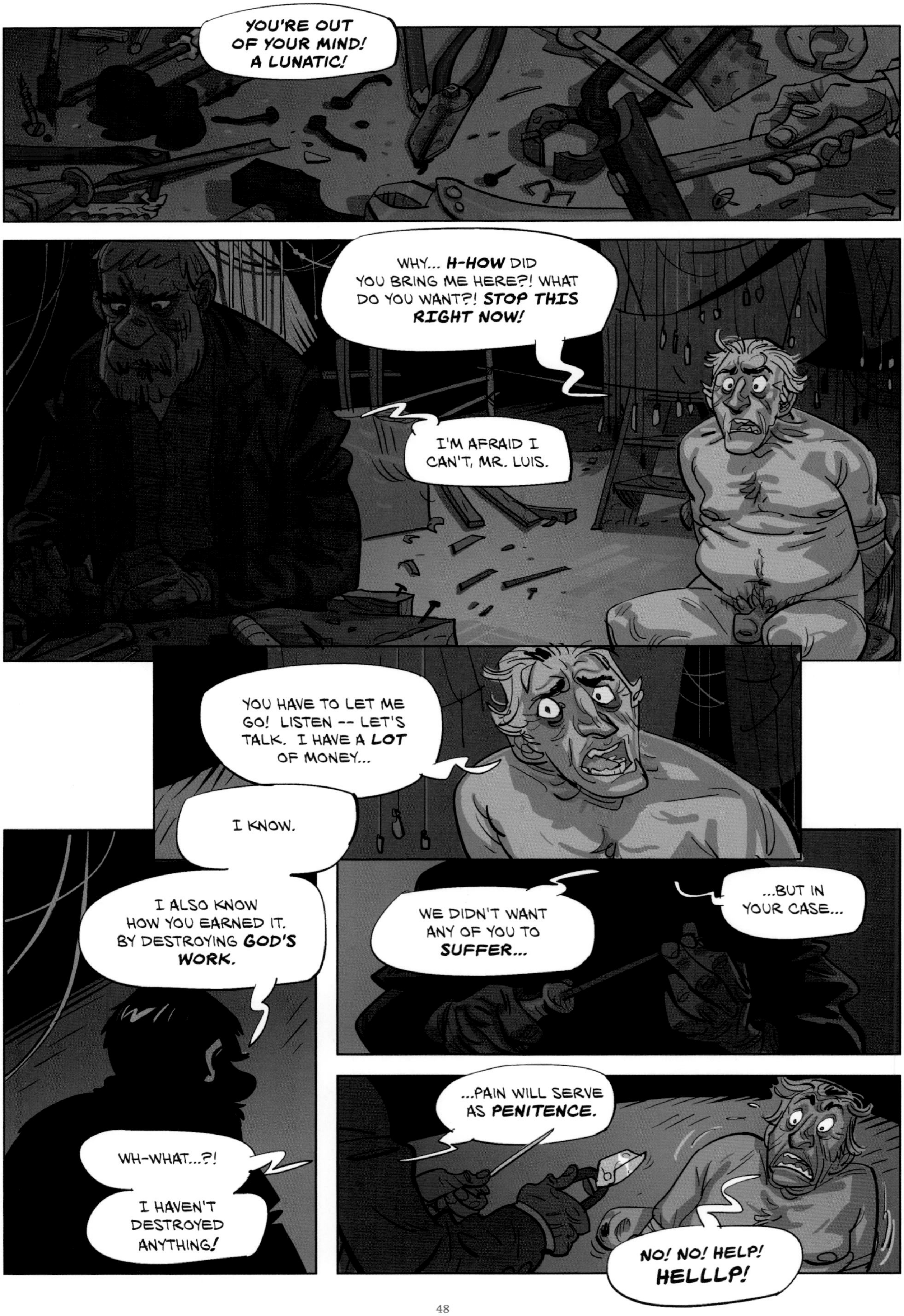

YOU'RE OUT OF YOUR MIND! A LUNATIC!
WHY... H-HOW DID YOU BRING ME HERE?! WHAT DO YOU WANT?! STOP THIS RIGHT NOW!
I'M AFRAID I CAN'T, MR. LUIS.
YOU HAVE TO LET ME GO! LISTEN -- LET'S TALK. I HAVE A LOT OF MONEY...
I KNOW.
I ALSO KNOW HOW YOU EARNED IT. BY DESTROYING GOD'S WORK.
WE DIDN'T WANT ANY OF YOU TO SUFFER...
...BUT IN YOUR CASE...
WH-WHAT...?!
I HAVEN'T DESTROYED ANYTHING!
...PAIN WILL SERVE AS PENITENCE.
NO! NO! HELP! HELLLP!

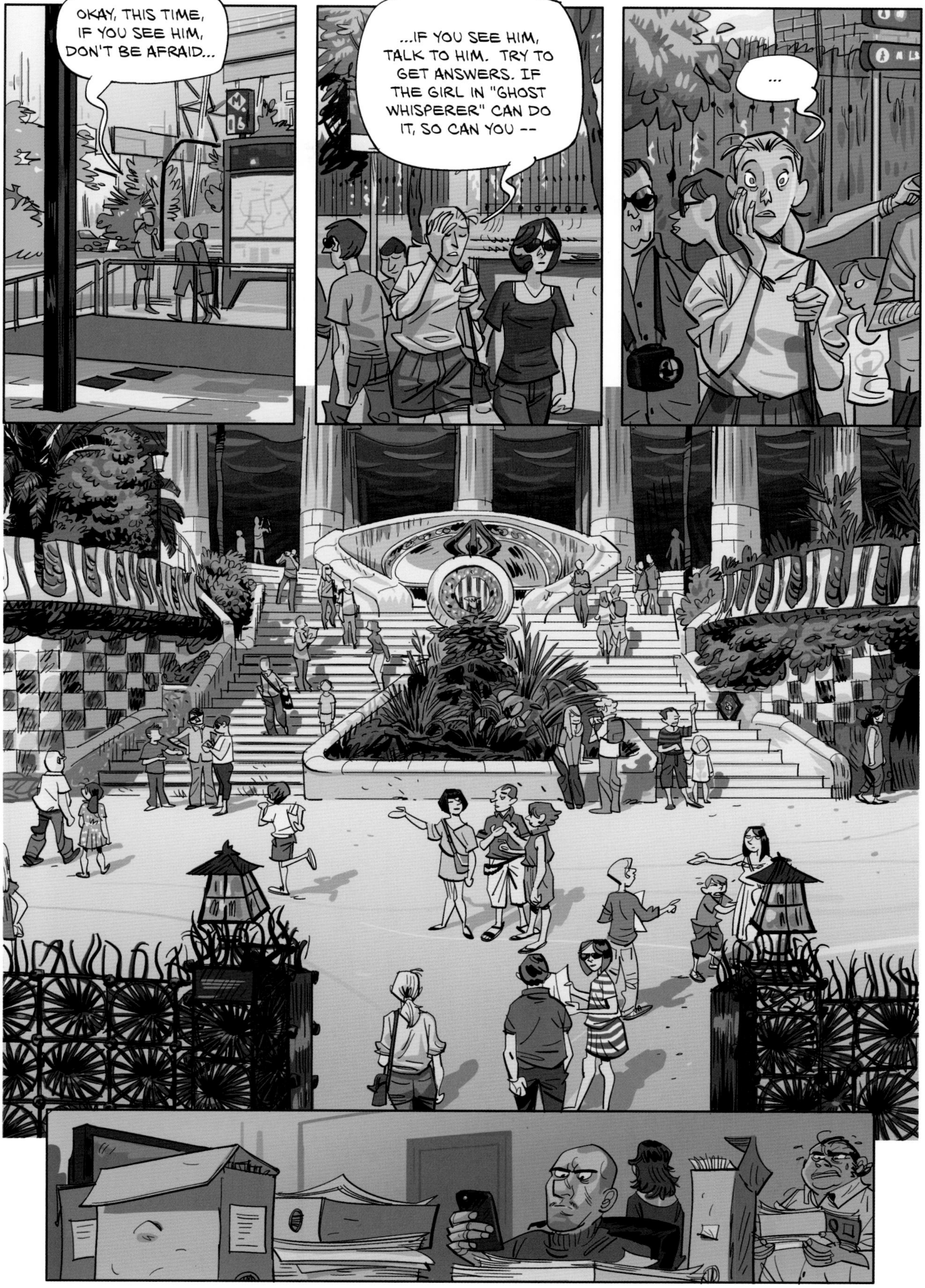
OKAY, THIS TIME, IF YOU SEE HIM, DON'T BE AFRAID...
...IF YOU SEE HIM, TALK TO HIM. TRY TO GET ANSWERS. IF THE GIRL IN "GHOST WHISPERER" CAN DO IT, SO CAN YOU --
...

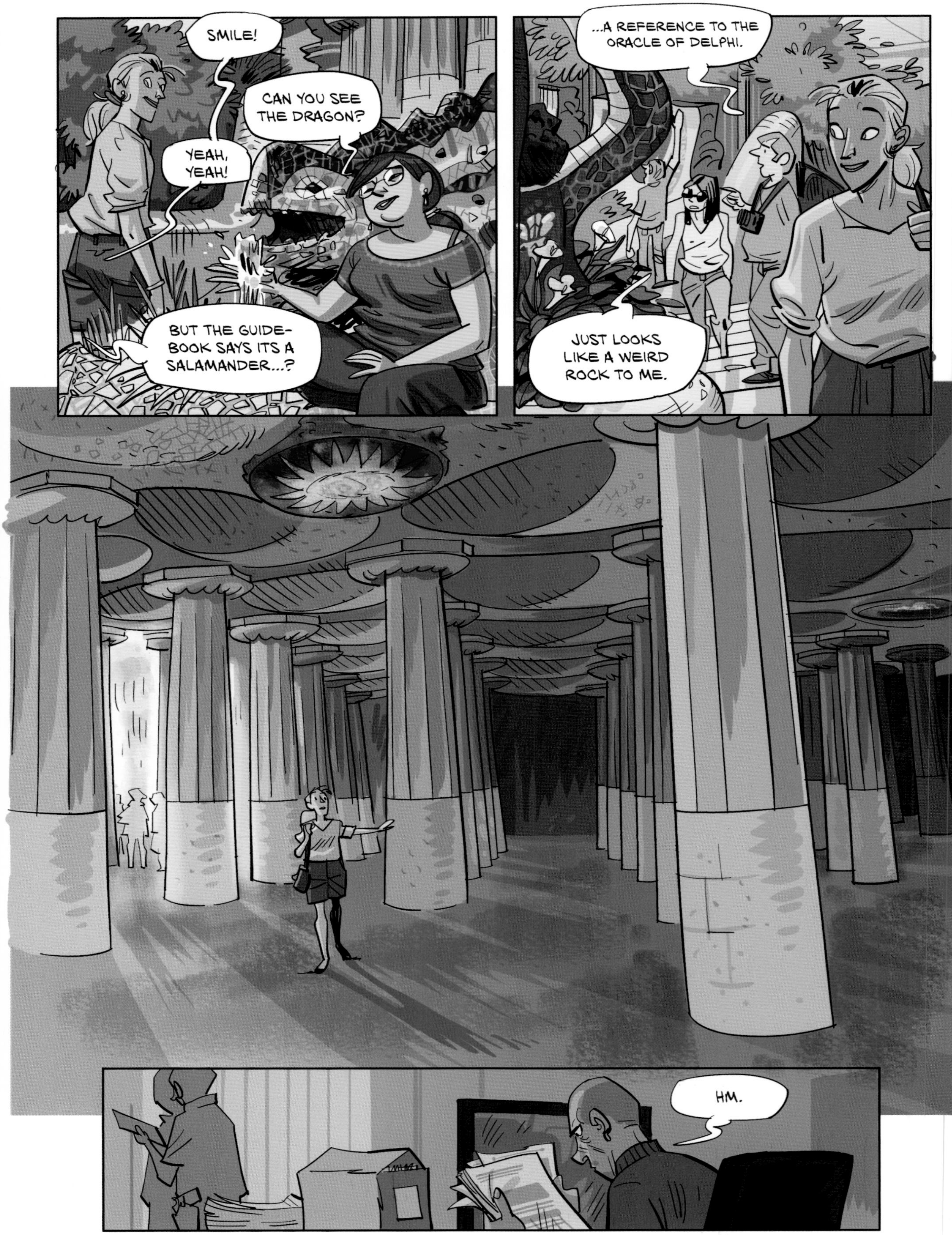
SMILE!
CAN YOU SEE THE DRAGON?
YEAH, YEAH!
BUT THE GUIDE-BOOK SAYS ITS A SALAMANDER...?
...A REFERENCE TO THE ORACLE OF DELPHI.
JUST LOOKS LIKE A WEIRD ROCK TO ME.
HM.

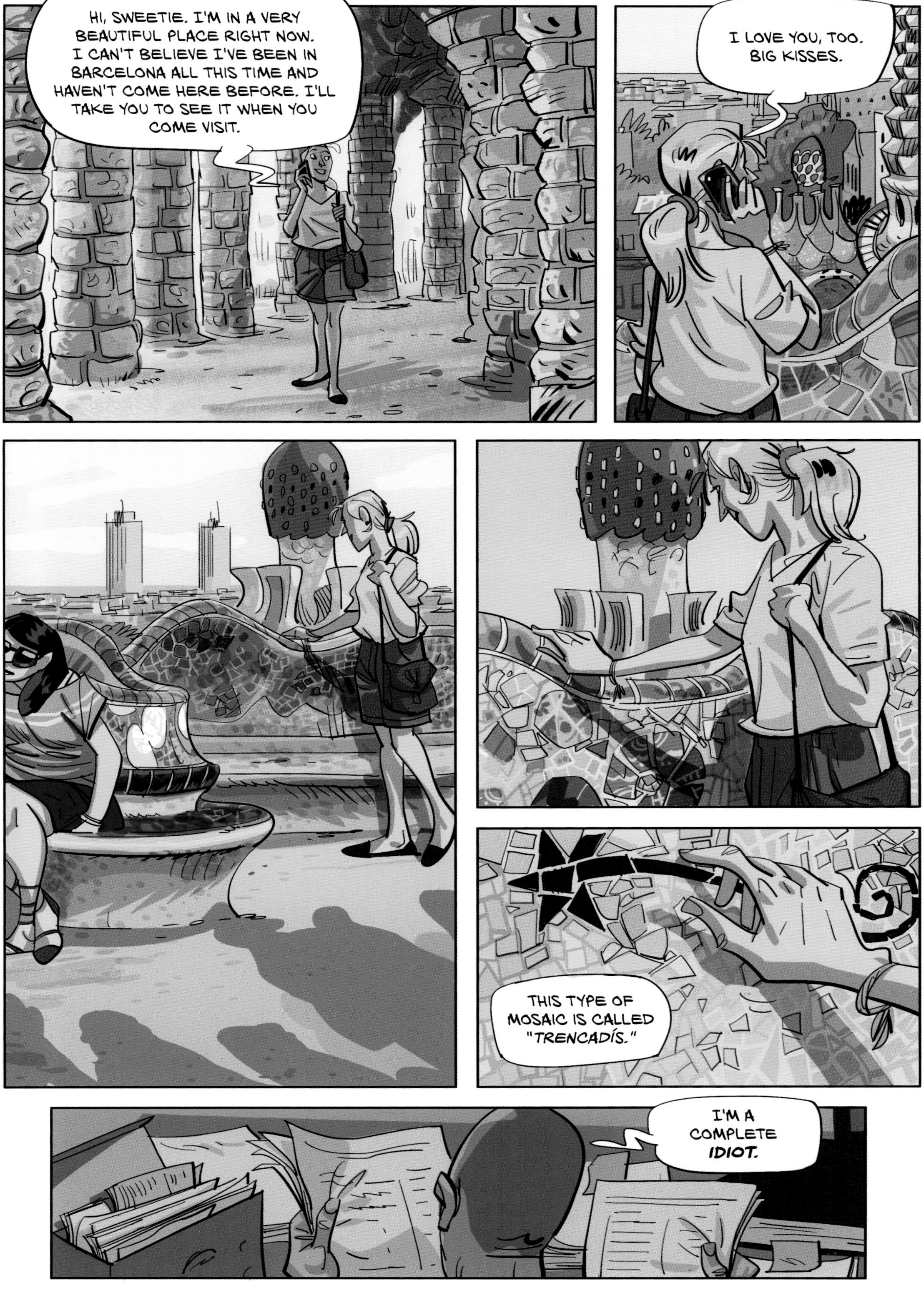
HI, SWEETIE. I'M IN A VERY BEAUTIFUL PLACE RIGHT NOW. I CAN'T BELIEVE I'VE BEEN IN BARCELONA ALL THIS TIME AND HAVEN'T COME HERE BEFORE. I'LL TAKE YOU TO SEE IT WHEN YOU COME VISIT.
I LOVE YOU, TOO. BIG KISSES.
THIS TYPE OF MOSAIC IS CALLED "*TRENCADÍS.*"
I'M A COMPLETE **IDIOT.**

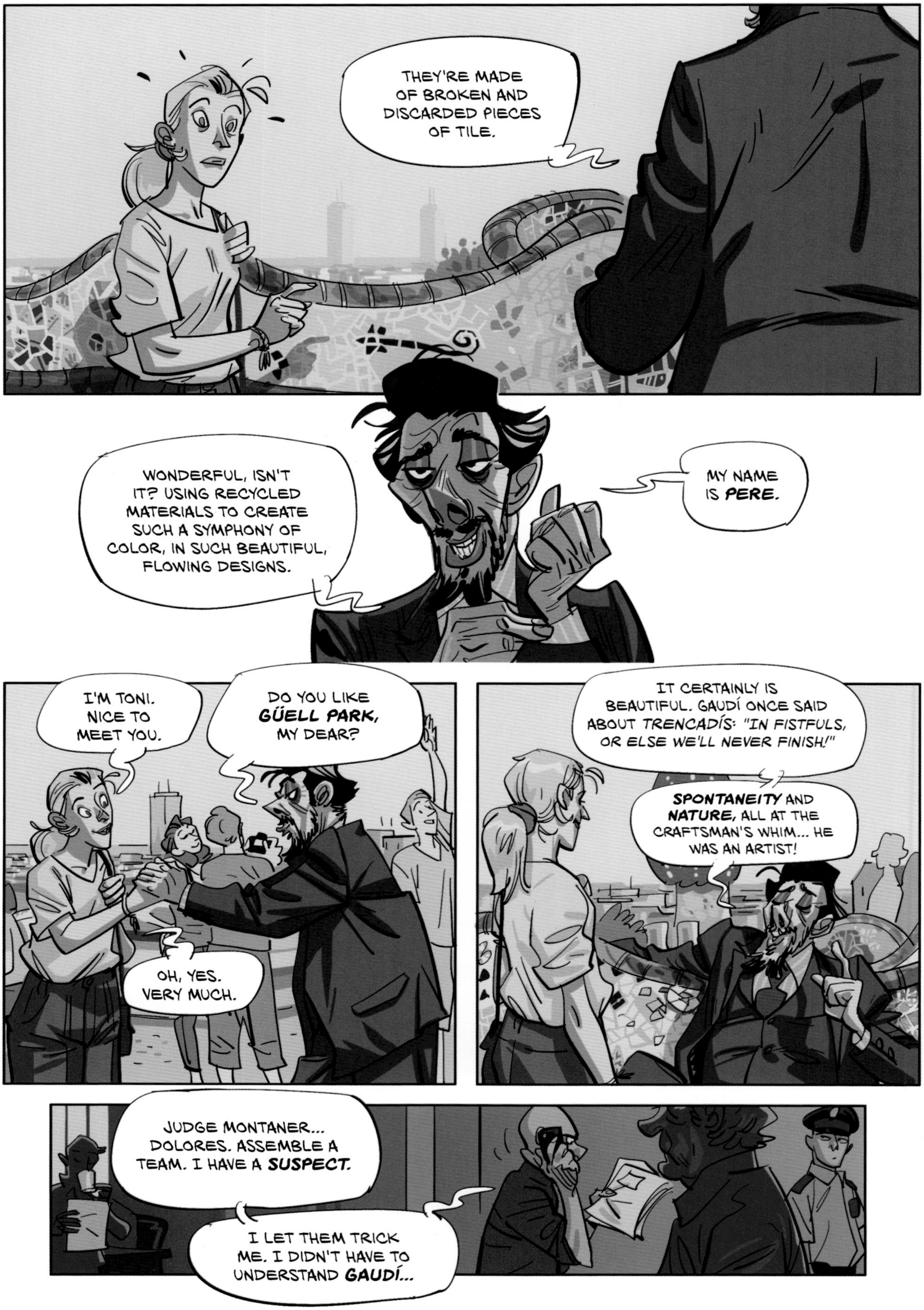
THEY'RE MADE OF BROKEN AND DISCARDED PIECES OF TILE.
WONDERFUL, ISN'T IT? USING RECYCLED MATERIALS TO CREATE SUCH A SYMPHONY OF COLOR, IN SUCH BEAUTIFUL, FLOWING DESIGNS.
MY NAME IS **PERE.**
I'M TONI. NICE TO MEET YOU.
DO YOU LIKE **GÜELL PARK,** MY DEAR?
OH, YES. VERY MUCH.
IT CERTAINLY IS BEAUTIFUL. GAUDÍ ONCE SAID ABOUT *TRENCADÍS*: *"IN FISTFULS, OR ELSE WE'LL NEVER FINISH!"*
SPONTANEITY AND **NATURE,** ALL AT THE CRAFTSMAN'S WHIM... HE WAS AN ARTIST!
JUDGE MONTANER... DOLORES. ASSEMBLE A TEAM. I HAVE A **SUSPECT.**
I LET THEM TRICK ME. I DIDN'T HAVE TO UNDERSTAND **GAUDÍ...**

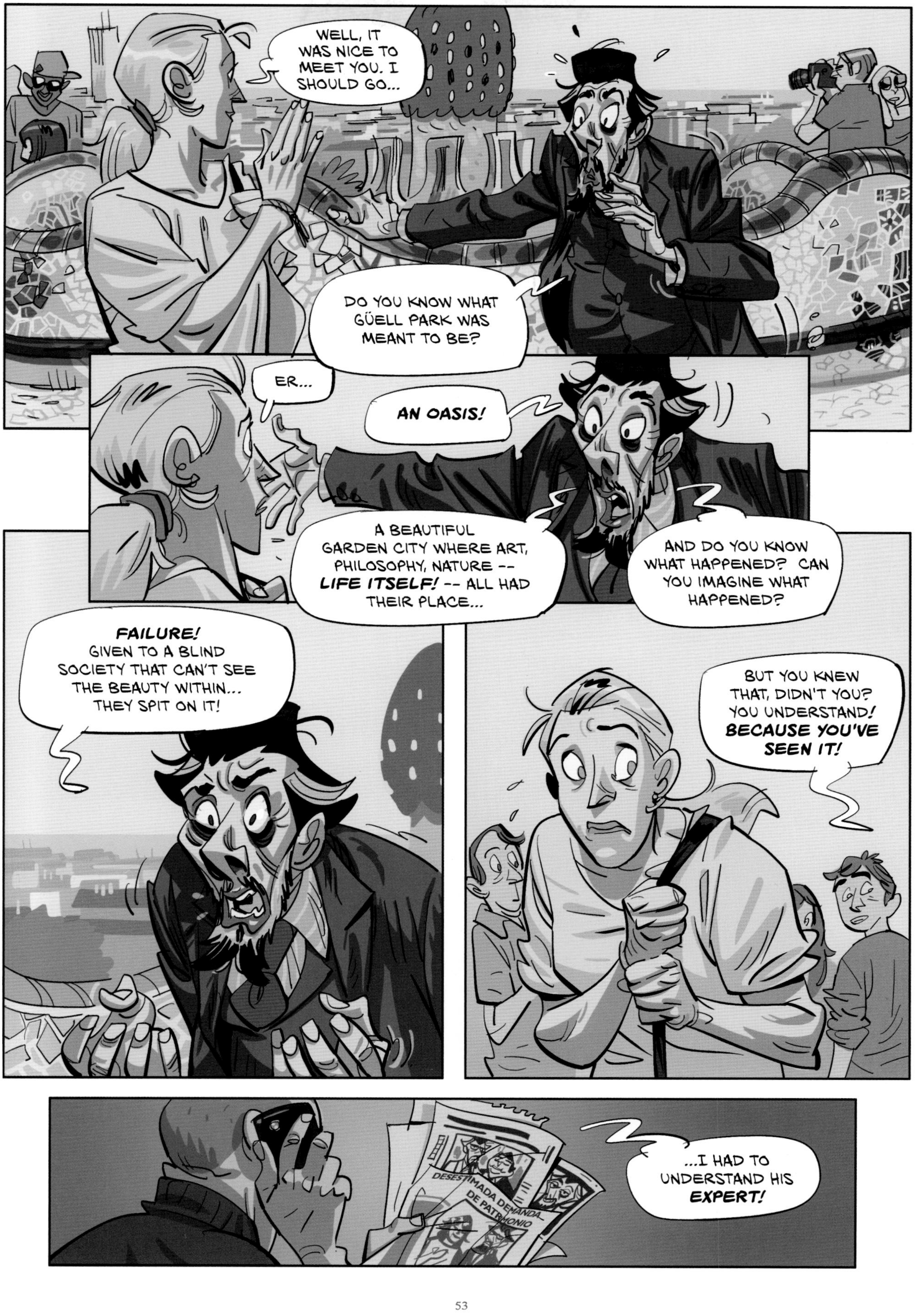
WELL, IT WAS NICE TO MEET YOU. I SHOULD GO...
DO YOU KNOW WHAT GÜELL PARK WAS MEANT TO BE?
ER...
AN OASIS!
A BEAUTIFUL GARDEN CITY WHERE ART, PHILOSOPHY, NATURE -- LIFE ITSELF! -- ALL HAD THEIR PLACE...
AND DO YOU KNOW WHAT HAPPENED? CAN YOU IMAGINE WHAT HAPPENED?
FAILURE! GIVEN TO A BLIND SOCIETY THAT CAN'T SEE THE BEAUTY WITHIN... THEY SPIT ON IT!
BUT YOU KNEW THAT, DIDN'T YOU? YOU UNDERSTAND! BECAUSE YOU'VE SEEN IT!
DESESTIMADA DEMANDA
...I HAD TO UNDERSTAND HIS EXPERT!

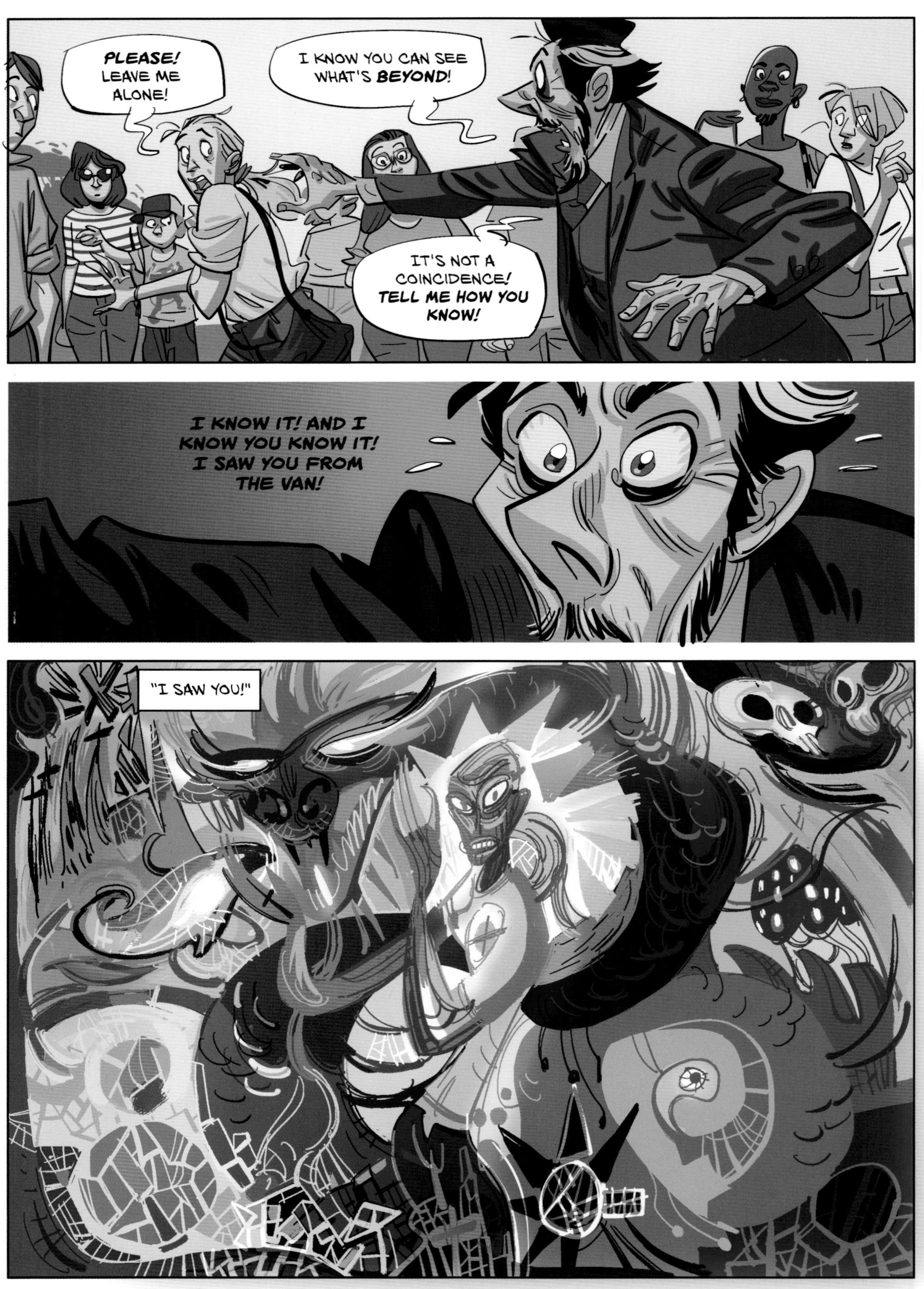
PLEASE! LEAVE ME ALONE!
I KNOW YOU CAN SEE WHAT'S BEYOND!
IT'S NOT A COINCIDENCE! TELL ME HOW YOU KNOW!
I KNOW IT! AND I KNOW YOU KNOW IT! I SAW YOU FROM THE VAN!
"I SAW YOU!"

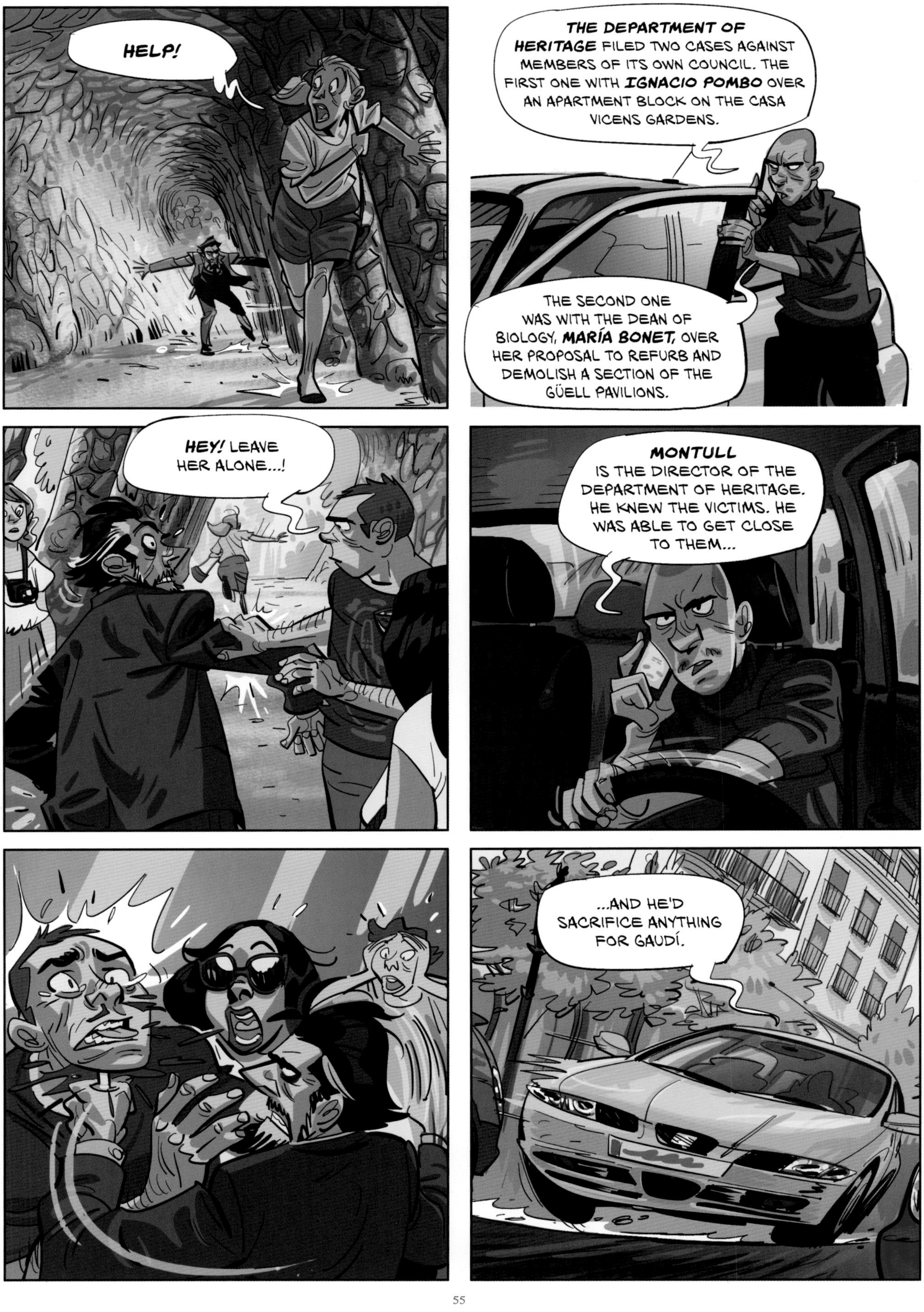
HELP!
THE DEPARTMENT OF HERITAGE FILED TWO CASES AGAINST MEMBERS OF ITS OWN COUNCIL. THE FIRST ONE WITH IGNACIO POMBO OVER AN APARTMENT BLOCK ON THE CASA VICENS GARDENS.
THE SECOND ONE WAS WITH THE DEAN OF BIOLOGY, MARÍA BONET, OVER HER PROPOSAL TO REFURB AND DEMOLISH A SECTION OF THE GÜELL PAVILIONS.
HEY! LEAVE HER ALONE...!
MONTULL IS THE DIRECTOR OF THE DEPARTMENT OF HERITAGE. HE KNEW THE VICTIMS. HE WAS ABLE TO GET CLOSE TO THEM...
...AND HE'D SACRIFICE ANYTHING FOR GAUDÍ.

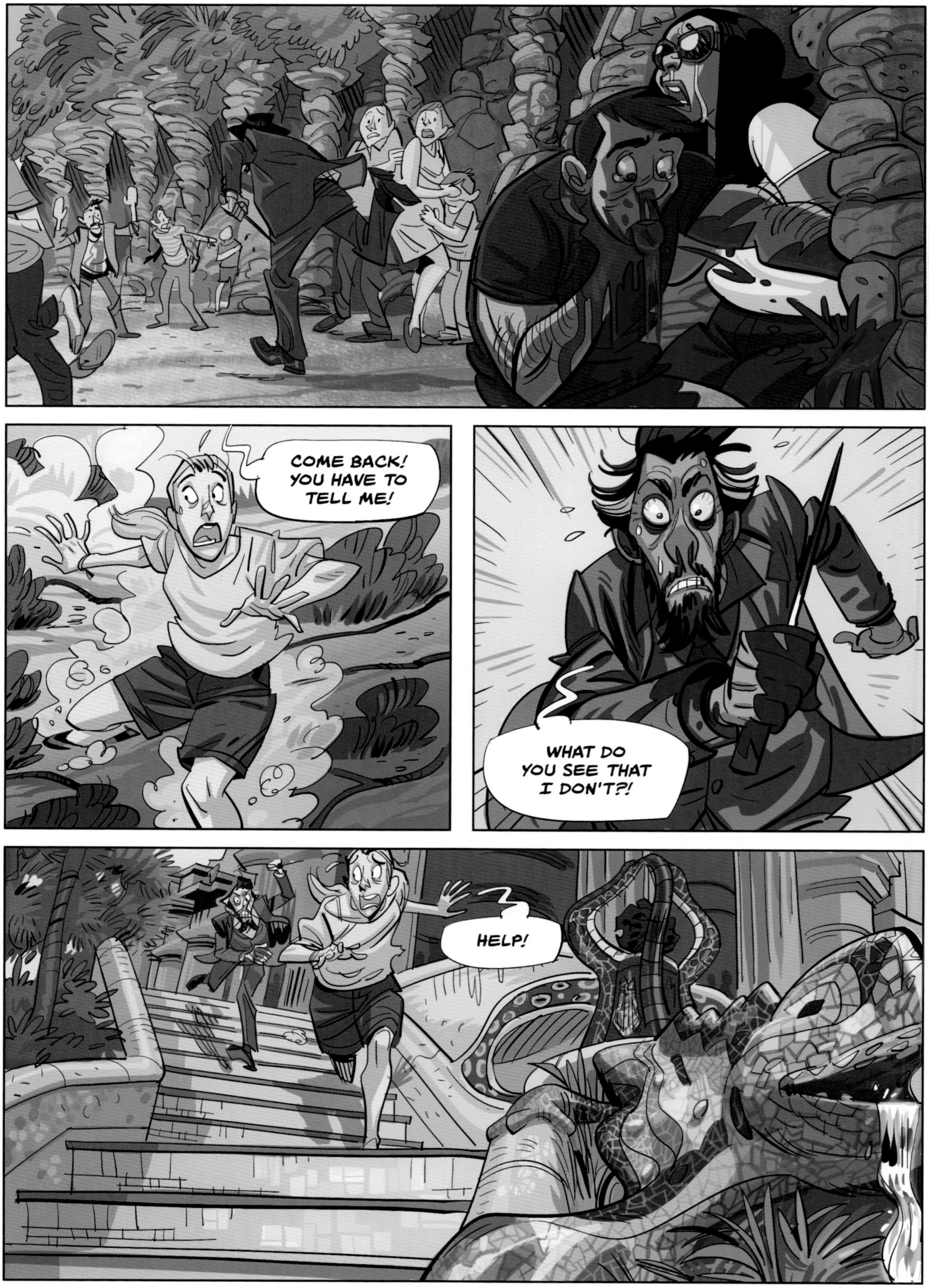
COME BACK! YOU HAVE TO TELL ME!
WHAT DO YOU SEE THAT I DON'T?!
HELP!

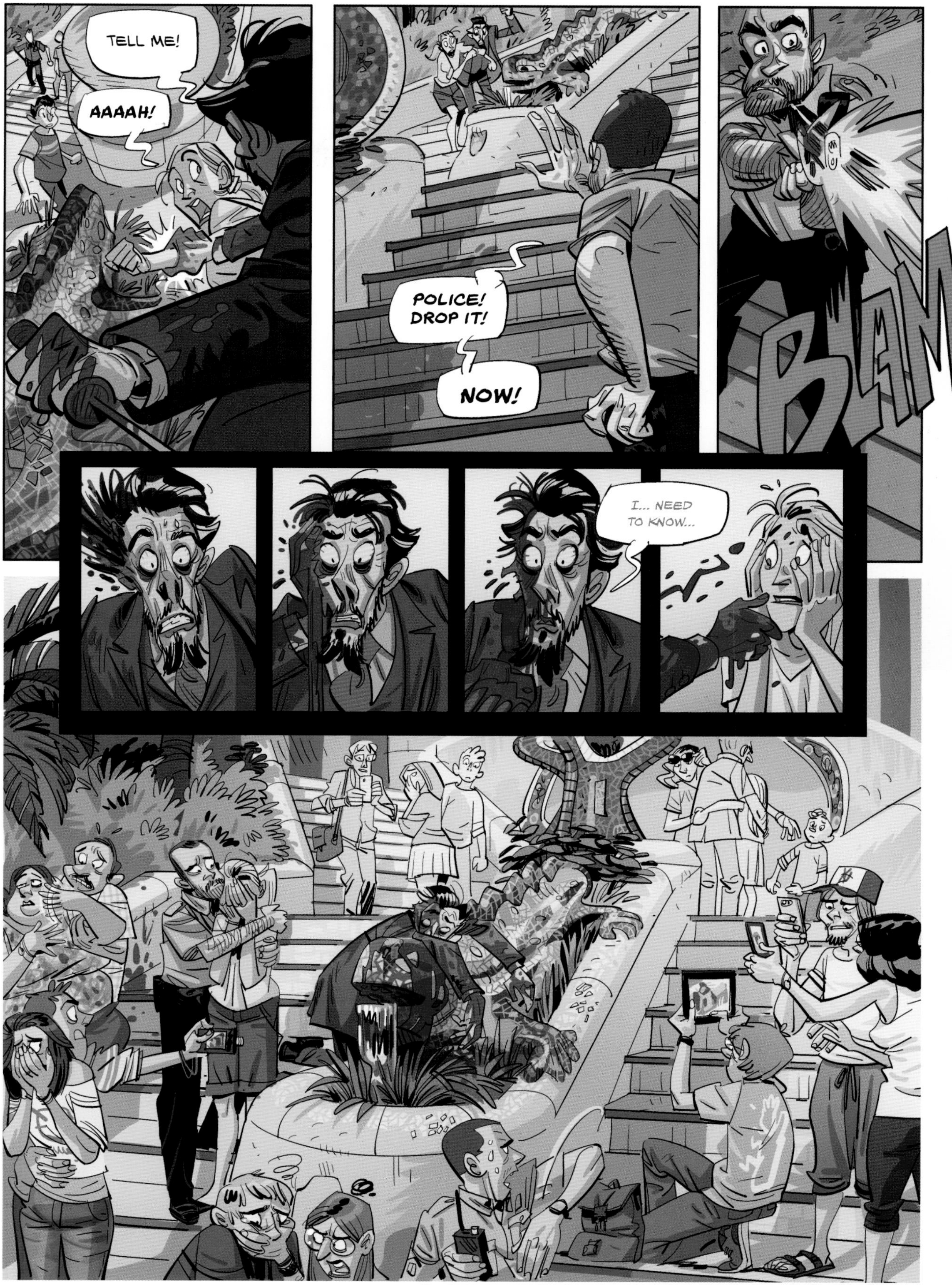
TELL ME!
AAAAH!
POLICE! DROP IT!
NOW!
BLAM
I... NEED TO KNOW...

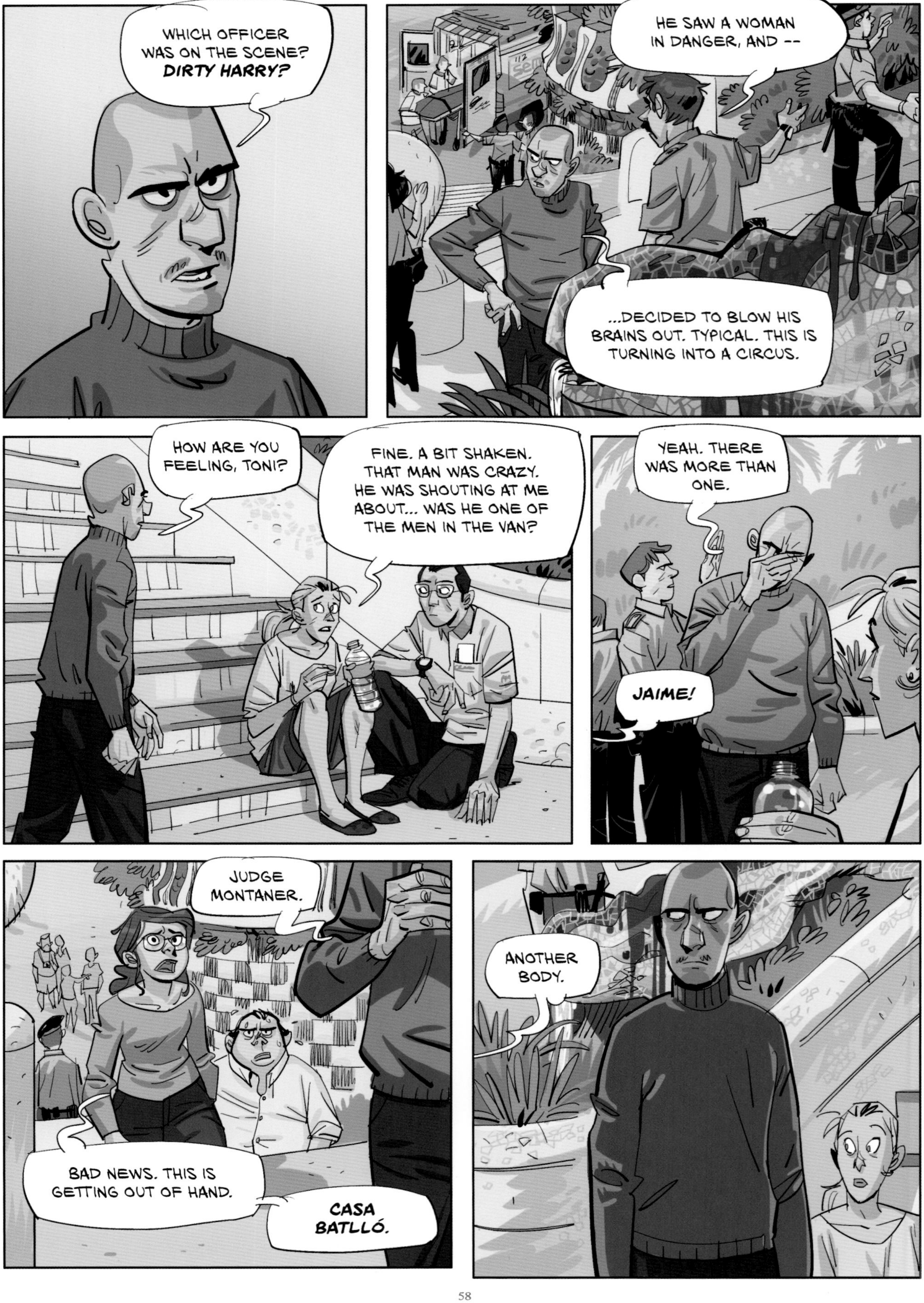
WHICH OFFICER WAS ON THE SCENE? **DIRTY HARRY?**
HE SAW A WOMAN IN DANGER, AND --
...DECIDED TO BLOW HIS BRAINS OUT. TYPICAL. THIS IS TURNING INTO A CIRCUS.
HOW ARE YOU FEELING, TONI?
FINE. A BIT SHAKEN. THAT MAN WAS CRAZY. HE WAS SHOUTING AT ME ABOUT... WAS HE ONE OF THE MEN IN THE VAN?
YEAH. THERE WAS MORE THAN ONE.
JAIME!
JUDGE MONTANER.
BAD NEWS. THIS IS GETTING OUT OF HAND.
CASA BATLLÓ.
ANOTHER BODY.

Chapter 3
Casa Batlló ♦ La Pedrera

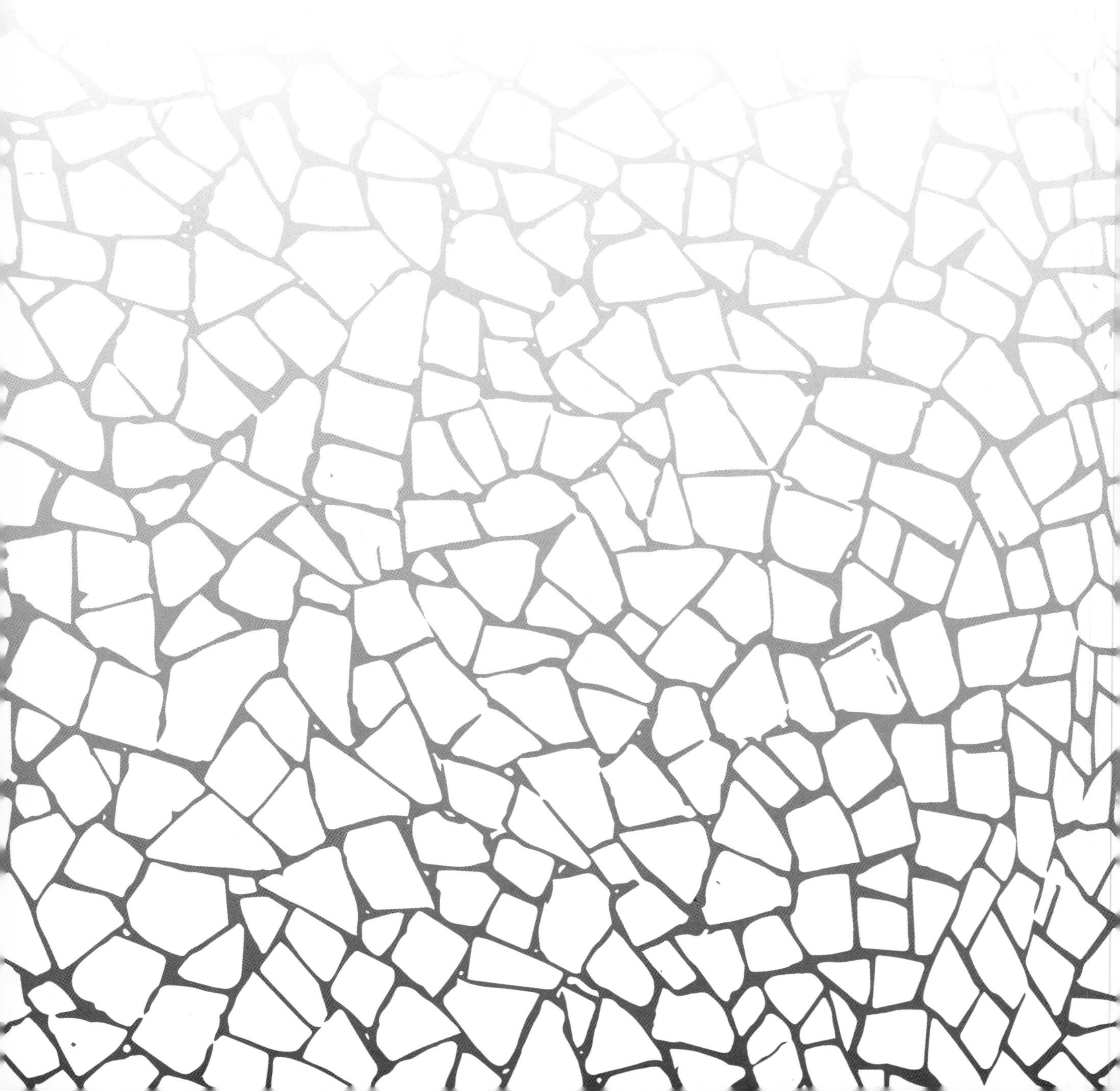

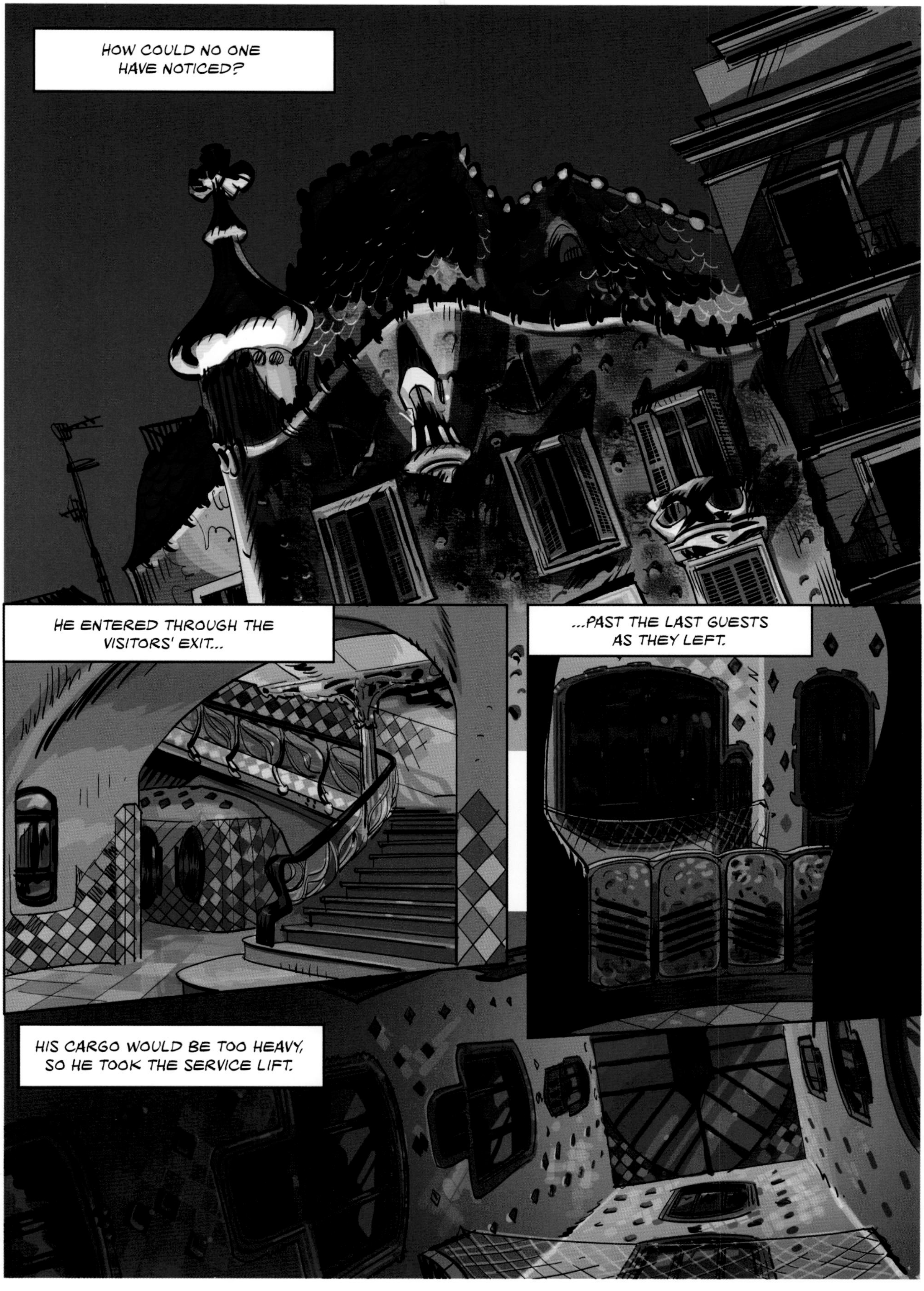
HOW COULD NO ONE
HAVE NOTICED?
HE ENTERED THROUGH THE
VISITORS' EXIT...
...PAST THE LAST GUESTS
AS THEY LEFT.
HIS CARGO WOULD BE TOO HEAVY,
SO HE TOOK THE SERVICE LIFT.

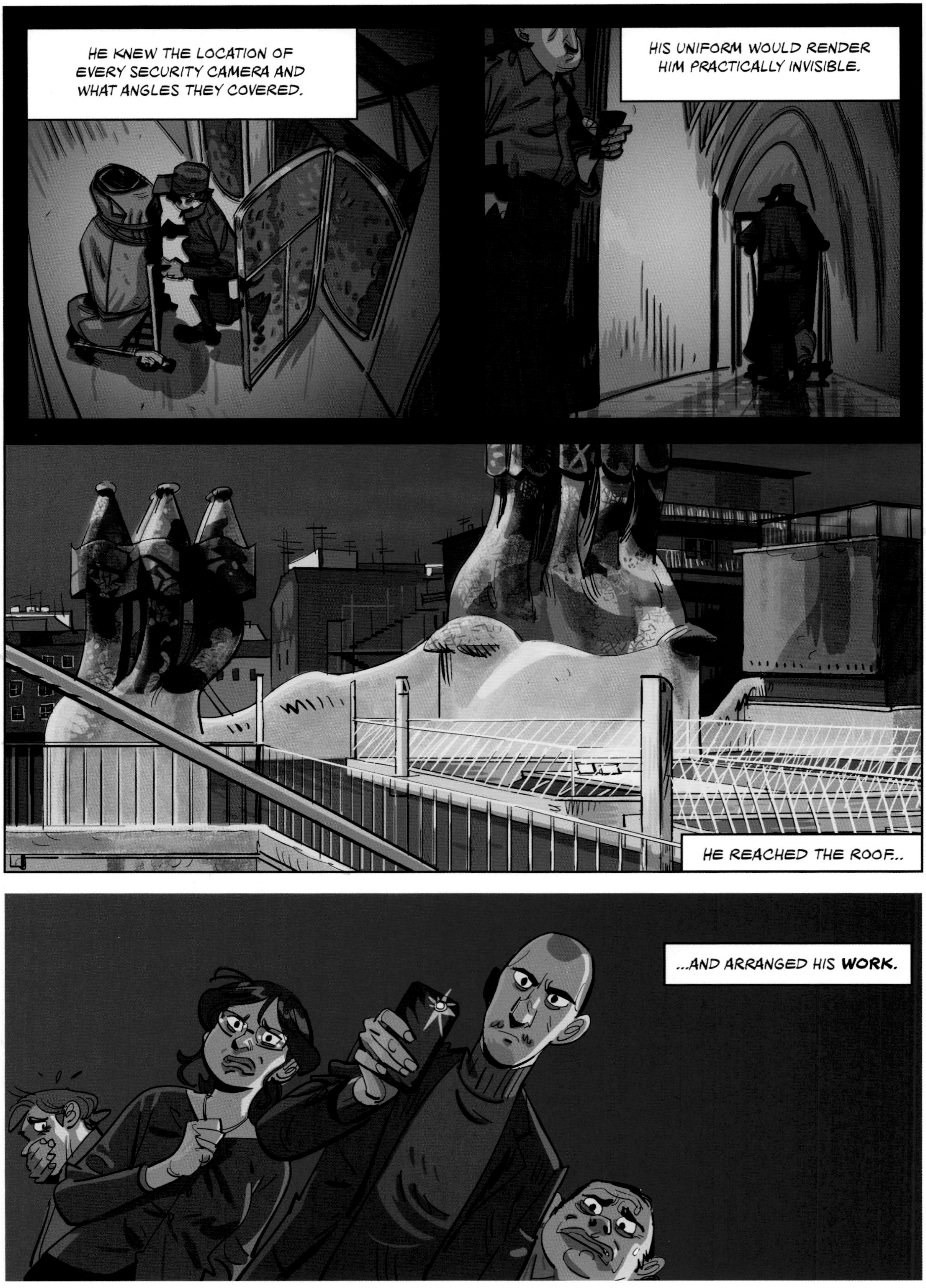
HE KNEW THE LOCATION OF EVERY SECURITY CAMERA AND WHAT ANGLES THEY COVERED.
HIS UNIFORM WOULD RENDER HIM PRACTICALLY INVISIBLE.
HE REACHED THE ROOF...
...AND ARRANGED HIS WORK.

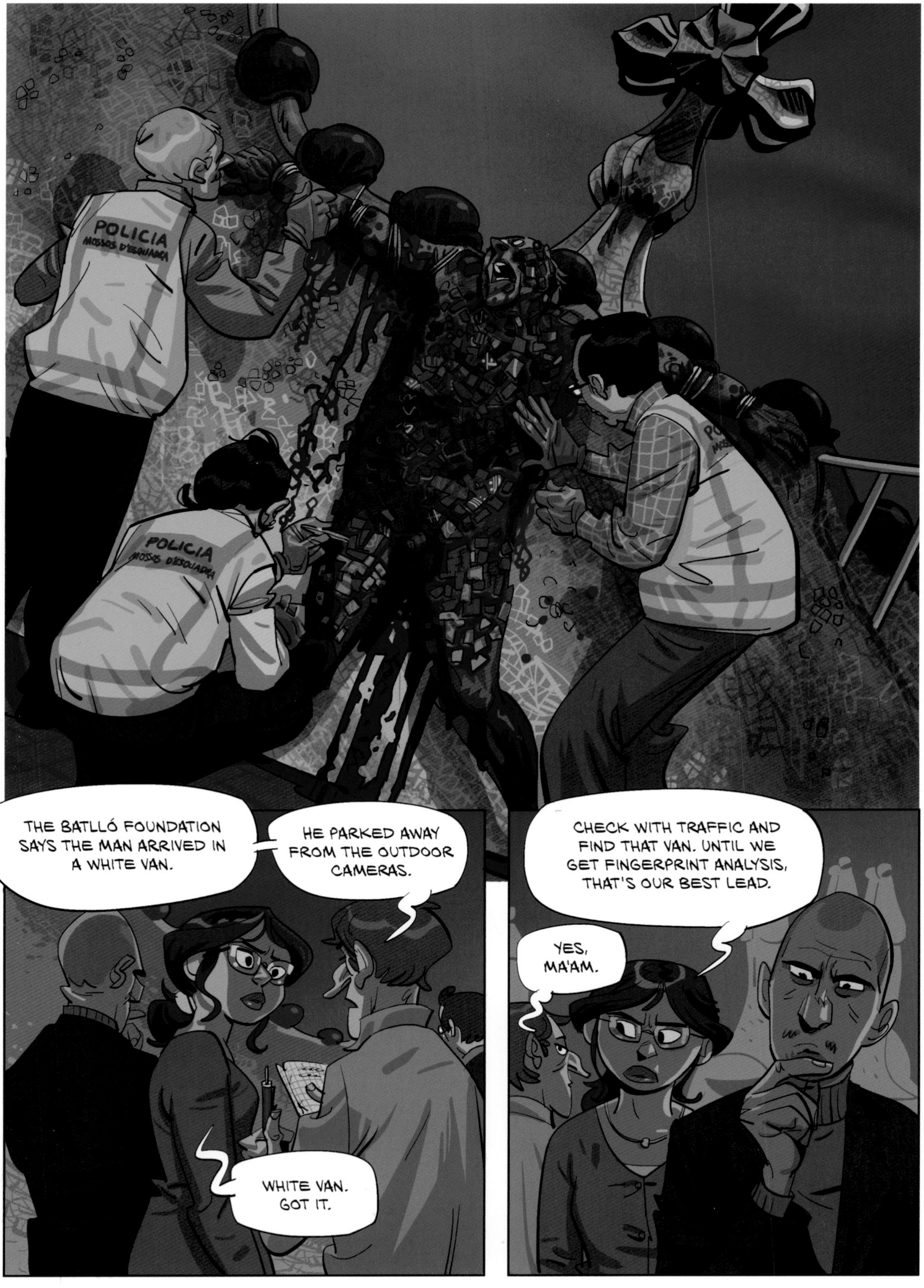
POLICIA
MOSSOS D'ESQUADRA
POLICIA
MOSSOS D'ESQUADRA
THE BATLLÓ FOUNDATION SAYS THE MAN ARRIVED IN A WHITE VAN.
HE PARKED AWAY FROM THE OUTDOOR CAMERAS.
WHITE VAN. GOT IT.
CHECK WITH TRAFFIC AND FIND THAT VAN. UNTIL WE GET FINGERPRINT ANALYSIS, THAT'S OUR BEST LEAD.
YES, MA'AM.

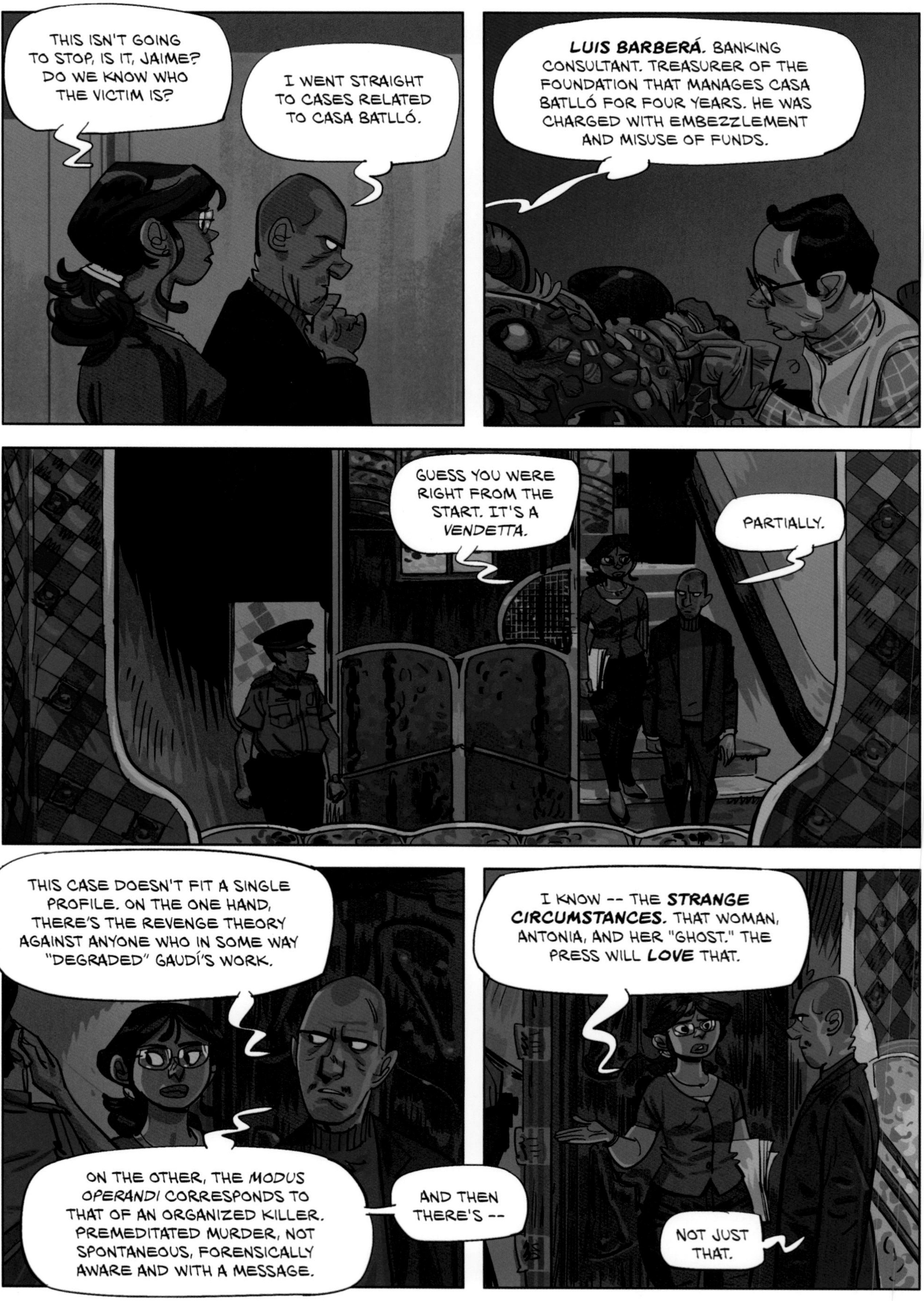
THIS ISN'T GOING TO STOP, IS IT, JAIME? DO WE KNOW WHO THE VICTIM IS?
I WENT STRAIGHT TO CASES RELATED TO CASA BATLLÓ.
LUIS BARBERÁ. BANKING CONSULTANT. TREASURER OF THE FOUNDATION THAT MANAGES CASA BATLLÓ FOR FOUR YEARS. HE WAS CHARGED WITH EMBEZZLEMENT AND MISUSE OF FUNDS.
GUESS YOU WERE RIGHT FROM THE START. IT'S A *VENDETTA.*
PARTIALLY.
THIS CASE DOESN'T FIT A SINGLE PROFILE. ON THE ONE HAND, THERE'S THE REVENGE THEORY AGAINST ANYONE WHO IN SOME WAY "DEGRADED" GAUDÍ'S WORK.
ON THE OTHER, THE *MODUS OPERANDI* CORRESPONDS TO THAT OF AN ORGANIZED KILLER. PREMEDITATED MURDER, NOT SPONTANEOUS, FORENSICALLY AWARE AND WITH A MESSAGE.
AND THEN THERE'S --
I KNOW -- THE **STRANGE CIRCUMSTANCES.** THAT WOMAN, ANTONIA, AND HER "GHOST." THE PRESS WILL **LOVE** THAT.
NOT JUST THAT.

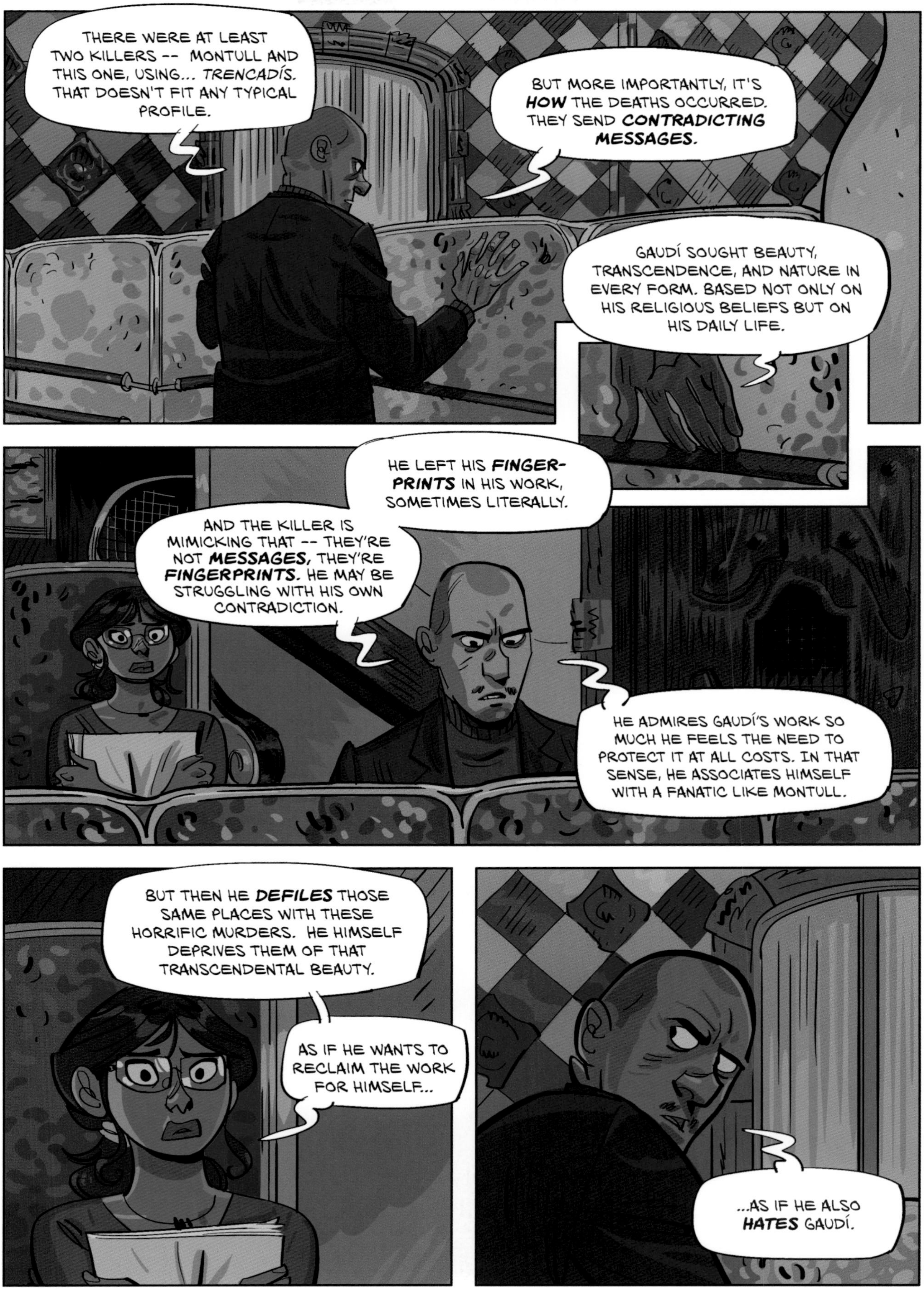
THERE WERE AT LEAST TWO KILLERS -- MONTULL AND THIS ONE, USING... TRENCADÍS. THAT DOESN'T FIT ANY TYPICAL PROFILE.
BUT MORE IMPORTANTLY, IT'S HOW THE DEATHS OCCURRED. THEY SEND CONTRADICTING MESSAGES.
GAUDÍ SOUGHT BEAUTY, TRANSCENDENCE, AND NATURE IN EVERY FORM. BASED NOT ONLY ON HIS RELIGIOUS BELIEFS BUT ON HIS DAILY LIFE.
HE LEFT HIS FINGER-PRINTS IN HIS WORK, SOMETIMES LITERALLY.
AND THE KILLER IS MIMICKING THAT -- THEY'RE NOT MESSAGES, THEY'RE FINGERPRINTS. HE MAY BE STRUGGLING WITH HIS OWN CONTRADICTION.
HE ADMIRES GAUDÍ'S WORK SO MUCH HE FEELS THE NEED TO PROTECT IT AT ALL COSTS. IN THAT SENSE, HE ASSOCIATES HIMSELF WITH A FANATIC LIKE MONTULL.
BUT THEN HE DEFILES THOSE SAME PLACES WITH THESE HORRIFIC MURDERS. HE HIMSELF DEPRIVES THEM OF THAT TRANSCENDENTAL BEAUTY.
AS IF HE WANTS TO RECLAIM THE WORK FOR HIMSELF...
...AS IF HE ALSO HATES GAUDÍ.

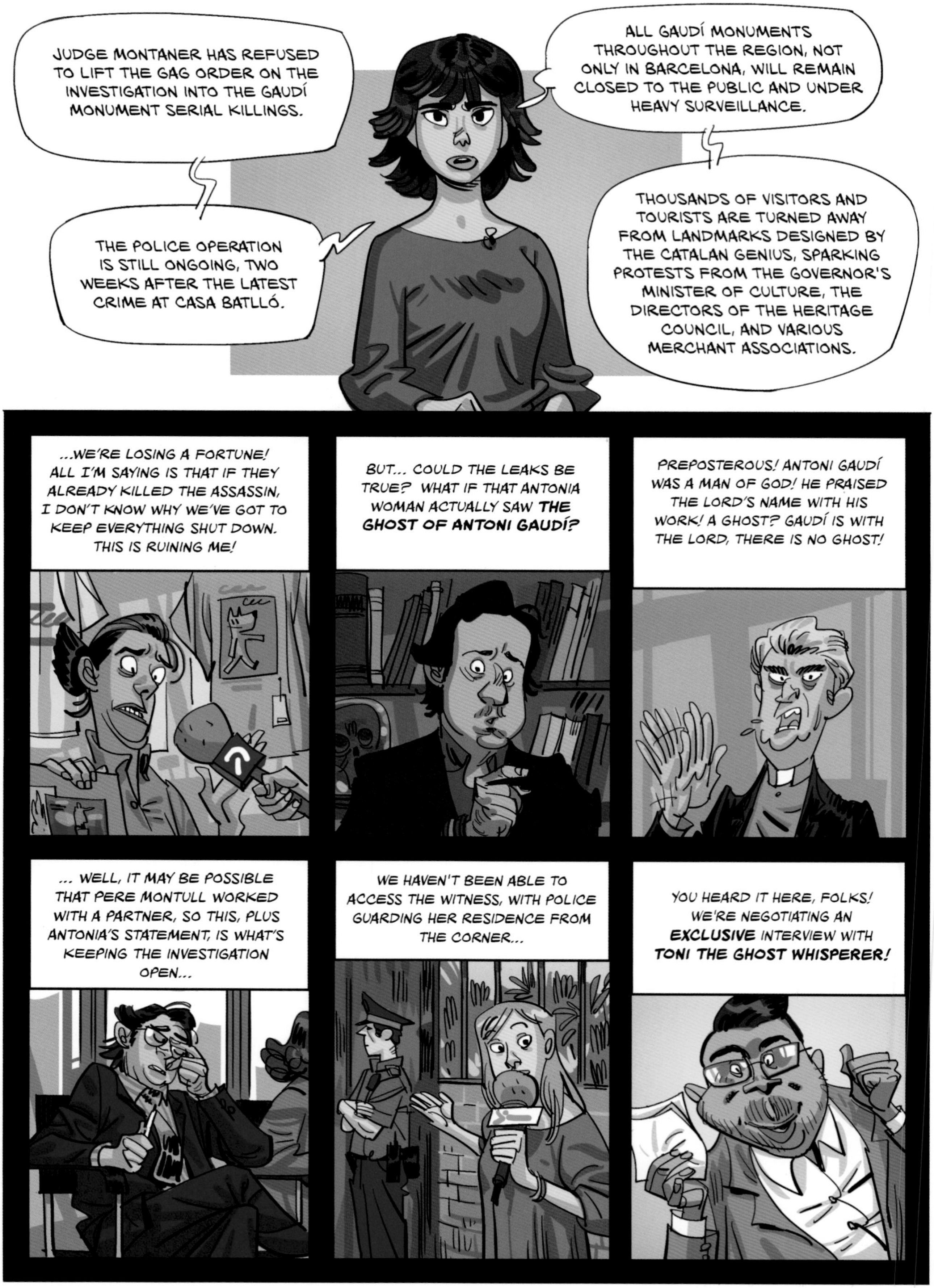
JUDGE MONTANER HAS REFUSED TO LIFT THE GAG ORDER ON THE INVESTIGATION INTO THE GAUDÍ MONUMENT SERIAL KILLINGS.
THE POLICE OPERATION IS STILL ONGOING, TWO WEEKS AFTER THE LATEST CRIME AT CASA BATLLÓ.
ALL GAUDÍ MONUMENTS THROUGHOUT THE REGION, NOT ONLY IN BARCELONA, WILL REMAIN CLOSED TO THE PUBLIC AND UNDER HEAVY SURVEILLANCE.
THOUSANDS OF VISITORS AND TOURISTS ARE TURNED AWAY FROM LANDMARKS DESIGNED BY THE CATALAN GENIUS, SPARKING PROTESTS FROM THE GOVERNOR'S MINISTER OF CULTURE, THE DIRECTORS OF THE HERITAGE COUNCIL, AND VARIOUS MERCHANT ASSOCIATIONS.
...WE'RE LOSING A FORTUNE! ALL I'M SAYING IS THAT IF THEY ALREADY KILLED THE ASSASSIN, I DON'T KNOW WHY WE'VE GOT TO KEEP EVERYTHING SHUT DOWN. THIS IS RUINING ME!
BUT... COULD THE LEAKS BE TRUE? WHAT IF THAT ANTONIA WOMAN ACTUALLY SAW **THE GHOST OF ANTONI GAUDÍ?**
PREPOSTEROUS! ANTONI GAUDÍ WAS A MAN OF GOD! HE PRAISED THE LORD'S NAME WITH HIS WORK! A GHOST? GAUDÍ IS WITH THE LORD, THERE IS NO GHOST!
... WELL, IT MAY BE POSSIBLE THAT PERE MONTULL WORKED WITH A PARTNER, SO THIS, PLUS ANTONIA'S STATEMENT, IS WHAT'S KEEPING THE INVESTIGATION OPEN...
WE HAVEN'T BEEN ABLE TO ACCESS THE WITNESS, WITH POLICE GUARDING HER RESIDENCE FROM THE CORNER...
YOU HEARD IT HERE, FOLKS! WE'RE NEGOTIATING AN **EXCLUSIVE** INTERVIEW WITH **TONI THE GHOST WHISPERER!**

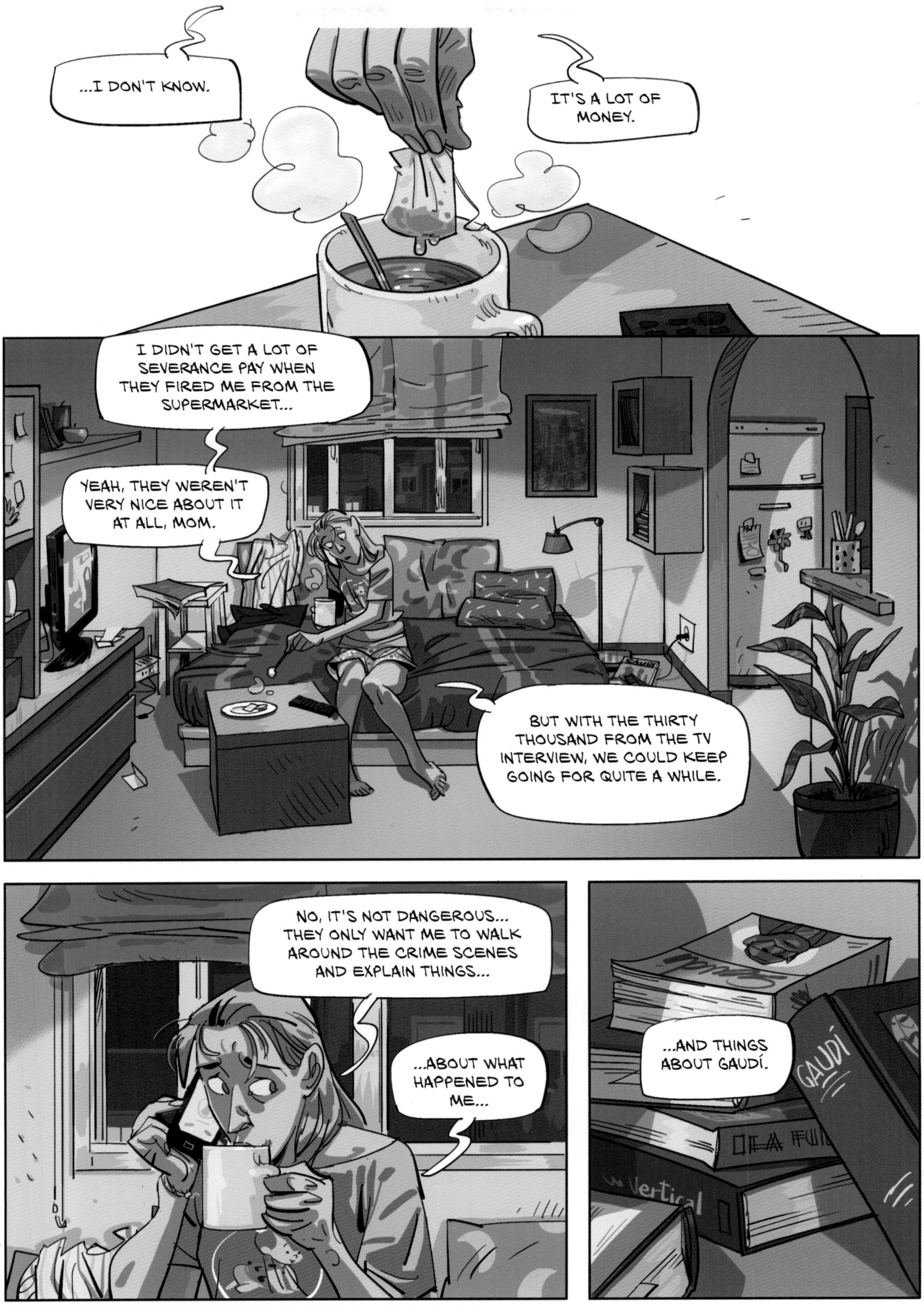
...I DON'T KNOW.
IT'S A LOT OF MONEY.
I DIDN'T GET A LOT OF SEVERANCE PAY WHEN THEY FIRED ME FROM THE SUPERMARKET...
YEAH, THEY WEREN'T VERY NICE ABOUT IT AT ALL, MOM.
BUT WITH THE THIRTY THOUSAND FROM THE TV INTERVIEW, WE COULD KEEP GOING FOR QUITE A WHILE.
NO, IT'S NOT DANGEROUS... THEY ONLY WANT ME TO WALK AROUND THE CRIME SCENES AND EXPLAIN THINGS...
...ABOUT WHAT HAPPENED TO ME...
...AND THINGS ABOUT GAUDÍ.
GAUDÍ
Vertical

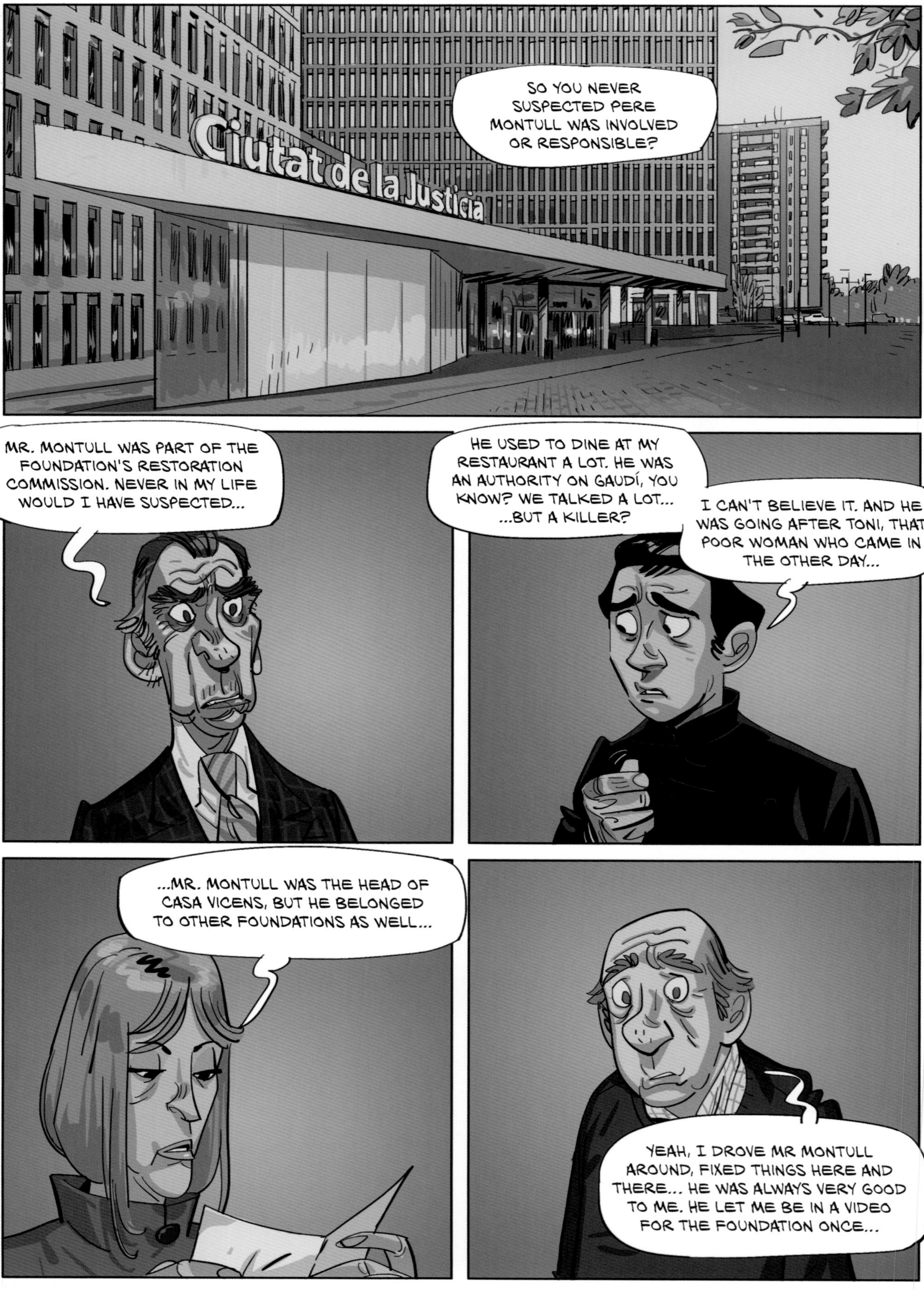
Ciutat de la Justicia
SO YOU NEVER SUSPECTED PERE MONTULL WAS INVOLVED OR RESPONSIBLE?
MR. MONTULL WAS PART OF THE FOUNDATION'S RESTORATION COMMISSION. NEVER IN MY LIFE WOULD I HAVE SUSPECTED...
HE USED TO DINE AT MY RESTAURANT A LOT. HE WAS AN AUTHORITY ON GAUDÍ, YOU KNOW? WE TALKED A LOT... ...BUT A KILLER?
I CAN'T BELIEVE IT. AND HE WAS GOING AFTER TONI, THAT POOR WOMAN WHO CAME IN THE OTHER DAY...
...MR. MONTULL WAS THE HEAD OF CASA VICENS, BUT HE BELONGED TO OTHER FOUNDATIONS AS WELL...
YEAH, I DROVE MR MONTULL AROUND, FIXED THINGS HERE AND THERE... HE WAS ALWAYS VERY GOOD TO ME. HE LET ME BE IN A VIDEO FOR THE FOUNDATION ONCE...

THAT MAKES FIFTEEN WITNESSES WHO'VE TESTIFIED.

FELLOW FOUNDATION MEMBERS, OTHER EXPERTS ON GAUDÍ, CONSERVATION SPECIALISTS... THEY ALL CHECK OUT CLEAN.

ALL HAVE *ALIBIS*.

I THINK WE'VE HIT A DEAD END, JAIME.

WHAT ABOUT THE FORENSIC ANALYSIS OF THE BODIES?

INCONCLUSIVE. I'M AFRAID TO SAY IT... THIS IS STARTING TO UNFOLD LIKE --

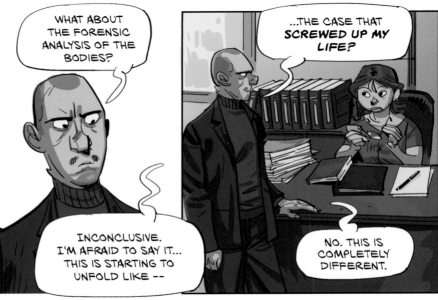

...THE CASE THAT *SCREWED UP MY LIFE?*

NO. THIS IS COMPLETELY DIFFERENT.

WILL YOU SIGN THE WARRANT?

TO SEARCH MONTULL'S HOUSE? YEAH, OKAY. YOU NEVER GIVE UP, DO YOU?

NOPE.

BUT YOU GAVE UP ON ME.

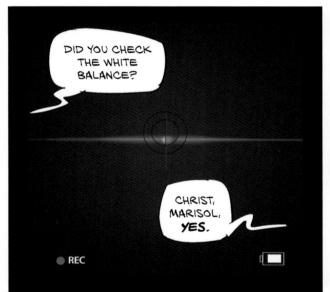

DID YOU CHECK THE WHITE BALANCE?

CHRIST, MARISOL, **YES.**

● REC

IF THE POLICE SAY ANYTHING...

MIKE, STOP ACTING LIKE SUCH AN AMATEUR. WE PAID A FORTUNE TO GET IN HERE. HOW'S MY FRAMING?

YOU'RE FINE. SHOULD I GO OUT AND TAKE SOME SETUP SHOTS?

SURE, BUT DON'T LET SECURITY CATCH YOU. THEY'RE CRACKING DOWN HARD ON VISUAL RIGHTS.

THEN WHAT SHOULD I FILM?

● REC

LET'S GO UPSTAIRS AND SHOOT SOME OF THE CHIMNEYS ON THE ROOF! THEY'RE PRETTY FAMOUS!

LOOK, PILI, I DON'T WANNA STICK AROUND HERE ALL DAY...

● REC

...LET'S JUST FINISH SHOOTING OVER THERE.

GET THE BALCONIES AND THE FAÇADE AS BACKGROUND FOOTAGE. TONI, YOU KNOW ABOUT THIS STUFF, RIGHT?

CAN YOU SAY SOMETHING ABOUT LA *PEDRERA* OFF CAMERA?

UH... SURE... I'VE NEVER BEEN HERE, THOUGH...

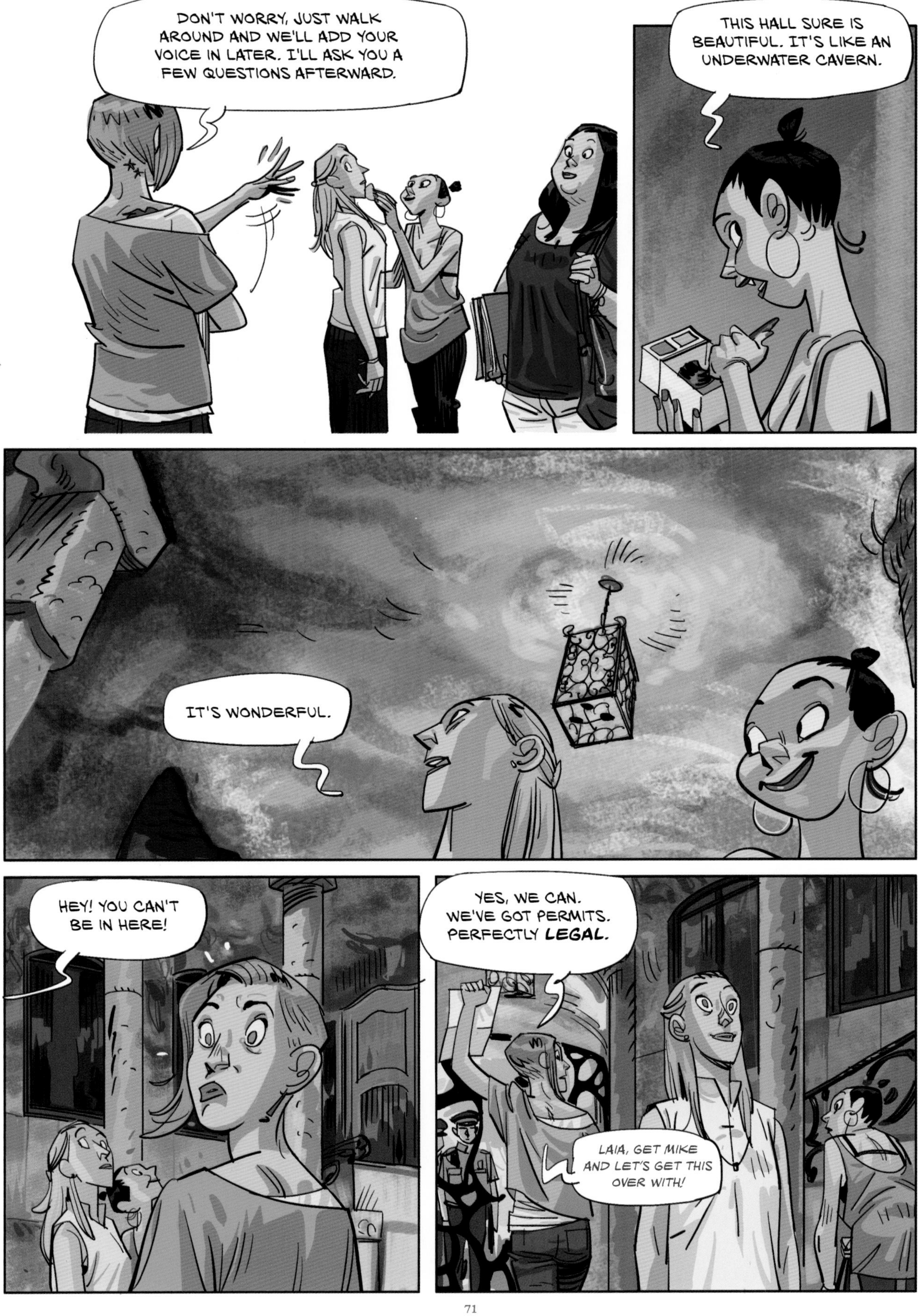

DON'T WORRY, JUST WALK AROUND AND WE'LL ADD YOUR VOICE IN LATER. I'LL ASK YOU A FEW QUESTIONS AFTERWARD.
THIS HALL SURE IS BEAUTIFUL. IT'S LIKE AN UNDERWATER CAVERN.
IT'S WONDERFUL.
HEY! YOU CAN'T BE IN HERE!
YES, WE CAN. WE'VE GOT PERMITS. PERFECTLY **LEGAL.**
LAIA, GET MIKE AND LET'S GET THIS OVER WITH!

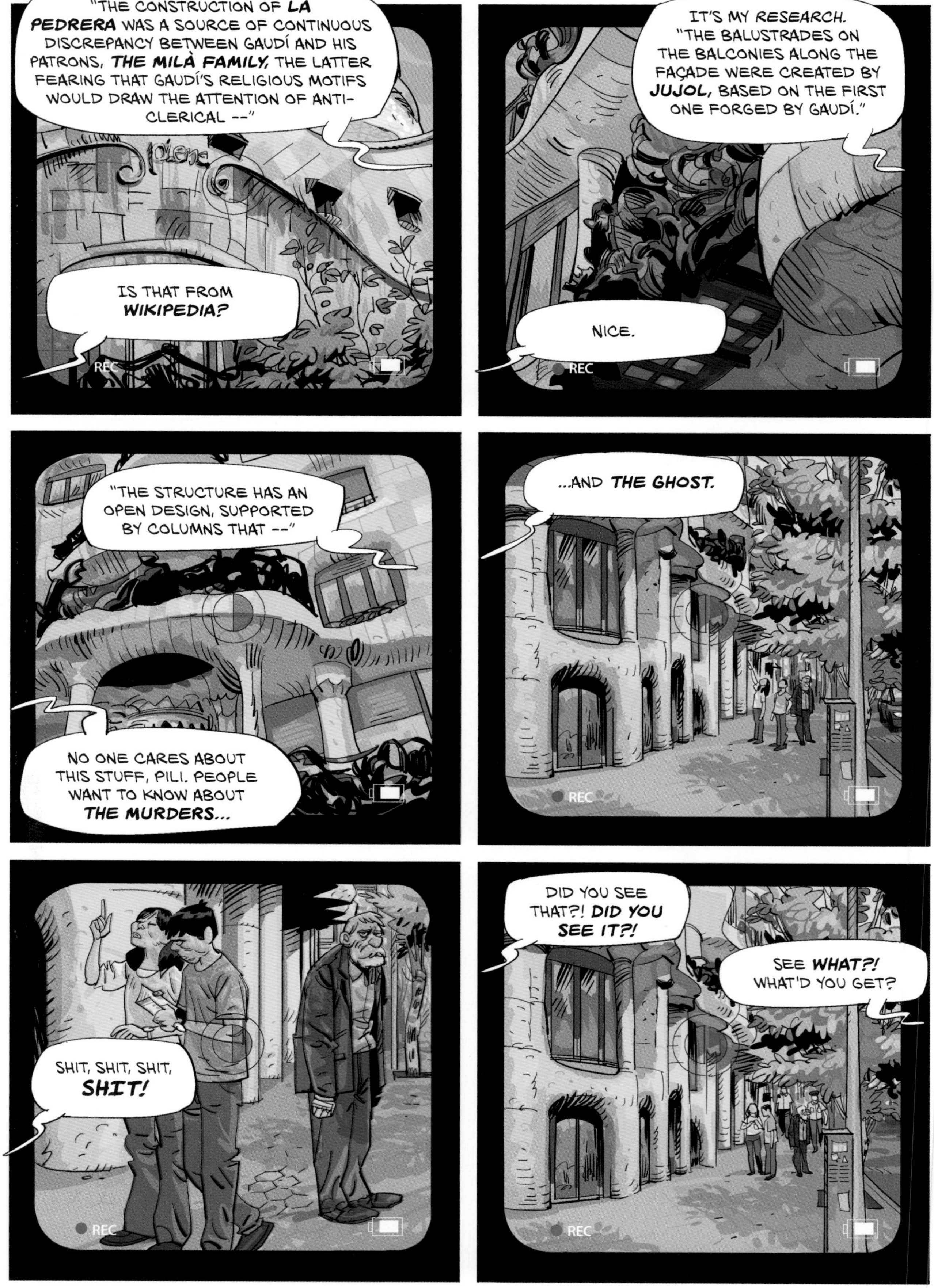
"THE CONSTRUCTION OF **LA PEDRERA** WAS A SOURCE OF CONTINUOUS DISCREPANCY BETWEEN GAUDÍ AND HIS PATRONS, ***THE MILÀ FAMILY,*** THE LATTER FEARING THAT GAUDÍ'S RELIGIOUS MOTIFS WOULD DRAW THE ATTENTION OF ANTI-CLERICAL --"
IS THAT FROM ***WIKIPEDIA?***
REC
IT'S MY *RESEARCH.* "THE BALUSTRADES ON THE BALCONIES ALONG THE FAÇADE WERE CREATED BY ***JUJOL,*** BASED ON THE FIRST ONE FORGED BY GAUDÍ."
NICE.
REC
"THE STRUCTURE HAS AN OPEN DESIGN, SUPPORTED BY COLUMNS THAT --"
NO ONE CARES ABOUT THIS STUFF, PILI. PEOPLE WANT TO KNOW ABOUT ***THE MURDERS...***
...AND ***THE GHOST.***
REC
SHIT, SHIT, SHIT, ***SHIT!***
REC
DID YOU SEE THAT?! ***DID YOU SEE IT?!***
SEE ***WHAT?!*** WHAT'D YOU GET?
REC

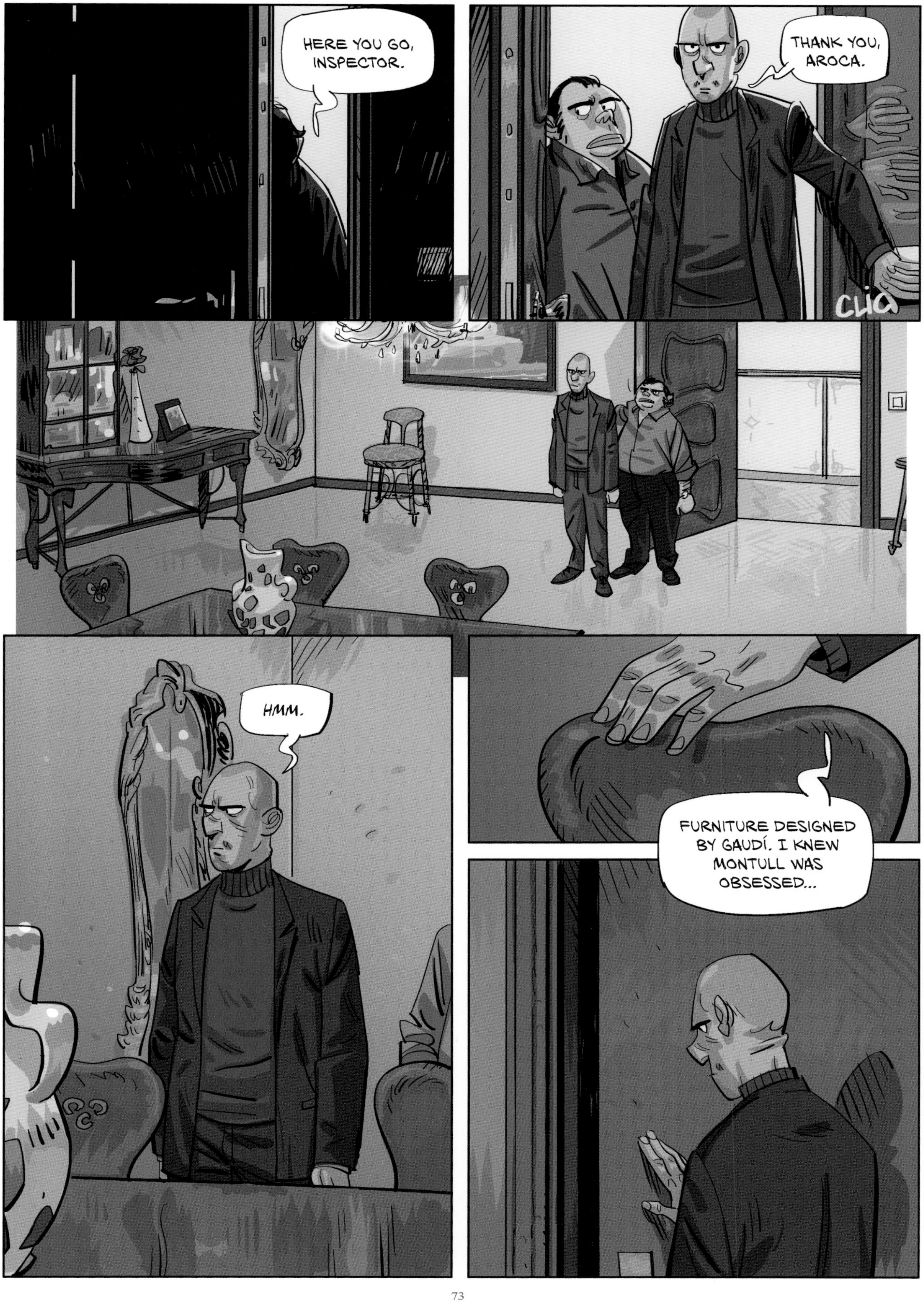
HERE YOU GO, INSPECTOR.
THANK YOU, AROCA.
CLIC
HMM.
FURNITURE DESIGNED BY GAUDÍ. I KNEW MONTULL WAS OBSESSED...

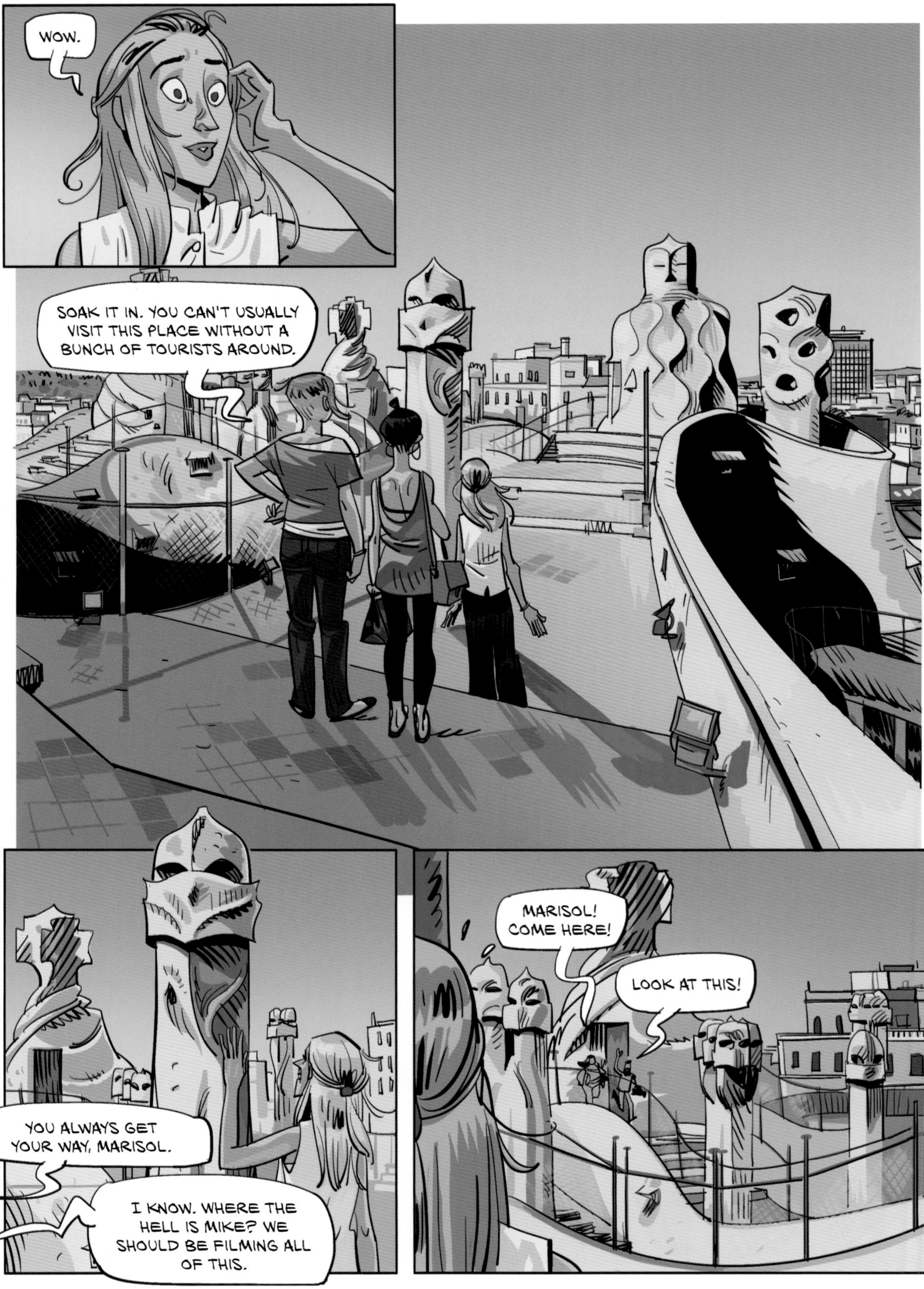
WOW.
SOAK IT IN. YOU CAN'T USUALLY VISIT THIS PLACE WITHOUT A BUNCH OF TOURISTS AROUND.
YOU ALWAYS GET YOUR WAY, MARISOL.
I KNOW. WHERE THE HELL IS MIKE? WE SHOULD BE FILMING ALL OF THIS.
MARISOL! COME HERE!
LOOK AT THIS!

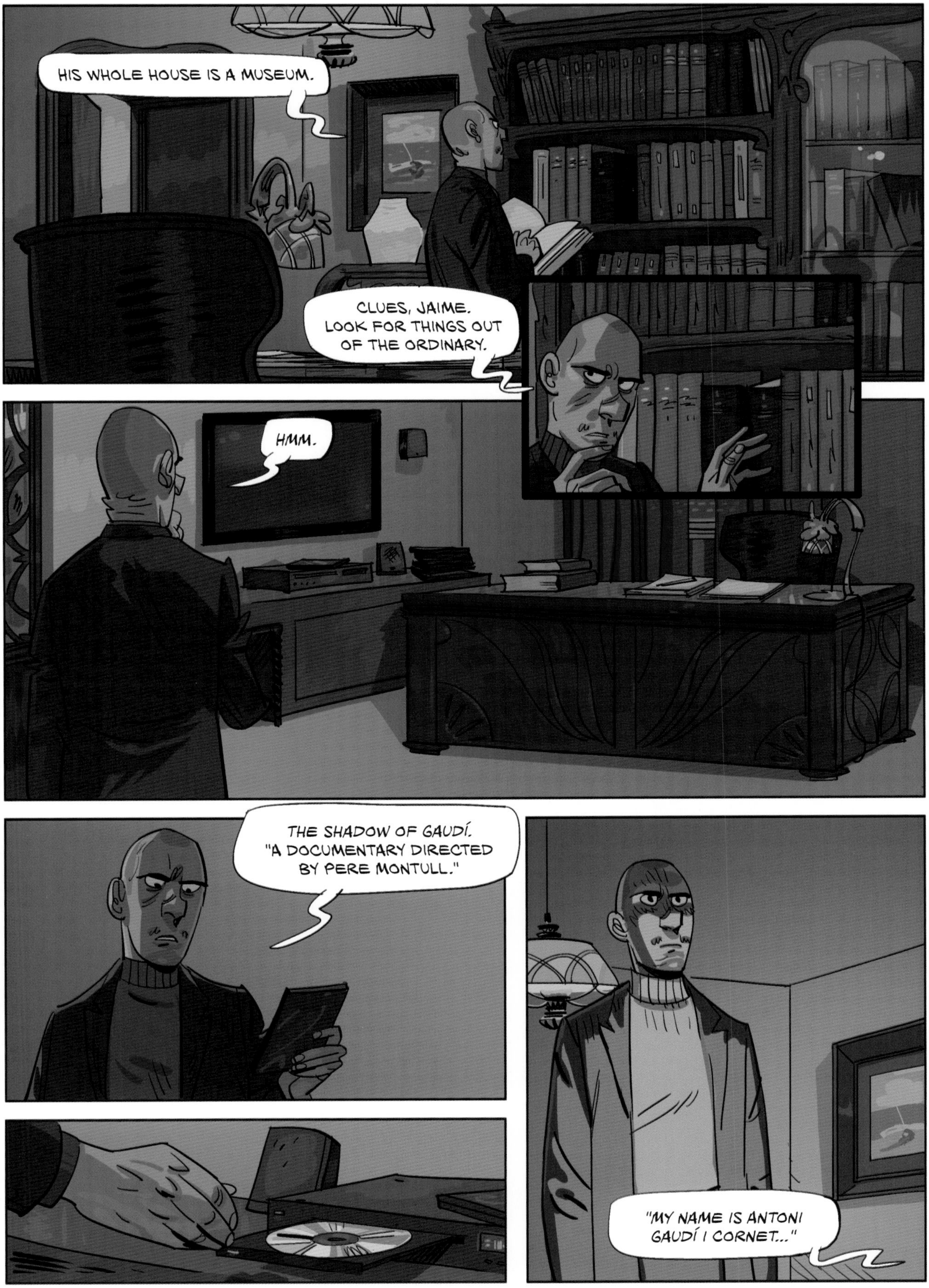
HIS WHOLE HOUSE IS A MUSEUM.
CLUES, JAIME. LOOK FOR THINGS OUT OF THE ORDINARY.
HMM.
THE SHADOW OF GAUDÍ. "A DOCUMENTARY DIRECTED BY PERE MONTULL."
"MY NAME IS ANTONI GAUDÍ I CORNET..."

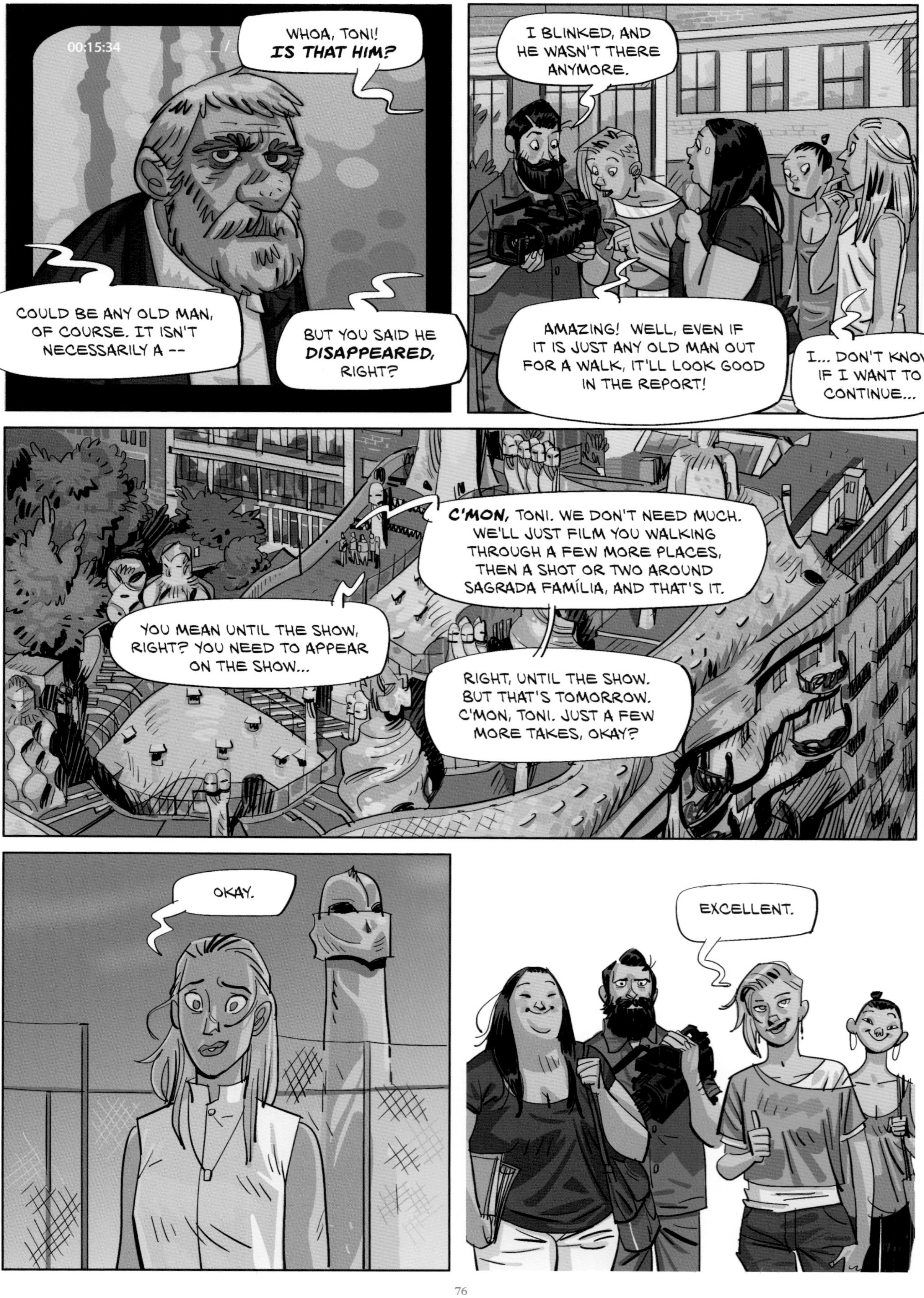
00:15:34
WHOA, TONI! IS THAT HIM?
COULD BE ANY OLD MAN, OF COURSE. IT ISN'T NECESSARILY A --
BUT YOU SAID HE DISAPPEARED, RIGHT?
I BLINKED, AND HE WASN'T THERE ANYMORE.
AMAZING! WELL, EVEN IF IT IS JUST ANY OLD MAN OUT FOR A WALK, IT'LL LOOK GOOD IN THE REPORT!
I... DON'T KNOW IF I WANT TO CONTINUE...
C'MON, TONI. WE DON'T NEED MUCH. WE'LL JUST FILM YOU WALKING THROUGH A FEW MORE PLACES, THEN A SHOT OR TWO AROUND SAGRADA FAMÍLIA, AND THAT'S IT.
YOU MEAN UNTIL THE SHOW, RIGHT? YOU NEED TO APPEAR ON THE SHOW...
RIGHT, UNTIL THE SHOW. BUT THAT'S TOMORROW. C'MON, TONI. JUST A FEW MORE TAKES, OKAY?
OKAY.
EXCELLENT.

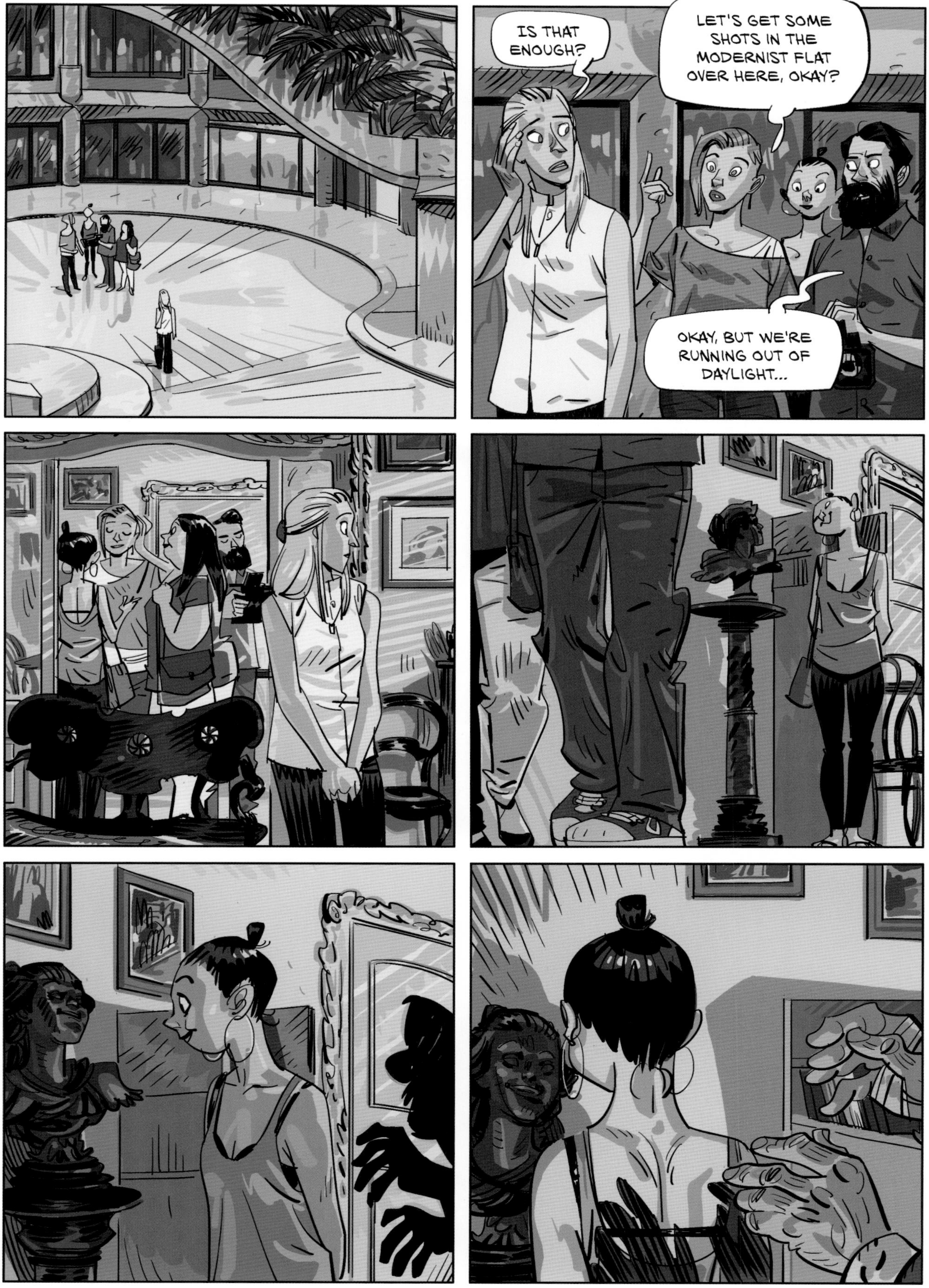
IS THAT ENOUGH?
LET'S GET SOME SHOTS IN THE MODERNIST FLAT OVER HERE, OKAY?
OKAY, BUT WE'RE RUNNING OUT OF DAYLIGHT...

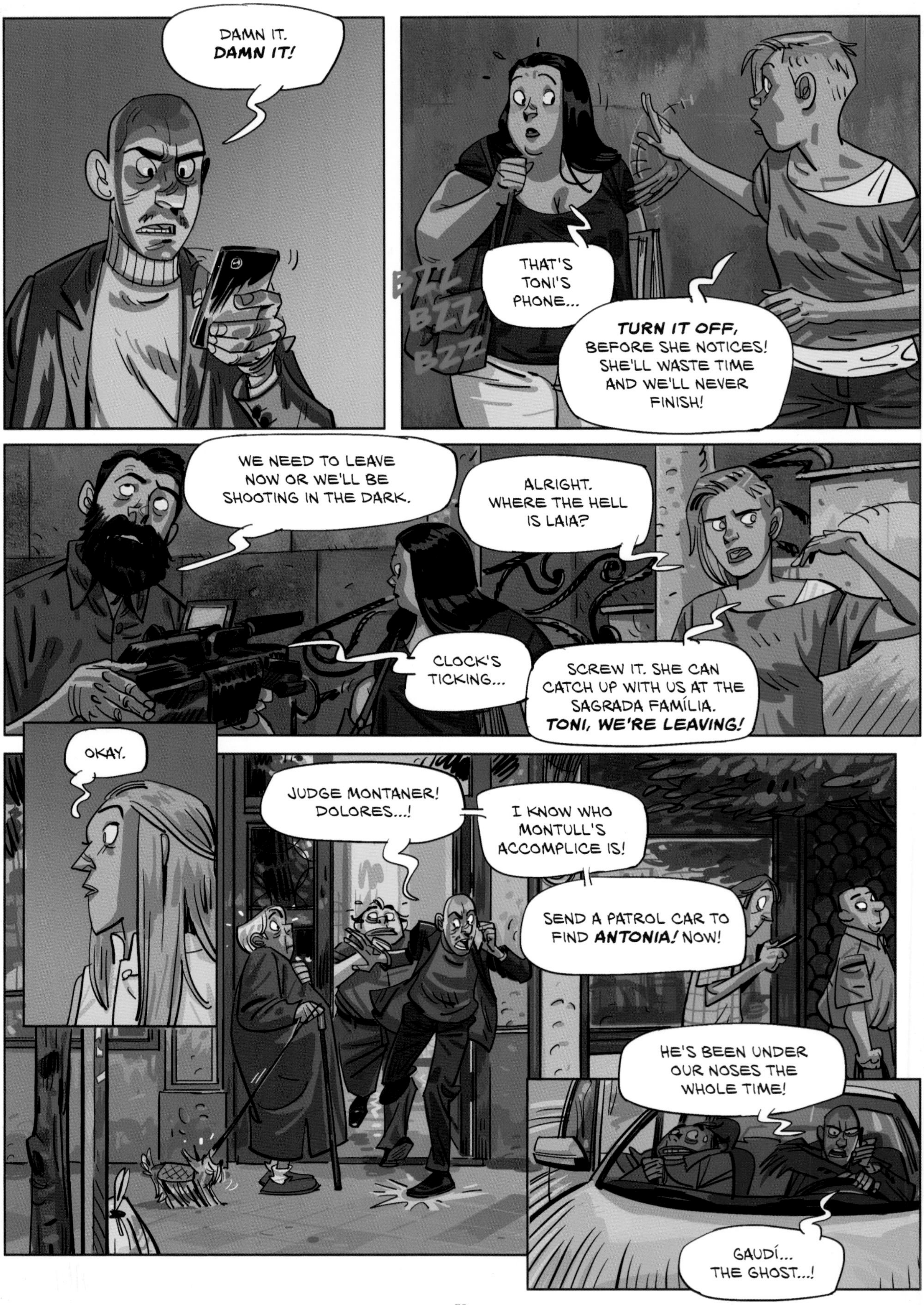
DAMN IT. DAMN IT!
THAT'S TONI'S PHONE...
BZZ BZZ BZZ
TURN IT OFF, BEFORE SHE NOTICES! SHE'LL WASTE TIME AND WE'LL NEVER FINISH!
WE NEED TO LEAVE NOW OR WE'LL BE SHOOTING IN THE DARK.
ALRIGHT. WHERE THE HELL IS LAIA?
CLOCK'S TICKING...
SCREW IT. SHE CAN CATCH UP WITH US AT THE SAGRADA FAMÍLIA. TONI, WE'RE LEAVING!
OKAY.
JUDGE MONTANER! DOLORES...!
I KNOW WHO MONTULL'S ACCOMPLICE IS!
SEND A PATROL CAR TO FIND ANTONIA! NOW!
HE'S BEEN UNDER OUR NOSES THE WHOLE TIME!
GAUDÍ... THE GHOST...!

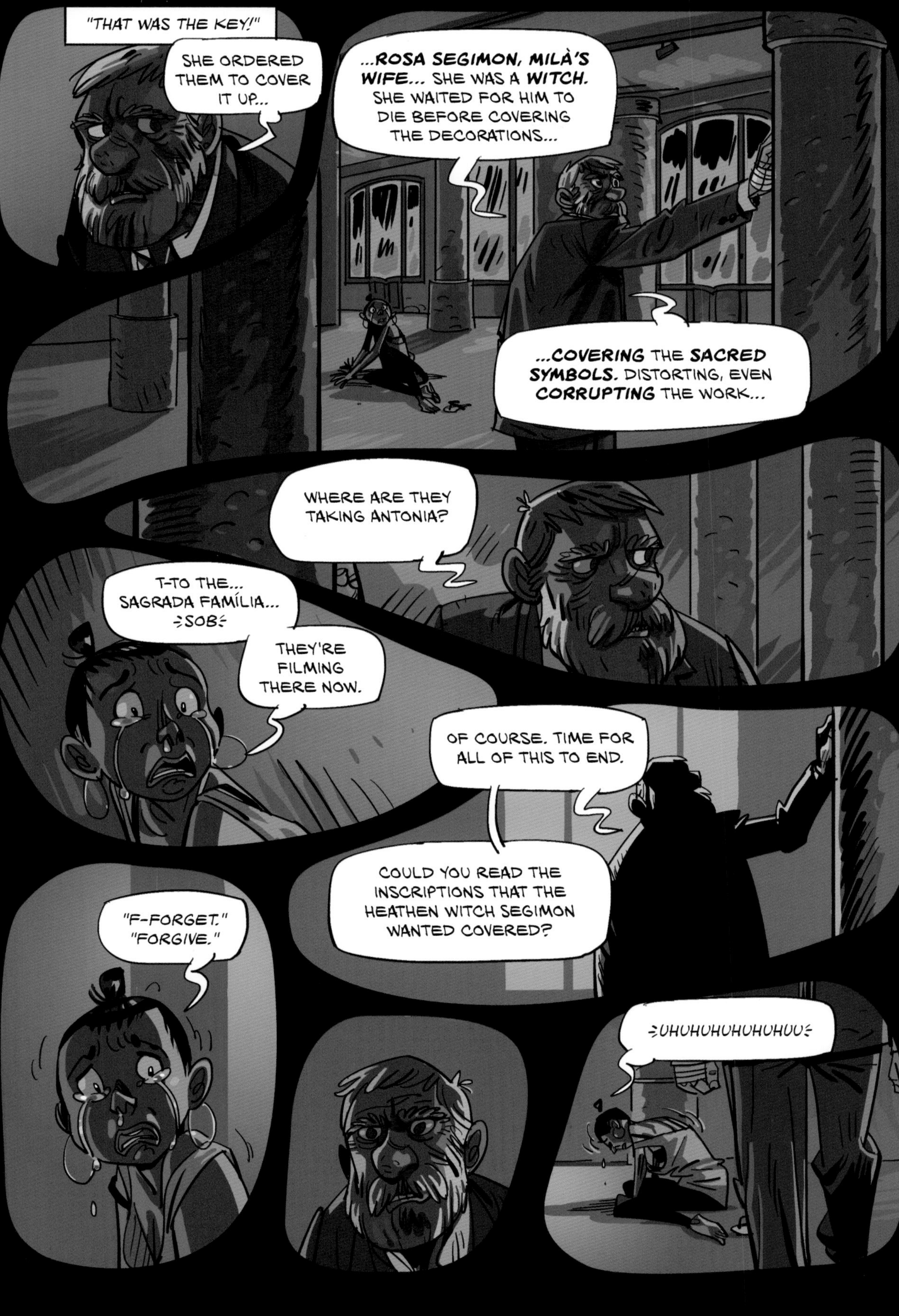
"THAT WAS THE KEY!"
SHE ORDERED THEM TO COVER IT UP...
...ROSA SEGIMON, MILÀ'S WIFE... SHE WAS A WITCH. SHE WAITED FOR HIM TO DIE BEFORE COVERING THE DECORATIONS...
...COVERING THE SACRED SYMBOLS. DISTORTING, EVEN CORRUPTING THE WORK...
WHERE ARE THEY TAKING ANTONIA?
T-TO THE... SAGRADA FAMÍLIA... SOB
THEY'RE FILMING THERE NOW.
OF COURSE. TIME FOR ALL OF THIS TO END.
COULD YOU READ THE INSCRIPTIONS THAT THE HEATHEN WITCH SEGIMON WANTED COVERED?
"F-FORGET." "FORGIVE."
UHUHUHUHUHUHUU

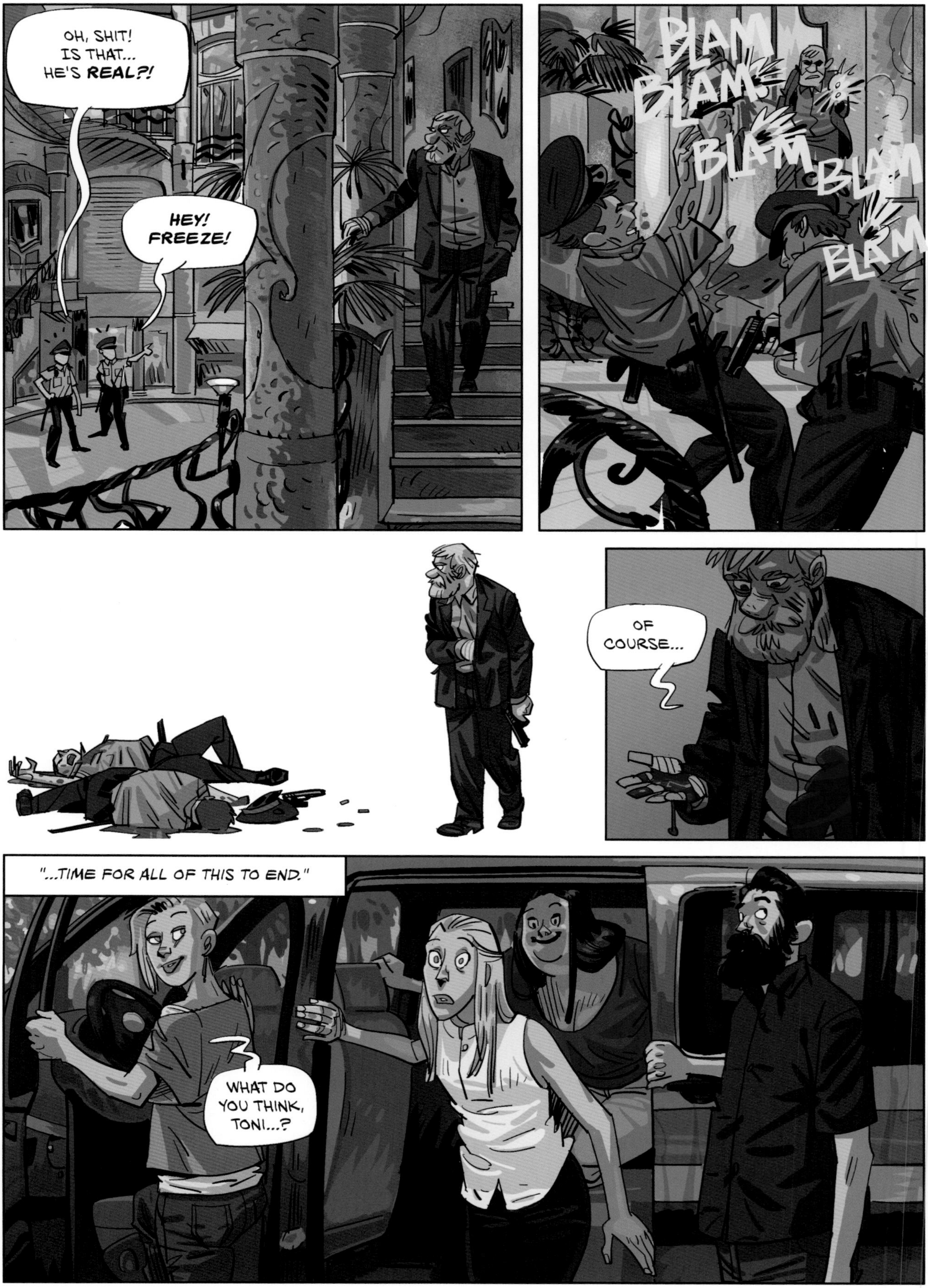
OH, SHIT! IS THAT... HE'S **REAL?!**
HEY! FREEZE!
BLAM BLAM BLAM BLAM BLAM
OF COURSE...
"...TIME FOR ALL OF THIS TO END."
WHAT DO YOU THINK, TONI...?

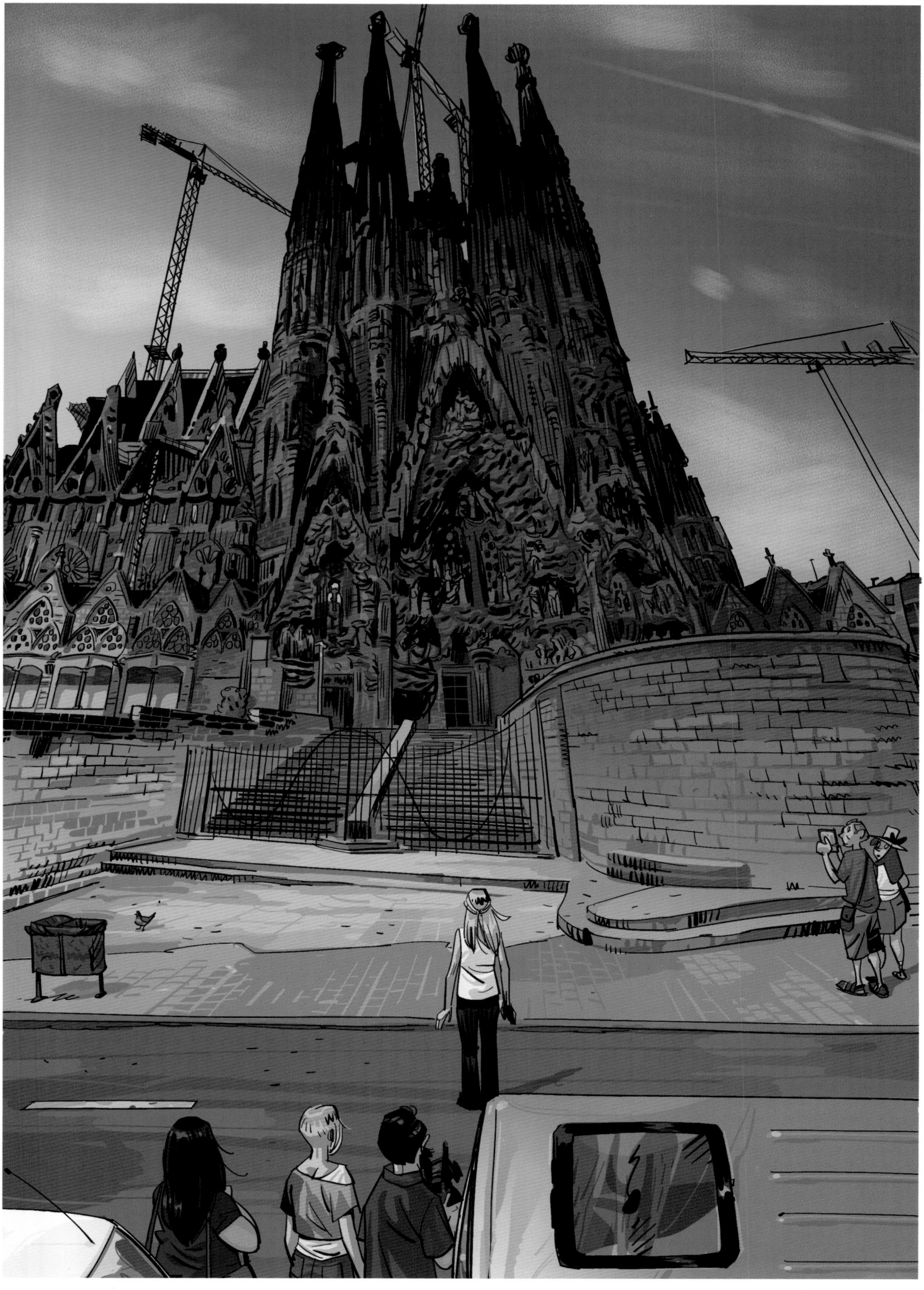

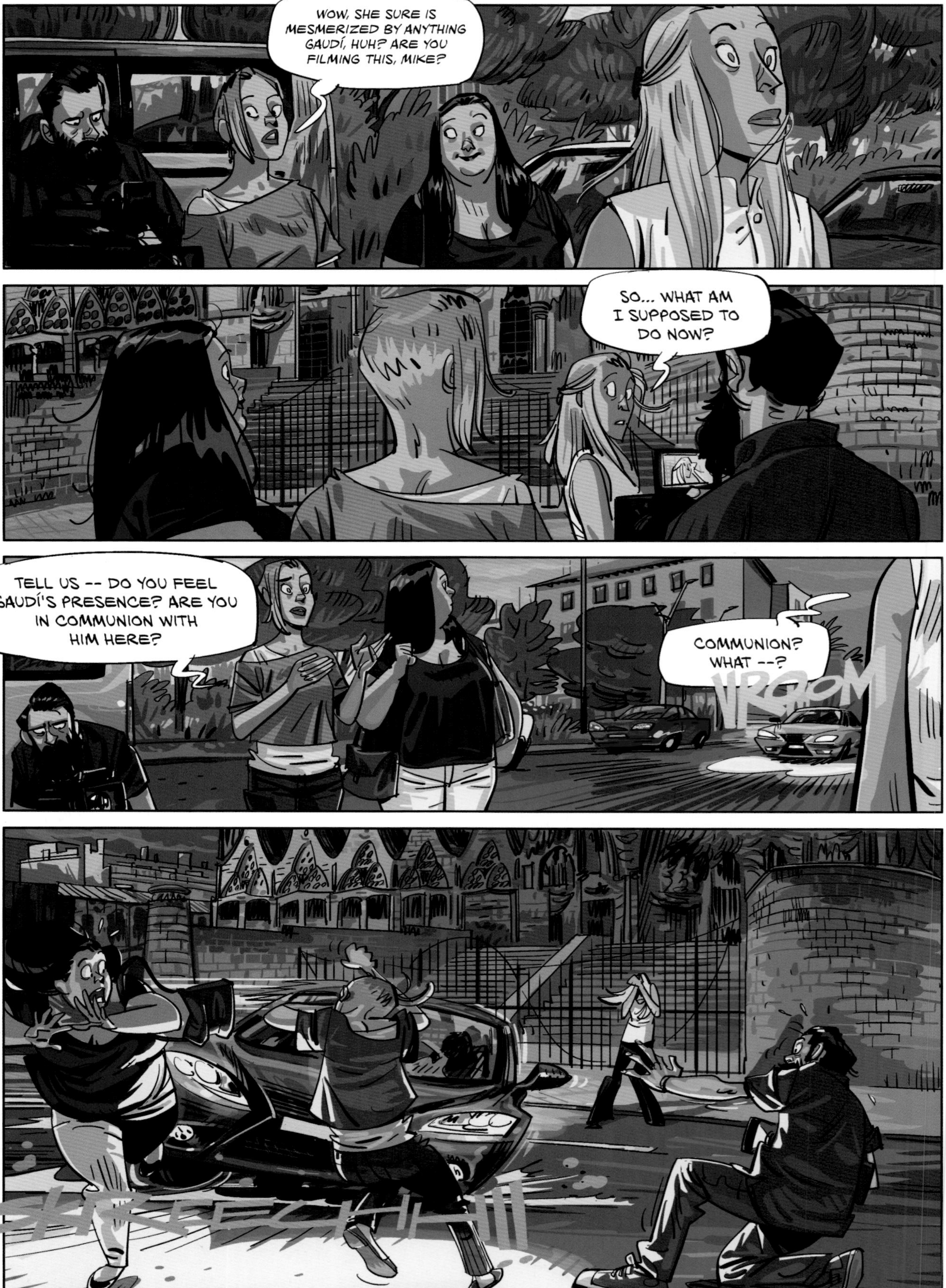
WOW, SHE SURE IS MESMERIZED BY ANYTHING GAUDÍ, HUH? ARE YOU FILMING THIS, MIKE?
SO... WHAT AM I SUPPOSED TO DO NOW?
TELL US -- DO YOU FEEL GAUDÍ'S PRESENCE? ARE YOU IN COMMUNION WITH HIM HERE?
COMMUNION? WHAT --?
VROOM
SKREECHHH!!

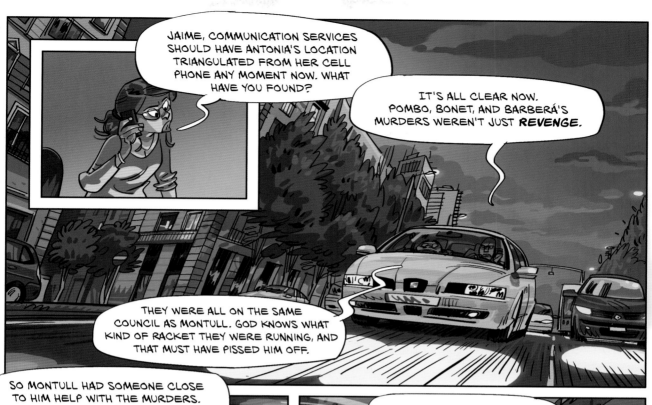

JAIME, COMMUNICATION SERVICES SHOULD HAVE ANTONIA'S LOCATION TRIANGULATED FROM HER CELL PHONE ANY MOMENT NOW. WHAT HAVE YOU FOUND?

IT'S ALL CLEAR NOW. POMBO, BONET, AND BARBERÁ'S MURDERS WEREN'T JUST *REVENGE.*

THEY WERE ALL ON THE SAME COUNCIL AS MONTULL. GOD KNOWS WHAT KIND OF RACKET THEY WERE RUNNING, AND THAT MUST HAVE PISSED HIM OFF.

SO MONTULL HAD SOMEONE CLOSE TO HIM HELP WITH THE MURDERS. SOMEONE WITH AN OBSESSION OF THEIR OWN -- THEY FUELED EACH OTHER! BUT THEN SOMETHING HAPPENED: *ANTONIA.*

FOR GOD'S SAKE, JAIME, **WHO IS IT?!**

FIND ANTONIA RIGHT NOW! SHE'S HIS OBJECTIVE! THE MAN WANTED TO *BE* GAUDÍ...

"...BUT **HATES** HIM BECAUSE HE **CAN'T BE!**"

EEEEKK!

BLAM

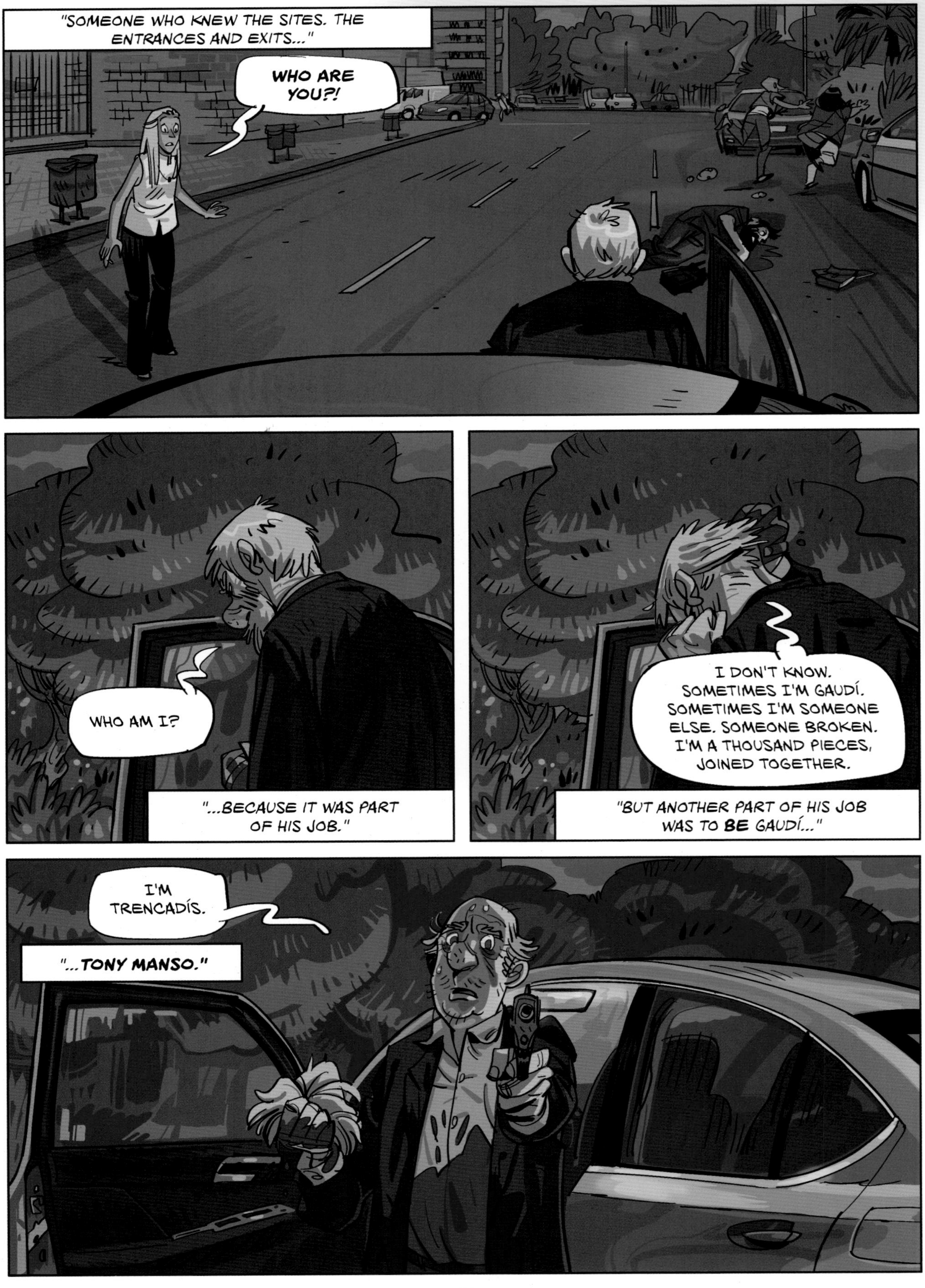
"SOMEONE WHO KNEW THE SITES. THE ENTRANCES AND EXITS..."
WHO ARE YOU?!
WHO AM I?
"...BECAUSE IT WAS PART OF HIS JOB."
I DON'T KNOW. SOMETIMES I'M GAUDÍ. SOMETIMES I'M SOMEONE ELSE. SOMEONE BROKEN. I'M A THOUSAND PIECES, JOINED TOGETHER.
"BUT ANOTHER PART OF HIS JOB WAS TO BE GAUDÍ..."
I'M TRENCADÍS.
"...TONY MANSO."

Chapter 4

La Sagrada Família

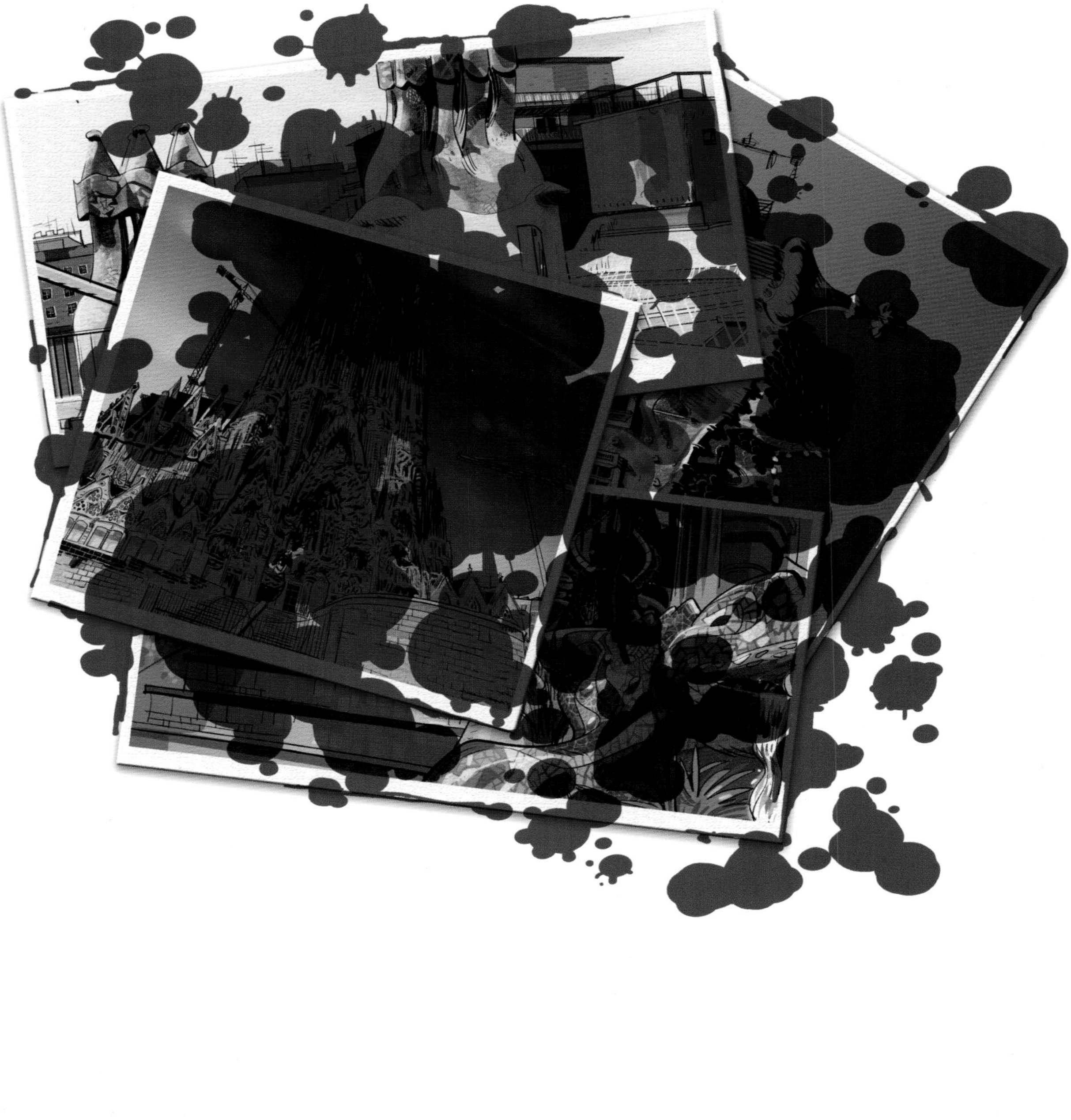

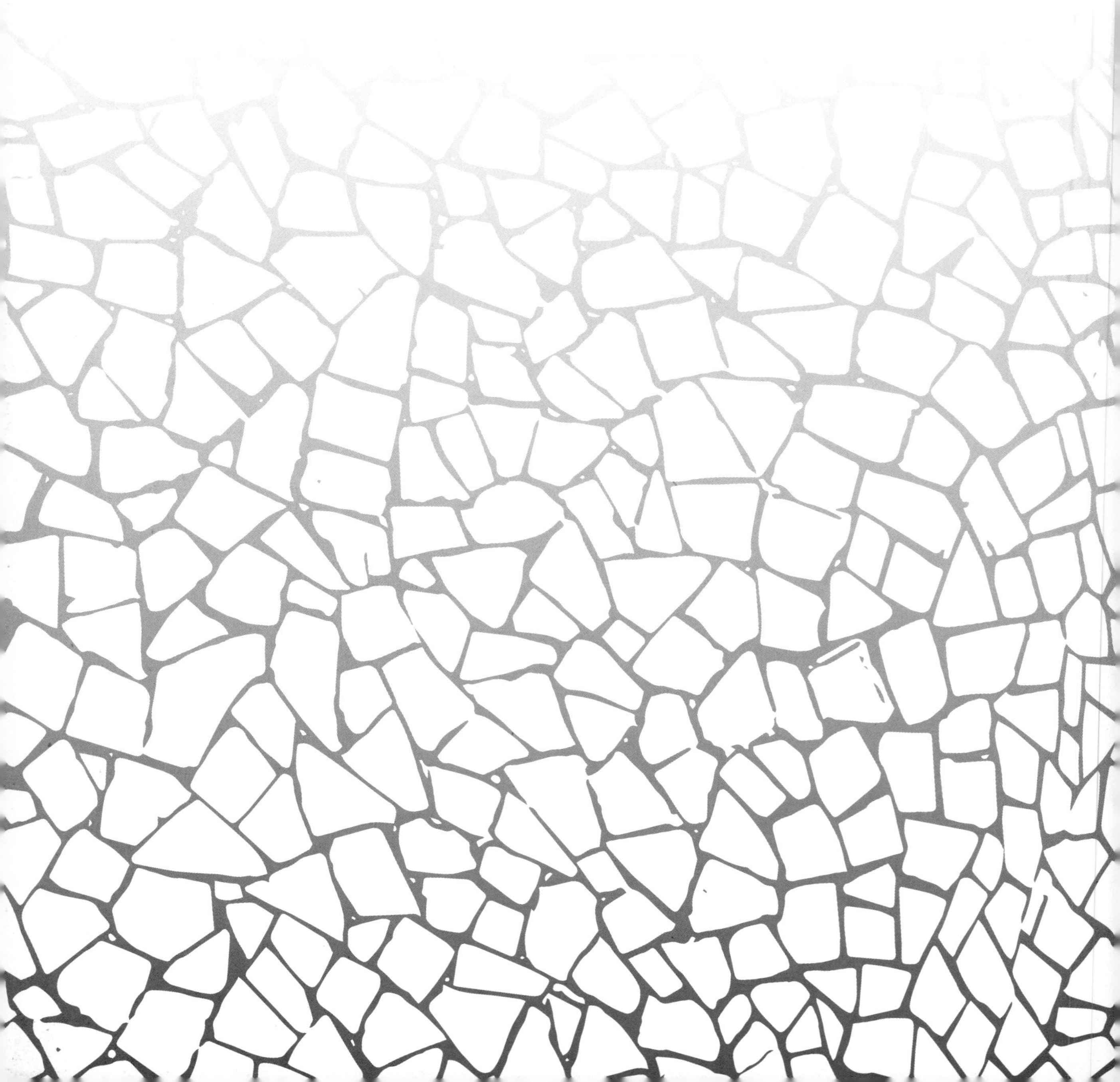

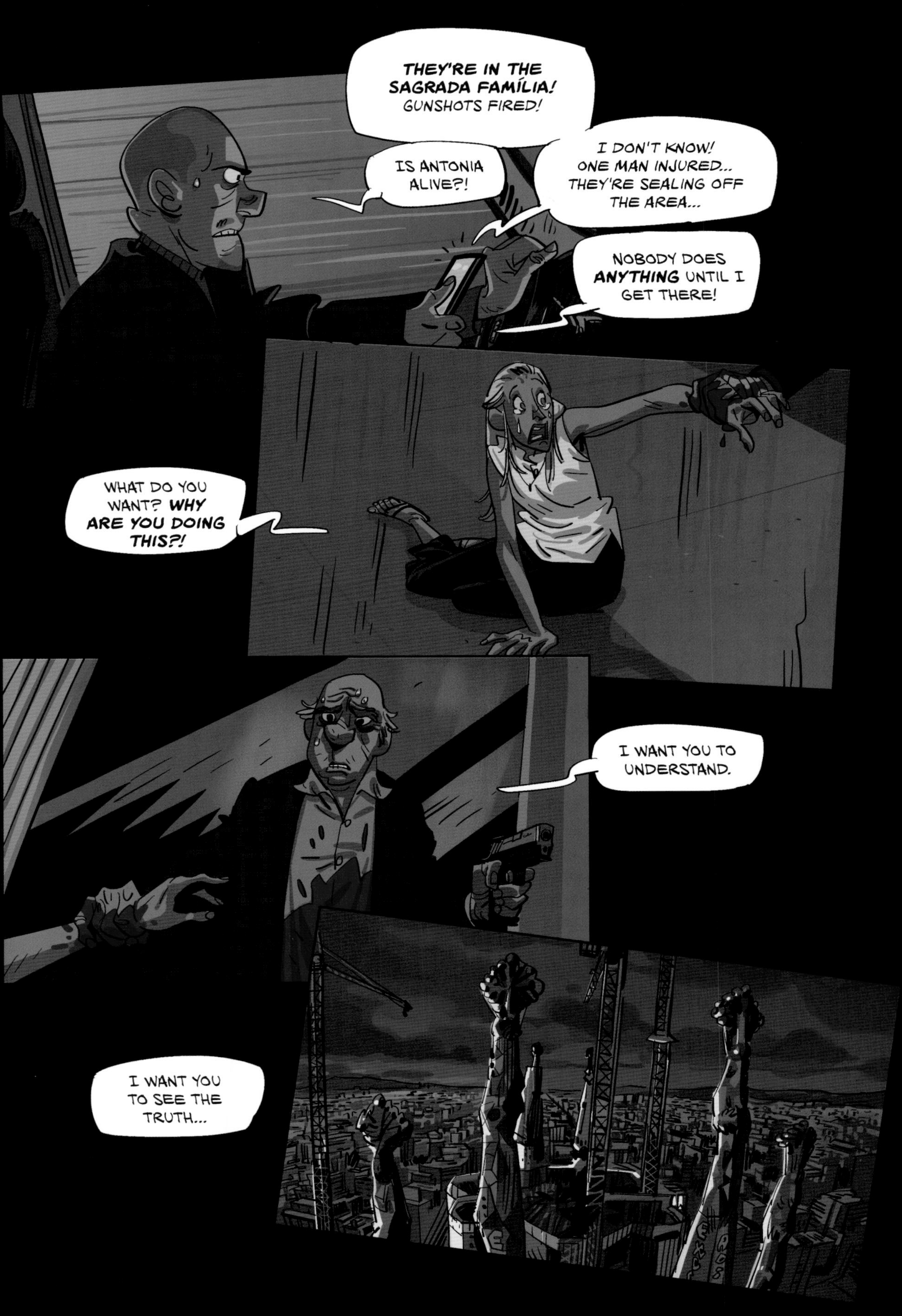
THEY'RE IN THE SAGRADA FAMÍLIA! GUNSHOTS FIRED!
IS ANTONIA ALIVE?!
I DON'T KNOW! ONE MAN INJURED... THEY'RE SEALING OFF THE AREA...
NOBODY DOES ANYTHING UNTIL I GET THERE!
WHAT DO YOU WANT? WHY ARE YOU DOING THIS?!
I WANT YOU TO UNDERSTAND.
I WANT YOU TO SEE THE TRUTH...

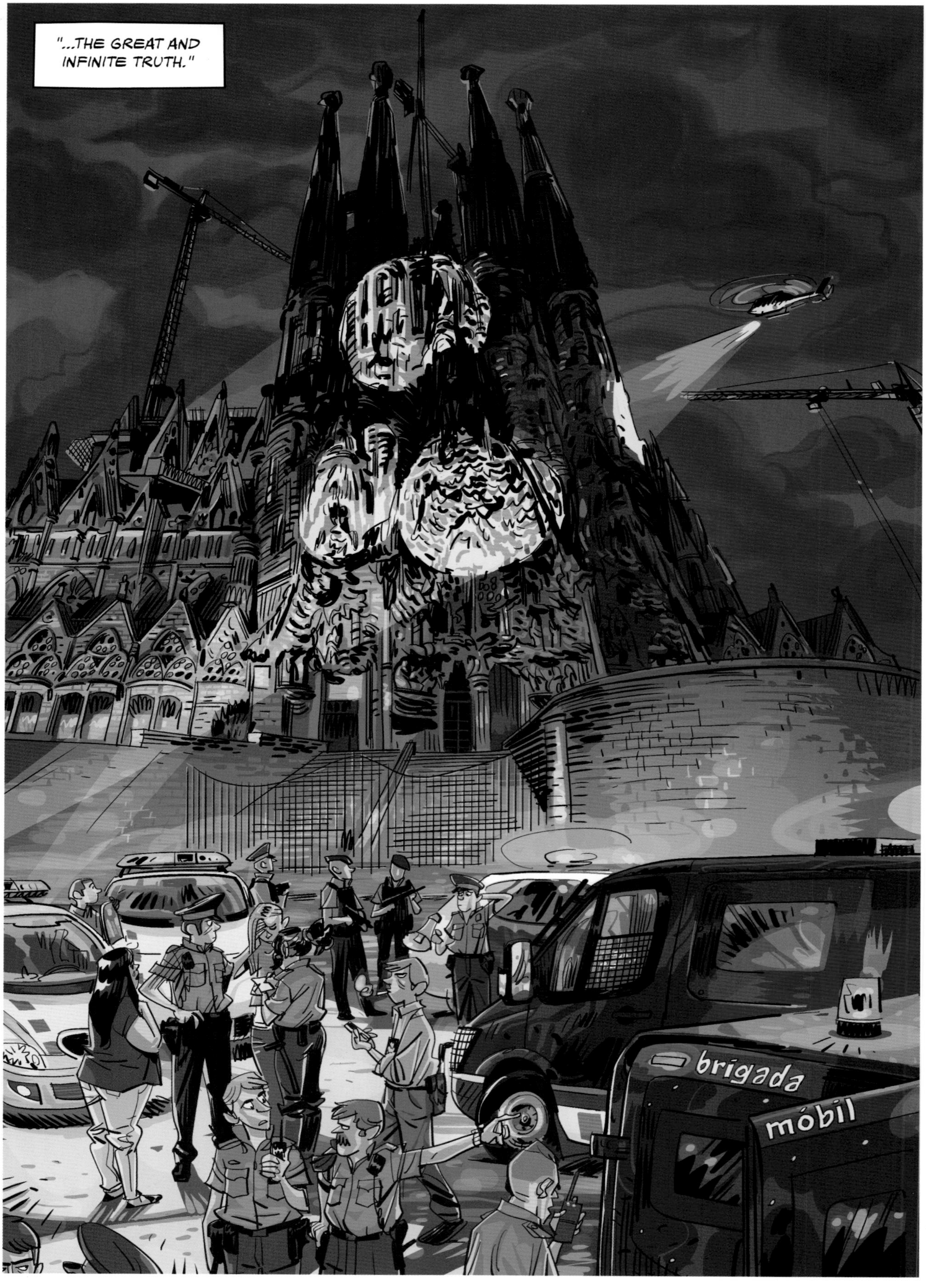
"...THE GREAT AND INFINITE TRUTH."
brigada
móbil

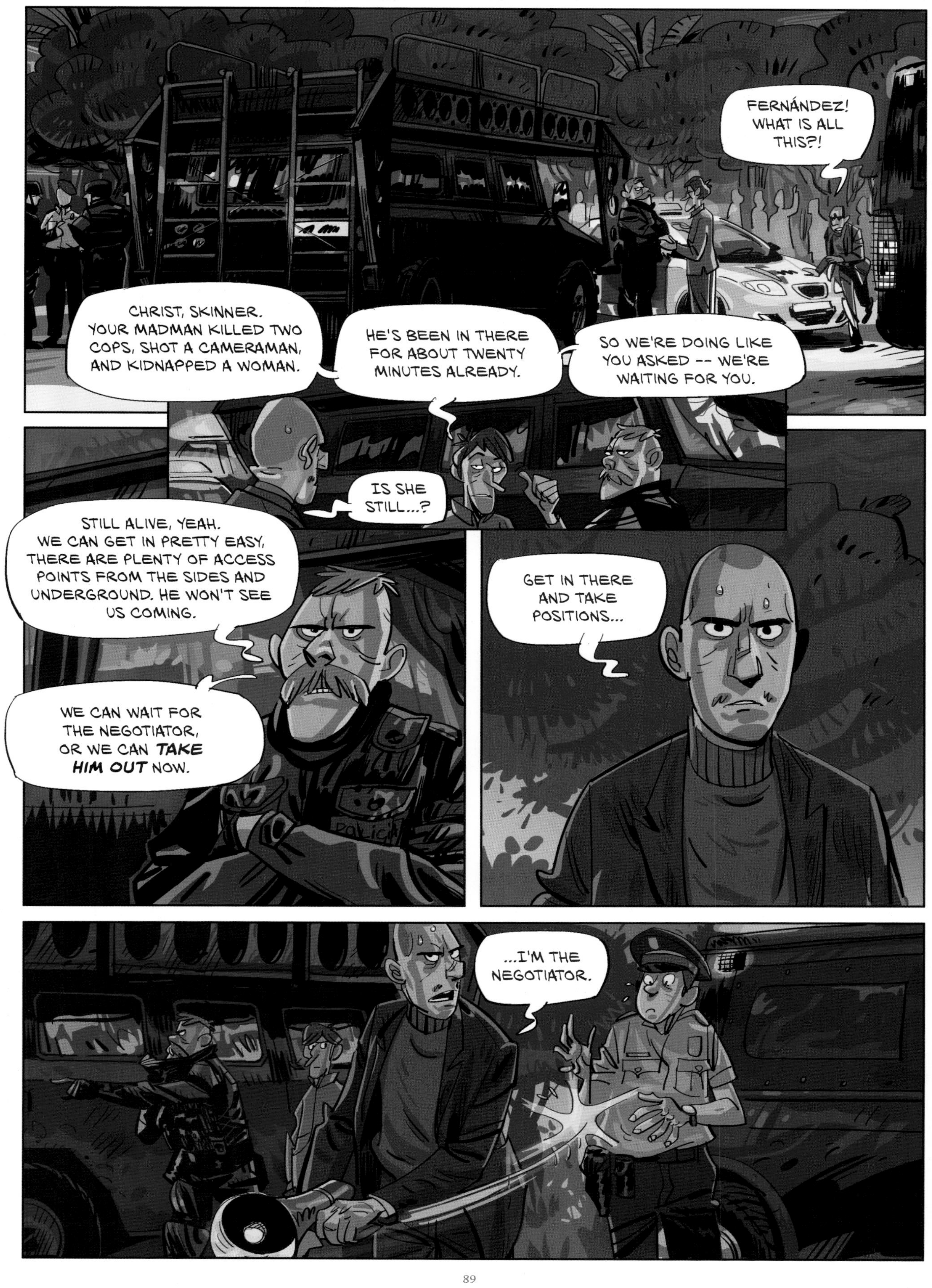
FERNÁNDEZ! WHAT IS ALL THIS?!
CHRIST, SKINNER. YOUR MADMAN KILLED TWO COPS, SHOT A CAMERAMAN, AND KIDNAPPED A WOMAN.
HE'S BEEN IN THERE FOR ABOUT TWENTY MINUTES ALREADY.
SO WE'RE DOING LIKE YOU ASKED -- WE'RE WAITING FOR YOU.
IS SHE STILL...?
STILL ALIVE, YEAH. WE CAN GET IN PRETTY EASY, THERE ARE PLENTY OF ACCESS POINTS FROM THE SIDES AND UNDERGROUND. HE WON'T SEE US COMING.
WE CAN WAIT FOR THE NEGOTIATOR, OR WE CAN TAKE HIM OUT NOW.
GET IN THERE AND TAKE POSITIONS...
...I'M THE NEGOTIATOR.

FAITH, HOPE, CHARITY. ALL THAT GUIDE US TO PERFECTION, YOU SEE?

THE RULER, THE CHISEL, THE COMPASS, THE HAMMER...

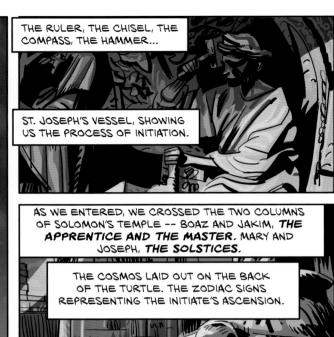

ST. JOSEPH'S VESSEL, SHOWING US THE PROCESS OF INITIATION.

THERE ARE SYMBOLS EVERYWHERE, AND THEY MUST BE INTERPRETED BY THEIR MANY FACETS.. THEY OPEN OUR MINDS TO GOD!

AS WE ENTERED, WE CROSSED THE TWO COLUMNS OF SOLOMON'S TEMPLE -- BOAZ AND JAKIM, *THE APPRENTICE AND THE MASTER.* MARY AND JOSEPH, *THE SOLSTICES.*

THE COSMOS LAID OUT ON THE BACK OF THE TURTLE. THE ZODIAC SIGNS REPRESENTING THE INITIATE'S ASCENSION.

ON THE COLUMN OF THE LORD'S GENEALOGY, THE HOLY FAMILY. THE FINAL REVELATION OF GOD MADE MAN. A JOURNEY MADE UNDER HIS WATCHFUL EYE.

THE ANGEL OF THE LAST JUDGMENT, BEARING THE FACE OF... OF OPISSO! A... A CARTOONIST! THE TAU OVER THE ETERNAL CYPRESS, THE FIRST LETTER OF "GOD" IN GREEK, THE NINTH CABALISTIC SEPHIROT OF THE SNAKE...

THE PELICAN OF THE EUCHARIST, AT THE FOOT OF THE CYPRESS, THE EGG OF BIRTH, AND THE LETTERS "IHS" -- "JESUS" IN GREEK, OR MAYBE AN ANAGRAM OF "ISIS, HORUS, SET"...? THESE ARE ALL SYMBOLS THAT WE MUST --

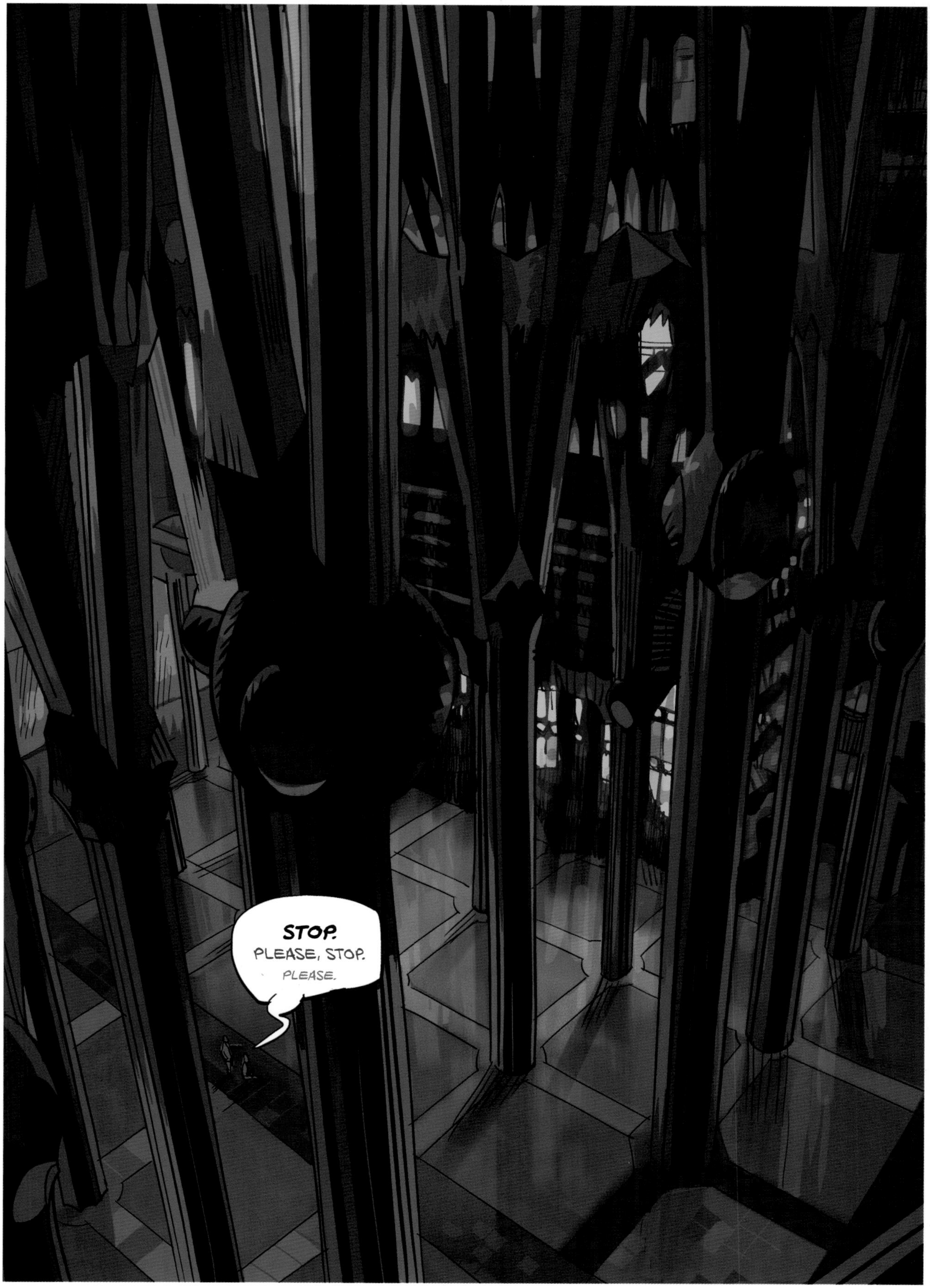
STOP.
PLEASE, STOP.
PLEASE.

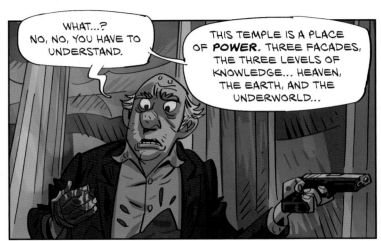

WHAT...? NO, NO, YOU HAVE TO UNDERSTAND.

THIS TEMPLE IS A PLACE OF **POWER**. THREE FACADES, THE THREE LEVELS OF KNOWLEDGE... HEAVEN, THE EARTH, AND THE UNDERWORLD...

I DON'T CARE! I DON'T WANT TO KNOW ANY OF THIS! LEAVE ME ALONE!

FORGIVE ME. I MEAN IT. ALL THIS PAIN, EVERYTHING I'VE CAUSED YOU... BUT YOU... YOU SAVED ME WHEN I WAS GOING TO KILL MYSELF, YOU KNOW?

THAT'S WHEN I KNEW I MUST GUIDE YOU. YOU WERE MY SIGN.

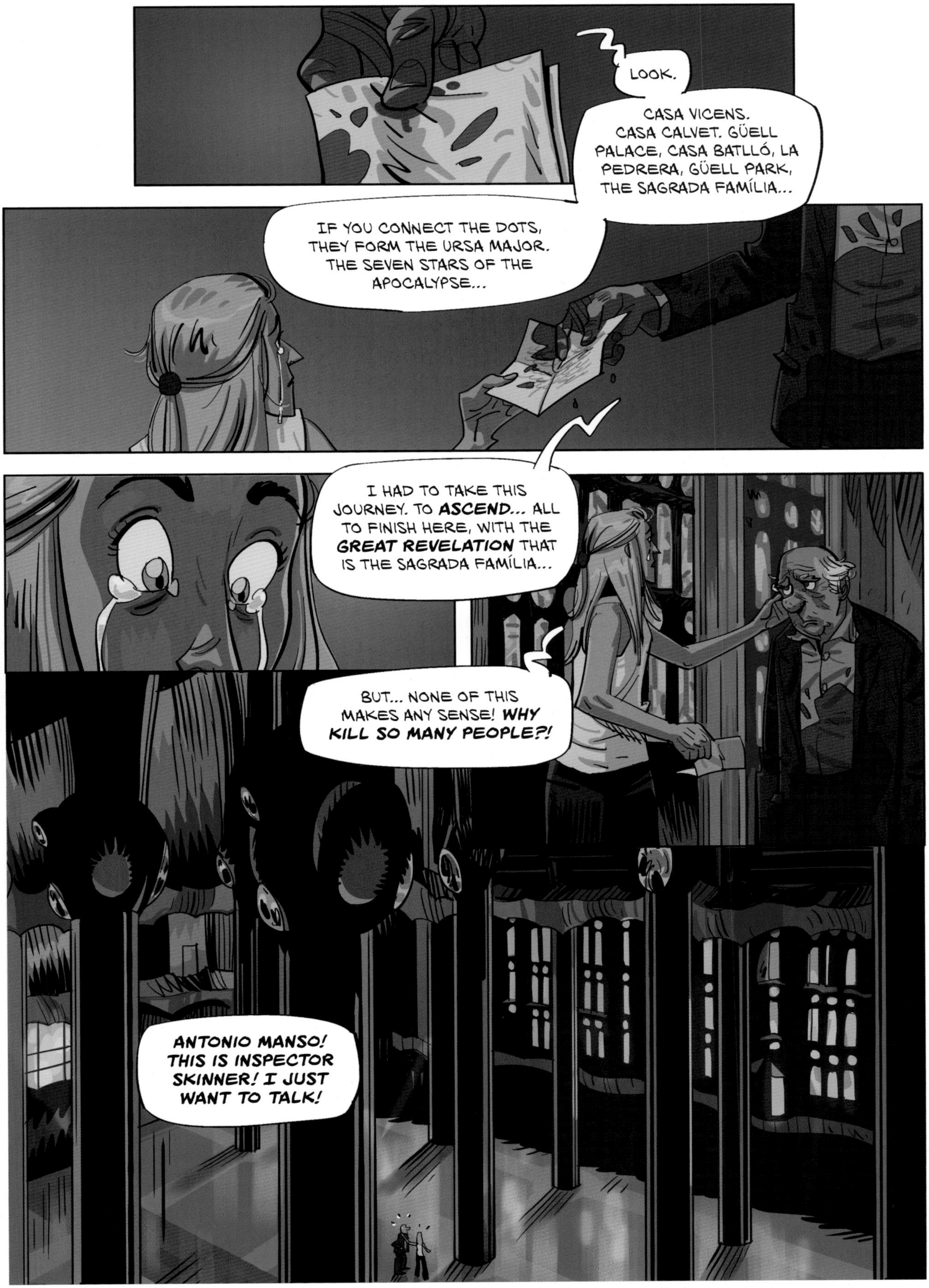
LOOK.
CASA VICENS. CASA CALVET. GÜELL PALACE, CASA BATLLÓ, LA PEDRERA, GÜELL PARK, THE SAGRADA FAMÍLIA...
IF YOU CONNECT THE DOTS, THEY FORM THE URSA MAJOR. THE SEVEN STARS OF THE APOCALYPSE...
I HAD TO TAKE THIS JOURNEY. TO ASCEND... ALL TO FINISH HERE, WITH THE GREAT REVELATION THAT IS THE SAGRADA FAMÍLIA...
BUT... NONE OF THIS MAKES ANY SENSE! WHY KILL SO MANY PEOPLE?!
ANTONIO MANSO! THIS IS INSPECTOR SKINNER! I JUST WANT TO TALK!

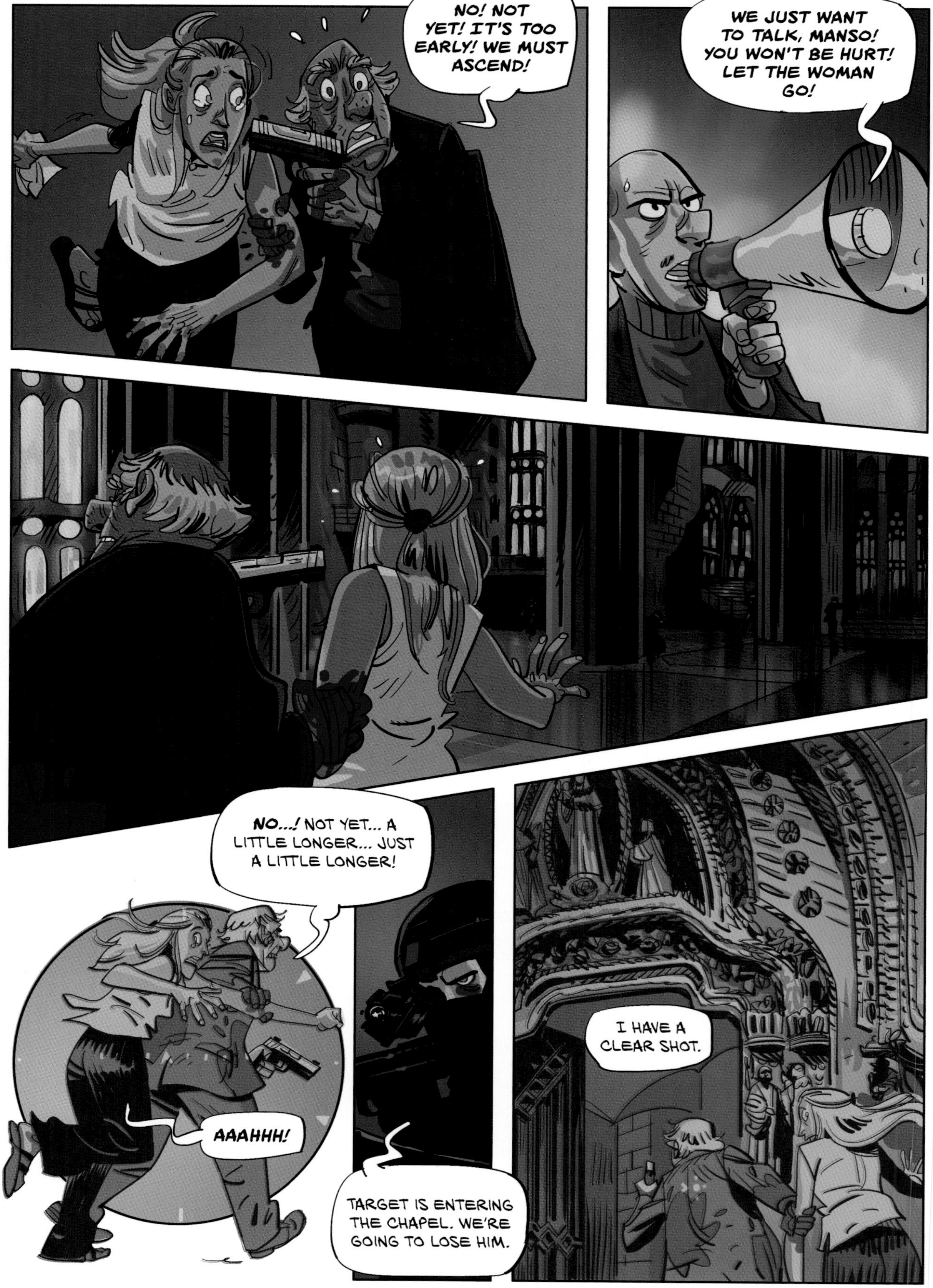
NO! NOT YET! IT'S TOO EARLY! WE MUST ASCEND!
WE JUST WANT TO TALK, MANSO! YOU WON'T BE HURT! LET THE WOMAN GO!
NO...! NOT YET... A LITTLE LONGER... JUST A LITTLE LONGER!
AAAHHH!
TARGET IS ENTERING THE CHAPEL. WE'RE GOING TO LOSE HIM.
I HAVE A CLEAR SHOT.

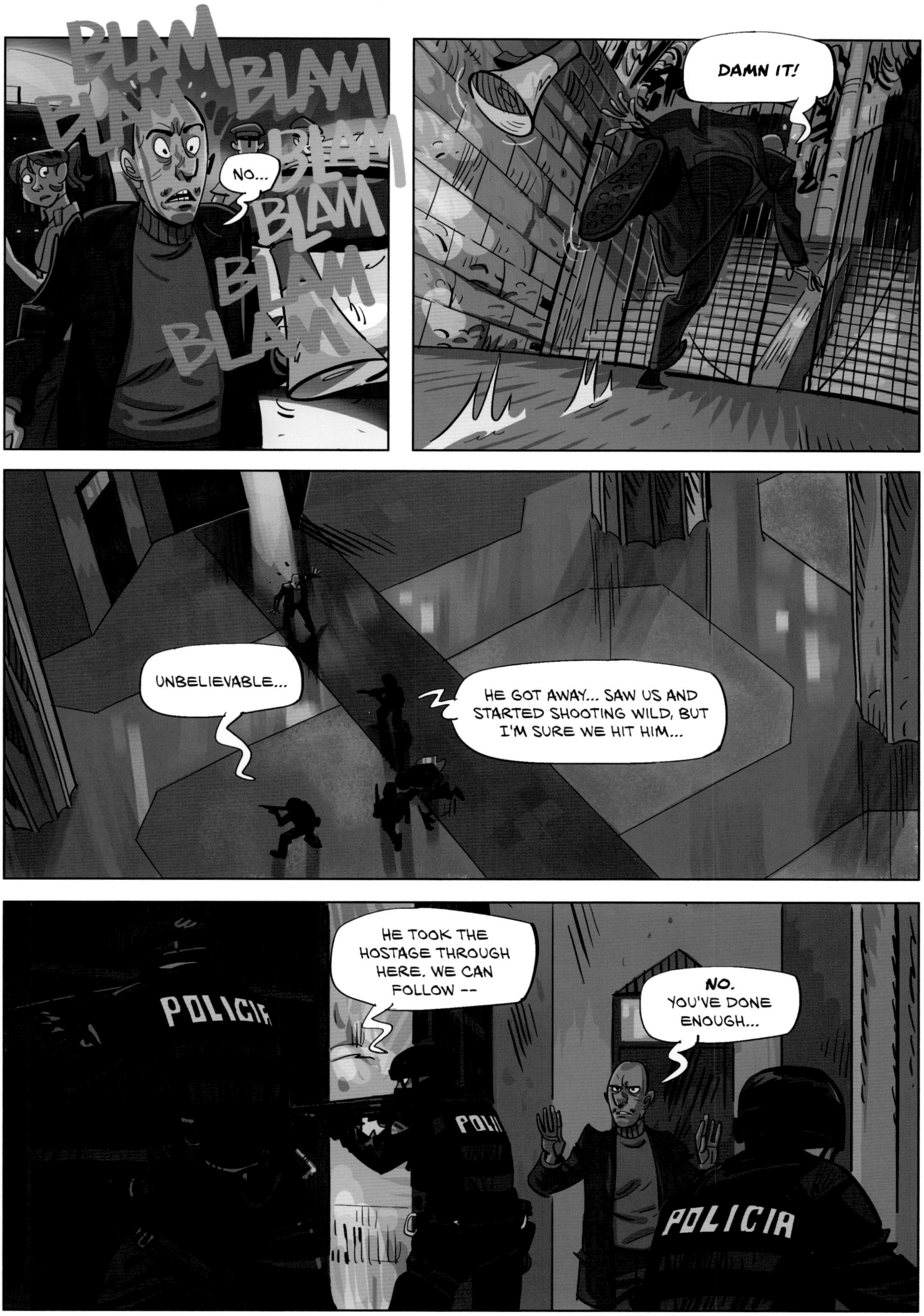
BLAM BLAM BLAM BLAM BLAM BLAM BLAM BLAM
NO...
DAMN IT!
UNBELIEVABLE...
HE GOT AWAY... SAW US AND STARTED SHOOTING WILD, BUT I'M SURE WE HIT HIM...
POLICIA
HE TOOK THE HOSTAGE THROUGH HERE. WE CAN FOLLOW --
NO. YOU'VE DONE ENOUGH...
POLI
POLICIA

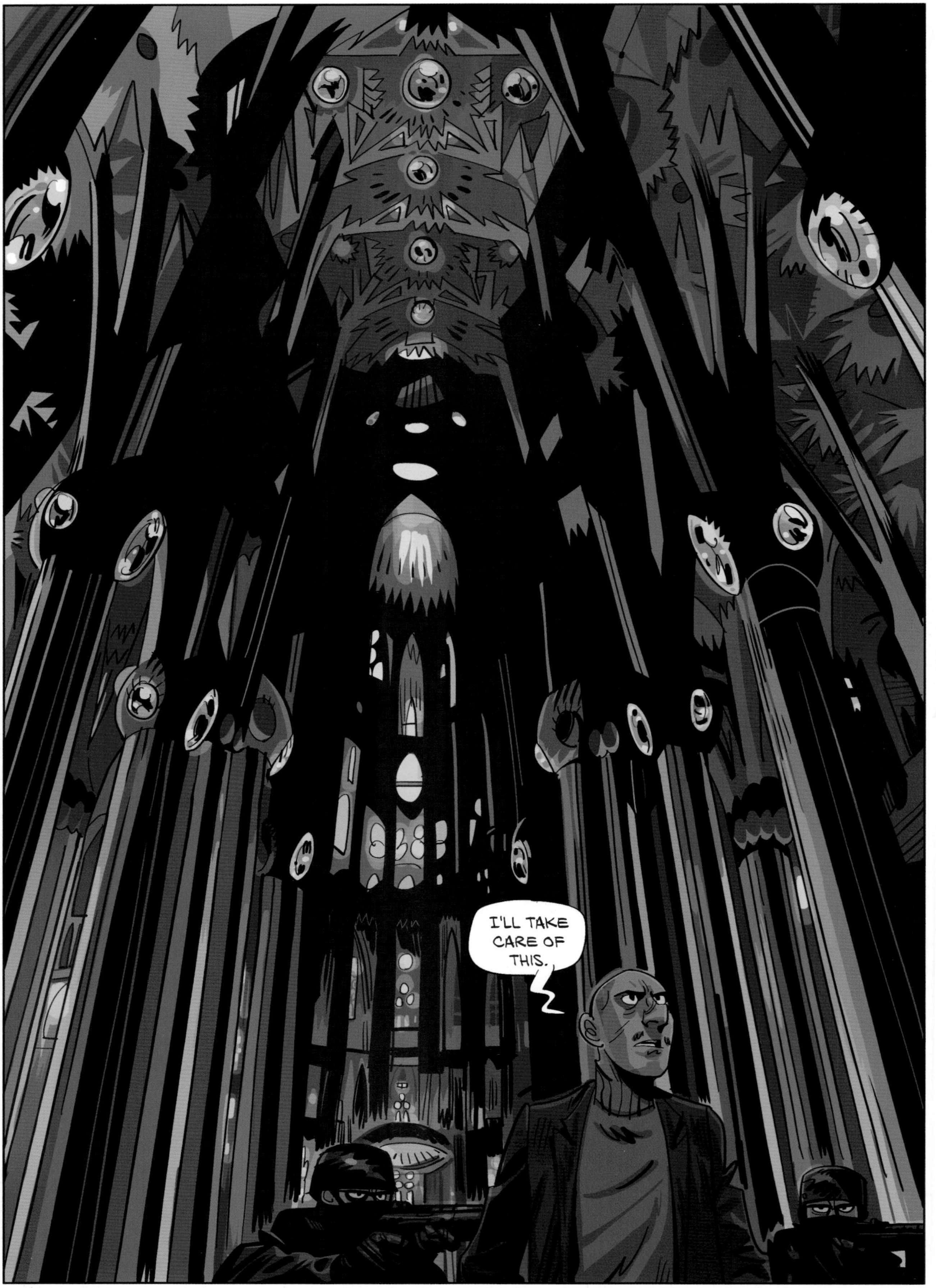
I'LL TAKE CARE OF THIS.

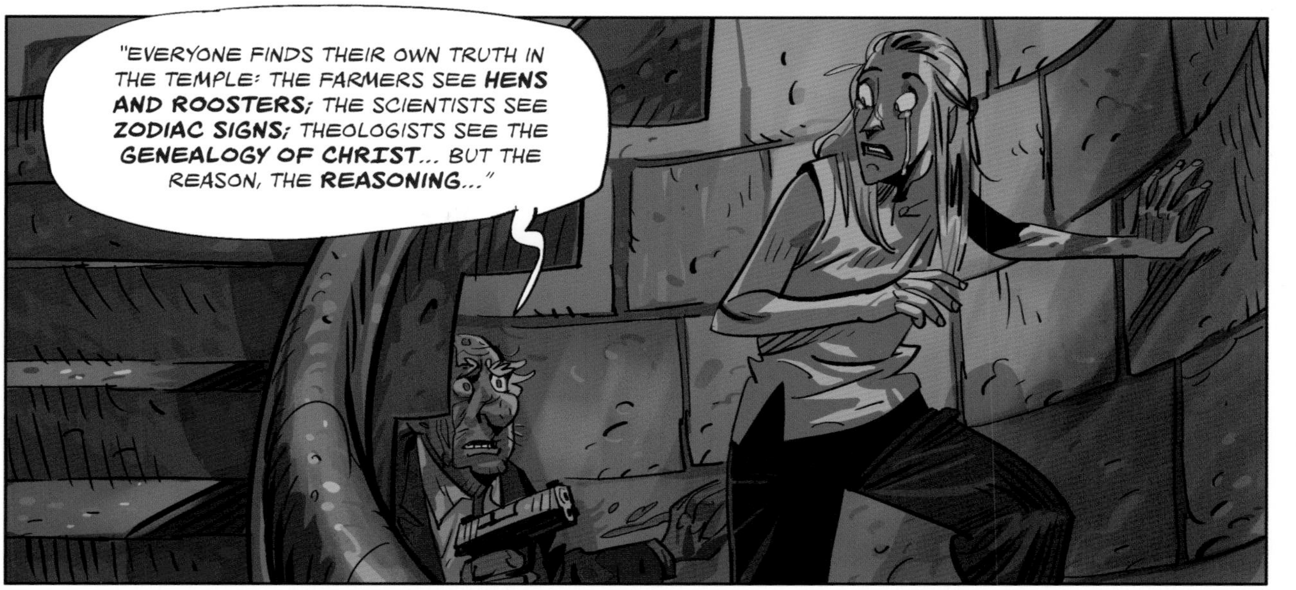
"EVERYONE FINDS THEIR OWN TRUTH IN THE TEMPLE: THE FARMERS SEE **HENS AND ROOSTERS;** THE SCIENTISTS SEE **ZODIAC SIGNS;** THEOLOGISTS SEE THE **GENEALOGY OF CHRIST...** BUT THE REASON, THE **REASONING...**"

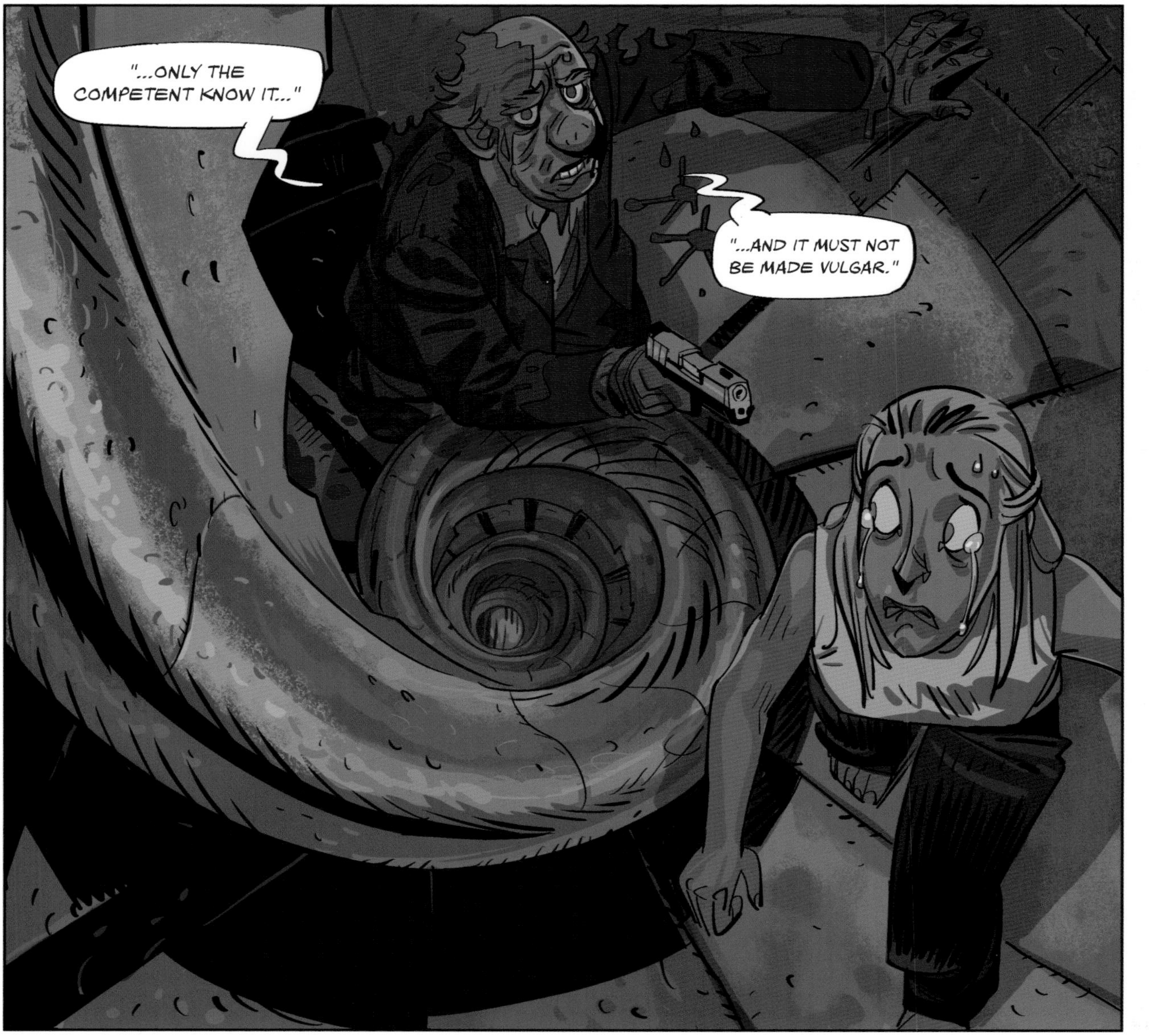
"...ONLY THE COMPETENT KNOW IT..."
"...AND IT MUST NOT BE MADE VULGAR."

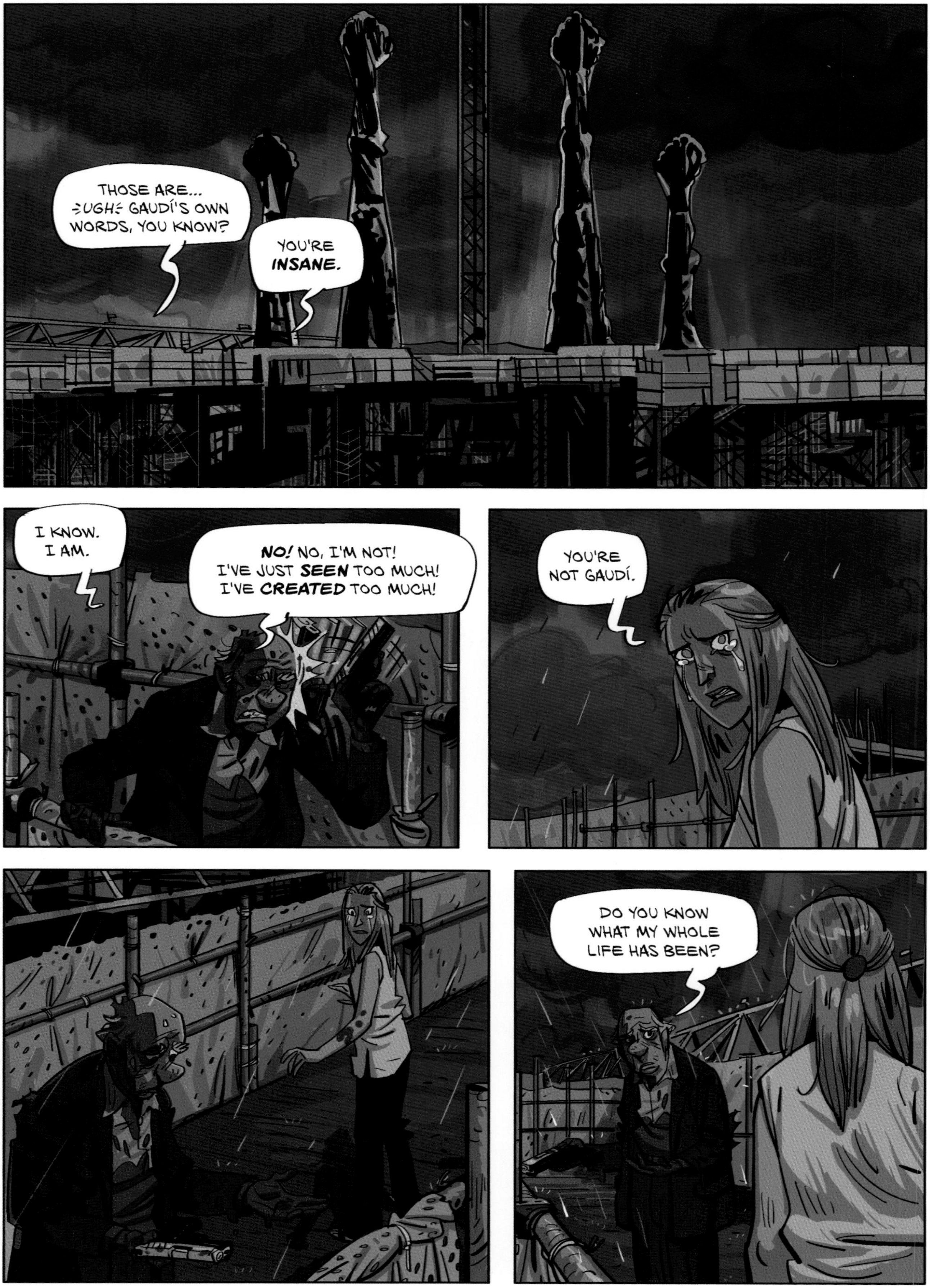
THOSE ARE... ≡UGH≡ GAUDÍ'S OWN WORDS, YOU KNOW?
YOU'RE **INSANE.**
I KNOW. I AM.
NO! NO, I'M NOT! I'VE JUST **SEEN** TOO MUCH! I'VE **CREATED** TOO MUCH!
YOU'RE NOT GAUDÍ.
DO YOU KNOW WHAT MY WHOLE LIFE HAS BEEN?

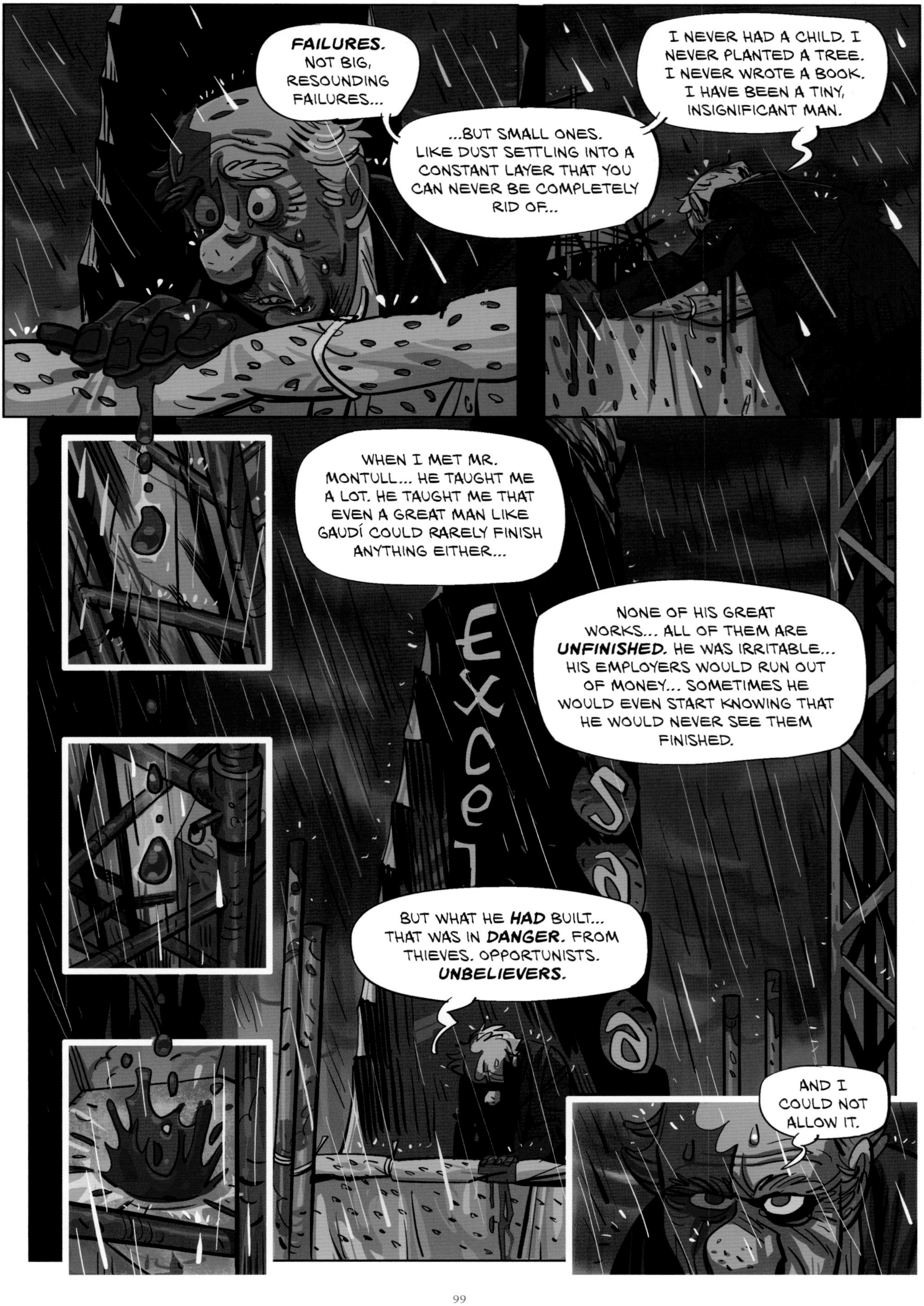
FAILURES. NOT BIG, RESOUNDING FAILURES...
...BUT SMALL ONES. LIKE DUST SETTLING INTO A CONSTANT LAYER THAT YOU CAN NEVER BE COMPLETELY RID OF...
I NEVER HAD A CHILD. I NEVER PLANTED A TREE. I NEVER WROTE A BOOK. I HAVE BEEN A TINY, INSIGNIFICANT MAN.
WHEN I MET MR. MONTULL... HE TAUGHT ME A LOT. HE TAUGHT ME THAT EVEN A GREAT MAN LIKE GAUDÍ COULD RARELY FINISH ANYTHING EITHER...
NONE OF HIS GREAT WORKS... ALL OF THEM ARE **UNFINISHED.** HE WAS IRRITABLE... HIS EMPLOYERS WOULD RUN OUT OF MONEY... SOMETIMES HE WOULD EVEN START KNOWING THAT HE WOULD NEVER SEE THEM FINISHED.
BUT WHAT HE **HAD** BUILT... THAT WAS IN **DANGER.** FROM THIEVES. OPPORTUNISTS. **UNBELIEVERS.**
AND I COULD NOT ALLOW IT.

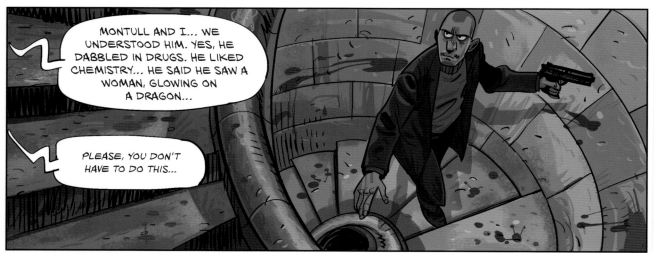

MONTULL AND I... WE UNDERSTOOD HIM. YES, HE DABBLED IN DRUGS. HE LIKED CHEMISTRY... HE SAID HE SAW A WOMAN, GLOWING ON A DRAGON...

PLEASE, YOU DON'T HAVE TO DO THIS...

YES, I HAVE TO FINISH SOMETHING, FOR ONCE IN MY LIFE.

I HAVE TO DO THIS. TO **PROTECT THE WORK.**

PROTECT THE WORK...?

HA!

YOU'RE NOT "PROTECTING" HIS WORK!

DON'T TRY TO TELL ME HOW MUCH YOU LOVE WHAT HE'S DONE, WITH ALL OF YOUR FLOWERY BULLSHIT EXPLANATIONS! YOU **HATE** GAUDÍ! ALL YOU'VE DONE IS **DESECRATE** HIS WORK!

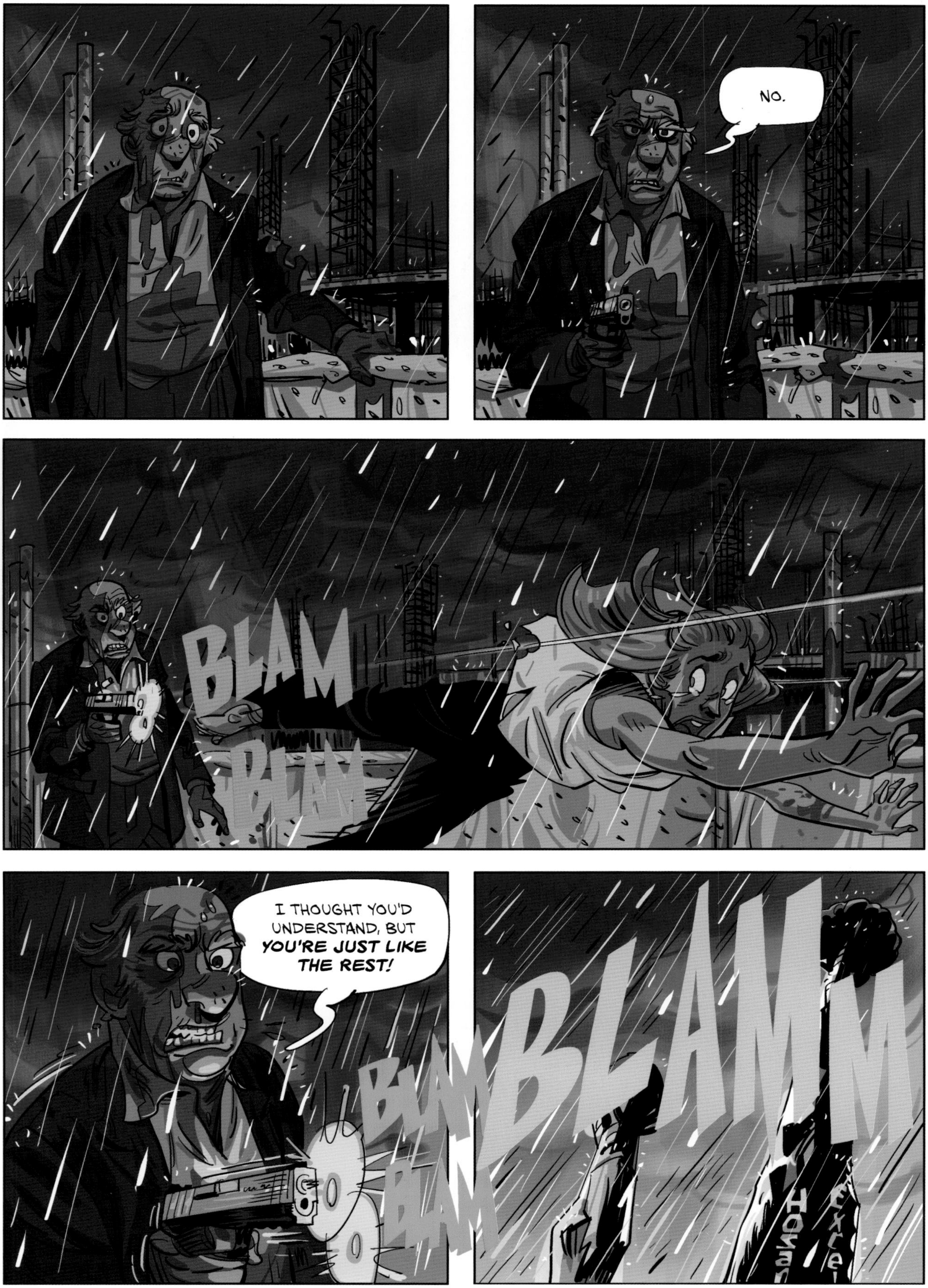
NO.
BLAM
BLAM
I THOUGHT YOU'D UNDERSTAND, BUT ***YOU'RE JUST LIKE THE REST!***
BLAM
BLAM
BLAMM

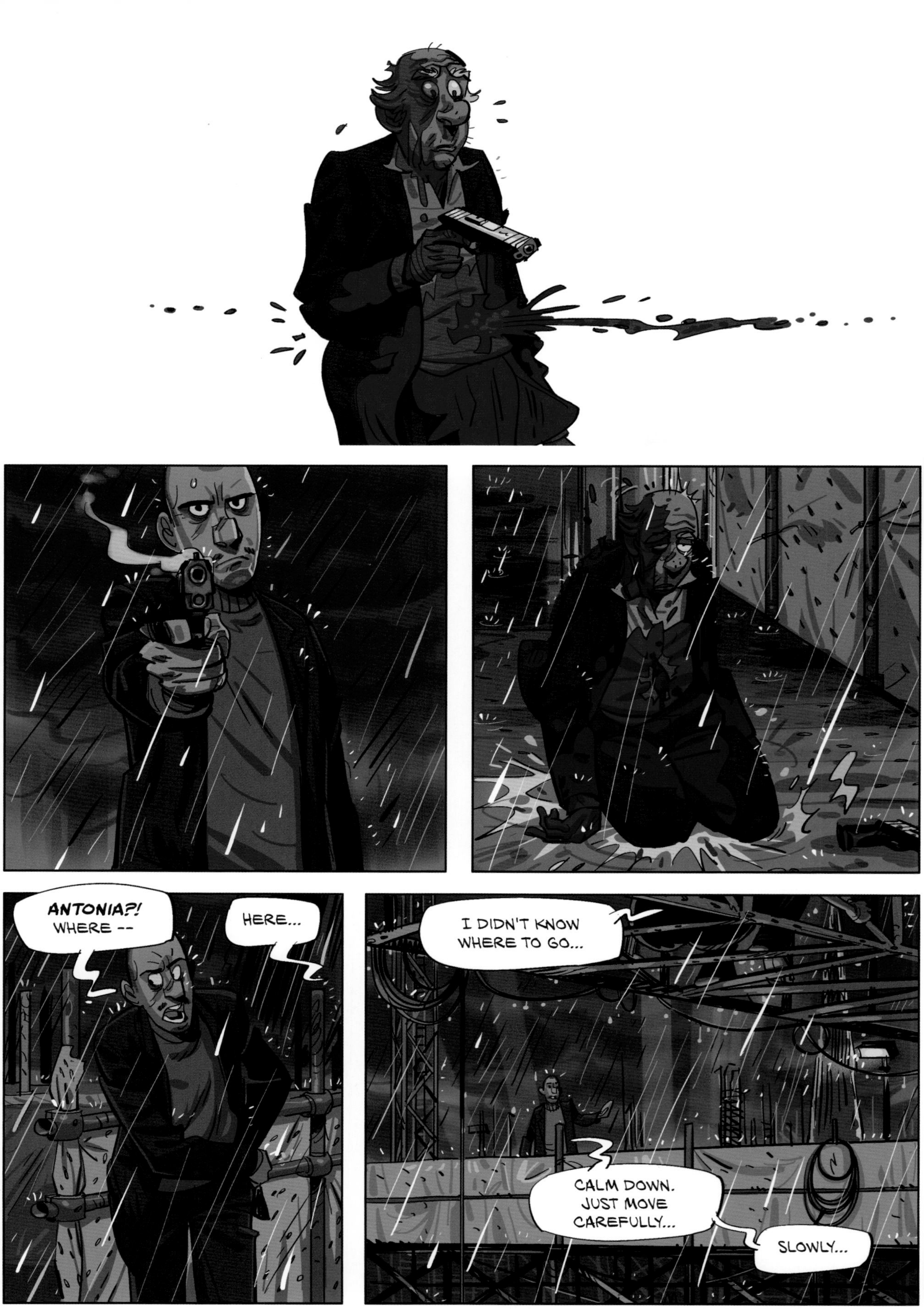
ANTONIA?! WHERE --
HERE...
I DIDN'T KNOW WHERE TO GO...
CALM DOWN. JUST MOVE CAREFULLY...
SLOWLY...

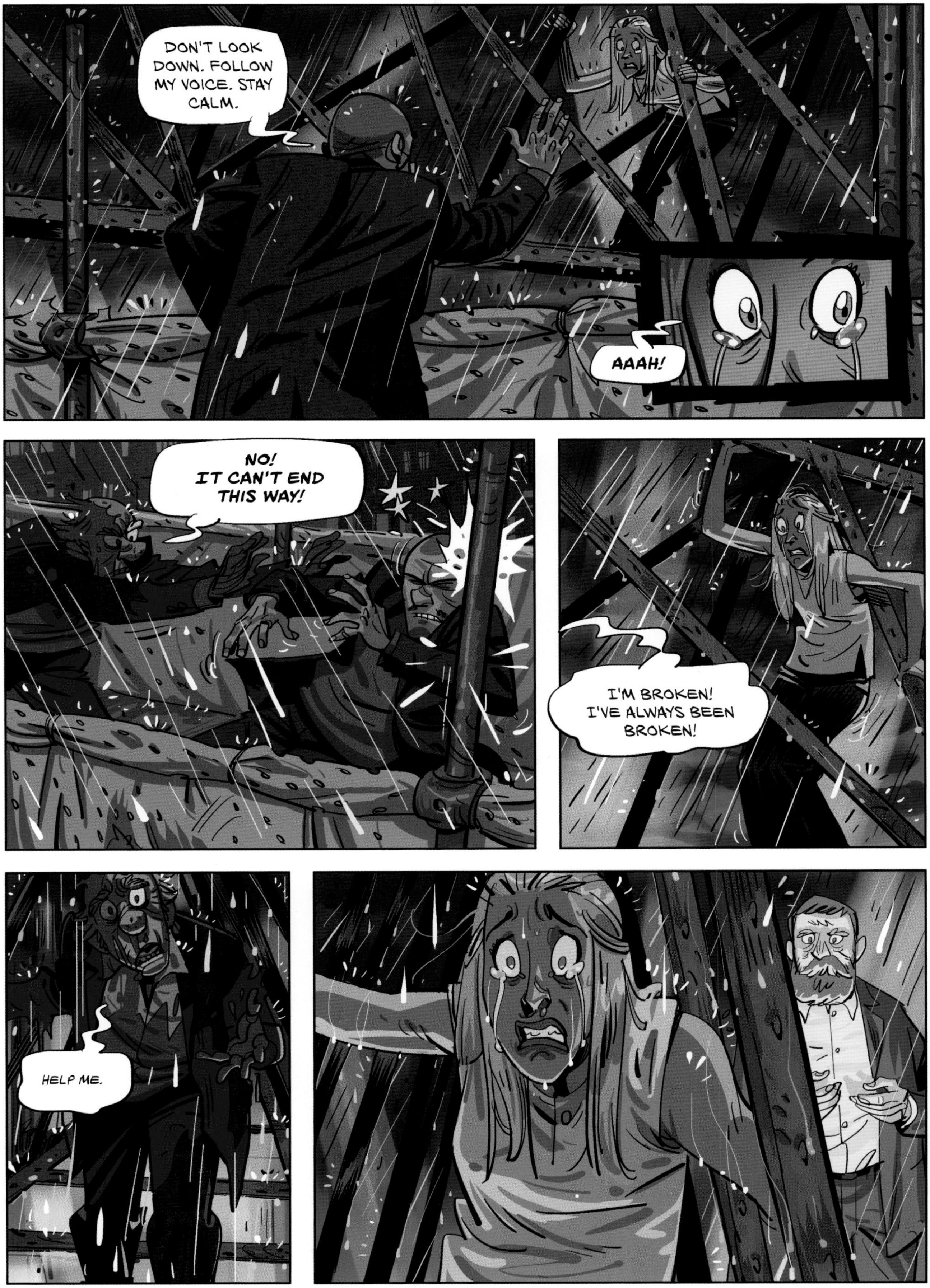
DON'T LOOK DOWN. FOLLOW MY VOICE. STAY CALM.
AAAH!
NO! IT CAN'T END THIS WAY!
I'M BROKEN! I'VE ALWAYS BEEN BROKEN!
HELP ME.

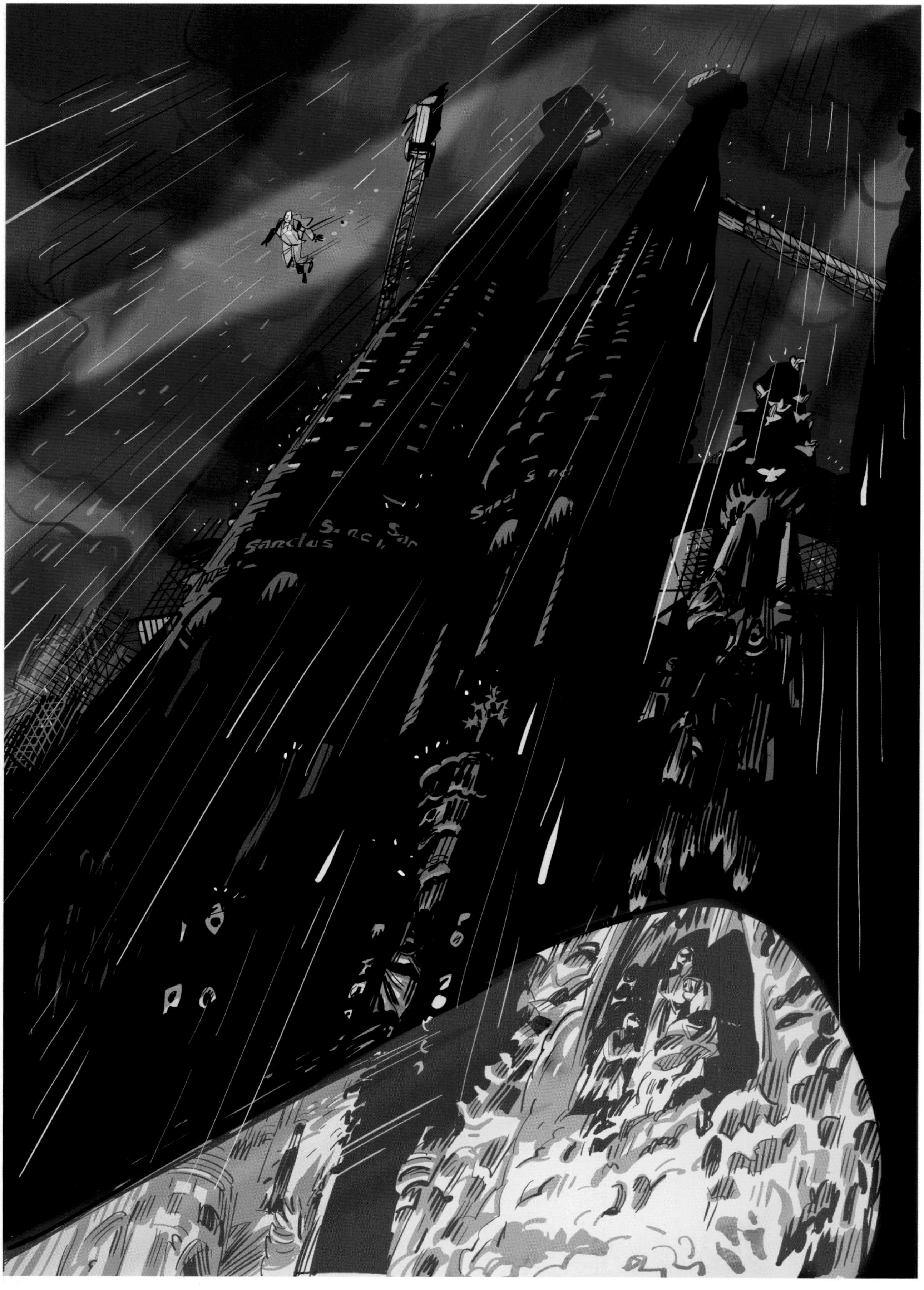
Sanctus

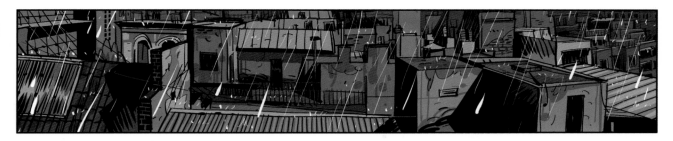

HERE. IT'S FROM A VENDING MACHINE, BUT IT'S NOT BAD.

THAT'S WHAT YOU SAID LAST TIME, INSPECTOR.

I DID? HOW ARE YOU FEELING?

I'M FINE, THANKS. BUT TELL ME... BE HONEST...

DID YOU SEE *HIM?* BEHIND THE CRANE...

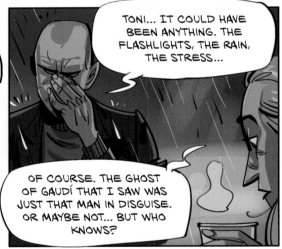

TONI... IT COULD HAVE BEEN ANYTHING. THE FLASHLIGHTS, THE RAIN, THE STRESS...

OF COURSE. THE GHOST OF GAUDÍ THAT I SAW WAS JUST THAT MAN IN DISGUISE. OR MAYBE NOT... BUT WHO KNOWS?

I REALLY DON'T CARE.

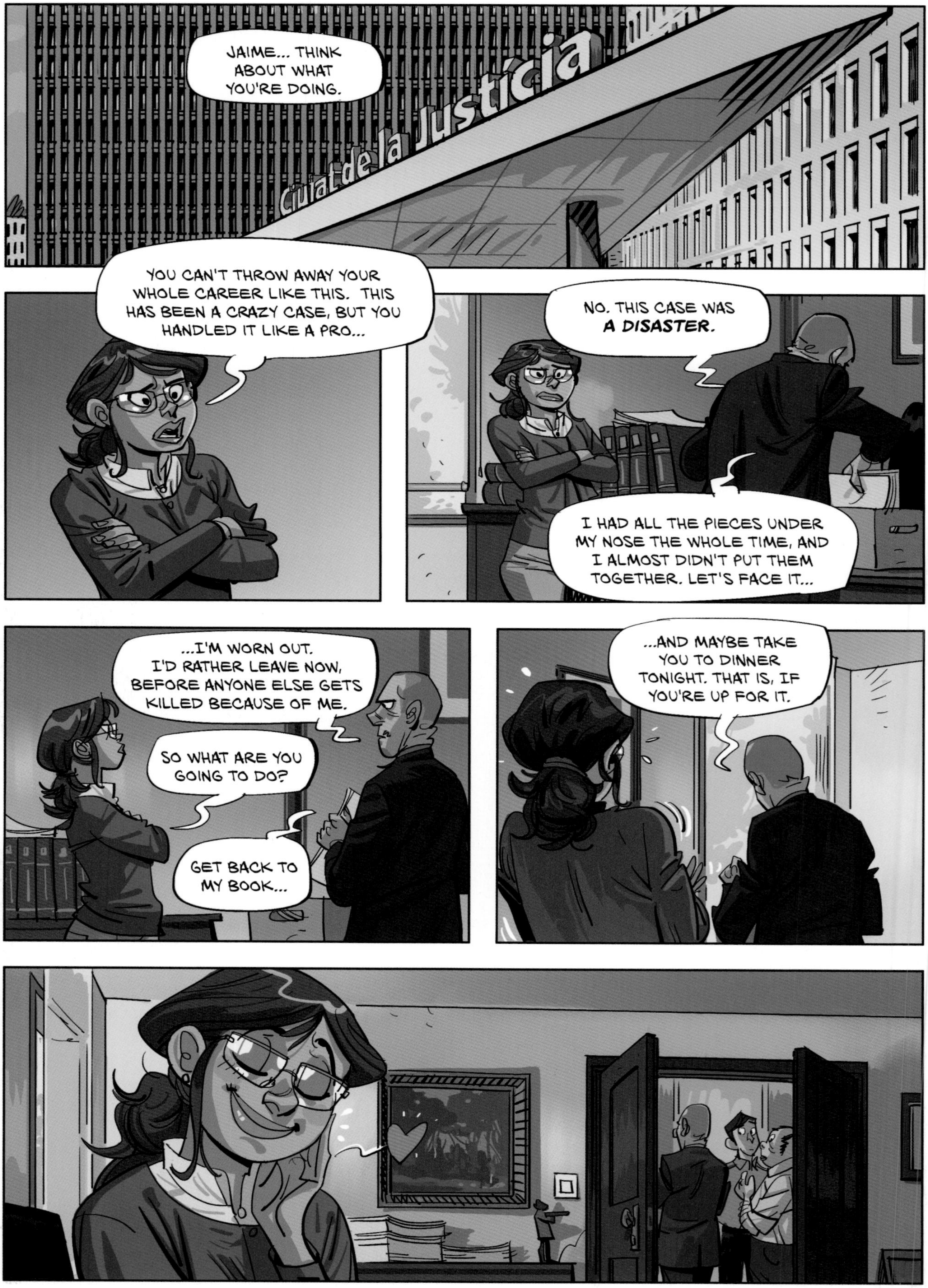
JAIME... THINK ABOUT WHAT YOU'RE DOING.
Ciutat de la Justícia
YOU CAN'T THROW AWAY YOUR WHOLE CAREER LIKE THIS. THIS HAS BEEN A CRAZY CASE, BUT YOU HANDLED IT LIKE A PRO...
NO. THIS CASE WAS ***A DISASTER.***
I HAD ALL THE PIECES UNDER MY NOSE THE WHOLE TIME, AND I ALMOST DIDN'T PUT THEM TOGETHER. LET'S FACE IT...
...I'M WORN OUT. I'D RATHER LEAVE NOW, BEFORE ANYONE ELSE GETS KILLED BECAUSE OF ME.
SO WHAT ARE YOU GOING TO DO?
GET BACK TO MY BOOK...
...AND MAYBE TAKE YOU TO DINNER TONIGHT. THAT IS, IF YOU'RE UP FOR IT.

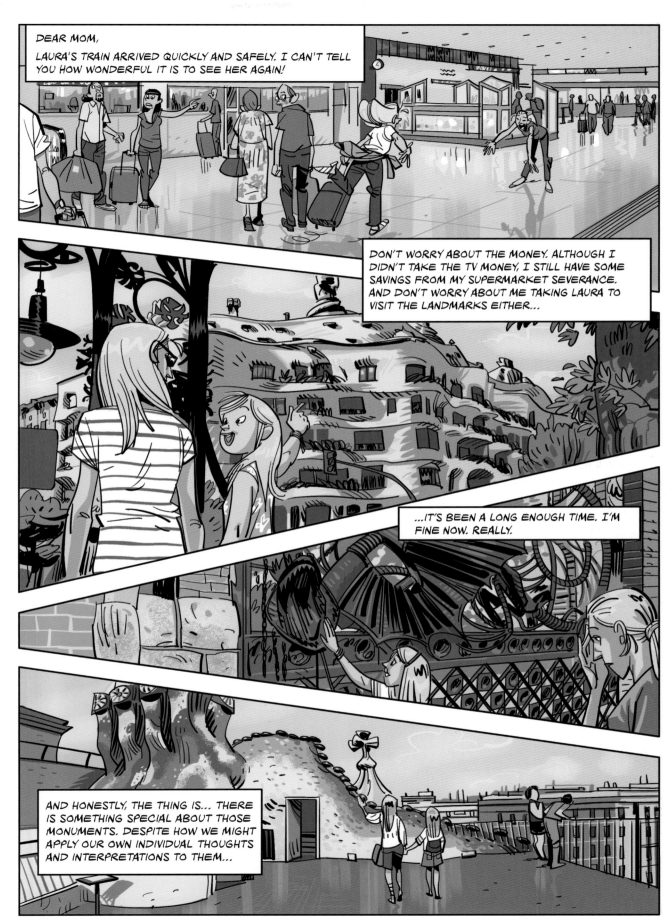

DEAR MOM,
LAURA'S TRAIN ARRIVED QUICKLY AND SAFELY. I CAN'T TELL YOU HOW WONDERFUL IT IS TO SEE HER AGAIN!

DON'T WORRY ABOUT THE MONEY. ALTHOUGH I DIDN'T TAKE THE TV MONEY, I STILL HAVE SOME SAVINGS FROM MY SUPERMARKET SEVERANCE. AND DON'T WORRY ABOUT ME TAKING LAURA TO VISIT THE LANDMARKS EITHER...

...IT'S BEEN A LONG ENOUGH TIME, I'M FINE NOW. REALLY.

AND HONESTLY, THE THING IS... THERE IS SOMETHING SPECIAL ABOUT THOSE MONUMENTS. DESPITE HOW WE MIGHT APPLY OUR OWN INDIVIDUAL THOUGHTS AND INTERPRETATIONS TO THEM...

EVEN IF THEY WROTE BOOKS FILLED WITH PRECISE EXPLANATIONS ABOUT HOW AND WHY GAUDÍ DID THINGS THE WAY HE DID...

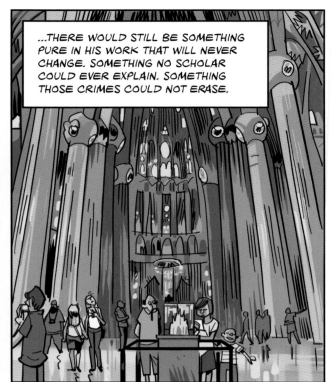

...THERE WOULD STILL BE SOMETHING PURE IN HIS WORK THAT WILL NEVER CHANGE. SOMETHING NO SCHOLAR COULD EVER EXPLAIN. SOMETHING THOSE CRIMES COULD NOT ERASE.

SOMETHING LIKE... A SPIRIT. LIKE A DREAM BURIED IN TIME.

A LIFE.

THE GHOST of GAUDÍ

Sketches and Designs

by Jesús Alonso Iglesias,
with additional notes by El Torres

Trencadís

Or the origins of *The Ghost of Gaudi*

This is possibly the most difficult and, at the same time, easiest story I have ever written.

It is difficult because, imagine, you're sitting there with your things, and Ricardo Esteban, who shares your obsession and pays for your rights, calls and says: "Let's make a book about Gaudí."

And then you say yes. And it takes you almost two years to write it.

Although Gaudí has always been part of those wonderful visits to Barcelona, I'd never looked much into his life. But now, of course, I had a story on my hands. I had to understand his architecture, enter his life. It was time to get down to business.

It was overwhelming. The dimensions of his oeuvre are gigantic, almost unfathomable.

However, I could not write a simple biography. It's not my favourite genre and, all that being said, I found myself unable to write an interesting story based on his life.

So it had to be fiction. Fiction about Gaudí, about his work. Lets see... an evil sect who wants to destroy the Sagrada Família? Done already. Next! The symbolism of his work as a door and key to a higher plane? Done already. Next! Satanists against the Catholicism of Gaudí's work? Done already. Next.

Overwhelming.

And in that way, I felt like each and every one of the characters in The Ghost of Gaudi. I hated and loved him at the same time. I dropped the books to the ground and was amazed when I could visit his works. I snuck into Casa Battló (but not like a killer) to see if it was possible to climb the stairs; I visited repeatedly, but the story still wouldn't come. I was about to tell Ricardo that I had given up. Then suddenly, it came to me. A murderer who hates and loves Gaudí at the same time. Who felt as confused and overwhelmed as I did. From these contradicting feelings came this plot.

It's all here: the need to understand and the ability to be fascinated, and the rage at not being able to understand everything. The magic and symbolic theories and the impressive form and presence that the most universal of architects gave Barcelona. But even so, the story was hard to pen. It was a complex trencadís of characters who had to enter and exit, clues and police plots that had to be credible. No ninjas jumping over rooftops. Ordinary people. Supermarket cashiers and bartenders and burnt-out cops.

So what made this story the easiest?

Jesús Alonso Iglesias.

If I think I'm meticulous and obsessive when I write, Jesús is even worse. Which makes my work easier. He carefully studies all the possible angles of each scene, documented not only by the few reference pictures I'd send him, but by continuing to research and look beyond the words.

And then he draws. He draws like the angels.

His characters breathe, walk, and take the dog out. His rooms are not just four perspective lines. People live in them, they have as much presence as the characters do, and you can read, for instance, the story of Antonia's life in her room. And furthermore, he dares to draw Gaudi's work and assimilate it into the story. The Ghost of Gaudi would have been impossible with any another draftsman. It simply wouldn't have been the same.

It was also both easy and difficult because of Ricardo's constant presence. Encouraging and spurring, as insistent as a child at an amusement park. "Is it ready yet?" As a good editor, he was there throughout the creation process. This story was originally called "Trencadís," which seemed to me a great name for a murderer obsessed with Gaudi who hacked his victims to pieces. But, as a good editor, he assured me that the alternate name, which is what this book is titled, would have more of a hook.

But, you know? We're only three pieces of a much larger trencadís, one that needs you, dear reader, to complete.

Enjoy it.

El Torres

Jesús:

There are ideas that arise as you read the script that need to be written down before they are forgotten. They'll be retouched later if necessary.

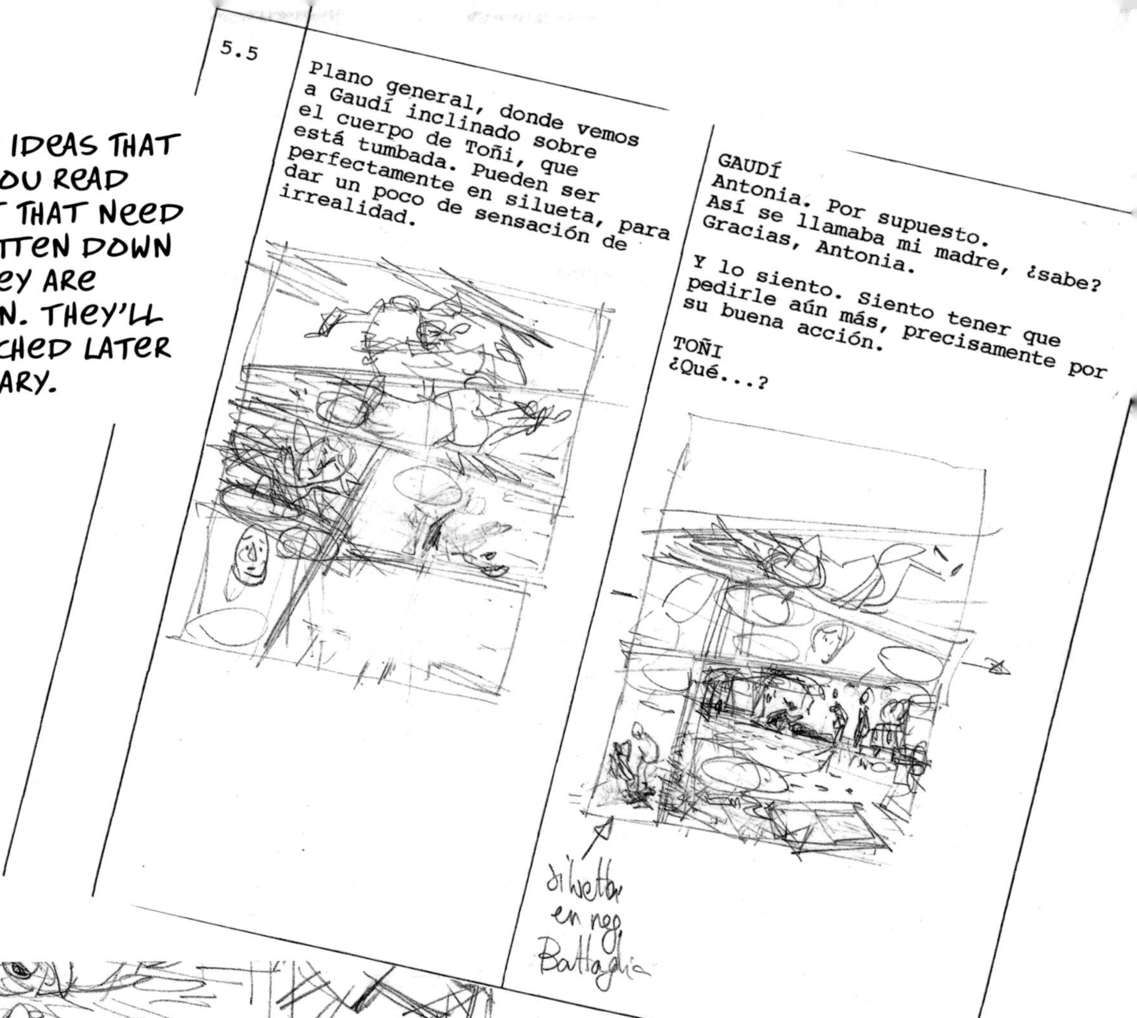
5.5

Plano general, donde vemos a Gaudí inclinado sobre el cuerpo de Toñi, que está tumbada. Pueden ser perfectamente en silueta, para dar un poco de sensación de irrealidad.

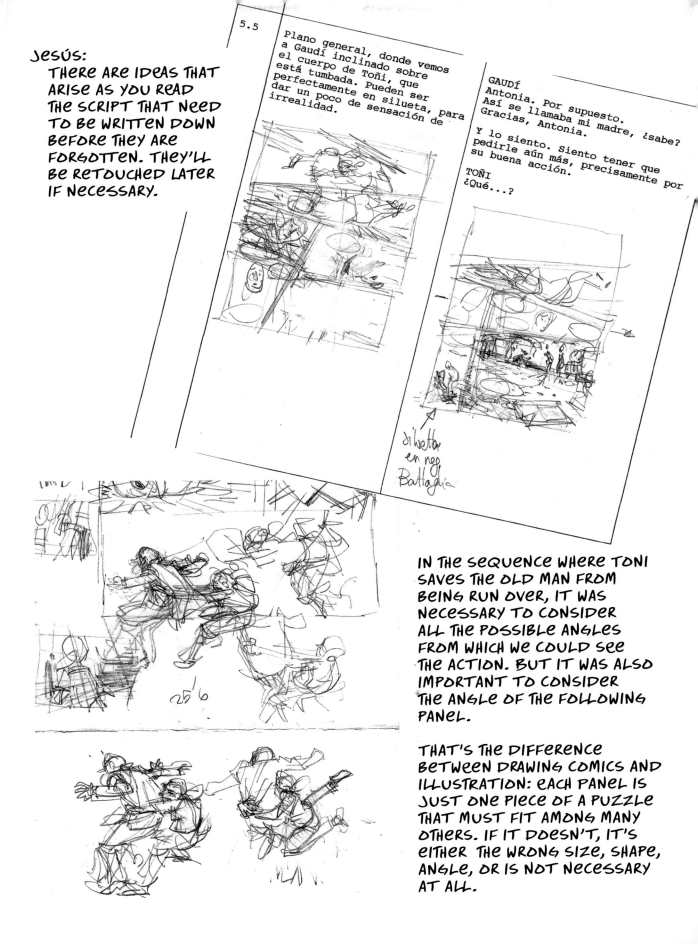

GAUDÍ
Antonia. Por supuesto. Así se llamaba mi madre, ¿sabe? Gracias, Antonia.

Y lo siento. Siento tener que pedirle aún más, precisamente por su buena acción.

TOÑI
¿Qué...?

silueta en neg Battaglia

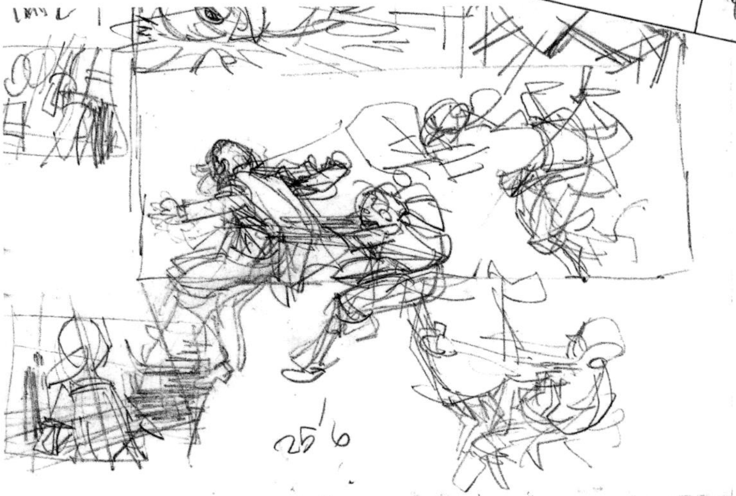

25'6

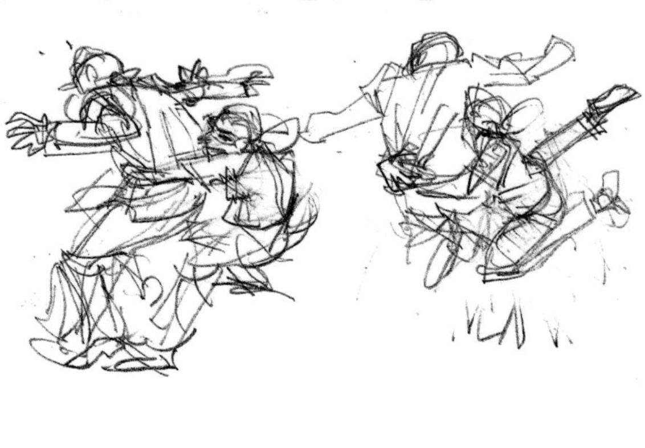

In the sequence where Toni saves the old man from being run over, it was necessary to consider all the possible angles from which we could see the action. But it was also important to consider the angle of the following panel.

That's the difference between drawing comics and illustration: each panel is just one piece of a puzzle that must fit among many others. If it doesn't, it's either the wrong size, shape, angle, or is not necessary at all.

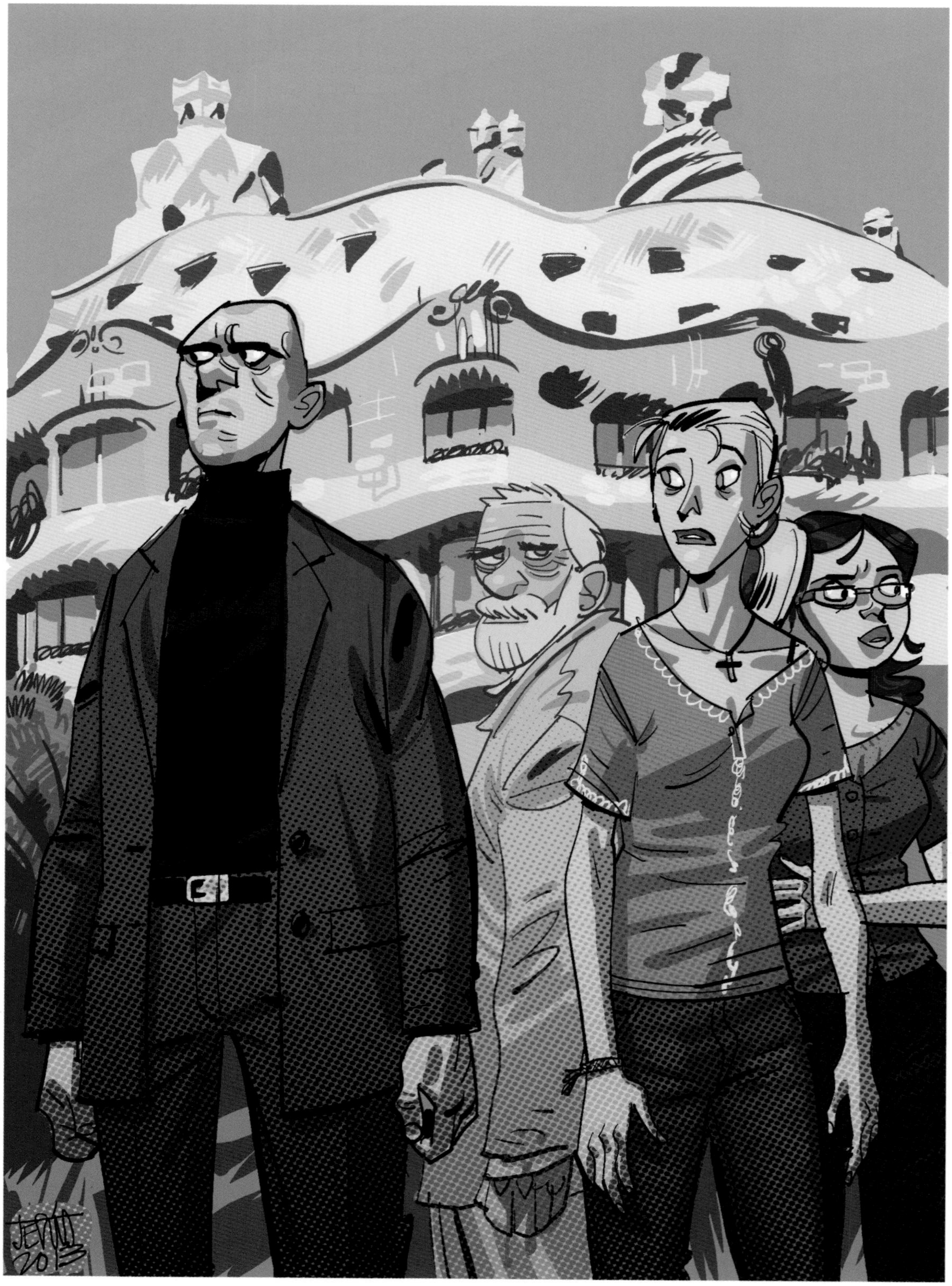

El Torres: Promotional drawing from Jesús, just after starting on the first pages of the book. Although it was used as an ad and the cover of a promotional brochure, we were both very clear that the actual book cover would be something completely different.

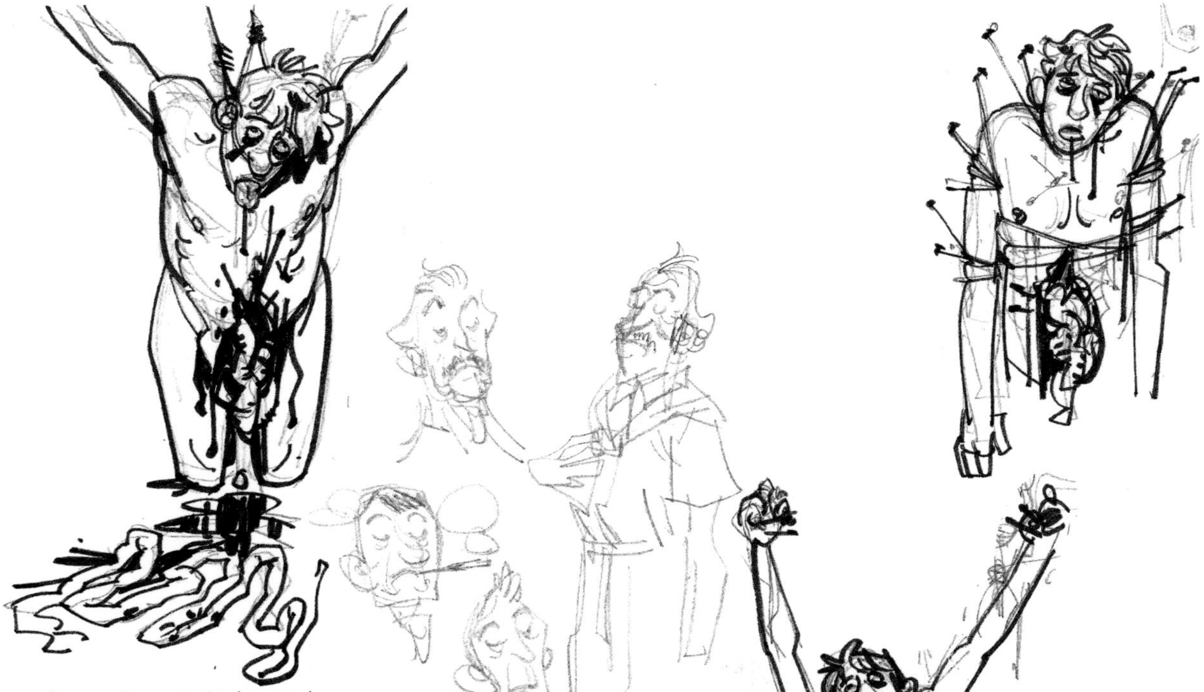

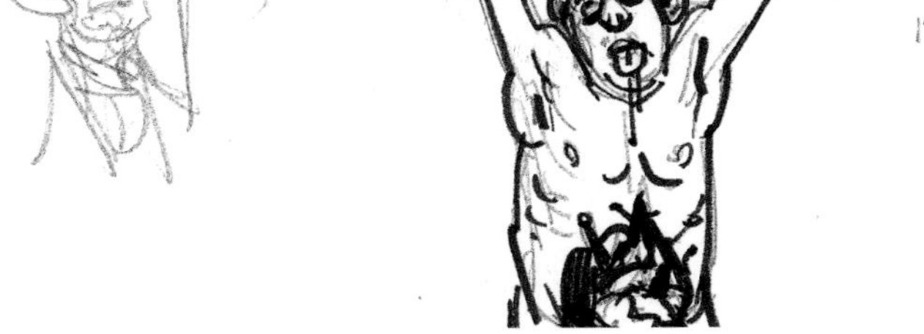

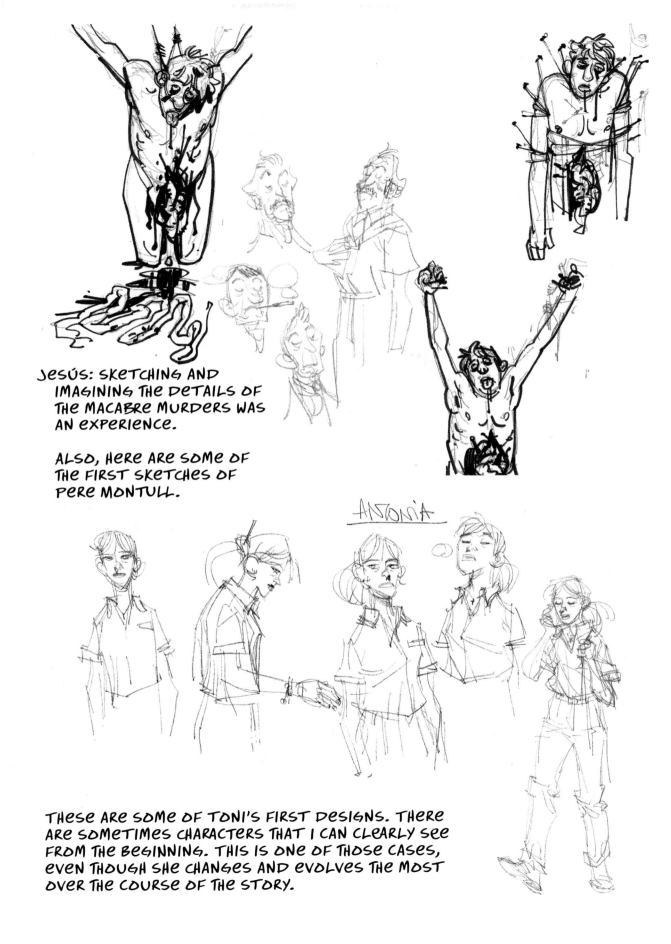

JESÚS: SKETCHING AND IMAGINING THE DETAILS OF THE MACABRE MURDERS WAS AN EXPERIENCE.

ALSO, HERE ARE SOME OF THE FIRST SKETCHES OF PERE MONTULL.

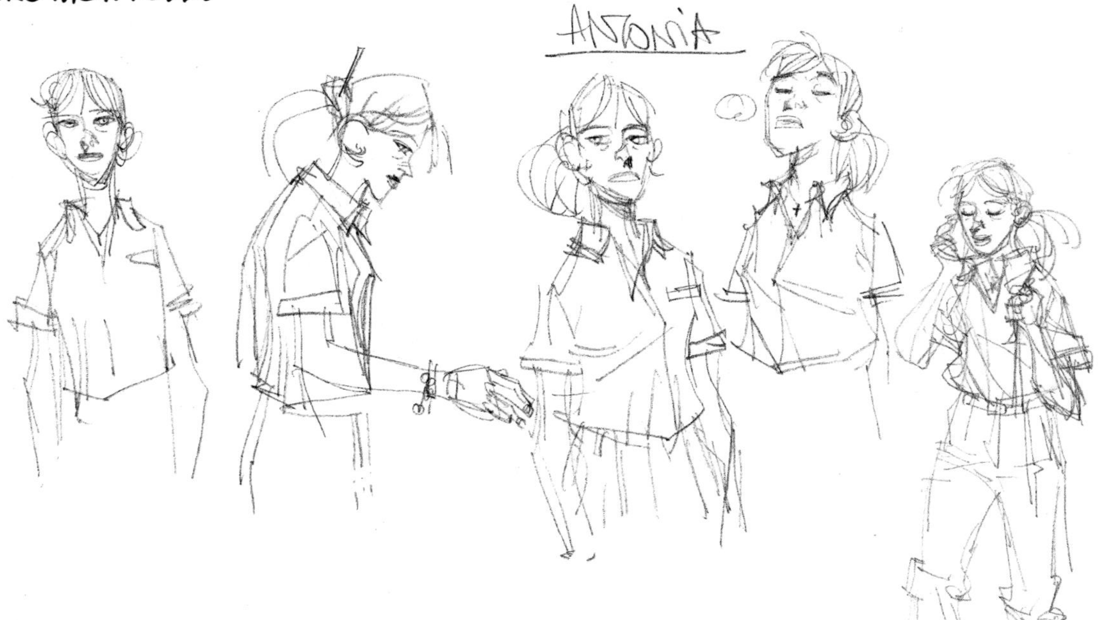
ANTONIA

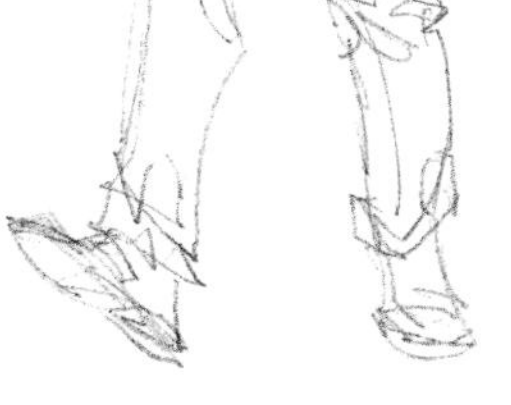

THESE ARE SOME OF TONI'S FIRST DESIGNS. THERE ARE SOMETIMES CHARACTERS THAT I CAN CLEARLY SEE FROM THE BEGINNING. THIS IS ONE OF THOSE CASES, EVEN THOUGH SHE CHANGES AND EVOLVES THE MOST OVER THE COURSE OF THE STORY.

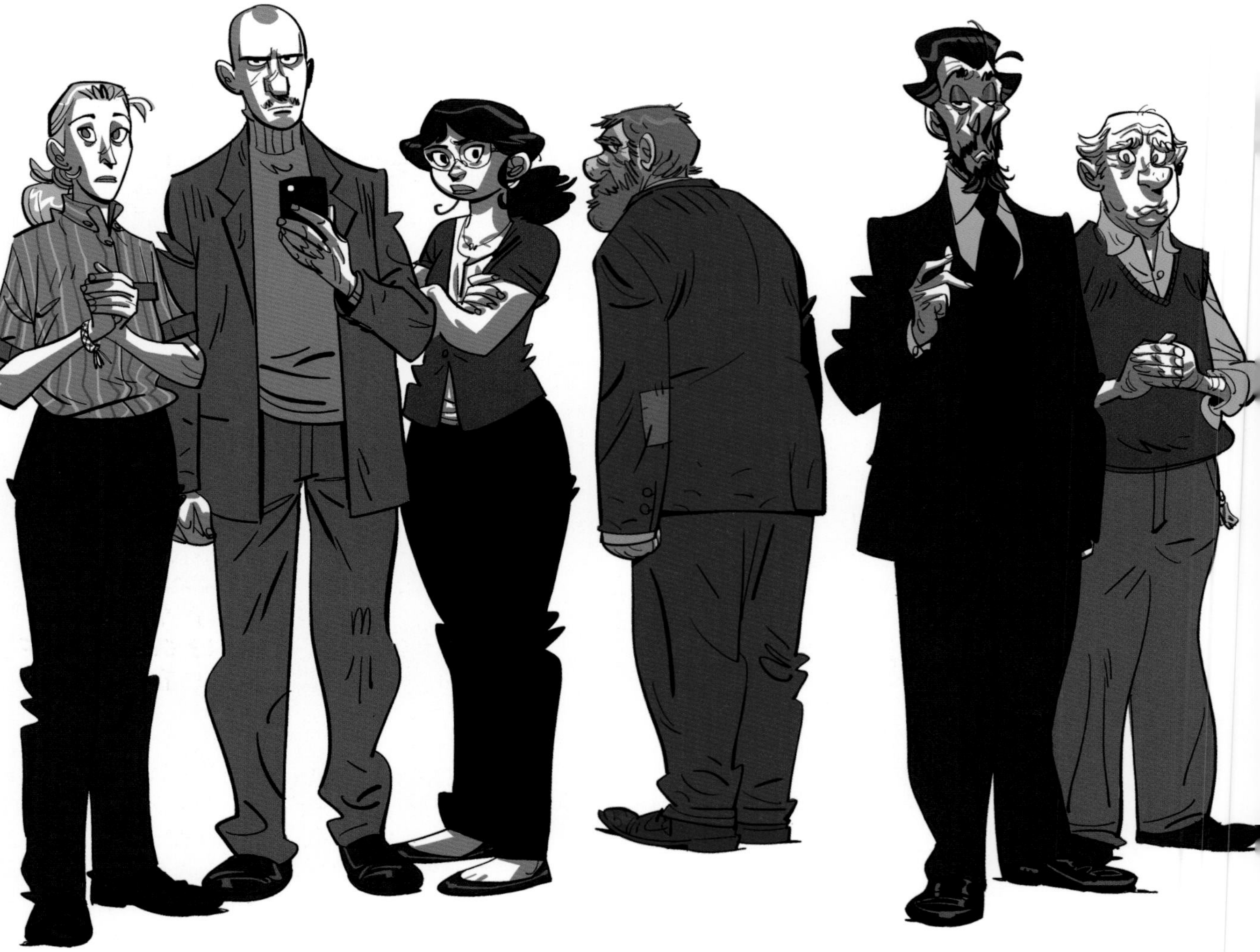

An illustration of the main characters in The Ghost of Gaudí.

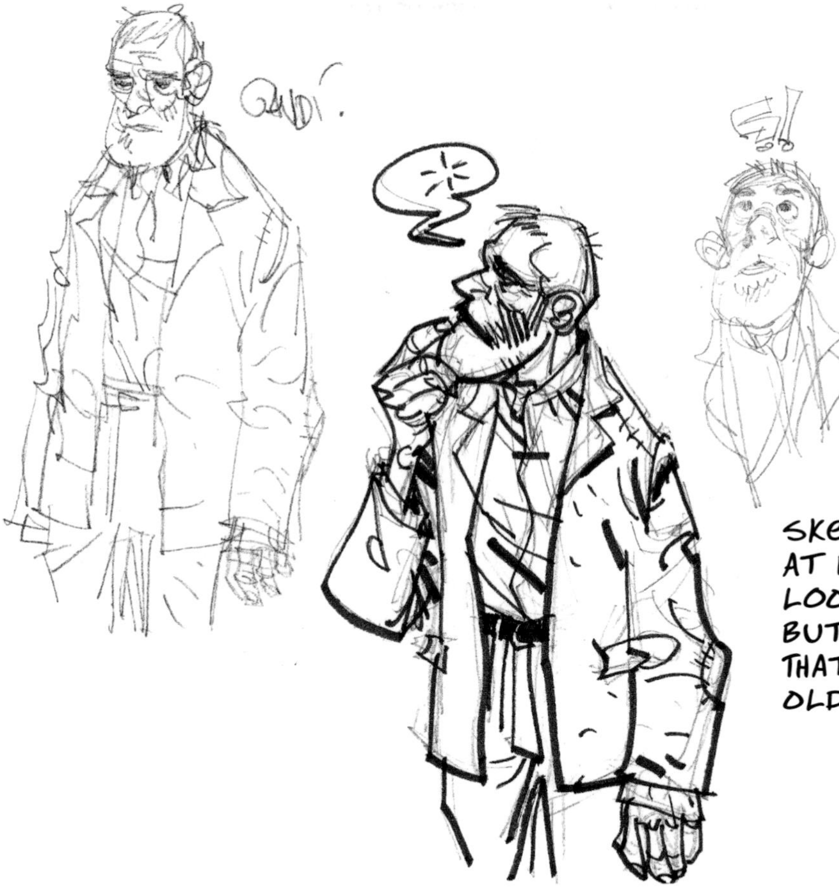
GAUDÍ.

SKETCHES OF GAUDÍ. AT FIRST THE CHARACTER LOOKED MORE HOMELESS BUT THEN CHANGED TO THAT OF A HELPLESS OLD MAN.

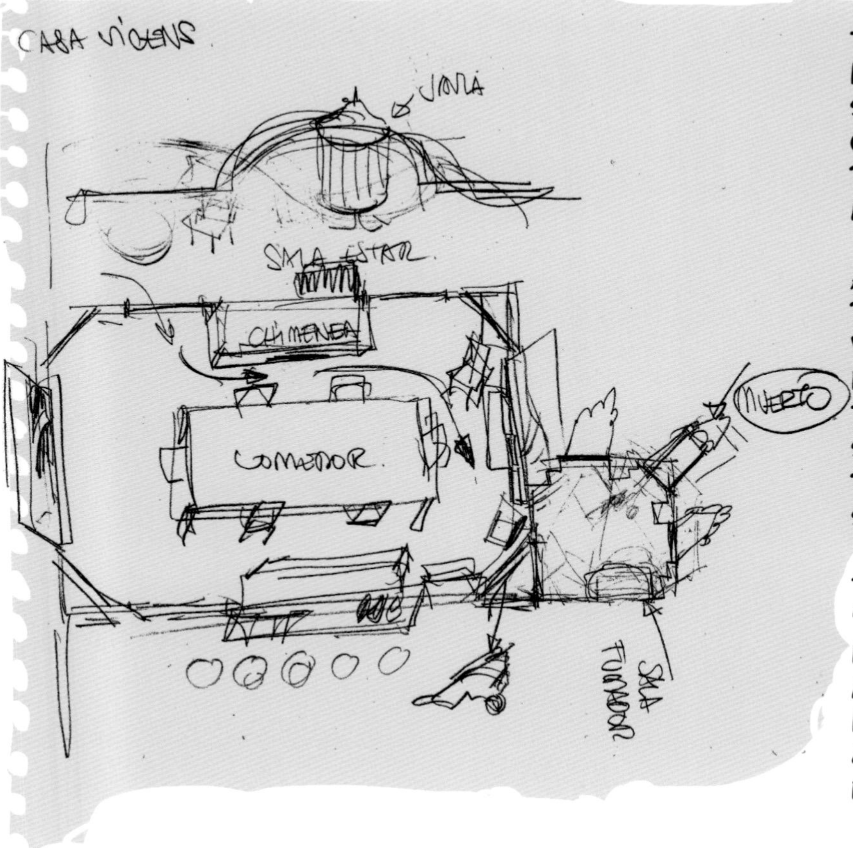
CASA VICENS
SALA ESTAR
CHIMENEA
COMEDOR
MUERTO
SALA FUMADOR

THE FIRST MURDER SCENE IN CASA VICENS INVOLVED STUDYING MANY PHOTOS... EXCEPT FOR THE CORNER OF THE ROOM WHERE THE BODY LIES.

AFTER A LONG SEARCH THROUGH PHOTOGRAPHS, VIDEOS, FILMS, AND FITTING THEM ALL TOGETHER, I WAS ABLE TO SKETCH A PLAN OF WHAT THE SET OF THIS MACABRE SCENE WOULD BE.

THAT'S ONE OF THE "PROBLEMS" WHEN COMING FROM ANIMATION: YOU ALWAYS LOOK FOR LOGIC IN THE INTERACTION OF CHARACTERS AND BACKGROUNDS.

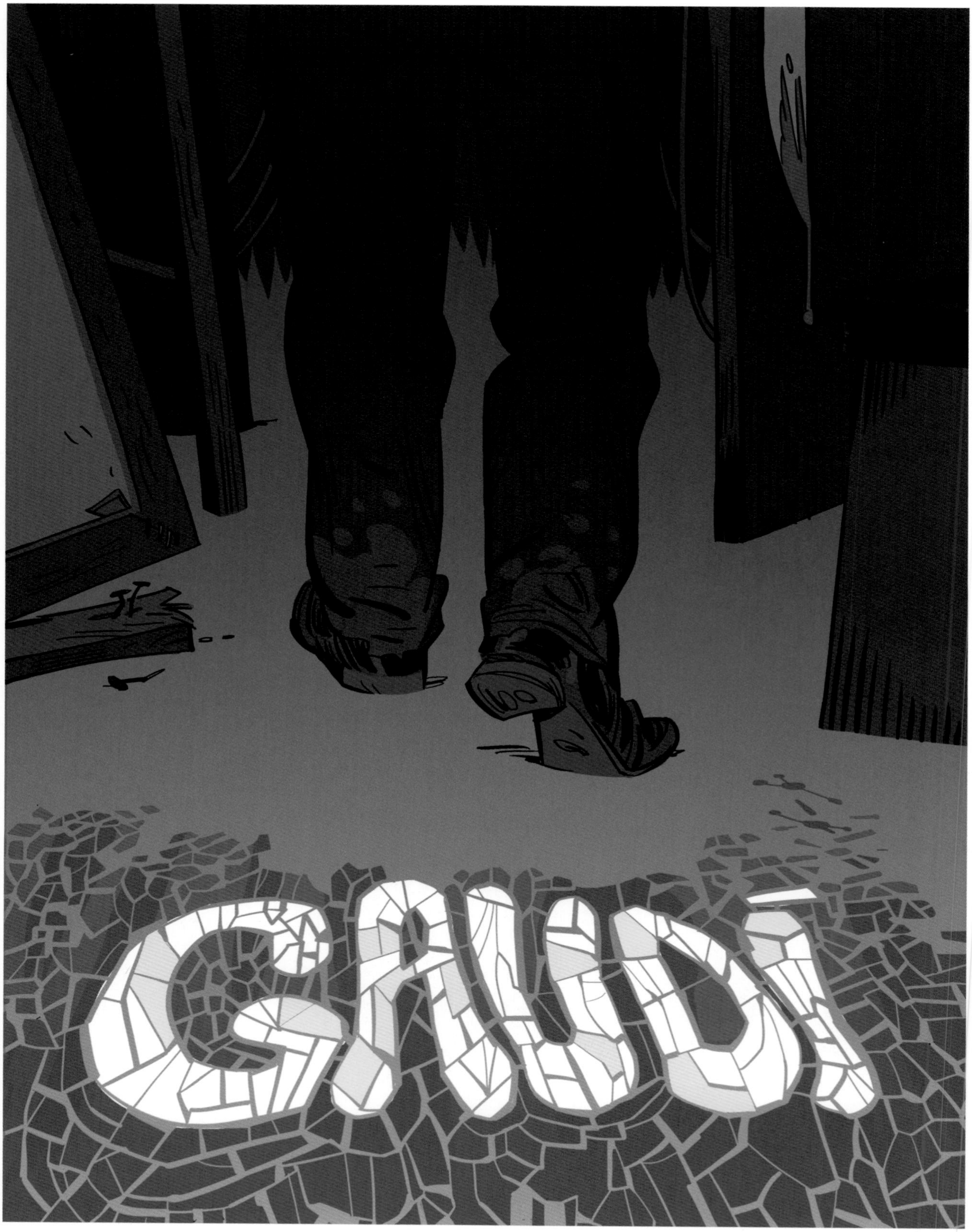
GAUDÍ

A rejected cover for The Ghost of Gaudí. *This was about to be the final cover... until Jesús showed us the art for the current cover of the book. The bloody trencadís is still one of my favorite designs for the logo.*

To the right, this is one of the first pages we got. Wow! We were on our way!

Soon afterward we changed it almost completely because Toni was "looking at the camera" a bit too much and looked a little tired for what we wanted to show.

Jesús made many alterations to the pages as we progressed with the story. Each panel has a lot of work hours behind it!

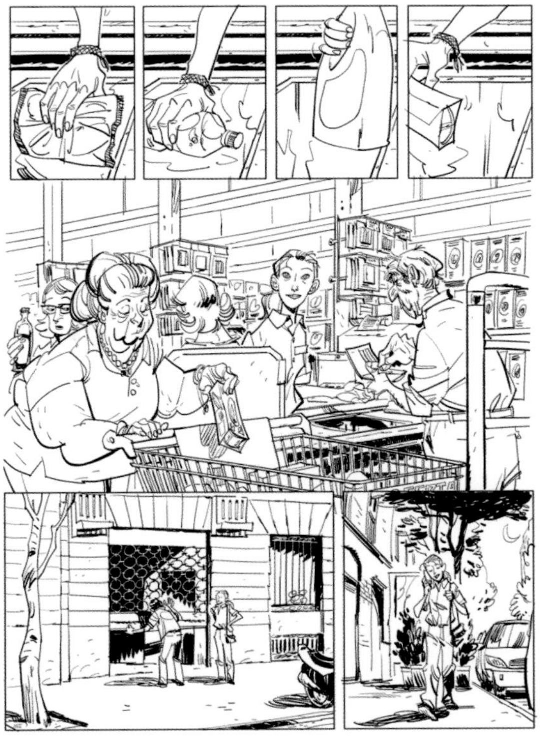

MONTULL IS ANOTHER ONE OF THOSE DESIGNS THAT WAS VERY ATTRACTIVE IN THE FIRST CONCEPTS BUT ENDED UP CAUSING MANY PROBLEMS WHEN I HAD TO DRAW HIM FROM CERTAIN ANGLES. SO MUCH SO THAT I HAD TO RESORT, IN AN AFTERNOON OF BOREDOM, TO MODELING HIM IN PLASTICINE TO GET A CORRECT 3-D VISUALIZATION. LESSONS TO LEARN.

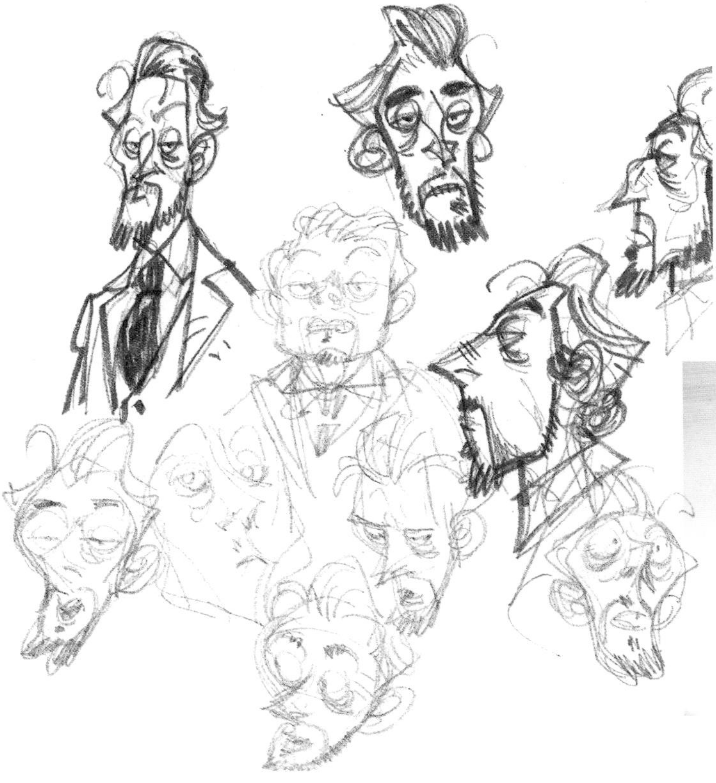

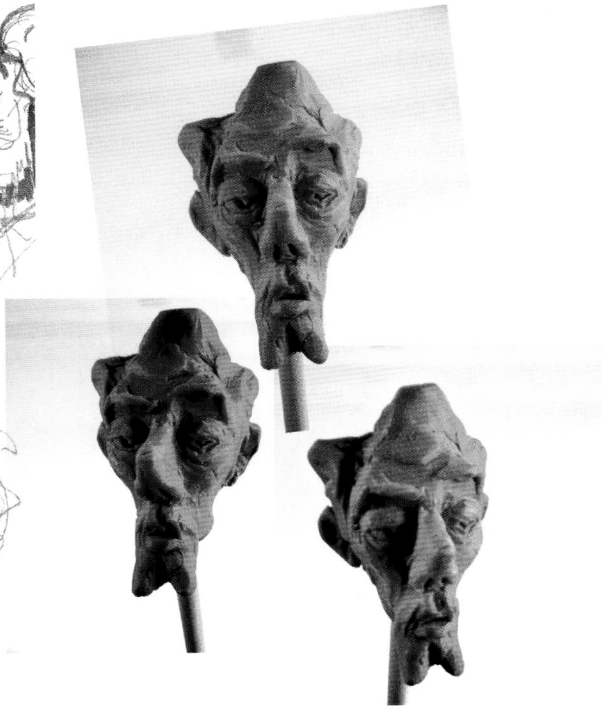

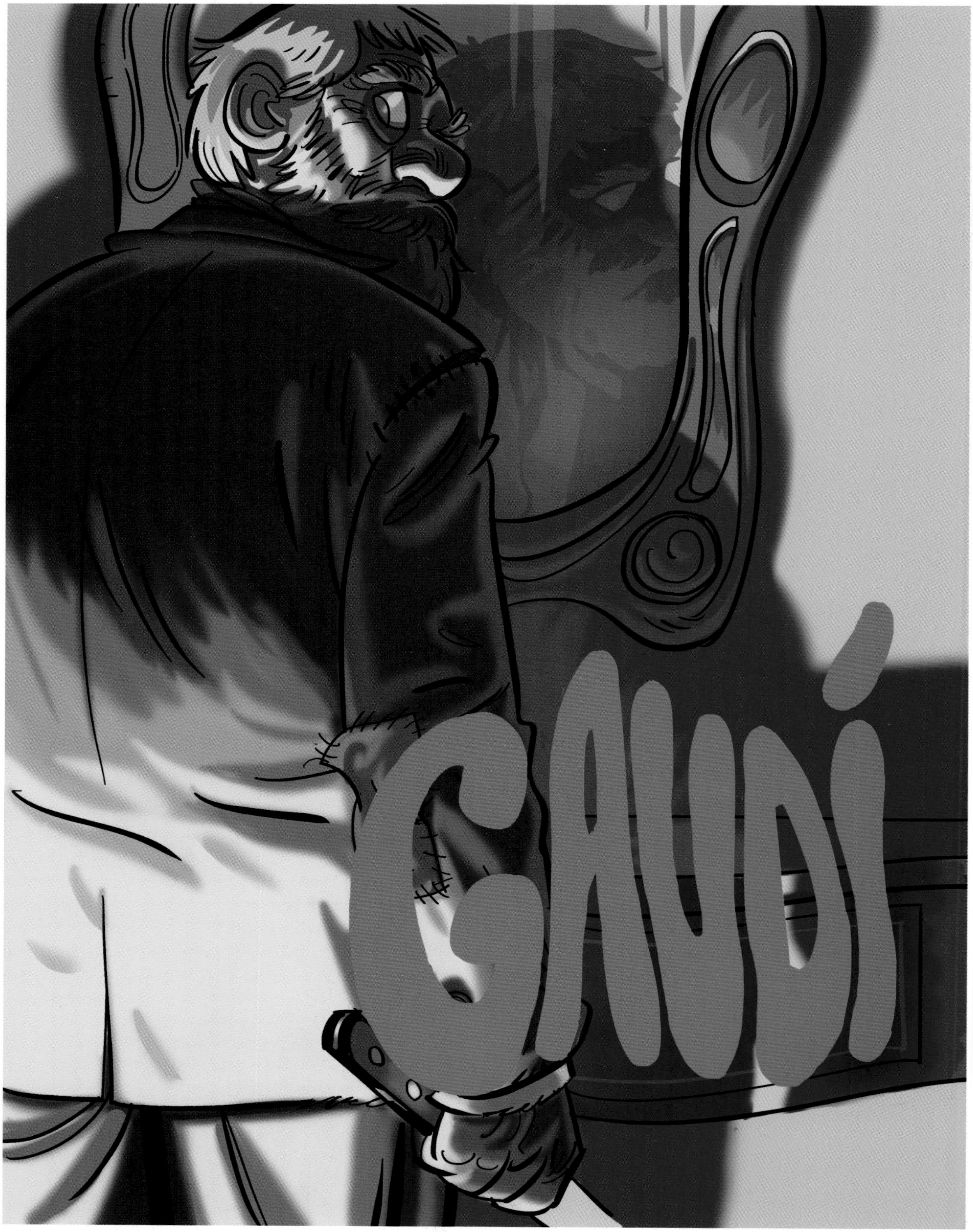
GAUDÍ

Another rejected cover for The Ghost of Gaudí. *The drawing is excellent, but I didn't like how it gave our killer such a spotlight right from the start. This could have caused the reader, having seen the cover, to build expectations that aren't in the book. Our publisher loved it, however.*

THE BALD INSPECTOR WAS ALSO PRETTY CLEAR FROM THE START. IN FACT, BEFORE READING THE REFERENCE ABOUT A REAL ACTOR THAT EL TORRES HAD SENT ME, I HAD ALREADY IMAGINED HIM. MAGIC HAPPENS!

A TIP FOR BUDDING ARTISTS: THINK CAREFULLY ABOUT CHARACTER DESIGNS BEFORE THEY ARE FINAL, OR THEY COULD BECOME TORTURE! IT HAPPENED TO ME WITH SKINNER'S DAMN NOSE!

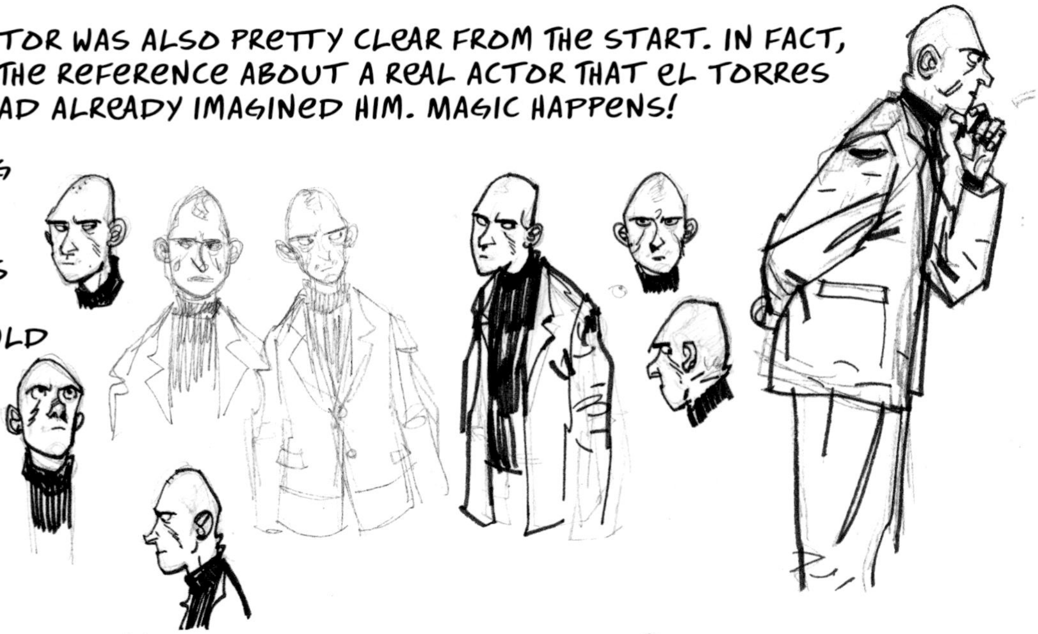

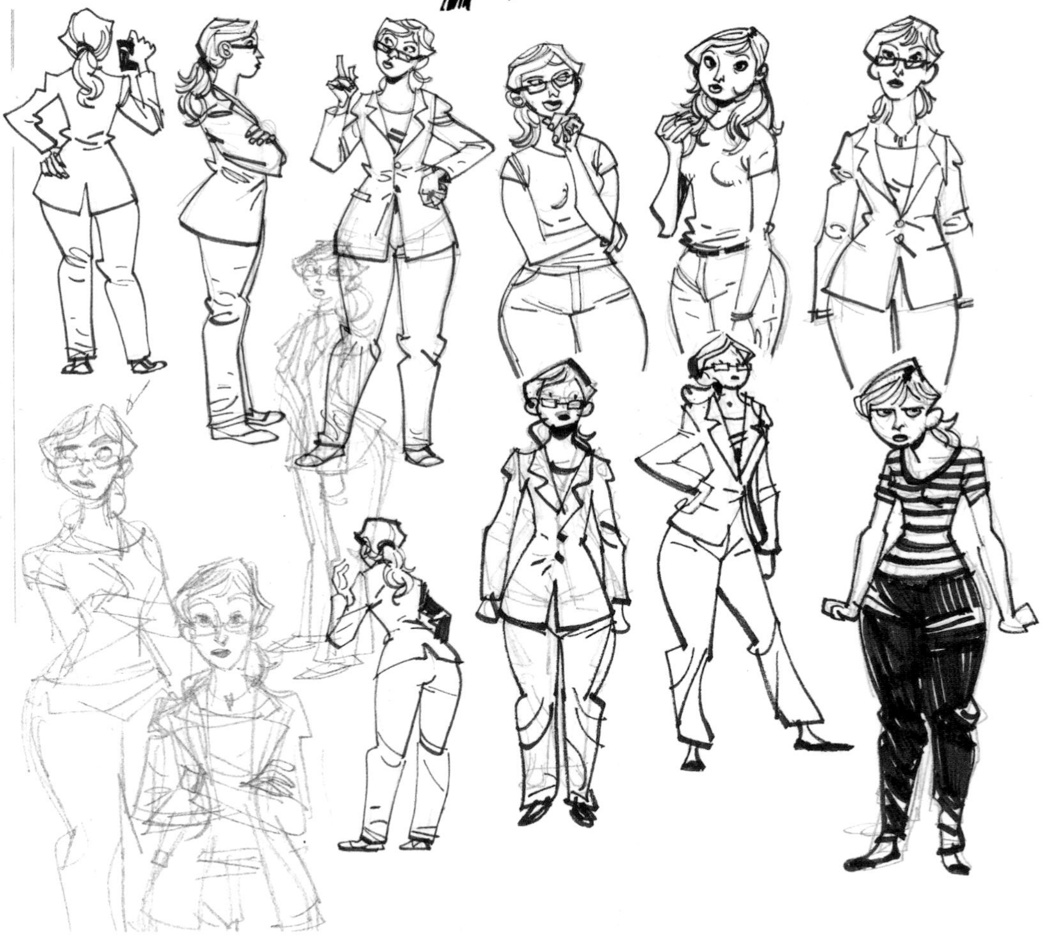

JUDGE MONTANER WAS A HARD CHARACTER FOR ME TO DESIGN (I'M VERY BAD WITH FEMALE HAIRSTYLES), AND I ENDED UP COPYING IT FROM A WOMAN I SAW IN A MEETING! IN THE END, SHE BECAME ONE OF MY FAVORITE CHARACTERS TO DRAW, DUE TO HER NATURAL CURVES AND INNOCENT SENSUALITY.

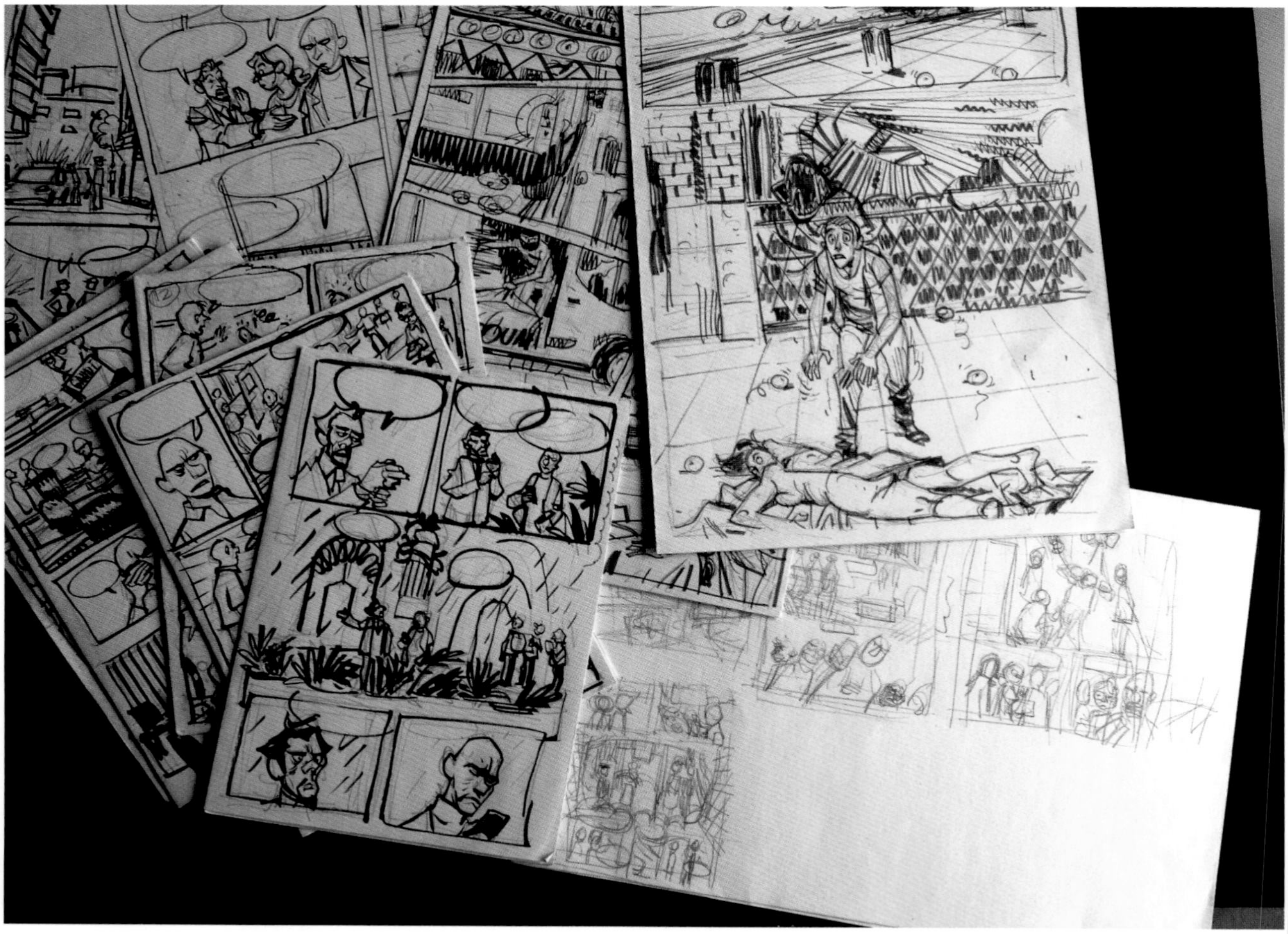

HERE IS A SERIES OF PAGES FROM THE STORY -- I USUALLY DO PAGE PLANNING IN SMALL THUMBNAILS TO AVOID GETTING UNCONSCIOUSLY LOST IN THE DETAILS. IF I'M SENDING IT TO THE SCRIPTWRITER AND THE PUBLISHER, I'LL MAKE THEM A LITTLE BIGGER AND REFINED.

I was so stuck at end of the story! It was clear that it needed a climax, something epic. But what should I do? Blow up the Sagrada Família? Another fire like the one that it suffered in 2011, due to an old man, or during the revolts of 1936? I couldn't stop mulling it over.

So I took advantage of a trip to Barcelona to visit the basilica and took some photos using Hipstamatic on my cell phone (yes, I'm that kinda guy).

And suddenly -- poof! Before my eyes, the end of the story appeared in a crane. This is that photo.

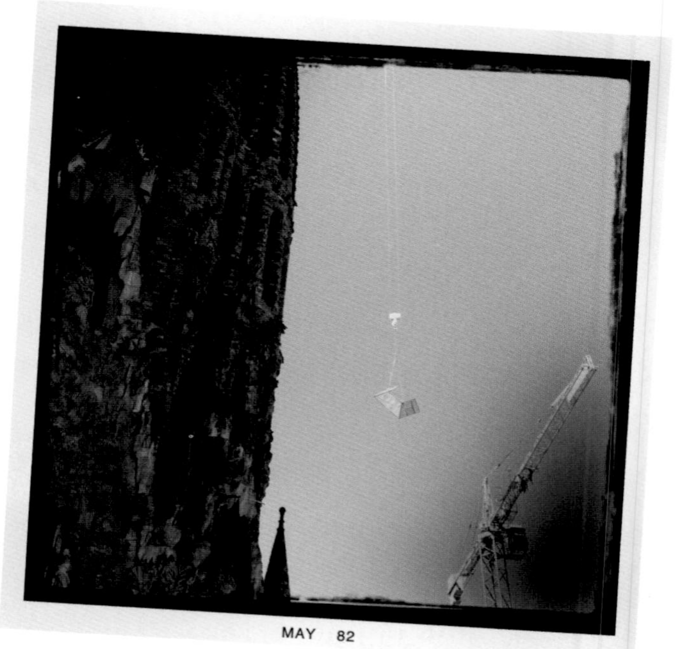
MAY 82

THE CREATORS

EL TORRES

One of the most prolific Spanish comic writers in recent years, El Torres's works have been released in the United States through companies such as Image Comics and IDW Publishing, and most recently through his own independent publishing company, Amigo Comics. His successful horror books include *The Veil*, *The Suicide Forest*, *Nancy in Hell*, *Drums*, and *The Westwood Witches*, all earning him the label "master of horror." Some of these books have been optioned for film and have been released in numerous countries, including France, Germany, the United States, Spain, and Japan. He currently lives in Málaga, Spain.

JESÚS ALONSO IGLESIAS

With a degree in fine arts, specializing in design, Jesús Alonso spent five years working in the Animation Studio Milímetros, SA, creating layouts, storyboards, and character designs for several TV series, such as *Pippi Longstockings*, *Renade*, *Street Sharks*, and *All Dogs Go to Heaven*, as well as animated features *The Three Wise Men* and *Dragon Hill*. He was soon assigned as preproduction chief with the series *Altair* and feature film *El Cid*. In addition to this narrative work, he has also worked in advertising, with companies such as Remo Asatsu, Remo D6, Bassat Ogilvy, ACH&Asociados, and Draftworldwide. In 2002 he began his career as a freelance illustrator, creating popular comics for the French and Spanish markets, including the renowned *Silhouette* with writer Victor Santos and *POS* with writer Pierre Paquet.

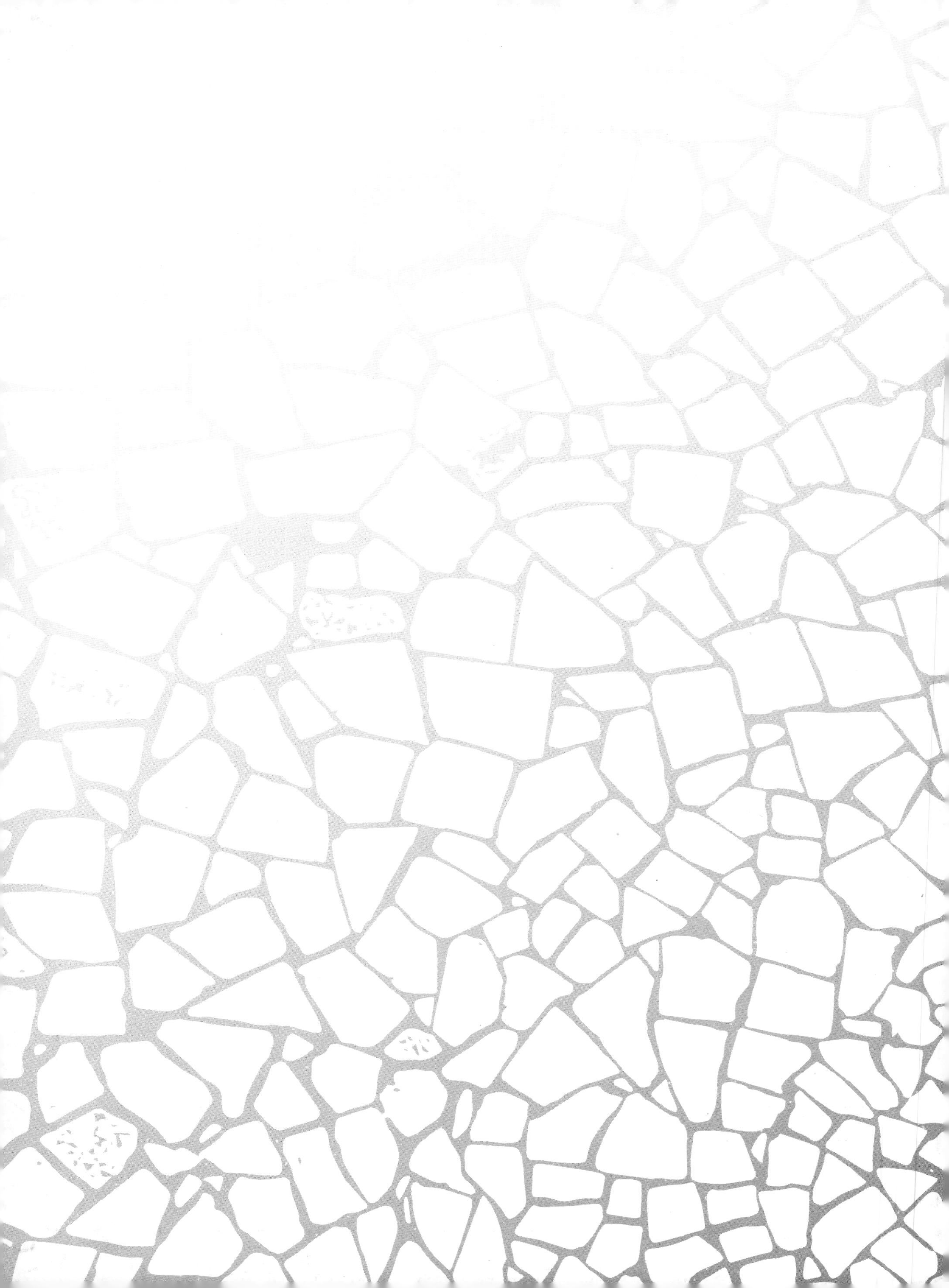